C000121274

A TALE OF STARS AND SHADOW

LISA CASSIDY

National Library of Australia Cataloguing-in-Publication Entry

Creator: Lisa Cassidy

Publisher: Tate House

ISBN: 9780995358997 (Printed)

ISBN: 9780648539209 (eBook)

Copyright © 2019 by Lisa Cassidy

The moral right of the author has been asserted

All rights reserved.

No part of this book may be reproduced in any form or by any electronic or mechanical means, including information storage and retrieval systems, without written permission from the author, except for the use of brief quotations in a book review.

Cover design: Jessica Bell

Map design: Oscar Paludi

Music and Lyrics: Peny Bohan

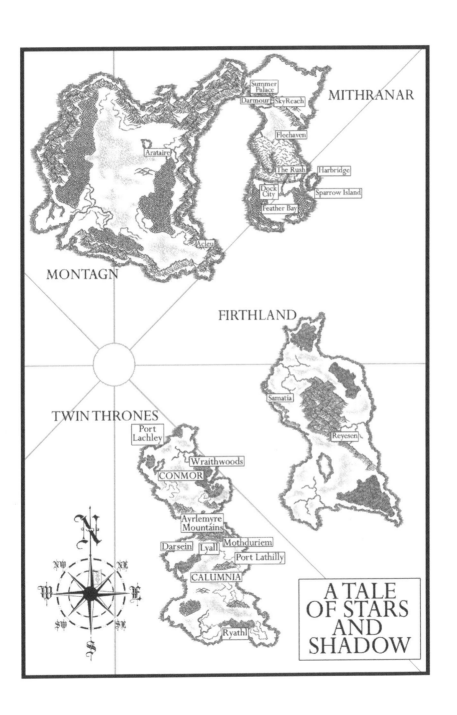

MITHRANAR

Summer
Palace
Darmour SkyReach

Fleehaven

Arataire

The Rush Harbridge

Dock
City Sparrow Island

Feather Bay

Acleu

MONTAGN

FIRTHLAND

Samatia

TWIN THRONES

Reyesen

Port
Lachley

Wraithwoods

CONMOR

Ayrlemyre
Mountains

Darsein Lyall Mothduriem
Port Lathilly

CALUMNIA

A TALE
OF STARS
AND
SHADOW

Ryathl

N

NW NE

W E

SW SE

S

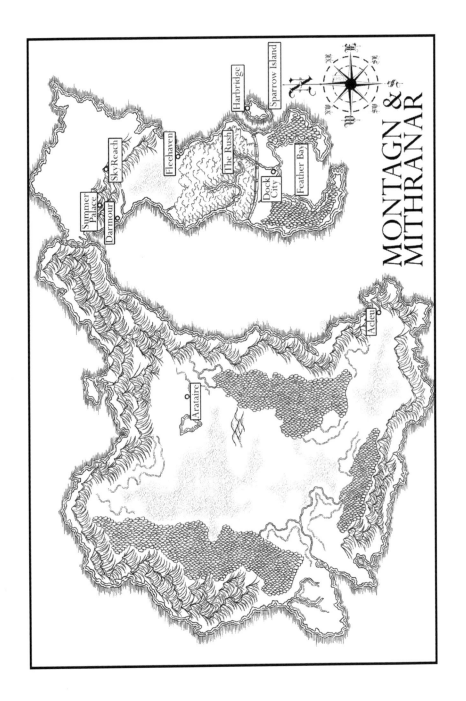

MONTAGN &
MITHRANAR

Summer Palace
SkyReach
Darmour
Fleehaven
The Rush
Harbridge
Sparrow Island
Dock City
Feather Bay
Arataire
Aclen

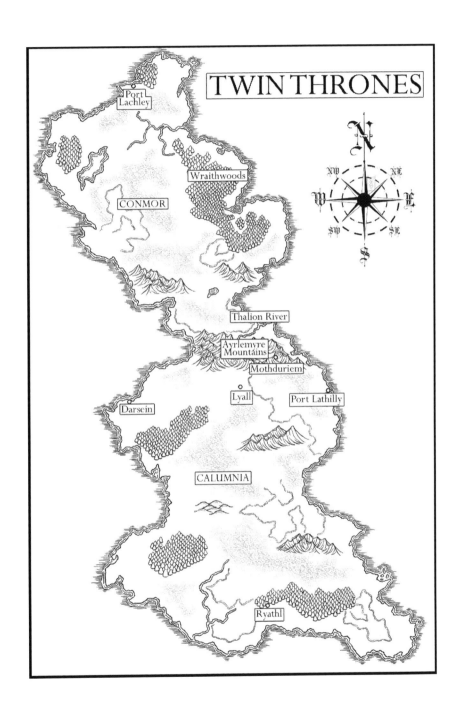

TWIN THRONES

Port Lachley

Wraithwoods

CONMOR

Thalion River

Ayrlemyre Mountains

Mothduriem

Lyall

Port Lathilly

Darsein

CALUMNIA

Ryathl

CHAPTER 1

*I*t was the deepest hour of the night.

Rain and wind lashed at Feather Bay, turning its usually tranquil surface into a turmoil of white-capped waves. Merchant ships anchored in the seething waters listed heavily, pulling up hard against their anchors, spray soaking their open decks.

The Shadowhawk stood still, hands folded loosely before him, voluminous cloak hiding his form. His attention focused on one ship amongst the many. Having arrived earlier in the afternoon with barely enough time to anchor before the storm hit, it had yet to unload.

Anticipation kindled in his stomach with a slow burn that he savoured like fine wine. As the sensation unfurled and spread through his body, he remained outwardly still, ignoring the rain driving into his masked and hooded face and the wind tearing and clawing at his cloak.

His gaze narrowed, tracking a moving pinprick of light on the deck—likely the handheld lantern of a crew member with the unenviable duty of checking everything remained locked down in the storm.

Abruptly the Shadowhawk shifted attention, warned by a flickering in the shadows of the narrow alley to his left. His hand slid to the narrow blade he wore tucked into the small of his back.

A man emerged. Familiar. Offering a slight nod as he came to stand at the Shadowhawk's side.

The Shadowhawk moved his hand away from the blade and slid his gaze back to the ship.

"We've been watching the docks since *The Merry Raven* berthed. Two Falcons on board, with a shift change every four hours. Next shift change should be dawn." The man's voice was pitched above the sound of the wind and held no trace of nervousness or uncertainty.

The Shadowhawk's lip curled. Only two Falcons. "And your group is in position?"

It was always a different group, each led by a different man or woman who knew nothing about the other groups. Each had a different way of communicating with him.

And none of them knew the Shadowhawk's face.

"Awaiting your word."

The Shadowhawk nodded. "Wait a half-turn then follow me out. Make for the cargo hatch at the stern."

IT WAS TOO DARK, the weather too wild, for anyone to notice the shadow slipping over the starboard railing of *The Merry Raven* and making straight for the main hatch leading inside. It lifted easily, a faint light glimmering from below, but nobody shouted or called the alarm.

The Shadowhawk dropped inside, crouching on the top step and securing the hatch behind him. Immediately the driving rain was cut off and he was left with only the roar of the wind and waves hurling themselves at the ship.

At the bottom of the ladder, two narrow passageways led in different directions. The light was coming from under the door of a cabin at the end of the passageway leading straight ahead—probably the captain's room.

The Shadowhawk turned left.

Darkness was his friend, and as he moved, he gathered the shadows around him, allowing them to shroud his cloaked form. He padded quickly through the ship, moving with the lurching of the floor under his feet. One lit cabin at deck level held a handful of sailors playing cards—presumably those on watch—but the rest of the crew should be below trying to sleep through the storm.

He turned away. He needed to find the sleeping crew. They would likely be positioned close to the cargo hold, and despite the sound the storm was making, he couldn't take the risk that they might hear him.

He'd done this many times before, and it didn't take him long to make his way down into the bowels of the ship and find the sleeping berth. Keeping the shadows close—anyone watching would see only moving darkness—he pulled the door closed and latched it.

At the quiet snick of the latch falling into place he waited, breathing to stay calm. But nobody inside roused.

He thought about going back up, locking in the captain and the sailors playing cards. But they were awake. If one of them heard him doing it or tried to leave... but the storm was loud. It was unlikely they'd hear anything happening down in the cargo hold. And if they did, well, merchant sailors weren't soldiers.

Decision made, he moved down the narrow passageway leading to the cargo hold. It was there he found his first obstacle—two armed Falcons standing guard on either side of the hatch.

Not that either of them would strike fear into anyone trying to get in.

The Shadowhawk couldn't help the sharp smile of amusement that spread over his face at the sight. One was half-leaning against the wall, his skin a green hue almost matching the colour of his wings, his left hand clutching his stomach. The other just looked bored. Their immaculate teal uniforms and silken wings contrasted sharply with the rough wood of the ship's interior and the dim light from two flickering torches further down the passageway, making them seem horribly out of place.

Briefly he considered sneaking past them in the shadows. He discarded the idea the moment he thought it. The seasick one was practically standing on the hatch and the lamplight was strong enough to make the shadows surrounding him look unnatural if he stepped into it.

A single steadying breath, and he summoned the deep, husky voice of the Shadowhawk. "I've got an arrow drawn and pointed at your heart. One move and I let loose."

He was unarmed apart from the knife at his back, the knife he never used, but they didn't know that—he was utterly hidden by the darkness beyond the pool of lamplight. The two Falcons jumped, the seasick one adding a shade of yellow to the green tinge of his skin. The other one's hand dropped to the hilt of his sword, but the Shadowhawk barked, "Don't! There's no need for either of you to die tonight. You know who I am. Do as I say and you live. Start walking backwards. Slowly. Arms up."

They shared a glance, neither willing to attack with the threat of an arrow coming out of the darkness at them, but still reluctant to leave their post.

"My patience is running out." His voice turned edgy, dark. "Start walking, or I loose this arrow. The second will follow before the remaining one of you can get anywhere near me."

His glance fell on the face of the seasick Falcon—a young man surely no older than twenty—and for a moment guilt tried to flicker. He squashed it ruthlessly.

After sharing another glance, the two Falcons began inching backwards up the passageway, hands in the air, their wings making their usually graceful movements awkward and clumsy in the confined space.

He moved them back until they reached a hold he'd spotted earlier, on his way from the sleeping berth. "Inside. Not a sound. Shut the door behind you. Go."

They hesitated only a moment longer, the seasick one swaying, clutching his stomach harder. The second one opened the door and shoved his comrade in before following suit. Once the door swung shut, the Shadowhawk moved quickly, dropping the bar over the doorway.

The sharp scent of penned sheep had hit him earlier as he passed the doorway—the hold where livestock were kept would be one that could be barred from the outside, holding back any panicked animal herd trying to flee. A perfect place to trap someone.

Besides, there was no small satisfaction in sticking the pretty winged Falcons in with stinking sheep.

Mouth curling in contempt at their uselessness, the Shadowhawk returned to the hatch leading to the cargo hold, listening hard through the rain drumming on the deck above. Nothing else loomed out of the darkness, so he opened the hatch and dropped through before pulling it closed and securing it from the inside. It should prove a good enough obstacle if the crew on watch worked out what was happening.

The two Falcons wouldn't be missed until shift change at dawn, still at least two full-turns away. Once that happened, he wouldn't have long before many more Falcons descended on *The Merry Raven*.

The sheer number of crates stacked in the hold gave him pause—but his informants on the docks had told him they were all full of supplies of wheat from Montagn. His eyes tracked the dim interior of the hold until landing on the unloading door at the stern.

He winched it open, ignoring its loud screech and the icy wind rushing in as the door splashed down into roiling ocean. Several two-man rowboats were waiting, rocking wildly on the storm-tossed waves. At the sight of the opening door, one of the boats came in closer.

It unloaded four men into the hold. Seasoned sailors all of them, with the way they easily jumped the gap from boat to hold, not even a glance at the raging ocean below their feet. At a nod from the Shadowhawk they began working, dragging crates over to be loaded onto the waiting boats.

By the time the third boat was full, shoulders and arms ached, but he gritted his teeth and increased his pace, forcing the pain to the back of his mind. When all the boats were filled with crates, he looked up at the sky. The rain and low clouds made it difficult to tell the time, but they couldn't have longer than a half-turn before dawn.

The first three boats were already almost back to shore as the fourth one turned and began following. The Shadowhawk straightened his aching back and looked up towards the citadel.

It was time to go. Any longer and he'd risk getting caught. And he was too smart for that.

Casting a regretful look at the remaining crates, he reached inside his cloak and drew out a carved wooden arrow, fletched in black. After carefully placing it on the floor by the hatch entry, he headed over to the cargo door and leaped across into the final boat. "Go, get out of here," he barked at the rowers. "We need to make it to shore before light or the Falcons coming for shift change will spot us."

The wind was bitingly cold and the water hadn't calmed. The two men at the oars struggled for what felt like ages against the strong current, the work made harder by how heavily laden they were. An edge of anxiety tugged incessantly at him despite his physical weariness—Falcons would be searching the water and shoreline relentlessly once they reached *The Merry Raven* at dawn and saw what had been stolen. And though he'd done this many times before, he never took for granted that one day he might be caught.

Dawn was a faint pink glow on the horizon when they finally dragged the boat up onto the sand of a beach on the western headland of Feather Bay. Panting, aching, and stiff with cold, they all clambered out and joined the hive of activity around the other boats already ashore. They'd been pulled up high onto the sand, and more helpers were there to unload them and carry crates away.

He recognised one of the rowers—a kahvi brewer in another life—and a handful of the others helping unload crates. It had been a while since he'd worked with this group, but they were well-practised and efficient.

Apart from leaders of each group, he didn't even know their names. And they had no more idea who he was than any other man, woman or child on the streets of Dock City. It was safer for all of them that way.

As each boat was unloaded, its crew pushed them back out into the water and rowed south. Once the sun rose, they'd be nothing more than one of the myriad fishing vessels out to get the morning's catch.

None spoke to the Shadowhawk as he began helping to move the crates from the fourth boat into the backs of two large wagons. Dawn began inching across the sky, and the wind lost some of its strength, the pounding rain dropping to a light drizzle. They were tying down the load on the second wagon when a familiar figure appeared, stalking towards him with her customary confident gait.

"You got my message." He stepped away from the wagon to speak with her, not wanting any of the workers to overhear.

"You would have been shit out of luck if I hadn't," she observed.

True, but letting her know too long in advance... that was risky. He shrugged. "You know why I don't give you more notice."

"Yeah, yeah." She lifted a hand from where it had rested on the hilt of the dagger she always wore on her belt, dark skin blending with the dim light as she dismissed his words with a sharp gesture. Even soaking wet from the rain she was calm and collected. "The first wagon is already sorted, and we'll have the rest away by midday. After I've taken the cut for my people, we'll get the rest up north to Mair-land for you."

That was the usual arrangement. He used his people to identify the ships to hit and steal the supplies from. Saniya's network hid and distributed the goods to those who needed it.

"You never have told me how your 'people' are different to the rest of Dock City or Mair-land," he said casually.

"And I never will."

He barked a laugh. Fair enough. "And that's why I'll never give you advance notice. I don't trust you."

It was her turn to laugh. "I don't give a flying flea's shit about your trust, Shadowhawk. It's enough to know that neither of us could operate without the other."

"Shadowhawk!"

He turned—the kahvi brewer was pointing southeast, where two winged figures were outlined against the ever-lightening sky, making directly for *The Merry Raven*. Scorn simmered in his gut—they'd clearly waited for the storm to calm before risking flight and completing their shift change.

"Didn't want to sprain a wing, I suppose." Saniya's voice mirrored his contempt.

He turned away, gaze following one of the wagons as it trundled away. Satisfaction displaced the scorn and the lingering cold and exhaustion. There had been enough wheat in those crates to replace the yield destroyed in a recent avalanche that had badly affected several villages who relied heavily on farming for survival.

But quick on the heels of his satisfaction came a burning shame. It wasn't enough. He should be able do more, and *hated* that he didn't have the courage for it. Sighing, he rubbed at the beginnings of a headache throbbing at his temples. Always the same argument with himself. It got old, and tiring.

"Go, get out of here." Saniya's sharp voice dragged him from his thoughts. "I'll make sure the last wagon is sorted before the Falcons start searching the beaches."

He nodded, taking a final glance at the remaining wagon before setting off with quick strides along the beach. Once out of sight of Saniya and the wagons he tugged off his mask, shoved it deep inside his tunic then shrugged out of the cloak and balled it up, tucking it under his arm.

By the time he reached the waking streets of Dock City, he was just one of the crowd. An average, unremarkable human.

CHAPTER 2

She'd allowed herself to keep one good memory from *before*. It was nothing special, and she rarely let herself do it, but sometimes, in her worst moments, remembering it would lift her depression just enough to allow her to breathe. To put one foot in front of the other. To get out of bed.

The other memories she'd wrapped up and buried—as far away as she could push them—in the back of her mind. Those had the power to leave her gasping on the floor, unable to think under an overwhelming tide of grief.

But this memory…

It had been a perfectly ordinary summer afternoon. She'd walked into her Callanan partner's house, through the back door and without knocking, as she'd done a million times before. Sari had been sprawled on the small, brightly coloured couch, one eye on her little son playing by the window and the other on a long sheet of parchment. Warm sunlight shone through the windows and the house smelled of tomatoes and salty sea air.

Sari was already looking up with a grin before Talyn stepped through the doorway, warned of her arrival by their instinctive awareness of each other's presence. Her pleasure at Talyn's arrival was clear despite the fact they'd only seen each other late the day before, arriving back in the city after their latest assignment. An echoing pleasure had beat through her. Always like that. In perfect rhythm.

"Ta!" Tarquin had heaved himself off the floor to wrap his chubby arms around her leg in greeting before going to join his father in the kitchen. A moment later, his voice drifted back, high-pitched with excitement, as he'd asked if he could help.

Roan was cooking dinner—the source of the tomato smell. "Staying for dinner, Tal?" he'd asked, waving a wooden spoon around and sending sauce splattering to the floor when she ducked into the kitchen to say hello. Tarquin had shrieked with laughter. Sari had rolled her eyes, Talyn's presence probably saving Roan from a sharp word.

She *had* stayed for dinner. They'd talked and laughed over the food, then while Roan put their son to bed, she and Sari had sipped glasses of wine out in the garden, enjoying the balmy night. It had been easy, and warm and *home*.

Her Callanan partner had died two months later.

A SHARP SIDEWAYS step from the restless mare beneath her brought Talyn crashing back to the present. The mournful howl of baying hounds faded into the distance as the hunting pack reached the other side of the valley and entered thick forest. She touched the reins lightly, holding her copper mare in check.

"FireFlare looks eager to run."

Talyn looked up at the man riding his grey stallion towards her, hoping he hadn't noticed her drifting off. She gave a casual shrug, summoning a teasing tone of voice. "She's the fastest here and she knows it. Greylord is going to have to get used to second place today."

There had once been joy—and smugness too—in having one of the finest pureblood Aimsir mares in the country, but that was gone along with everything else. It was hard to remember what those things had felt like.

Ariar Dumnorix threw back his head and laughed. "Remember your place, Cousin. I am Horselord, *and* several years older than you."

His laughter eased something inside her. The ruling Dumnorix blood were a close-knit, powerful brood of whom much was expected, but there was something magical in the way they gave each other strength. She'd needed that desperately when she left Port Lathilly for Ryathl a year earlier—not that they had any idea.

Ariar's shock of golden hair, glinting with red highlights in the sun, wasn't typically Dumnorix, but his unusually luminous blue eyes marked him clearly as one of them. Bright as starlight in a clear night sky. All Dumnorix had those bright eyes, a physical manifestation of that hint of magic that ran through all their veins.

"You wouldn't want me to let you win, now would you?" Talyn's gaze roamed over the assembled nobility gathered on the plains outside Ryathl, waiting for the hounds to get the scent of a fox. "Uncle wouldn't like that."

"I can't believe he's managed to drag himself out of that draughty palace for the afternoon." Ariar's incredulousness was exaggerated, but a smile still curled at Talyn's mouth as they both glanced towards Aethain Dumnorix, ruler of the Twin Thrones. It was impossible to be completely depressed with Ariar around. She'd once been just like him.

The king was in his mid-fifties, his curling black hair still showing no signs of grey, his amber eyes sharp and intelligent in a handsome, rugged face. Ariar constantly ribbed his elder cousin for his serious and reserved nature. Talyn was more forgiving—she shuddered at the thought of the heavy responsibility the king of the Twin Thrones must bear.

"Six thrices, Talyn, you're not paying a jot of attention to what I'm saying, are you?" Ariar's voice interrupted her reverie. "Please tell me you're not mooning over Tarcos Hadvezer."

Talyn started, cursing herself again. She had to stop drifting off. Ariar's gaze was far too knowing for her comfort. She took his jibe and ran with it, summoning an irritated scowl. Tarcos was sitting his horse near the king. "I do *not* moon. Ever. End of story."

The distant baying of the hounds cut across Ariar's response, and FireFlare leapt into a gallop before Talyn could even dig in her heels. She settled down in the saddle without thought, doing her best to give in to the momentary freedom of her mare's speed and the wind whipping past her face.

The Twin Thrones Aimsir were legendary for their riding prowess and the speed and agility of the horses they rode—used as a mobile archer force in battle, they spent peacetime hunting to supply the northern villages of Calumnia during the long, rugged winters when they were mostly cut off from the rest of the country. It was in tracking, chasing down and killing the dangerous kharfa—massive animals with thick hides used for clothing and meat that could supply an entire family for a week—that Aimsir had developed their skills in horsemanship and archery.

Growing up in the north, it had been inevitable that Talyn would become Aimsir, and now it was impossible to remember a time when she hadn't been one, even though she'd left home and the unending plains in the north that were the Aimsir heartland to join the Callanan the moment she was old enough.

Ariar—who'd never left the Aimsir and had commanded them as Horselord for three years now—passed Talyn on Greylord within moments and took the lead as they raced across the open plains towards the forest in the distance. Aethain was in between Talyn and Ariar on his own Aimsir stallion, two of his Kingshield guards keeping close, their focus on their charge, not the hunt.

But FireFlare was rapidly closing the distance.

Talyn edged the mare out to the left, the wind tearing through her raven hair and bringing tears to her eyes. They gained steadily on the king until FireFlare was flying past him and closing in on Ariar. An echo of the old Talyn came rising to the surface, and she whipped her knife out from her belt, flipped it neatly, and tapped Ariar on the back of the head with the hilt as FireFlare raced by.

Greylord had the faster acceleration but FireFlare was swifter than anything alive over longer distances.

"Cheat!" Ariar roared good-naturedly at her, the wind ripping his words to shreds.

FireFlare edged ahead of the pack, with Ariar closest behind, followed by Aethain and the handful of his Kingshield guard that could keep up as they hit the forest and pushed through.

The nobles were left far behind.

The baying hounds had a fox cornered in a wide clearing not far beyond the tree line. Talyn reached back for her bow, Ariar barely three strides behind her. Dropping the reins and controlling FireFlare with knees alone, she yanked an arrow from the quiver on her back, knocked the bow, and...

The hiss from behind froze her mid-draw.

Panic sprawled up through her chest in a torrent so forceful she literally couldn't think. Then her logical brain caught up.

Ariar had fired in the second before Talyn could. It was just his arrow flying through the air behind her.

It hit the fox cleanly, two breaths before Talyn loosed her arrow, which buried itself in the fox's side inches away from Ariar's. Talyn guided her mare around in a wide circle, slinging the bow back across her saddle and trying to return her breathing to normal before her cousin noticed. Fortunately he was too busy letting out a loud whoop of triumph to do so.

That was when the ruler of the Twin Thrones burst into the clearing, reining his horse in with easy skill once he saw the fox was already dead.

"What was with the hesitation?" Ariar complained. "I thought you weren't going to let me win."

Her heart plummeted when she realised he'd noticed. The panic threatened to return. She cleared her throat and lifted her left hand. "My wrist is still a little sore. Besides, I did win, FireFlare beat you here."

"*Liar.*"

Talyn resolutely shoved the voice away. She was currently in a phase of pretending it didn't exist.

"But Ariar's arrow landed first. He takes the win," Aethain said, approval in his voice as he nodded at Ariar. Her cousin grinned in delight.

"Thank you both for the outing," Aethain continued. "Can you join me for lunch tomorrow?"

"I can't. I'm sorry, uncle," Talyn apologised. He wasn't technically her uncle—her mother was his first cousin—but the diminutive was easy. Those of Dumnorix blood never used titles when speaking to each other, even if one of them did sit on a throne with two countries under its rule. "I won't have another day off for a while."

"Of course. The next posting assignments are decided next week." Aethain's amber eyes brightened. "I'm sure Lark will put you somewhere important given your background. You must be excited."

She wasn't. In fact, the very idea terrified her. The Kingshield posted new recruits to guard details every six months. A broken wrist in sparring practice had gotten her out of the last one—the first since she'd left the Callanan and joined the Kingshield—but that excuse wasn't going to work again.

"I can't come either. I'm off back to the mountains." Ariar looked cheerful at the idea. "More brigands to slay, that sort of thing. We'll do dinner when I get back though."

Aethain frowned. "Nothing too serious I hope?"

"Not at all," Ariar assured him. "In fact, we're planning an assault on one of their main supply bases near Port Lathilly." A sideways glance at Talyn. "One of the Callanan informants there came through in a big way."

She gritted her teeth. Ariar's look told her the informant was one she and Sari had developed before her partner's death. She tried to be glad their hard work in finding him had paid off, but she failed miserably. Her hands had tightened unconsciously on the reins, the leather cutting into her skin. She almost welcomed the pain.

Aethain's amber eyes settled on her a moment, as if he sensed some of her distress despite the mask she wore. But eventually he nodded. "Good work. Keep me apprised of the outcome."

With that, he wheeled his horse around to turn back for the castle.

"Talyn?" Ariar asked, looking concerned. He knew the story, they all did, but after a year she'd developed a good enough pretence that they thought she'd moved on. The last thing she wanted was for them to realise how broken she actually was.

"Try not to get hit by a poorly-aimed brigand arrow," she said lightly. "Ryathl can be a drag without you around to liven things up."

"Don't I know it! You just stay here and polish your pretty King-shield sword like a good little guard and I'll be back quicker than you think." Lightly meant, there was still a hint of confusion in her cousin's tone. Ariar would never understand why she'd left the life of an Aimsir to be a Callanan, and now a Kingshield. With a wink, he wheeled his horse and galloped away after the king. Soon after he was surrounded by his own Kingshield guard, who'd been left trailing valiantly in his wake.

Talyn let out a breath. Being amongst her relatives made her stronger, calmer. But it also meant having to summon the effort to maintain a semblance of what she'd been before. Now, left alone in the clearing, she was both relieved and tired.

Sighing, she turned FireFlare back towards the city. She had just enough time to wash off the smell of horse and change before a promised meet up with friends in the city.

And somewhere between now and then she'd need to summon the strength for more pretending.

That came sooner than she'd hoped. She emerged from the clearing well behind Ariar and Aethain to find Tarcos Hadvezer, the Firthlander prince living at Ryathl court, waiting for her.

As per custom between the Firthlander warlord and the king sitting the Twin Thrones of Calumnia and Conmor, Tarcos had come to Ryathl three years earlier to live at court. Technically, he was a hostage, but nobody ever used that word. The Twin Thrones held sovereignty over Firthland, but Aethain, and his father and grandfather before him, essentially allowed the Firthlanders to run themselves.

And to ease the sting, the Dumnorix often sent one of their brood to Samatia for a similar purpose. Ariar had spent five years there when he was younger.

Tarcos' smile was reserved, but his hazel eyes were warm against his dark skin. Unlike the wild hair and beards of the fierce Firthlander Bearman detachment stationed with him in Ryathl, he was clean-shaven and wore his dark hair cut short.

He caught her gaze, and his faint smile widened slightly. She gave him a quick smile as she rode up to him. They'd been lovers on and off since they'd met during a brief assignment that Talyn and Sari had been given in Ryathl, but it had never been anything serious. There was no room in her for anything serious, not anymore, and he seemed happy with that arrangement.

Not that her uncle would be unhappy if they were serious. A match between her and a Firthlander prince was about as perfect as it came, and she supposed one day it would be official. Imagining that day was utterly impossible. But she liked Tarcos a lot.

"Is your uncle going to ensure you're posted to his guard detail?" he asked eagerly as they began riding together back to the city.

Talyn winced. She wished everyone would stop bringing that up. "No. In fact, he'll do the opposite. We're Dumnorix, Tarcos. Neither of us would appreciate him pulling strings on my behalf."

Thank everything for that.

Tarcos sensed enough in her tone to let it drop, instead turning the subject to the hunt. She liked that about him—that he knew when to let things lie. And while she chatted with him about who had come first and last in the hunt, her mind turned over her options for how to manage what was coming the next week.

Part of her rankled at the endless drill and sparring that had been her life in the year since joining the Kingshield. A much larger part was terrified she wouldn't be able to handle returning to active duty. If anything happened like it had just then—when the sound of an arrow firing had frozen her and cost her the win—she'd never forgive herself. A lapse like that on active duty could lead to the death of her charge.

Another sparring injury would be too obvious. No other ideas came to her, short of asking her uncle to intervene. That would mean telling him the truth, a conversation that was even more terrifying than getting posted to a detail in the first place.

Tarcos seemed to sense her distant mood and left her at the city gates with a warm kiss and a promise to take her to dinner the next night.

Her melancholy mood followed her all the way back to the Kingshield barracks, despite the ride and time with her Aimsir mare. Once she'd washed, she found herself standing at the window of her shared room. Outside, the sun was setting, soft orange rays lighting the courtyards and gardens of the Kingshield barracks in amber.

Idly, she placed her palm on the window, savouring its cool touch. In the drill yard below, warriors wearing the black uniforms of the Kingshield called out to each other as they sparred. The emblem on their chests—a hundred tiny stars stitched into the shape of twin crossed swords—gleamed amber; almost as bright as the real things.

Like stars in a night sky.

Burn bright and true.

The Dumnorix oath. She held that thought, kept holding as she breathed in deep.

Leaving the Callanan to join the Kingshield at twenty-five was far from unheard of. The Kingshield—solely responsible for the protection of the ruler sitting the Twin Thrones and all others of Dumnorix blood—only accepted the elite from across the various Calumnian and Conmoran fighting units.

But being Kingshield wasn't something Talyn had ever planned on. She'd only ever wanted to be Callanan, to experience the thrill of battle, weapon in hand and adrenalin pumping through her veins. It had meant leaving her family farm and the quiet life her Dumnorix mother had won for herself when she'd withdrawn from court and its politics upon choosing to marry a commoner. It meant leaving the Aimsir and the joy of a fast gallop and the open plains. None of that had mattered, she'd wanted to be Callanan so badly. After all, it was in her blood. Her mother had been Callanan—the Dumnorix line was littered with Aimsir, Callanan and SkyRiders.

But after Sari... she'd tried but couldn't do it. She'd fled the Callanan and gone to the Kingshield.

But what they didn't know—her little secret, one that could destroy her if it got out—was that she didn't want a posting. She wasn't at all certain she wanted to be in a fight ever again. Wasn't certain she could handle it.

But she couldn't let it go either.

Curling her hand into a fist of frustration—would she ever stop dwelling?—Talyn stepped away from the window and cast around for her cloak.

She was already late to meet her friends.

SARI HAD BEEN Talyn's Callanan partner, but they'd had many close friends amongst the Callanan before Talyn's abrupt departure, two in particular. It made the idea of spending time with Leviana and Cynia equally painful and comforting, and Talyn could never decide which was the stronger emotion. Most of the time it just hurt.

Leviana Seinn was the only child of the wealthy and powerful Lord Rodrich Seinn, who had doubled his wealth and power overnight when he'd married her mother, one of the Firthlander warlord's cousins. Talyn had met Leviana in Ryathl her first week after leaving home in the north, during a dinner hosted by Aethain.

After that night, Talyn quickly decided she hated all such events. Too many prying eyes and questions on topics she found too boring to even contemplate. Leviana had been gorgeously dressed, a popular member of the young, elite set of Ryathl court whom Talyn had absolutely zero interest in joining.

It had taken those members a total of about three breaths to give up on courting the friendship of the newest and most mysterious Dumnorix family member in town. Talyn supposed her conversation on the relative merits of daggers versus sais—at some point she was going to have to choose her specialist Callanan weapon—might have had something to do with that.

She'd therefore been astonished to see Leviana standing amidst the small group of Callanan recruits the next morning at Callanan Tower.

"Well, parties are all very exciting and everything, but I have to do something with myself." She'd correctly read Talyn's shocked expression. "Can't sit around my father's mansion all day for the rest of my life. I'd go mad with boredom."

Throughout their apprenticeships and all the years since, Leviana had maintained her involvement in the social set, often disappearing at night for parties or dinners, but she'd become a friend like all those in the small group training together had. She was also one of the fiercest fighters Talyn had ever encountered, especially given her tiny stature.

And while Talyn and Sari had essentially partnered by the end of that very first day, it hadn't been until graduation as full Callanan Warriors four years later that Leviana and another member of their small group—Cynia Leed—had formalised their partnership.

Leviana and Cynia were already there when Talyn entered the overly-warm interior of their favourite inn. Both women smiled and waved Talyn over. As pint-sized as her partner, Cynia was also half-Firthlander, but whatever noble blood ran in her family was distant and generations back. She'd grown up on her family's small farm just west of Ryathl.

Off duty, Leviana was wearing a beautifully tailored dress which brought out her eyes and shining dark hair. Her shoes were similarly stunning. In contrast, Cynia wore a simple shirt and breeches, with the sleeves of her shirt rolled up to the elbows. They made a disparate sight.

"How many knives have you managed to conceal in that thing?" Talyn asked as she took a seat. She couldn't see any. In full uniform, Leviana usually had about ten of her signature weapons stored in assorted positions around her body. It had become a game to guess where.

"Six."

Talyn snorted. "No way."

"I can show you if you like?" Leviana offered, beginning to reach down the back of her neck.

"No, that's fine." Talyn lifted her hands in surrender.

"I can confirm." Cynia rolled her eyes. "She's already explained to me where each of them is. To be honest, it sounds uncomfortable."

"Pfft. What's a bit of discomfort in comparison to being prepared?"

"For what?" Cynia asked. "A sudden brigand attack in the middle of Ryathl?"

"You never know," Leviana said airily.

Cynia shook her head, then turned to Talyn, a teasing note to her voice. "Tarcos not with you?"

"Tarcos had plans with some friends of his," Talyn said firmly, shutting down Leviana before she could say whatever it was she was about to. If Leviana had her way, they'd have been married the moment they met. The words 'perfect match' were often bandied about. Talyn detested those words.

"That's good. It means we get some time with you, Tal." Cynia smiled. "How have you been?"

Talyn shrugged as she leaned back further into her seat. This was the first time she'd seen them in months—they'd been away in the west on assignment. "I'm good. The posting assignments happen next week."

"You're more patient than I am." Leviana made a face. "I'd have quit in high temper by now. Everyone knows how good you are. How is it they've still got you in drill training?"

"You know they only post recruits twice a year. They like to make sure we're thoroughly trained in guard procedures," Talyn said mildly.

"They should have posted you the moment your wrist healed. Your record speaks for itself." Cynia was the ruthlessly practical one and saw through Talyn far more clearly than Leviana.

Unconsciously, the fingers of Talyn's right hand crept to her now fully-healed left wrist. She fought to keep her face bland, not wanting to confirm any suspicions Cynia might have about that injury. "Cynia—"

"You're one of the best." Leviana burst out. "It's a waste for you to be shut up in the Kingshield barracks doing nothing but polishing your sais. You and Sari were the best of the best—no Callanan out there could match you. That hasn't changed."

Under the table Talyn's hands curled into fists. "I don't want to talk about this."

"Talyn." Leviana's voice softened. "I—"

"We *thought* we were the best!" Talyn shot to her feet, trying but failing not to shout. "And she died for it."

The chatter filling the inn paused temporarily, those sitting closest swivelling in their direction to see what the fuss was about. Anger gone as quickly as it had come, she sank back into her seat, exhausted. "Please, I don't want to talk about it."

Cynia silently reached over the table and took her hand. "Sorry."

Talyn shook her head. "I'll be posted next week, all right? Enough." She needed to change the subject. "Have you been given a new assignment yet?"

"No, actually." To Talyn's never-ending relief, Leviana took the segue and ran with it. "It's nice to be back in the city and have a break. I've missed so many parties—you wouldn't believe all the gossip I've had to catch up on."

Talyn smiled, trying to lighten the mood. "Do you have any idea where they'll send you next?"

"We hear word there's a trip to Montagn coming up," Cynia said, keen interest edging her voice.

"Montagn?" Talyn perked up. She'd never been there, but that was true of most residents of the Twin Thrones. A sprawling empire across the sea to the distant north, Montagn sat west of the small kingdom of Mithranar, her father's birthplace.

While trade was vibrant between Montagn, Firthland, the Twin Thrones, and to a lesser extent Mithranar, successive rulers of the Twin Thrones had historically refused to send a crown representative to Montagn for one compelling reason.

They used slave labour.

Cynia seemed to be following a similar train of thought. "I'm not sure what's changed, or if anything has. This would be a Callanan liaison assignment only—not a formal crown representative—aiming to build relationships with the Montagni army."

"Even so," Talyn muttered. Like all her family, she believed the mere idea of slave labour—the thought that the life of a person could be bought and paid for—was utterly abhorrent.

"Whoever goes will likely have a chance to see Mithranar too," Cynia added.

"I still struggle to get my head around the idea of people with wings." Leviana sounded fascinated by the idea.

"It's not all that different from our SkyRiders," Talyn said. "And apparently they helped King Alendor during the Firthlander war."

Leviana and Cynia shared a quick glance. Peace had reigned between Firthland and the Twin Thrones for generations, but the time of war hadn't been entirely forgotten, nor had the consequences. Aethain allowed Warlord Hadvezer a lot of freedom to rule, but the fact remained Firthland was effectively a vassal state of the Twin Thrones.

Those like Leviana and Cynia, who were the product of inter-marriages between citizens of the two countries, hadn't escaped the occasional ire directed their way by those who liked to dwell on the past.

"If we got the Montagni assignment, we might get to see a winged person." Cynia nudged Leviana excitedly. "They have magic too, don't they? Do you know much about that, Tal?"

"My father never talked about it much, but I think the winged folk do have some kind of magic." She nodded. "He told me once it's different from Callanan magic though."

"It's odd how little we know about them, right?" Leviana frowned. "They really keep to themselves."

Talyn had never thought about it like that, but Leviana was right. And her father had always been so reluctant to talk about his home.

"It might be a self-preservation thing," Cynia suggested. "They're a fairly small country with a great big powerful neighbour. Keeping a mysterious air, particularly about their magical abilities, might make anyone think twice about invasion."

"You really want to go that far away?" Talyn asked, trying to relax her grip on her glass. The idea would have once enthralled her—she and Sari would have leapt at the chance for such an adventure. Somewhere inside her that excitement was still there... she just didn't know how to reach it anymore.

"It would be so exciting to see a new place, and it's only for a year," Cynia said. "But the First Blade isn't likely to send junior warriors. She'll probably send one of the Callanan masters."

"You should go for it anyway," Talyn advised. "You might not get it this time, but they'll know you're interested and hopefully they'll remember that next time it comes up."

"Good advice." Cynia flashed her a smile.

A brief silence fell as they sipped ale and soaked in the lively atmosphere around them. Though they hadn't seen each other in a while, Leviana had written often, and Talyn looked over at her as she remembered the big news her friend had announced in her most recent letter.

"How is your mother?" she asked. Leviana had been an only child until her parents had announced several weeks earlier that they were expecting. It was a shock to everyone given their older ages, but Leviana had nonetheless sounded thrilled at the idea of a baby sibling.

"She's well, according to the healers. Father is desperately hoping for a boy." Leviana scrunched up her face. "Then he might have the proper heir he's always wanted."

Talyn and Cynia shared a look. Leviana's parents hated that she'd chosen to join the Callanan and pressured her constantly to leave. Her friend didn't talk about it much, but the pressure had to be stressful.

"Be careful, Levs," Cynia warned softly.

"Why? It will be perfect. I'll have a cute little baby sibling to fuss over and they'll stop harassing me about leaving the Callanan."

Leviana's voice indicated she wanted to talk about this about as much as Talyn wanted to talk about Sari, so Talyn pushed her half-empty mug away and rose. "I have early drill in the morning, so I should probably get going."

Leviana's face fell, but neither of them challenged her abrupt departure. Cynia offered a cheerful wave. "We'll make sure to come find you before we head out on our next assignment."

"Make sure you do." Talyn managed a smile, then turned and pushed her way through the crowd, letting out a breath of relief when she reached the warm evening air outside.

By the time she walked back through the busy city streets to the Kingshield barracks, weariness tugged at her muscles. She grew tired so quickly these days. Shaking off that depressing thought, she went through the gates, turning left for the barracks. But she'd only taken a couple of steps when one of the new recruits came running up.

"Guard Dynan?" he asked. "The First Shield wants to see you."

"Now?" She frowned. The overall commander of the Kingshield rarely conducted business outside of daylight hours. It was even rarer that he called junior guards to his office for one-on-one meetings.

"Yes, Guard Dynan. He asked me to wait for you here and send you straight up."

Once the recruit had run off, she stood, hesitating. A summons like this probably meant she was about to get early advice on the posting they'd decided for her, the courtesy no doubt due to her Dumnorix blood.

"This is a good thing."

Her fingers crept to her wrist again. She hated the indecision that had her wavering in the middle of the Kingshield yard, hated that a big part of her wanted to ignore the summons and hope it just went away. And now she'd run out of time to come up with a way to get out of a posting.

"You'll be fine."

Firmly ignoring the voice in her head, she straightened her shoulders and turned for the building where the First Shield had his quarters.

It was going to be fine.

CHAPTER 3

The door to the First Shield's rooms stood open. After straightening her black tunic and settling the leather weapons' belt at her waist, Talyn knocked and entered.

First Shield Lark Ceannar sat behind his desk, an expression of intense focus tightening his rough-edged features as he studied the parchment in front of him. His left hand hovered over it, blue ink pearling on the tip of the quill he was holding, an instant away from dripping down onto the page. Behind him hung the Dumnorix house sigil—the crossed swords on a black background wreathed in amber starlight and flame.

Ceannar wasn't nobility. He'd joined the Kingshield from the Calumnian army and risen through the ranks over many years, earning his place at the top. She'd seen him on occasion at palace functions, but they'd officially met only once, the day she'd been formally accepted into the Kingshield. She had little to form a solid impression of him outside the gossip of her fellow guards—that he was a good administrator, but blunt and uncompromising. He was also rumoured to have been one of the finest fighters the Kingshield had ever had.

"Sir?" she prompted him when it became obvious he hadn't heard her knock.

Ceannar glanced up and waved her silently to one of the chairs before his desk. She closed the door and sat, trying not to shift uncomfortably as his attention returned to the parchment. Several minutes passed, and three drops of the ink—she counted—before he finally scratched something on the page and put it aside.

Then he looked up. Faded brown eyes focused on her face, his look giving her the impression she had his entire attention, whatever the parchment contained completely forgotten. "I read through your file earlier, Guard Dynan. You've been with us just over a year, now?"

"Yes, sir." She nodded.

"Your father travelled here as a sailor when he was a young man, then stayed after meeting your mother?"

"Yes, sir. He fell in love with our country, as much as my mother." Mithranar remained somewhat of an exotic mystery to most of those in Firthland and the Twin Thrones, particularly as it was home to the winged folk—humans with wings that allowed them to fly. Only the sailors who plied their ships back and forth with trading goods knew much about them. No member of the winged folk had yet to step foot in either capital of Ryathl or Port Lachley that she was aware of.

But Ceannar already knew all this. It was starting to feel like he was easing into something, and he wouldn't be doing that if it was something good. She tried not to tense.

"Your record is impressive. You were an Aimsir rider from age twelve—startlingly young, even for a Dumnorix—before leaving the north at sixteen to join the Callanan." His gaze remained unwaveringly on hers. "You have been described without exception as one of the most skilled Callanan to ever wear the green cloak. Why leave all that to join the Kingshield?"

The question was delivered bluntly. Despite herself, she couldn't hold that gaze. Her eyes dropped to her lap. "I'm sure you already know that I lost my partner, sir."

There was a moment of silence, but his blunt tone didn't change when he spoke again. "I am aware. What happened was tragic. But why leave and join the Kingshield? Was it because of your connections with the royal family?"

That was exactly why, but not in the way Ceannar thought, and she struggled for a satisfactory answer that wouldn't give away what she was hiding from everyone. "Not really, sir. My mother formally removed herself from court and any political influence when she chose to marry my father. I was raised far from the court, and I don't have any formal status here."

"But you've had audience with the king a number of times since your first arrival in Ryathl? You even attended the hunt with His Majesty and Lord Ariar yesterday."

"Yes, sir." She shifted, uncertain of where this questioning was headed. "Political influence or no, they are family, and now that I am living in Ryathl I like to spend time with them."

Ceannar nodded as if her words answered something, though she couldn't imagine what. He leaned back in his chair and folded his arms over his chest. His sleeves were rolled to his elbows and a long scar was visible snaking up from his left wrist to elbow. "I have a question for you, Guard Dynan."

"Yes, sir?" she asked warily.

"How does one of the most skilled Callanan fighters of her generation break her wrist sparring against a Kingshield Aimsir recruit with no background in weapons' skills apart from his bow?"

It hit her like a blow. All the warming up, the going over her history, it had all been to lower her guard, but she hadn't expected that it would be for *this* question. She froze, trying to come up with something to say. "I—"

"Don't even think about lying to me. Do that, and you're out, Dumnorix family member or not."

His voice and expression were merciless, giving her no wriggle room and no time to think. Reluctant admiration filled her, despite the panic beating at her bones. "I made a mistake, slipped and fell badly. It happens."

That was technically true.

"You fell badly on purpose and you know it. Quit hiding from yourself, Talyn."

She firmly pushed the voice away. Ceannar was still watching, clearly not satisfied by her answer and waiting for a better one. She desperately tried to think of something to say that would satisfy him without revealing how broken she was. "It was a lapse of concentration. It happens sometimes when I... when I remember what happened."

A muscle ticked in his jaw. "You won't be part of the posting assignments going out next week, Guard Dynan."

She shot up in her chair, astonishing herself at the indignance sweeping through her. "Why not, sir?"

"You're being given a different assignment." He held her gaze. "I am deploying you to Mithranar. The Acondor crown has requested a Kingshield guard be sent to Mithranar to assist in building their soldiers' capability in guarding and close protection."

Thick silence fell as Talyn processed Ceannar's words and then replayed them over in her mind to make sure she was hearing him properly. Then, she shifted in her chair, trying to keep the confusion from her face. "Why do they want a Kingshield guard now? And anyway, sir, I'm a new Kingshield without any active guard experience, wouldn't it be best to send a—"

"Let me be clear on something." That merciless gaze was back. "I'm not giving you a choice here. You accept this assignment and all it entails right now, before we go any further, or I have a conversation with your uncle about my doubts regarding your injury and fitness for duty."

Her lip curled. "You're blackmailing me."

Something flashed in his eyes, so briefly she barely caught it, but it might have been unease. "On the contrary. I'm your superior officer and I'm giving you an order. Do you accept?"

"Yes." She spoke without needing to think about it. She couldn't have Aethain find out about her, the idea of it terrified her more than anything else, because it would make her brokenness real—if others knew, she wasn't sure she'd ever come back from it. And that prospect was scarier than agreeing to go to a distant country without knowing why or what for.

"Good." But the unease flashed over his face again, stronger this time. "Before I go on, our discussion here tonight must remain within this room. I need your assurances on that."

Talyn glanced around, several things becoming clear. Why he'd summoned her at night. Why his clerk hadn't been outside when she arrived. "I've sworn my oath to the Kingshield, sir. I would never betray that." She frowned. "Speaking of, why is this request from Mithranar even being considered? The Kingshield only protect Dumnorix family members."

Ceannar's gaze fastened on her even more tightly, and he paused again, as if reconsidering a decision already made. "The youngest Acondor prince—Cuinn Acondor—is a member of the Dumnorix family."

Her mouth opened. Closed. She tried not to shift in her chair. Failed. Her astonishment deepened, the unreality of the conversation making her wonder if she wasn't dreaming. There was a Dumnorix in the Mithranan royal family?

The First Shield read the look on her face, saw her struggle to form words, and continued. "I accept this comes as entirely unexpected news, Guard Dynan. Nobody outside this room is aware of Prince Cuinn's Dumnorix heritage. There are good reasons for this, none of which I intend to go into with you. Suffice to say my initial intention was to deny the Mithranan request. This was also the king's decision—the Kingshield are not to be farmed out to other armies. Our specialist expertise is for the benefit of the Twin Thrones only."

Talyn cleared her throat. "So my uncle doesn't know about Prince Cuinn?"

"Only I know. And all previous First Shields." Ceannar gave her a look. "And now you."

Wonderful. "Then your decision to deny the request makes sense, sir." What didn't make sense was him telling her this.

"That's where it gets tricky." He sat back in his chair, idly rubbing at the scar on his arm. "When the request was discussed at our regular council meeting with the king, the Callanan First Blade asked that the king and I change our minds. She asked that we agree to what Mithranar was asking for and send someone to gather information on their behalf—the Callanan appear to have recently developed a significant interest in a Mithranan individual called the Shadowhawk. The First Blade pointed out that the request from Mithranar offered the perfect cover for someone to go there and investigate."

"Sir, I..." She reached up and rubbed at her forehead, trying to make sense of the myriad of questions that wanted to spill out of her. At least it was now clear why she'd been chosen for this, and why Ceannar was sending her despite his doubts about her—he was being pressured from outside. Not only that, but as ex-Callanan she had the skills they needed for this. "Who is the Shadowhawk?"

"The First Blade indicated that he's a criminal, one whose activities have them worried. I'm afraid I don't know much more than that." His expressionless face told her nothing either. What could the Callanan have that would make them so worried about a Mithranan criminal they'd risk conducting a secret investigation in a foreign country?

"Ooh, something odd is happening here, Tal."

The voice—Sari's voice, she finally admitted to herself—whispered through her mind, and she pushed it aside, determinedly focusing her attention on Ceannar as he spoke again.

"You will go to Mithranar officially as a serving Kingshield officer," Ceannar continued. "As far as the king and First Blade are concerned, you are being loaned out—by me—to the Callanan to investigate the Shadowhawk on their behalf."

Sari's voice wasn't wrong. None of this made sense. "Sir, I'm sorry, but I left the Callanan. I'm not one of them anymore. I feel uncomfortable—"

"It's this or a conversation with your uncle, Guard Dynan," he reiterated sharply.

Silence filled the room for a moment. Anger curled under her fear. She'd never liked being backed into a corner, and now she was essentially putting herself there. Self-contempt and fear swirled inside her stomach in a bitter mix.

"Prince Cuinn is Queen Sarana's youngest son." He spoke when she didn't protest any further. "I assume he'll already have some sort of guard, so you'll do your best to join that unit, or at least be involved in their training." He flashed an unexpected smile. "The First Blade now owes me quite a large favour without realising her request provides the perfect reason for me to send a Kingshield to Mithranar."

She cleared her throat. "What about Queen Sarana's other sons? Won't they need a Kingshield detail?"

"Cuinn's relation to the Dumnorix line comes from his father. He has a different father from his other siblings."

She blinked. "Sir, you don't think the queen might suspect I'm there for other purposes than just training their soldiers? Especially if you and the king have agreed to her request without asking for anything in return."

The first glimmer of approval appeared on his face. "Your uncle has considered that. You are being provided to Queen Sarana in return for a shipment of izerdia, which is setting off for Port Lachley as we speak."

A handsome return indeed—izerdia was crucial to any sort of explosive material used in a range of purposes from mining to war. And it wasn't cheap. However, that wasn't the only problem she could foresee. "If I'm to be officially training Mithranan soldiers in close protection skills to guard the royal family, I'm not sure what opportunity I'll have to investigate a criminal. In my experience, criminals don't operate in the same sphere as royal families."

"I pointed out as much to the First Blade." Ceannar shrugged. "She pointed out that being in Mithranar at all was a damn sight better than investigating from Ryathl."

"Yes, sir." She nodded acknowledgement of that. "What about the fact I'm one of the Dumnorix? Izerdia aside, you don't think the Mithranans might take exception—if not suspect my true purpose—if they found out a member of the royal family had been sent to train their soldiers?"

"There's no reason for them to find out unless you tell them. Most of the Twin Thrones doesn't even know who you are since your mother left court before you were even born." Ceannar stood. "As is usual for a Kingshield posting, you'll be deployed to Mithranar for a year. I can promise you now that following this assignment you'll be re-assigned here in the city if that's what you wish."

Talyn's mind reeled. Away for a year. Away from everything familiar to her. Away from her Dumnorix family. Maybe it would be good, to travel so far away from all the memories, from the gaping hole inside her.

"Guard Dynan?"

"Sir?" That heavy gaze was on her again, leaving her no room to look away.

"I was never a Callanan, but I have some understanding of the depth and nature of a Callanan partnership bond." He paused, that gaze on her the sharpest it had been all meeting. It shifted to her left wrist, then back to her eyes, flaying her to the bone. "Tell me that you can still be what you once were. The First Blade pushed hard for this, but tell me I'm not making a mistake sending you alone on such a complex mission without support."

"I..." Her fingers curled on the chair, everything in her wanting to scream aloud that she was terrified the answer to his question was no. "I'll be fine, sir." She spoke with a confidence she didn't feel. Guilt swamped her at what amounted to a lie, followed quickly by fear. If she was wrong and something happened to Prince Cuinn... more than just her secret would be out.

He nodded, releasing her. "You've been booked on a ship leaving tomorrow evening. I apologise for the haste. Good luck, Guard Dynan."

"Yes, sir." She turned for the door.

"One more thing." His voice stopped her.

"Sir?"

"Prince Cuinn likely knows nothing about his Dumnorix heritage." Ceannar paused. "In fact, his blood may not be obvious to you in the same way I understand it is with your relatives here. His Dumnorix heritage comes from a distant branch of the family tree that has been separate from yours for generations."

Her eyebrows shot skyward without her permission. A distant branch not connected to the one ruling the Twin Thrones. How was that possible?

Ceannar ignored her response and continued. "Cuinn's line have never had a Kingshield guard because it has always been safer that nobody know of their existence. Cuinn is the last remaining of that line. You are to do everything in your power to keep him from learning it. And before you ask any more questions—don't. Remember that nobody outside this room is ever to know what I've just told you." He returned to sit behind his desk. "Dismissed, Guard Dynan."

"Yes, sir." After a beat, and still not quite understanding any of what she'd just been told, Talyn turned and walked out the door.

AFTER HER CONVERSATION WITH CEANNAR, Talyn toyed briefly with the idea of going to the palace to inform her uncle of her assignment. In the end she decided against it. Ceannar had heavily implied that the king and First Blade knew she was the one fulfilling the Callanan request. No, her uncle knew already. And he'd left Ceannar to tell her.

Sighing, she entered her room and sat down to write a long letter to her parents. She wouldn't even have time to travel north and see them before she left.

Her mother wasn't going to be happy.

She wondered what her father would think about her being sent to his homeland. He had never spoken much about Mithranar, but growing up, she'd sometimes caught him staring off towards the north, a yearning in his eyes she hadn't understood until she was older. She'd asked him about it once, and he'd told her with a smile that he was sometimes homesick.

"They have such beautiful music in Mithranar, baby girl," he'd said as he picked her up and cuddled her to his chest.

"You just miss the music, Da?"

"Well, I had friends there too."

"Do you want to go back?"

He'd laughed and swung her around. "Not on your life. Why would I ever want to leave my girl?"

She wondered what it was her father had yearned for, what he'd been missing, what made him so sad.

Maybe she'd find out.

TARCOS APPEARED in her doorway late the next morning. She already had most of her things packed, and a single bulging bag sat beside the door.

"What's going on?" He smiled a greeting.

Talyn straightened from tidying her cot and tucked strands of black hair behind her ears. "I was called into the First Shield's office last night. I've been given an assignment."

"I see." He came closer, reached out to take one of her hands. She fought the urge to shake it off—not because she disliked his touch, but because he was too close, his smile too intimate. "How do you feel about that?"

"It's about time," she said with false confidence. "But the assignment isn't part of the regular posting cycle. He's sending me to Mithranar."

Tarcos's smile faltered. Genuine puzzlement lit up his hazel eyes. "Mithranar? That doesn't make any sense. Unless... is one of your family traveling there?"

"No. Queen Sarana requested a Kingshield to help train her soldiers in close protection." While Tarcos was her lover, he was also a Firthlander prince, and she knew without asking Ceannar wouldn't want her divulging the true reasons for her assignment. "She's paying through the nose in izerdia for it, too."

He let out a breath, a frown creasing his forehead. "Talyn, you left the Callanan, and I'm one of the few people who understands why. Travelling so far away, from your friends and family, to an unfamiliar place? You should tell your uncle you don't want to go."

She squeezed his hand before giving in to the urge to break away. "They're my orders. I don't want anyone treating me specially just because I'm related to the king," she said. "And I particularly can't afford anyone thinking I'm backing out because I'm not up to it."

"That's a legitimate concern, despite how furiously you deny it. You've been out of action for over a year," he said stubbornly.

"They're my orders," she repeated, stung. Tarcos never pushed her about what had happened—his quiet steadiness was what drew her to him. He was smart too, and like her, he felt things deeply, more deeply than he ever let on to the world. That bond made her feel safe with him, something she'd needed after what had happened. "And it's not like I've been sitting around doing nothing for the past year. I've trained every single day. I'll make sure those Mithranan soldiers are taught well."

He sighed, then moved forward to wrap his arms around her. "I hate the idea of you leaving. You know I only worry about you because I care."

"Ceannar did promise me I would be reassigned here when I returned. And it's only for a year," she murmured against his chest.

"Well that's a little better." A warm smile.

She stepped out of the hug, taking his hand and tugging him over to sit on the cot beside her. "You'll write to me, won't you?"

"As often as I can," he promised, hazel eyes searching hers. "I don't want to lose this, what we have. All right?"

She nodded. "I'll be back before you know it."

"I've seen one of the winged folk once, you know." A smile tugged at his mouth, and his hand reached out to cup her cheek and draw her closer.

"Really?" she breathed into his kiss, moving to tug the hem of his shirt from his breeches.

"Some official visit to Samatia when I was young." He deepened the kiss, voice turning husky. "Are your roommates going to come back?"

"Not for at least another full-turn. They're at drill." She grazed her fingers across his ribs where she knew he was ticklish, winning a laugh from him, needing to lighten his momentary gravity.

"Wretch," he muttered, loosening the ties on her vest.

"You love it," she murmured as she pushed him down on the cot.

CHAPTER 4

*T*he Shadowhawk entered the apartment he used and unbuttoned his sweat-soaked shirt before crossing to the bucket in what passed for a bathing area and splashing water on his face and chest. The bucket was nearly empty and its contents growing stagnant. He made a face—he'd have to get more from the well down the street next time he was here.

The hustle and bustle of Dock City streets three levels below filtered through the thin walls. Long habit made him glance at the apartment's only window, checking that the tattered curtain completely covered the grimy glass, before dropping into the room's only excuse for a chair. It would almost be more comfortable to stand, he thought sourly.

It had been a long night spent roaming the streets, scouting, searching, making sure that neither City Patrol nor WingGuard had found any of the hidden crates of wheat.

The tang of smoke on the air was strong this morning—his neighbour must have just finished one of his potent cigars. The Shadowhawk thought briefly about asking for one. Smoking might take some of the edge off that wired yet exhausted feeling that often swamped him. But no, interaction with the neighbours was an unnecessary risk.

A familiar knock at the door had him reaching instantly for the mask under the chair—one of several he kept hidden around the place. Only one man knew this as the Shadowhawk's apartment, and his knock was distinctive. Nobody else visited him here. His neighbours paid little attention to the scruffy, quiet man who moved about at odd hours and rarely seemed to be home.

It was a risk, anybody knowing the Shadowhawk's location, but this man had information sources he needed. One of a handful of information brokers that worked the underbelly of Dock City, their services offered to criminals, citizens and City Patrol alike, this one refused to meet anywhere but privately in the Shadowhawk's apartment. The Shadowhawk was only partially reassured by the fact that if a broker turned on one client, he'd lose every single other one in a heartbeat and probably end up dead in an alley. He'd made certain that even if this man did sell him out, he wouldn't be able to tell the Patrol or Falcons much other than the location of his apartment and what he looked like in a mask and cloak.

Checking the mask was in place, the Shadowhawk stood behind the door as he opened it so that nobody passing in the hall outside would catch sight of him, then closed it as soon as the man was inside the room.

"Navis." The Shadowhawk spoke flatly, disapproval in his tone. "You were here last week. You should have left it longer before returning."

"I would have preferred to. But I've learned something of potential use to you." His voice was smooth, carefully-controlled. The Shadowhawk rarely identified emotion in that voice, and when he did, he was left with the distinct impression it was deliberate. Navis was a professional, keeping himself well-paid by finding information and selling it to those who wanted it, yet staying alive no matter how dangerous the people he dealt with. The Shadowhawk had chosen Navis from amongst the brokers he knew because of that professionalism… and because of his access to winged folk circles.

A mark in the 'reasons to be uneasy' column. A human having the sort of access Navis did to the winged folk shouldn't be possible.

"What is it?"

"The Twin Thrones are sending one of their Kingshield guards to join the WingGuard as an official liaison." Navis raised a hand before the Shadowhawk's questions could spill out. It irked him the man could predict him so well—nobody else in the world could. "The Kingshield are the best of the best... they only take the elite from across the Twin Thrones' various fighting units."

A curious development, but it wasn't clear why Navis thought it might be interesting to the Shadowhawk. "Why? To enhance relations with Mithranar?" That would make the most sense. Montagn was a constant, overwhelming presence to the west. If their ahara decided he wanted Mithranar... well, there wasn't much that could stop him apart from a little bit of geography and potentially Prince Mithanis.

"Perhaps," Navis said. "But the Kingshield are trained for personal protection. Not liaison or diplomacy. I've never once heard of them doing anything else."

"And you would have?" he asked pointedly. The depth and range of Navis' knowledge worried him as much as he found it useful.

Navis said nothing to that, his typical response when the Shadowhawk pressed into areas he didn't want to discuss. Controlling his irritation with an effort, the Shadowhawk said, "So you're suggesting the Twin Thrones has some interest in protecting the Acondor family, or at least building the WingGuard's protection capability? If not that, they'd be sending a different kind of warrior, no?"

A quick flash from under the hood. Was Navis surprised he'd come to that conclusion so quickly? "It seems odd, and I couldn't begin to think why, but yes, that was my conclusion."

"Who was the source of the request? Did the Twin Thrones offer or did someone here request the Kingshield?"

"I don't know that yet."

A beat of silence. "What does this have to do with me, Navis?"

"It's an oddity. And oddities usually mean there's something bigger at play. I thought you'd want to know."

The Shadowhawk studied him for a long moment, searching for a hint of betrayal, a twitch of dishonesty, or even a clue as to whether he knew more than he was letting on.

But there was nothing.

With a sigh, he dug inside his tunic, pulling out one of the handful of coins he kept secreted there. "It's interesting, Navis, but I can't see how your information is actually useful for me. That's all you're getting."

Navis caught the tossed silver coin and it disappeared inside his cloak with a swiftness that the Shadowhawk's eyes couldn't track. "A pleasure as always, Shadowhawk."

ONCE HE WAS GONE, the Shadowhawk returned to the chair, wincing as its hard edges pressed into his hip. He'd played it casual with Navis, not wanting to let on how unsettled his news made him. A foreign warrior being sent to join the WingGuard—it made no sense.

Just as quickly as he'd sat down he rose to his feet, unable to sit still. As little sense as it made for the Acondor family to request a Kingshield liaison, it made even less sense that the Twin Thrones would just offer one up.

So, the Acondors had requested it. But why? What internal power play between the queen and the elder prince had resulted in this *oddity*, as Navis had called it?

The Shadowhawk's jaw clenched. He worried about what this meant. He tried so hard, so damn hard, and the effort exhausted him. Most of the time he hated himself for what he did, what he hid, what he *didn't* do.

His life was a house of cards, one that would collapse under the slightest strain. The coming of this Kingshield warrior could upset the balance and destroy his carefully structured existence.

He shook himself then, straightening his shoulders and pulling on a fresh shirt. Aside from their futile attempts to catch him, the Wing-Guard had nothing to do with the Shadowhawk—this foreign warrior's focus would surely be on protection and training, not on anything else in Mithranar. There was no reason why his activities would be affected or threatened.

But there was something... a faint tremor deep in his gut. The coming of this warrior was going to change things.

But how?

He would have to find out. He couldn't trust Navis—he couldn't trust *anyone*—so he'd have to find out another way.

After all, he *was* the Shadowhawk. Despite his secrecy, his connections spread deep throughout Dock City. There were ways he could make sure the coming of this foreigner didn't upset his work.

It was far too important.

CHAPTER 5

A settling of the ship's motion woke Talyn from sleep. Judging from what the captain had told her the previous night, this probably meant they'd entered Feather Bay, the main port of Mithranar.

Pushing back the rough blanket that had made her skin itch all night, she dressed quickly, leaving her bag sitting at the foot of her bunk as she left the tiny cabin.

Thick, warm air hit her as she climbed the ladder to the deck. A glance around showed early morning fog beginning to clear as a hot sun burned through. She rounded the pilot's cabin and stepped down towards the prow.

Her stride faltered and she came to a stop.

One hand absently reached up to rub at her eyes to make sure she was actually awake and not sleepwalking. Consciousness established, her legs carried her forward, right up to the prow of the ship. There she stood, legs spread wide for balance, wide-eyed gaze staring in astonishment.

Feather Bay was a turquoise harbour cradled by narrow headlands to the east and west reaching miles out into the ocean. To the north, tall forested hills rose into the sky, the tops of some of the taller ones still hidden behind the morning's foggy haze. They weren't as magnificent as the Ayrlemyre mountain range she'd spent so many years in, but their size wasn't what was so impressive about them.

They held a city between their slopes and peaks.

She blinked, open-mouthed, at the intricate web of turrets, balconies, and towers that soared high above Feather Bay, stretching far back into the land. Dragging her eyes downwards, she re-focused her gaze on the port.

From what she could tell, there was only a single area of relatively flat land—it stretched north from the shoreline for maybe two or three miles, and out along the eastern and western headlands that weren't as hilly, but thickly forested.

The city up in the hills beyond the harbour was jaw-dropping, but the flat ground below... she couldn't find a speck of visible surface under the ramshackle city that covered it, making it impossible to tell whether it was sand or dirt or something else underneath. Much bigger than Ryathl, it was so closely packed in together she wondered how anyone *breathed*.

Separating the port city from the one in the hills above it was a high wall that reached up to the level of the lowest buildings of the hill city. But calling it a *wall*... there was no word she could think of to adequately describe the magnificent, glimmering marble structure that riveted her gaze. Thoroughly opaque, it hid everything behind it from view.

A gushing waterfall thundered down over the wall to the east from a gloomy space between two hills that seemed to contain the thickest cluster of graceful buildings. It crashed down into a wide, flowing river that cut the town in two and flowed out into the bay.

This was Mithranar?

A faint chuckle sounded at her left shoulder, making her start. She turned at the captain's approach—she'd been too stupefied with wonder to notice it. At least, that's what she told herself. But in truth she wasn't as sharp as she'd once been.

"It's always like that, the first time people see the place," he said, giving her a sympathetic smile.

"My father never..." she mumbled, then cleared her throat and looked over at him. "It's amazing."

"It's a pretty sight, no doubt about it."

Her eyes returned to the city above the wall, squinting against the glare of the sun and the distance. The ship was closer now, edging in to its berth, and most of the fog had burned off. Movement caught her gaze—a figure up on one of the balconies close to the top of the wall. They were carelessly balanced right on the very edge, made tiny by the distance, covered in a bright green cloak.

She gasped without thought when the figure suddenly dived from the balcony, plummeting straight down.

Then, halfway through the descent, the cloak unfurled.

Talyn's mouth dropped as she saw that it wasn't a cloak at all, but a pair of magnificent green wings. The flyer slowed quickly, wings flapping lazily until he or she hovered in mid-air. With a final great flap, they landed on a lower balcony and disappeared inside.

"I take it nobody told you about the winged folk?" The captain's chuckle once again penetrated her stupefaction.

"Well, yes, but..." Talyn had *believed* that winged folk existed, but to actually *see* them was another thing entirely. "I had no idea."

He laughed. "The citadel—that's the city up in the hills over Dock City, above and behind the wall—is their home. Look."

Turning to where he pointed, Talyn stared even higher up into the sky. Upon closer inspection, what she had initially taken for a higher than usual number of brightly coloured birds floating in the skies above the citadel were winged people.

"It's... I don't have words," she breathed, eyes fixed on the sight. Hundreds of pairs of wings glinted in the afternoon sun in almost every colour of the rainbow.

The captain nodded, stroking his moustache, clearly enjoying her reaction. "All the winged folk live up there in the citadel. Those without wings, humans, live down here in Dock City. That great bloody wall represents more than an architectural marvel. The two societies don't get along very well."

"Why not?" she asked distantly, still watching the winged people.

He shrugged. "Winged folk don't just live above the humans because they can fly—they actually believe they're superior to the rest of us. There are a lot of poor families living in Dock City, but you'd be hard pressed to find a poor winged folk family."

She frowned, not sure if she understood his meaning correctly, but when she turned away from the sight before her, he was already walking away, calling out orders to his crew.

"Oh Sari, I wish you could see this," she murmured, swamped by a wave of melancholy so strong her shoulders bowed. For once, the voice in her head wasn't there, and she wasn't sure whether to be relieved or sad.

She shifted her gaze to the people swarming around the docks. Her ship had been guided to a berth on the western side of Feather Bay. Dock City crowded the shoreline right up to where the headlands narrowed, split only by the river to the east.

In the bright sunlight, the water sparkled. While the homes of Dock City were built from wood and sandstone, the graceful towers rearing above the wall looked to be the same creamy marble as the wall itself, reflecting all the brightness and colour of the day. She wasn't sure she'd ever seen anything so wondrous.

It was hot, though, the thickness of the air palpable. She was already sweating through her longvest and shirt. Such humidity was completely unfamiliar—Talyn was more accustomed to the bitterly cold air of the mountains and the salty, dry warmth of Calumnia's east coast.

Once they were docked, she returned briefly to her cabin to grab her bag then headed for the gangplank. The captain was waiting for her on the barnacle-encrusted dock below. Off the ship, the citadel was so far above ground level that she could only barely make out the top buildings when she craned her neck back as far as it would go. The marble wall reared like a monster over Dock City, probably two or three miles distant.

"Why the wall?" she asked the captain.

"I'm not sure." He shrugged. "There's some story behind it, I think, but I've never been told it."

She followed the captain down to the end of the jetty, where he entered a large building to file his paperwork with the harbour master. It was even hotter and muggier amongst the clustered crowds and away from the sea breeze. Sweat beaded her forehead and dripped uncomfortably down her back. Breathing felt almost like drinking soup.

The harbour swarmed with workers, none of them winged. The Mithranan accent was a lilting, musical one, the sound reminding her sharply of her father's voice. She got a few odd glances, mostly at her clothing—the men she saw all wore light shirts, all but a few without sleeves. Those with sleeves had them rolled up to elbows. The occasional woman that wandered into sight wore loose clothing too, dresses and skirts or loose pants that swung when they moved.

The captain spent a few minutes filing while Talyn waited outside, eyes constantly scanning her surroundings, drinking in everything around her. It was like nothing she'd ever experienced before, from the unfamiliar accent, to the soupy air and the utter strangeness of a hill city. A deep breath sucked in an almost overwhelming odour of people, sewerage, animals, vegetation and trade goods, overlaid with a scent of flowers.

She wasn't sure whether feeling so utterly adrift was a good thing or a bad thing. At least Sari's voice in her head had temporarily gone away.

A partially ripped piece of parchment attached to a nearby post caught her eye. Glancing inside to check on the captain—he was frowning over a form that looked only half complete—she wandered over to read it. It was barely legible, and she had to squint to make out the words. It seemed to be addressing the unfairness of winged folk extravagance when so many were poor down in Dock City.

At the bottom, it was signed by a single letter—an S—bisected by a jagged lightning bolt. A single arrow, smaller than any she'd ever seen used, pinned the parchment to the post. It was simple, fletched in black, and had the same lightning symbol etched into the shaft. Her eyes narrowed in thought, brain springing to life without permission.

"Seems like you've found your Shadowhawk already."

Talyn bit her lip. The voice was back. Despite her best intentions, she found herself responding. *"Maybe. Let's not jump ahead."*

"You always say that."

"And I'm generally right."

"I'm thinking someone who's barely literate."

"Or making themselves appear that way."

"Good point. We shouldn't jump ahead."

"Guard Dynan?"

Talyn's eyes slid closed and she took a deep breath before turning to face the ship's captain. He was clutching an unloading schedule, frowning as if he'd called her name a few times already. She tried to erase all traces from her expression that she'd just been talking to a ghost in her head. Sari had been so quiet on the ship journey, Talyn had hoped that maybe her voice was fading away.

Guess not.

"Come on." He motioned. "They told me someone's been sent to meet you. I'll take you to him, then I've got to hurry back. We need to be unloaded and loaded back up again by the dawn tide tomorrow."

She managed to keep up with the stocky captain as he weaved his way through the crowded dock area, pushing easily through the bustle. Nobody seemed to care about being jostled in the crowds, as if it were simply taken for granted. People shouted and called to each other, their voices mixing with the shouting of street vendors wheeling carts and the traders who had stalls along the docks. It was deafening, and Talyn had to fight the temptation to put her hands over her ears.

Finally, they turned onto a wide road leading directly towards the bottom of a steep path that had been cut into the massive wall. It wound up in slow curves to the citadel at the top—an architectural marvel indeed.

She'd barely had time to notice it when three men came sprinting out of a square full of people and stalls—a marketplace—to her right, one of them clutching a bulging sack. They were moving so fast that the one with the sack slammed right into her. Unprepared, she went sprawling onto the dusty road, rolling instinctively to break her fall.

They'd sent the captain stumbling too, the closest runner smoothly yanking the satchel from the man's shoulder as he went—the one containing all his ship's paperwork.

The three men kept running, not looking back as they crossed the road and disappeared around a nearby corner. Talyn was on her feet a second later, glancing towards shouts coming from a second group of men in pursuit. Wearing matching brown uniforms, they weren't moving nearly as fast as their quarry as they tried to shove through the now-agitated crowd that had gathered and was spilling out of the busy marketplace.

"Bastards!" the ship captain swore after the fleeing men, seeming to have temporarily forgotten she was there. "Goddamn City Patrol will never catch them."

She glanced from him to the street across the road where the men had disappeared. Without thinking about it any further, she hefted her bag and sprinted after them.

They'd already made the mistake of fleeing down a much quieter street—there were only a handful of people moving in each direction along it, easy for her to avoid as she ran. She was halfway down the street when they rounded a corner ahead.

She increased her pace, hurtling around the blind corner and hoping there was nothing or no one beyond to run into. There wasn't, and by the time she rounded it, she'd halved the distance between her and the thieves.

"Reckless, Tal."

One of them lagged, face red and glistening with sweat as he glanced back. Without breaking stride, she swung her duffel bag off her back and hurled it at him. It crashed into his back and he went down hard, banging his head on the ground as he fell. Ahead, his companions paused, but when he didn't get up immediately, they turned and kept running.

Talyn left her bag and continued the pursuit. Sprinting harder without the weight of her bag, heart pounding in her chest, dust flying from her boots, she closed the distance. As she got within throwing range, she considered taking them both down with a throw of her sais, but quickly discarded the idea—potentially maiming two strangers without understanding the situation better might be considered a faux pas on her first day in a foreign country.

"You think?" Sari asked dryly. *"Why are you even chasing these fools?"*

The two men jerked abruptly to the right and into the doorway of what looked like an empty shopfront. Her boots skidded in the dust as she turned and went after them, bursting through the doorway at a full sprint. One man was waiting for her, but she'd expected that and instantly dove forward. The whisper-soft hiss of a knife passing through the air inches from the top of her head brushed by her as she hit the ground and rolled to her feet in one movement.

The second man had been hiding in the corner, and now he broke and ran for the open doorway. Talyn spun, kicking the door so hard it slammed into the man's back as he scrambled over the threshold. He fell forward into the street, and Talyn turned as the third man—the knife-thrower—yanked open the shutters on a window on the opposite side of the room.

He was scrambling up onto the edge when she reached him, grabbed his legs, and yanked hard. He kicked out at her, forcing her to let go. Avoiding another kick, she moved in and placed the sharp point of her sai at the base of the man's spine.

"Get back inside or you'll never walk again," she warned.

He swore, and Talyn stepped away as he let go of the window frame and dropped to the floor. She made a sharp gesture with her sai. "On the floor. Facedown. Hands on the back of your head."

She studied him as he complied, alert for any indication that he was about to make another move to flee or attack. He was maybe her father's age, maybe younger—it was hard to tell given his scruffy beard and threadbare clothing—his whole body rigid as he lay down and stared mutinously at the floor, jaw clenched. The sack he'd presumably stolen, along with the captain's satchel, lay on the floor under the window.

For a moment there was nothing but the sound of her heartbeat thudding in her chest. Three men taken down in the space of moments. The first time she'd been in a fight since... the first time she'd ever been in a fight without Sari at her back.

Sweat slicked every inch of her skin and soaked through the back of her longvest. Her muscles burned from overexertion. She'd pulled something in her left calf—the result of losing the sharp edge she'd once had—but her body had known the steps even if her mind had been too afraid to take them. The grief was like a live creature clawing through her chest, and she wanted to bend over and start howling like a baby.

The sound of shouts outside gave her something to focus on, and by the time two men in matching brown uniforms stepped inside, blinking against the dim interior, she'd managed to regain some composure. Even so, the first one through the door gave her an odd look. "Who are you?"

"Talyn Dynan." She sheathed the sai and offered a hand. "I'm Kingshield from Calumnia. Who are you?"

"We're City Patrol. What—" The older of the two men was gruff, red-faced and sweaty, ignoring her outstretched hand. The younger, more eager one, spoke over him in panting breaths.

"I'm Lidrin and this is Rolf." His face scrunched. "What's a Kingshield—I've never seen anything like what you just did? And what brings you to Mithranar?"

Rolf shot his companion a hard look, holding it until the younger man dropped his gaze, then turned his attention back to Talyn. "Would you mind stepping outside so our watch officer can speak with you?"

"Of course." Talyn followed Rolf outside into the sunlight, blinking rapidly until her eyes adjusted, while Lidrin went for the man on the floor. Two more men in brown were tying the wrists of the man she'd hit with the door, and another was standing nearby, hand firmly on the shoulder of the thief she'd dropped in the road with her duffel. His hands were already tied behind his back and her bag was at his feet.

"Reckon the patrol captain will make us hold them in the cells?" One of the Patrolmen looked at Rolf.

"Theac wouldn't have," another one muttered. "They were just hungry, is all."

"Not just that." Rolf nodded his head at the scraggly man Lidrin was struggling to drag outside. "This one's part of the Shadowhawk network. I almost caught him last year when they robbed the coal shipment."

Talyn's eyes went straight to the prisoner who'd thrown the knife at her with such deadly accuracy. Unlike the other two he was spitting curses at the Patrolmen, shoulders writhing as he fought the rope around his wrists.

"That's why I chased those fools, Sari. Instinct."

There was no reply. Her attention was caught by the arrival of another Patrolman along with her ship's captain. From the way everyone around her looked at the new Patrolman—despite his small, lithe stature—she supposed this was the watch officer.

"Sir, this is Talyn Dynan from Calumnia," Rolf said. "She says she's something called a Kingshield."

The man's hazel eyes widened slightly in surprise. He looked Talyn up and down, clearly unsure what to make of her presence. "I'm Watch Officer Andres Tye. Thank you for your help."

"I second that," the captain said in relief. "You have my thanks, Guard Dynan. Losing those papers would have cost me badly."

"They're just inside along with whatever these men stole." She lifted a questioning eyebrow at Tye. Beside her, Rolf gestured, and one of the Patrolmen ducked into the house.

"It was bread from one of the stalls at the market." Tye's expression was an odd mixture of regret and frustration. "It's the second time this week we've caught thieves at the markets in broad daylight."

The Patrolman reappeared from inside the house, passing the captain's satchel back to him and then opening the sack for Tye's inspection. The scent of fresh bread wafted out. Unbidden, Talyn's stomach growled. She hadn't eaten much for breakfast and the exertion of the chase and fight had made her hungry.

"Lucky you didn't throw your sais at them. They were just hungry," Sari observed.

Being hungry didn't give you licence to steal, but there was something about the look of the men she'd just hunted down that made her uneasy at having helped catch them. Before Talyn could manage a reply, either to Sari or Tye, a sweep of air washed over them, warm and redolent with the scent of flowers. Instantly all Patrolmen's eyes shot upwards. The prisoners' too. The Shadowhawk member's expression turned flat and hateful, one side of his mouth curling in contempt.

Three winged men dropped gracefully out of the sky, their outstretched wings furling gracefully in the narrow quarters of the street. Sleeveless teal vests fitted their upper bodies, a winged emblem etched in scarlet silk on their shoulders. Breeches in deeper blue, but also edged in scarlet, fitted neatly into ankle-high leather boots. Elaborately carved sword hilts—each one different—poked out from where they wore their weapons strapped down their backs between their wings.

Talyn stared, unsure whether it was their beauty or the fact that she was seeing winged people up close for the first time that had her so frozen. Before she realised what was happening, the City Patrolmen melted away, taking the prisoners and her ship's captain with them.

By the time she'd registered they were leaving, all she caught were the black looks they shot in the direction of the winged folk on their way down the street. She turned back, acutely aware of the dust and scuff marks on her previously immaculate uniform. Not to mention the sweat glistening on her face and plastering her shirt to her skin.

"You must be the foreigner."

Her gaze fixed on the winged man who'd spoken. His short-cropped hair was brown, bare arms wiry and strong. Extra muscle bulked up his shoulders, likely because of the massive dark-red wings that hung loosely from his back.

Beauty and grace had been the first two things that came to her stunned mind at the first sight of winged folk so close, and though the grim set of this one's features took away some of his natural beauty, he was nonetheless striking. Almost at odds with his expression was the musical lilt to his voice—it was hard to concentrate on his words when they were being spoken in such a lovely way.

"I'm Guard Talyn Dynan of the Kingshield, yes." She saluted for good measure.

"Jehran Ravinire. I'm the Falcon, overall commander of the Mithranan WingGuard." He eyed her carefully, piercing dark eyes making it hard to stand still under the scrutiny. "I hope you're not going to be more trouble than you're worth, Guard Dynan."

She fought the impulse to glance at the dirt on her pants or look back into the empty store. "How's that, sir?"

"You've barely even arrived, and you're already involved in a scuffle."

"I was just helping out the City Patrol, sir."

"Leave their job to them in the future," he said gruffly, then turned and began striding away. He did not introduce the other two men with him—both younger but with matching expressions of reserve. The look they sent her way expressed almost identical degrees of contempt, but they were lifting in the air before she could even process it, let alone respond.

Shrugging, she hefted her bag and went after Ravinire.

She caught up to him as he turned back into the wide avenue leading to the base of the wall and he kept moving until they reached the bottom of a long, winding path leading upwards that had been seamlessly chiselled into the wall—she could barely contemplate how thick the structure must be. The path was wide, leaving room for plenty of people to be moving in both directions.

Not that there were many.

Ravinire glanced at her, then started up the path. Talyn followed obediently.

It was a hard walk. The path was steep and seemed to go on forever. Still, Ravinire walked with her the entire way rather than flying as he so easily could have done. It was a detail she didn't fail to notice—she just wasn't sure whether it indicated respect or a desire to emphasise the fact she couldn't fly like him.

Her legs began to ache about halfway up, the muscle in her calf tugging painfully each time she pushed off it, and her shoulders and back followed suit not long after. Gritting her teeth, she kept up with Ravinire's merciless pace anyway. One thing all Callanan learned was enduring physical discomfort. She might be out of fighting shape, but her will could get her through almost everything. Almost.

As they approached the top, she began to be glad she wasn't afraid of heights. The city and harbour grew smaller and smaller below them, the drop precipitous with no railing along the path's outer edge to prevent an accidental fall.

Then, they rounded a corner and were at the top. It *was* thick—at least two carriage-lengths across—and it ran east and west into the distance as far as she could see. The drop was dizzying, but the view south out into Feather Bay utterly stunning.

She stopped, letting her eyes drink it all in.

North were unending forested hills, as far as she could see. And above her, perched amongst the upper slopes of the hills, was the citadel. No part of it that she could see reached lower than the top of the wall where she stood. The drop was precipitous—a single glance down onto the dark green forest canopy had Talyn's stomach swooping.

A marvellous trick of architecture made the buildings clinging to the upper slopes of the forested hills seem neither fragile nor precariously balanced. Instead they simply looked like a natural part of the hillside.

Walkways—most taking the form of graceful marble bridges, finely-carved wooden ladders, or swinging rope bridges—led off in all directions, connecting the buildings of the citadel in a glittering spiderweb. There didn't appear to be order to any of it, but it was nonetheless beautiful.

"You'll be based up here given your status as a representative of the Twin Thrones." Ravinire finally spoke. "It may look daunting, but you'll find it easy enough to get around via ladders and walkways."

"Yes, sir. I'm sure I'll be fine." And fitter than she'd ever been. The sweat was pouring off her after the walk, soaking through the material of her vest and breeches and plastering her hair to her skull. She must've made a wonderful sight.

Another nod, and then Ravinire was off again, presumably expecting her to follow. They travelled upwards via a gruelling series of ladders and walkways, and through so many corridors that Talyn was soon utterly lost.

Some of the platforms were open to the air, and were filled with gardens, pools, or training yards. Others were closed in—from what she could see these served as living quarters, shops, eating places or inns. None of it looked separated. Residences perched between a tailor's and a café in one open walkway, and a public garden formed the roof of another large home.

And winged folk. Swooping past or drifting slowly in the afternoon heat. Travelling from place to place through the air. Conversation all around. Utterly wonderful in its strangeness.

"Are there tensions between the City Patrol and the WingGuard, sir?" she asked as they walked. She'd seen it before, plenty of times. Local army barracks rarely liked it when the Callanan were sent to assist with a problem in the area—be it an increase in bandit activity or particularly violent crime. They considered it interfering rather than assisting. And the Callanan *hated* it when Kingshield pulled rank over a situation by using their mandate of being responsible for protecting the monarch.

"What makes you think that?" He glanced back, expressionless.

She searched for a diplomatic turn of phrase. Shrugged when nothing came to her and decided to be blunt instead. "They disappeared as soon as you arrived, sir, and I caught the looks they were throwing you and your men."

He nodded. "Half of the Patrolmen are in the pocket of the Shadowhawk. If it were up to them, they'd probably have let the thieves go."

At another mention of the Shadowhawk, she wanted to probe further, but the closed look on Ravinire's face prevented her. They headed steadily east, towards the enormous waterfall plunging down between two hillsides, eventually emerging from a long corridor onto an open platform.

A wide bridge spanned a narrow gap between two hillslopes to a particularly stunning collection of buildings clustered together on the other side. The waterfall thundered just underneath the bridge, the source of several puddles of collected spray across its marble surface. The spray was wonderfully cool on her sweaty skin, tasting fresh and clean where it landed on her tongue and lips.

"The palace," Ravinire said curtly. "It houses the royal family and includes barracks for a full flight of the WingGuard—the flight dedicated to the protection of the crown. The walkway is guarded by four sentries at all times. A password is needed to be allowed in."

"How often are the guards changed?" Talyn asked. "And how useful are they, when someone could presumably fly into the area without going anywhere near this bridge?"

Ravinire looked at her, something that looked almost like the beginnings of respect flashing in his eyes. "Every three hours. And the guards are designed to keep humans out, not winged folk. I'll show you to your quarters, and then take you to organise your command. There'll be a bit of walking, so you may want to consider cooler clothing."

Her what? "My command?"

"Yes. A full WingGuard flight consists of four wings. The queen and the two elder princes have a wing each assigned to their protection, and the fourth is used as protection for the five Queencouncil members. Prince Cuinn, however, for various reasons, has never had a personal guard. You'll be heading up a new wing being created for him." He stepped out onto the bridge. The sentries at the other end parted to let them through without comment, though the looks they directed at Talyn were far from welcoming.

"I wasn't aware that I would be placed in command of a unit," she said, then cursed herself for arguing—fortunate chance had landed her exactly where Ceannar had wanted her to be, in Cuinn's detail. "My understanding is that I was to be training your soldiers."

"Fortunate chance? I'm not so sure."

"You have specific training that the WingGuard lacks, so it makes sense to put you in command of the new unit." He flashed her another unreadable glance. "You won't find it easy. There aren't any women in the WingGuard. It's not considered suitable for women to fight here."

Her eyebrows lifted. No wonder Ravinire looked so sour about her arrival. He—or whoever had made the official request to her uncle—probably hadn't thought to specifically request a male Kingshield. "Have there been any specific threats on the royal family, sir?"

"No."

"Can I ask why you've requested a Kingshield liaison, then?"

"That wasn't my decision," Ravinire said, a hint of ice in his tone.

She stopped, forcing him to halt also. Best to deal with this straight away—she didn't want lingering resentment with her superior officer if she could help it. "You don't want me here," she said bluntly.

He glanced at her, not rising to the bait. "I have heard good things about the Kingshield."

"But you didn't ask for one. Worse, I'm a woman." She kept her voice even, pointing out fact rather than challenging him. Then she kept the lie just as smooth. "Let me assure you I am only here to provide assistance to your WingGuard in close protection skills. Your queen paid a high price for it in izerdia—I promise you I'll do everything I can to live up to it."

"Understood." He continued walking.

She sighed, then ploughed after him. "If there haven't been any specific threats against the family, has the environment here changed in some way?" She tried asking her 'why now' question a different way. Ceannar either hadn't known or wouldn't tell her. Maybe Ravinire would. "I can't protect your prince or train your WingGuard properly without fully understanding what I need to guard against."

Ravinire stepped off a bridge and climbed a steep set of stairs to another terrace. This one looked out over a thickly forested hillside—they were so high up that a glance over the railing showed her nothing but green. "The prince won't be able to meet with you until later, but I will help you with the establishment of your wing." He neatly avoided her question.

"Six thrices, Tal, what is going on?"

She squelched Sari's voice as Ravinire stopped outside a blue wooden door. It stood slightly open, and he waved her inside. "These rooms are set aside for guests of the royal family, although they don't often get used because they're so far from the central area of the palace. I assigned one to you because it is close to the barracks I've set aside for your wing."

"So they're all empty?" She gestured towards the other doors along the terrace.

"That's right. You'll have privacy."

"Why aren't I in the barracks with my wing?"

"You're a guest of the crown," he said curtly. "I'll leave you to settle your things and change. I'll be back in a half-turn. If there's anything else you need, you can let me know then."

She tried not to be astounded when he spread his wings and leaped off the side of the terrace, but failed miserably. She *did* manage to hold back from going to gape over the railing after him.

Pushing the blue door open wider, she walked in on a sitting room that housed a lounge and a fireplace, with a desk and chair for work. Beyond an archway was a bedroom with a large bed and chest of drawers, the space filled with light from a window set in the roof over the bed. From the bedroom, a smaller arch led into a bathing room.

The sparse but tasteful setup of the room suited her perfectly. Maybe spending a year here wouldn't be so horrible after all. It certainly beat sharing a barracks room with anyone but Sari—something she'd struggled bitterly with since joining the Kingshield.

Not that she had any clue why a fireplace was necessary in this oppressively humid country. Or, for that matter, the thick doona on the bed.

It was slightly cooler up in the citadel, though, and she stripped off her sweat-soaked longvest with relief. The silence was complete—Ravinire had been right about the privacy.

She tried not to be unsettled, telling herself it was simply the result of being in an unfamiliar place. Ravinire's casual words that she would command a protection detail worried her, though. Whoever the members of the detail were, they weren't likely to welcome a foreigner being placed in charge of them, especially a woman and one without wings.

But the root of her unease was the fact she'd never been in command before. She had learnt all about it in the Callanan, but never actually been in charge of a unit. And the one time she had decided to make a call—

She shook her head, trying to pull herself back from sliding into the pit of despair that had become so familiar. She was Callanan no longer. She was Kingshield now, and it was her job to protect.

To busy herself, she washed quickly in the bathing room before digging through her bag and pulling on a fresh tunic, a lighter one designed for the summer months in Calumnia. The sleeveless black vest fell to just below the top of her breeches, held in place by a black leather swordbelt that unusually held no sword—instead twin sais were sheathed in the small of her back. To the uninitiated, they looked like oversized forks: a three-pronged weapon with the middle prong a good two inches longer than those on either side.

While Leviana adored her knives like they were her children, and Cynia was a better markswoman with her bow than most Aimsir Talyn had ever met, Talyn's signature weapon was her sais. Primarily a defensive weapon—perfect for a Callanan, who needed to disarm and hold more often than they needed to kill—the points of hers were sharp enough to kill if necessary.

Not that she couldn't use most other weapons when needed.

She brushed out her sweat-soaked hair and re-bound it in a long plait, her gaze falling on her discarded tunic as she did. She picked it up to fold it, lightly fingering the myriad of tiny amber stars etching out the shape of a pair of crossed blades over the heart.

Like starlight. That was how people described the unusual brightness of the Dumnorix family's eye colouring. And so the emblem worn by all the Twin Thrones' fighting forces was made of stars, always in the colour of the ruling monarch's eyes. A direct mirror of the Dumnorix house sigil—crossed swords on a black background wreathed in amber.

While the Callanan wielded a magic that allowed them to use their body's energy to summon a shield that could protect them from any type of attack, the hint of magic running through Dumnorix blood was less specific. It expressed itself—almost universally—in a natural and powerful charisma, strength and skill with weapons and a self-assurance bordering on arrogance, as well as an instinctive awareness of and connection to each other. And some Dumnorix, like Talyn and her mother, were born with Callanan magic too, making them formidable warriors.

She allowed herself to draw strength from that, from being one of them. So far, it had been all that kept her going.

Burn bright and true.

She would hold to that, would *make* herself hold to it. And maybe it would save her.

CHAPTER 6

A knock came at her door just as she'd finished tightening the laces on her boots.

The Falcon, who wore an impassive expression she was quickly coming to understand was his usual demeanour, stood back to allow her to leave. She shut the door behind her, and he wordlessly passed her a key. She took it and locked the door before tucking it away in a pocket.

"Is this the only one?" she asked.

"It is."

She fell in with him as he began walking. "You said before that you're the overall commander of the WingGuard, sir? The Falcon?"

"In the absence of a Ciantar, yes."

Talyn had no clue what that meant, but let it go. "And the Wing-Guard is the fighting force of the winged folk?"

"Yes." He hesitated. "But most folk, particularly the humans, refer to us as Falcons."

"Is there a human army?"

"Not as such. The City Patrol are responsible for maintaining order in Dock City and our larger towns in the north, but they are not trained for battle." He glanced her way. "Like your Callanan, as I understand it?"

"Not quite, sir. Like you, our country is at peace, so yes, the Callanan are focused on investigating violent or criminal behaviour where local army posts or guards can't control it or don't have the resources, but we *are* trained for battle. In times of war, we're a specialised, elite fighting unit."

"We? I thought you were Kingshield?"

She cursed herself for the dangerous slip of the tongue. She'd never have made a slip like that before, risking triggering Ravinire's suspicions about her other purpose in Mithranar. *Damn it.* "Kingshield only take the best warriors from across the Twin Thrones' various fighting forces, sir. I was Callanan before I joined the Kingshield."

He nodded, accepting that. "I already have one Falcon assigned to your new wing, but I would prefer you chose the rest yourself from outside the WingGuard."

Her confusion deepened. She cleared her throat. "I thought you said a flight of the WingGuard is responsible for the protection of the royal family?"

"You listen well," he said dryly. "A flight dedicated to protection and five other flights make up Mithranar's army. Almost seventeen hundred warriors in total."

"Seventeen hundred. He calls that an army?"

"I'm sorry, sir." Talyn stopped in the middle of the open-air corridor they were traversing. "I don't mean to be obtuse, but I don't understand. If the WingGuard are the only warriors Mithranar has, where are the other soldiers for my wing coming from?"

"If you can reign in your impatience just a little longer, your questions will be answered shortly, Guard Dynan," he said briskly.

"Is he deliberately trying to confuse you as some sort of test? This is all very odd, Tal."

"You don't say."

"Yes, sir," Talyn replied out loud, and they started walking again.

Ravinire seemed to reconsider his terseness a short time later, because he spoke again as they crossed the bridge and left the palace. "As you are not familiar with our country, our behaviour and reasoning will not always be obvious to you. Suffice to say, for now, that I feel it would be best that Prince Cuinn's guard not come from amongst the WingGuard."

"Yes, sir."

She didn't dare ask why.

TALYN WAS UTTERLY LOST by the time they emerged into the hot sunlight at the top of the wall and set out down the steep wall path. She followed without complaint, though not without a deep inward sigh.

Walking back up the wall for the second time in the same day was thoroughly unappealing, particularly after clambering up and down what felt like an endless series of ladders and narrow staircases in the citadel. Her legs muscles burned, her left calf was outright stabbing in pain with each step now, and she thought a blister might be coming up on her right little toe.

At the bottom, Ravinire strode with purpose through a bustling tangle of streets, clearly knowing where he was going. The sounds and smells of Dock City engulfed her, the humidity as thick as if she wore another cloak, her skin again becoming slick with sweat.

And the people.

It was a crowded city—they thronged the streets, moving in several directions at once without clear streams of movement. It wasn't easy to keep focused on Ravinire's quickly moving stride. Especially when she couldn't fail to notice the dark looks thrown their way.

People didn't like the Falcons. She wondered at the source of it. While the army, particularly local regiments, liked to consider the Callanan elitist and superior, they were widely respected amongst the people of Calumnia and Conmor. Talyn had certainly received her share of hatred and contempt from the thieves, rapists and murderers she and Sari had captured, but there had always been the counterpoint of genuine appreciation from the local citizens that those criminals had preyed on.

Eventually Ravinire turned down what appeared to be a main street—it was full of carts, horses and people, and a cloud of tiny buzzing insects hovering around crates of overripe fruit nearby was so thick that several flew into her mouth. She spat them out and switched to breathing through her nose.

"*I hate bugs.*"

"*Lucky you're not here then.*" Talyn grimaced as she swiped at another bug before it sailed into her mouth.

Ravinire stopped outside a long wooden building, before a series of uneven steps leading up to a double-doored and open front entrance. Two armed men in a familiar brown uniform stood to either side of the open doorway, both of them saluting—reluctantly—as Ravinire walked through.

Interesting. They disliked the Falcons, but clearly accepted Ravinire's authority without protest. The Patrolman on the left gave her a curious glance as she followed the Falcon inside.

"We've walked through the Wall Quarter into the Wealthy Quarter—this is the City Patrol headquarters," Ravinire explained as they entered a cool, dim foyer. "There's a station in each quarter, but this is the biggest. It's also where the main city jail is housed."

Talyn's gaze went to the cluttered desk directly ahead, where two Patrolmen sat. Although *sprawled* would be a better description. No strict military posture there, and neither looked like they could run half a block without turning bright red and keeling over. The one on the left was at least double her age, with thinning hair and sweat glistening on his face. He hefted himself to his feet at Ravinire's appearance, managing a sloppy salute. "Falcon. I'm Watch Officer Dirrus. The pardonables are down to your right, sir. We've separated them out of the main holding cells for you."

Ravinire nodded acknowledgement and turned to Talyn. "Down that hall you'll find the cells holding petty criminals that are to be considered for pardon by the queen. Choose as many as you want, and they'll be pardoned and sent to the citadel to join your wing."

Only years of training and discipline allowed Talyn to keep a straight face. "Sir, are you asking me to choose *criminals* to form a guard detail?" She felt the need to tack on, "For Prince Cuinn?"

"That's right." He hesitated. "None of the City Patrol were willing to volunteer for your wing, and as I said, I'd prefer Prince Cuinn's detail not be formed by a significant number of Falcons."

She wasn't entirely sure he wasn't playing some kind of prank on her. But this was the head of the WingGuard and he'd yet to demonstrate even a hint of a smile, let alone a sense of humour. No, he must be serious. And she was a soldier whose job it was to follow orders, no matter how strange they seemed.

"To be clear, sir," she said as politely as she could manage. "You want me to go and choose men from those cells to form a protective guard detail?"

"That's right. I haven't got all day, Guard Dynan. Best get to it." Impatience edged his voice. The two Patrolmen on the desk were doing their best to pretend like they weren't straining to listen to every word of this conversation.

She turned on her heel without a word, half-expecting laughter to break out behind her. But none came. She ached for Sari at her side so badly her chest physically hurt. Her partner would have known how to manage this situation with her crisp confidence and lack of patience for tomfoolery.

Instead Talyn was alone as she stepped through the doorway into the cells and stopped abruptly, waiting for her eyes to adjust to the dimness. A ripe stench filled her nose and she stifled the urge to put a hand over her face. Instead, she tried to breathe through her mouth. Once her eyes adjusted, a line of cells was visible running down either side of the hall that stretched out before her. There were maybe fourteen in total. Each cell had a single barred window situated high in the wall—the room's only light source—and was large enough to hold about three or four prisoners.

They were not unlike the cells at Callanan Tower or the city jail in Port Lathilly where she and Sari had spent plenty of time. Except for the smell. And the rotting straw that was used to floor the cells. And the stifling, oppressive heat that nobody had bothered to ease by opening a window or a door.

Talyn had barely taken two steps when the sound of a fight broke out from a cell down at the end of the hall. Shouts echoed and then a man grunted in pain. She recognised that sound—it was the grunt a fighter made when they were hurt but ignoring the pain so they could focus on survival.

After a glance behind to confirm neither of the Patrolmen on the desk were bothering to come and check on what was happening, she headed down the row. In the last cell on the right a bear of a man was being set upon by three of his fellow prisoners. His great muscles bulged as he sent one of his attackers flying into the wall. A second hit him with a piece of rusted pipe, and he staggered backwards, blood spurting from his nose and spraying his opponent.

"Hey!" A loud bellow came from the cell opposite. "Guards! Guards!"

Impressed by the voice's strength and note of command, Talyn spun towards the cell's occupant with interest. Stocky and broad-shouldered, he was going soft in the belly and his short-cropped hair was more grey than brown. His forearms were scarred, nose crooked like it had been broken several times, and he held himself like a soldier, despite the belly and the bloodshot eyes that spoke of poor diet and too much time in the city's taverns.

"What's going on?" Talyn asked him.

He scowled, looking her up and down as if wondering what the hell a *woman* was doing in the cells. "What the hell do you care?"

"If you want me to help him, you'll tell me, and be quick about it," she snapped.

The scowl only deepened. "Halun refused to be an enforcer for one of the overseers that runs the docks. He arranged to have Halun locked up in here, and then paid those prisoners to beat the snot out of him." He spat. "No doubt some coin went to one or two Patrolman's sticky fingers too, just to make sure they all ended up in a cell together."

She glanced back. Halun was cornered in the back of his cell. One of his cellmates was down, it looked like permanently, but the bear of a man was bleeding and clearly coming to the end of his strength. If she left him there, he could die. No Patrolmen had yet appeared despite the bellows of the prisoner opposite.

A bitter mix of shock and disgust curled in her. What kind of place was this? The criminals held prisoner in Callanan Tower were never treated this way, as if they were no better than animals.

She turned and jogged back out to the main foyer. Ravinire leaned against a wall nearby, wings brushing the floor, ignoring the dark looks being surreptitiously shot in his direction. She marched up to the desk. "The prisoner named Halun is being beaten half to death."

"There's nothin' we can do about that." Dirrus shrugged. "He can't leave that cell until someone pays his bond or he gets pardoned. Nobody has shown up on his behalf."

The man's blatant disinterest in the fate of the prisoners, not to mention Ravinire's equally apathetic attitude, had her gritting her teeth. Criminals generally weren't good people, but treating them like animals made you as bad as they were. "Fine," she snapped. "I choose him for my wing. Get him out of there."

In her head, Sari's voice roused, but Talyn slapped it back down, her anger making her strong. For the moment there was no despair, no aching for her partner, just determination. Dirrus heaved himself to his feet, gesturing for the younger man to join him. She chafed as they strolled down the hall, pulling out keys as they went. Ravinire said nothing.

On reaching the cell, the younger Patrolman drew his sword while Dirrus opened the cell and yelled for its occupants to stop fighting. The big man was crouched against the back corner, fending off attacks with his arms and fists. Blood ran freely from a broken nose and a nasty gash on his bald head.

The other two prisoners backed off when Dirrus entered, barking, "Get up, Halun. You're being pardoned. Come on, move it!"

Warily, Halun rose to his feet, surprisingly agile for such bulk. Under the blood and grime his skin was a lightly tanned brown. Talyn had never seen such a man before. It wasn't only his bulk—a curious pattern tattooed in green ink almost entirely covered his left cheek.

Halun said nothing as the Patrolmen hustled him out of the cell and down the corridor. The man in the opposite cell was trying very hard not to look like he was watching the proceedings. She kept her posture casual as she wandered over to stand before him. Instantly his gaze switched to her, flat and suspicious.

"What's your story?" she asked him.

"None of your damn business."

She jerked a thumb in Halun's direction. "Why try to help him?"

His look conveyed the same feeling his previous response had stated aloud with a touch of threat added. *Don't push me*, it warned. She was unmoved. She'd dealt with drill instructors even saltier than this one... in fact, that was exactly what this man reminded her of. A drill instructor.

Leaving him to his grumpiness, she turned away to walk slowly up and down and study the occupants of the other cells. On the surface, they were a charming mix of hapless, dead-eyed or simply world-weary and beaten down. None of them struck her with any confidence as men who could move and run, let alone learn to be a soldier. Reaching the last cell on the left, she paused, eyes lingering on its two occupants.

The first was a youth, closer to fifteen years than twenty by the look of him. Graceful but dirty hands covered his face where he sat hunched in the corner. Even curled around himself like he was, it was clear he was thin, too thin, and lank black hair hung tangled around his jaw. The slight shaking of his shoulders indicated he was sobbing.

The second prisoner was older, around Talyn's age. His narrow face was set in a perpetual expression of distrust, and he was pacing the cell incessantly, eyes scanning the windows and bars.

"What are you in here for?" she asked him.

The pacing man spat. "What's it to you?"

Nice. Talyn wasn't entirely sure why she'd stopped. These men were no different from the criminals she'd encountered for years. They certainly weren't warrior material.

"Are you done yet?" Ravinire's voice came from the entrance.

Talyn stifled a sigh of irritation, stubbornness keeping her there more than anything else. If this was to be her wing, she wasn't going to let Ravinire force her into choosing men for the sake of it. Her gaze returned to the boy in the corner. Something about these two made the back of her neck prickle in a way that none of the other prisoners she'd seen had.

Of course, that could be because the shifty one was a murderous psychopath.

"What are your names?" she asked them.

The young man in the corner didn't even look up. The other one smirked, repeating, "What's it to you?"

Talyn met his eyes, refusing to look away until he smirked again and shrugged. "Kid's name is Corrin. Hasn't stopped weeping like that since they bought him in. Gotta be something missing between the ears, if you know what I'm saying."

"It's not like that!" The youngster looked up suddenly, a fierce glare on his bony face. "Just leave me alone."

"What are you in here for?" Talyn asked again.

Corrin ignored her while the other shrugged, affecting disinterest. His pacing continued, but he didn't turn his back to her once. She'd seen something in the flash of Corrin's green eyes when he'd looked up. The same echo of it was hidden under the other prisoner's cocky demeanour, in the nervous twitch of his fingers and the refusal to show his back to her.

They were broken. Just like she was. And she didn't want to be broken. She needed some ray of hope that one day she could be herself again. Live again. Maybe this was a place to start.

"Captain Dynan?" Ravinire's musical, but irritated, voice sounded from the end of the hall.

With an inwards shrug, she stepped away from the bars and gestured to the younger Patrolman hovering just behind Ravinire. Were there seriously only two of them in the building? "These two. And the one down the end."

The Patrolman baulked. "Theac Parksin? I don't think so. The Patrol Commander will have my hide if I let him go."

"He's in the pardonable cells, isn't he?" she asked, eyebrow raised.

The Patrolman looked at Ravinire in mute appeal and received a stony look in return. With a heavy sigh, he walked down to unlock Theac's cell and motion him out. Then, plodding so slowly it set Talyn's teeth on edge, he returned to unlock the cell holding Corrin and the pacing man.

Talyn followed them out—Theac, Corrin, and his cellmate were ushered through a door on the other side of the foyer, and it swung closed behind them. She could only presume that's where Halun had been taken too. Dirrus was back at the desk, slumped in his chair and pretending to read a piece of parchment in front of him.

Ravinire lifted an eyebrow. "Only four?" he asked. "I thought I'd made it clear you were to put together a full wing? That's sixty warriors, Captain, plus talons."

She hadn't a clue what a talon was, but that was far from the most ridiculous thing about his sentence. "No disrespect sir, but you didn't bring me here to fish sixty prisoners out of the cells. And if you did, I'm telling you right now I can't train sixty men at one time effectively, even if they already had some semblance of basic training, which criminals most certainly do not."

Nil reaction. This man would win big at cards. "I expected at least enough for a full detail of ten soldiers."

"There weren't ten prisoners in there that looked to have the makings of a soldier, sir."

"You mean hardened men like the crying boy?" His lifted eyebrow conveyed volumes, and she struggled not to wilt under it.

"I understood you were leaving the choice up to me, sir," she said evenly. "You could have chosen them yourself." In fact, she didn't understand why he hadn't, why he was going through his whole charade.

Ravinire didn't respond to that, instead heading for the exit as he spoke. "They'll be brought up to the citadel this evening, washed and given fresh clothes and taken to the barracks I've assigned to your wing. You can get started with them first thing tomorrow."

"Yes, sir." She cleared her throat. "Can I ask when I'm to meet the prince, sir?"

"When he can accommodate you."

They were halfway to the door when a thought occurred to Talyn, a sharp reminder that her purpose in Mithranar was twofold. "Wait, sir, what about the three men from yesterday?"

"What men?" he snapped, all patience clearly gone.

"The thieves I chased down. Are they being held here?" One of them at least had known how to throw a knife—he could be useful. Particularly if he was part of this Shadowhawk's network, whatever that meant. She'd need sources if she was to investigate properly.

Ravinire looked at Dirrus, who was doing his level best to avoid attention. "Well, Watch Officer?"

"Don't know what you mean, sir," he muttered.

"Three men were arrested yesterday for stealing bread from the markets," Talyn said, stepping towards him. "Where are they?"

"They're not pardonables."

"Are they here?"

"Captain Dynan!" Ravinire's impatience had moved to outright irritation.

"One of them knew how to fight, sir," she said, turning back to him. "You're the one who just said four wasn't enough."

"Dirrus!" Ravinire barked.

The Patrolman's eyes dropped. "They're not here."

Ravinire's face tightened. "Then where are they?"

"Arrested in a different quarter, I suppose." Dirrus' resentful gaze switched to Talyn. "Markets you said? Probably being held by the Market Quarter Patrol then. All's I know is they're not here."

And that was all Ravinire's patience was going to give them. With a deeply irritated sigh, he turned and stalked from the building. Talyn had no choice but to follow—there was no way she'd find her way back to the wall walk alone, let alone her room up in the palace guest wing.

The sun was setting, a wondrous deep orange glow over the ocean, as Talyn followed the Falcon back up the wall. They spoke barely two words the rest of the way back, and he left her outside her room with nothing other than a terse, "I'll be back to collect you in the morning."

Standing inside her rapidly darkening and empty room, she took a deep, steadying breath. The utter solitude at least meant she didn't have to pretend or put up a façade.

Not until the following day, anyway.

CHAPTER 7

*T*alyn was up and dressed when Ravinire appeared at her door early the next morning. Sleep had been hard to come by. That wasn't unusual—often she woke, screaming, from nightmares —but the uncertainty of what the day would bring had only added to her restless night. Her instinct was to ignore the strangeness around her and focus on her job, protecting the prince and learning more about this Shadowhawk figure. Achieving either of those things was going to be hard enough, and there were no guarantees she'd get there.

But enough of her Callanan instincts remained that it was hard to ignore the oddness, not only of Mithranar, but of the circumstances of her being here. A secret Dumnorix prince. A Kingshield guard being used to do Callanan work. A Mithranan commander so opposed to having his own soldiers form Prince Cuinn's detail he wanted her to train criminals instead.

"*Maybe it's not him,*" Sari suggested. "*Maybe it's what he's been ordered to do.*"

Ravinire's knock on the door forestalled Talyn's reply, and she opened the door to find him standing there, wearing the same impassive expression of the day before.

"I'll take you to the wing," he said brusquely. "You're on your own from there."

"Yes, sir," she said, falling into step as he strode away, again expecting her to follow. If Ravinire was representative of winged folk in general, they certainly seemed an arrogant lot.

"Your wing's assigned barracks are adjacent to a drill yard, and there's only one entrance by foot to the area. Keep in mind, any of the winged folk can enter from higher or lower levels at any time."

Which made the barracks essentially un-guardable. She put the thought aside for the moment, asking a question that had been playing on her mind all night after her rather frosty reception. "How does the prince feel about me being here, sir?"

"That's something you'll need to discuss with him."

"And his feelings on having a protective detail made up of humans? Led by a human woman?" If this prince was anything like Ravinire or the other winged folk she'd briefly met, he'd likely treat the idea as a joke at best, an outright insult at worst. That would make protecting him properly difficult—a Kingshield guard needed to build a rapport, a trust, with their charge. That wouldn't happen if he didn't respect her. Although if he had Dumnorix blood, it might make him more amenable to her, even if he didn't understand why.

"Except from what Ceannar said you likely only share a great-great-grandmother or father," Sari commented. *"He might not notice at all."*

"Humans or winged folk, you won't be able to do much with only five warriors," he said pointedly.

Talyn bit her lip. Complaining wasn't her style. She told herself this was no different than the way Callanan apprentices were treated when they first started, or new Kingshield guards for that matter. She was a warrior—it was her job to take orders, no matter how high-handedly they were delivered. Besides, once she'd spent longer here and learned more of Mithranan culture, things might start to make more sense.

Ravinire said no more as they followed the long corridor away from Talyn's room that turned into an open walkway. He stopped by a ladder leading down and gestured for her to go first. At the bottom, another open walkway led to a marble arch with a wrought iron gate set into it. High marble walls ran to the left and right of the gate.

"Beyond are your wing's barracks. The key I gave you to your room will open this gate. Your training yard is fully equipped. If there is anything additional you need, please send a request through me."

"Yes, sir." She added an extra note of crispness to her voice.

Ravinire hesitated. "As I told you yesterday, most here don't believe there is a need for Prince Cuinn to have his own guard, including, I warn you, the prince himself. He will never inherit the throne, and as such, is safe from the more obvious threats."

The words were suddenly falling out of Ravinire's mouth, and she pushed at the opening, trying to wring as much information as possible from him. "And what are the less obvious threats, sir? If I am to be responsible for protecting him, I need to know that."

The Falcon's face closed over. "There is nothing definitive that I can tell you, Captain Dynan. When and if I get information, be assured that I will pass it on to you."

"I'm a Kingshield guard, not a captain," she said sharply, reacting to his sudden reserve.

"You're in charge of a WingGuard wing. That makes you a captain here. I'll come and find you later when it's time to introduce you to the prince."

With that he was gone, spreading his wings and leaping into the air.

Talyn put the key in the lock and turned it. The gate opened with a squeal of rusted metal and she went through, closing it behind her. The sun was warm on her skin as she headed along the narrow walkway. Despite the early hour, the humidity had her sweating already, like she was walking through a bowl of hot steam. The precipitous drop on either side looked down over a lower level of the citadel and beyond only green canopy.

She paused to watch as three winged folk swept through the air below her, colourful wings glittering as they turned mid-air and dropped down onto an open balcony. Musical laughter drifted up on a slight breeze, fading as they disappeared inside.

"Imagine being able to fly like that." A hint of yearning threaded Sari's voice.

Talyn huffed out a breath and kept walking. *"If I'd wanted to fly, I would have become a SkyRider instead of a Callanan warrior."*

The path ended on the western edge of a rectangular stone courtyard. Leaves and other debris covered the paved surface, and the walls of the building lining the northern side of the platform were unpainted and bare. The other edge, directly ahead of Talyn and to the south, looked out over a precipitous drop. They were miles high in the air, a carpet of trees far below.

She didn't spend more than a brief moment surveying the scenery, though, instead turning her attention straight to the five people scattered nearby. Their lack of military bearing was the first thing that arrested her. They sat slumped, sprawled or halfway asleep in various spots that couldn't have been farther from each other if they'd made a deliberate effort to stay distant.

Which they probably had.

Sari's laughter tinkled in her head. A smile rose to her face in the instant before she realised Sari wasn't actually there. Talyn was alone in the empty yard. Instead of letting the despair overwhelm her, she shifted her focus to her new wing—and looked straight to the one she didn't recognise, slouching against the wall to her left.

His sea grey wings trailed against the ground, and if it weren't for Halun, he would easily be the strangest-looking person there. His dark skin, silken chestnut curls and handsome features were partially ruined by the studied indifference of his expression.

This must be the single Falcon Ravinire had decided to assign to her wing. He was as pretty as the others she'd seen, but she saw no trace of warrior in his bearing or the lack of muscle tone in his bare arms. He met her appraising look with a faint smile that said he cared absolutely nothing for her opinion of him, either good or bad.

The next one was the oldest of the group—the one she'd pegged as an ex-soldier with a paunch. He eyed Talyn with disdain, arms crossed firmly over his chest. At least he was sitting up straight... ish.

Halun was larger than the first two put together. He wore a sleeveless jerkin over the bulging muscles of his chest and arms and light cotton breeches that ended, torn off, at his calves. Sweat glistened on his bald head, and he stared at Talyn unblinkingly. Purple bruising decorated his jaw, right eye and crooked nose, an interesting counterpoint to the green of his tattoo.

The boy sat scrunched against the wall, arms wrapped about his knees, mirroring the posture he'd had in the cell—utterly despairing. He gave Talyn a quick, darting look, then his eyes returned to his boots. At least today he wasn't crying.

The last of them was sprawled on a stone bench. Every part of him screamed insolence. He was the smallest of them all, with short-cropped blonde hair and a lean, wiry body. His lips curled in a sneer as Talyn's gaze moved to him.

For a moment she was frozen, unsure how to proceed against such apathy, if not outright hostility. Her fingers curled at her side as she forced herself to take a deep, slow breath. She was Dumnorix. People responded to that whether they realised what they were doing or not. She'd never been forced to use that charisma and confidence before—hadn't wanted *or* needed to—but now she was going to have to find a way.

"I am Captain Talyn Dynan, and I'm a Kingshield guard from the kingdom of the Twin Thrones. The Falcon has informed me I'm your wing captain, and I hope he's told you that we will be responsible for Prince Cuinn's protection." She paused. "Please introduce yourselves one at a time."

The silence hovered, thickening as time passed and nobody spoke. Talyn waited them out. It was a test, to see which of them would break first. She had her money on... a small flare of triumph went through her when her guess proved right.

"Kingshield? That's a nice, fancy title," the wiry man sneered.

She swivelled her gaze to him. "And your name is?"

He snorted, crossing his arms over his chest and leaning further back. The insolence was staggering, and she had to remind herself she was dealing with criminals, not soldiers. That was fine. She'd dealt with plenty of criminals before.

"His name is Zamaril." The older man spoke. "They call him 'Lightfinger' on account of he's a renowned thief."

"I'm the best thief Dock City has ever seen," Zamaril said lazily, sprawling even more insolently, if that was possible.

"Is that so?" She kept her voice casual, letting his attempts to rattle her slide off her shoulders. "How does the best thief Dock City has ever seen get himself caught?"

He scowled, shifting his glance away. Score one for Talyn. "I was ratted out by another thief."

Talyn nodded, turned to the older one. "And you are?"

"Theac Parksin," he grunted. "Former Patrol Captain of the Poor Quarter."

"Former?" She lifted an eyebrow.

He cleared his throat and spat. Delightful. She heaved an inward sigh and turned to the giant. "Your turn, Halun. What did you do before landing in the cells?"

His stare remained unblinking.

"He doesn't talk," Theac said eventually. Then he shrugged. "Not that I've ever heard anyway."

Zamaril sniggered. Talyn shot him a look before returning her gaze to Halun. The big man met her gaze fearlessly. There was no threat or challenge in his look though. He didn't mean her ill, he just refused to open himself to her. "Can't talk or won't talk?"

"How the hell should I know? I don't give a flea's shit either way," Theac muttered.

She gave Halun a little nod, as if to say, *that's all right*, then she switched her gaze to the youngest. "You?"

He lifted his head from his knees. "Corrin, ma'am," he said nervously. "I've..." He cleared his throat. "I've never fought before, but I can use a knife."

"A knife?" Zamaril burst out laughing. "What idiot decided you'd be of any use in a guard detail?"

She spun, quick as a flash. "Tell us, Zamaril. What use will *you* be?"

He scowled, looking away again. He was all attitude, this one, but so far he backed down each time she challenged him. She hoped there

78

was a spine in there to be unearthed. "From today onwards, we are a unit, a team. First rule is—we don't insult team members. Is that clear?"

The thief had dissolved into sulky silence. Talyn suppressed a sigh, edged her voice with granite. "Is *that* clear?"

"Whatever." He shrugged.

"And Corrin, it's not 'ma'am. It's 'Captain." She took a breath, struggling to keep hold of her patience as she turned to the final member of the wing. "You. Name."

The winged man had been busy smoothing the feathers in his left wing, boredom written all over his face, but he straightened as she addressed him. "Tiercelin Stormflight, Captain. I joined the Falcons three months ago when I turned twenty-one. After completion of my basic training, the Falcon assigned me here."

Three months of training was all the WingGuard received? She'd been a Callanan apprentice for four *years*. She widened her gaze to encompass them all. "Have any of you actually met the prince?"

Silence. Zamaril was examining his fingernails with an air of superiority that was beginning to grate on Talyn's nerves. Eventually Tiercelin cleared his throat. "Yes, Captain. My family and his are close friends. My father sits on the Queencouncil."

He spoke the words as if they were meant to impress her. They didn't. "Do any of you have any combat training?"

Theac and Tiercelin raised their hands.

Another silence.

"Apart from Halun, have any of you ever been in a fight before?"

Tiercelin dropped his arm. Theac kept his raised. Zamaril was now picking at the skin around his left thumb. Corrin hadn't lifted his head since she'd addressed him directly.

This was going superbly.

"That's fine, we'll start from the beginning," she said briskly. "First I'd like to understand where your individual strengths lie. I understand we have time before we meet the prince later today."

"You mean when *you* meet the prince?" Tiercelin cast a horrified glance at the humans gathered around.

"No. *We* are meeting the prince." It made no sense to protect someone when they didn't know who you were. The Dumnorix family knew each member of their guard personally.

"Delightful." Zamaril smirked. "I can see it now—Good afternoon Your Highness, I am Zamaril Lightfinger, the thief who has plagued your city for the past ten years. Your life is now in my hands."

"We're just pathetic humans." Theac glowered. "We don't go anywhere near the royal family."

Zamaril sat up quick as lightning, genuine anger rippling across his face as he regarded Theac. "Speak for yourself, old man," he spat.

"Who are you calling old?" Theac barked, half-rising from his seat.

"Knock it off!" Talyn snapped. "One more insulting word out of any of you, and you can go right back to the cells where I found you!"

Theac ignored her, shouldering his way past and barrelling down on the thief. Zamaril slipped off the bench, using his agility to scale half the wall and laugh tauntingly at the older man.

"Hey!" Talyn shouted. "Do either of you actually *want* to go back to the cells?"

Theac gave Zamaril a parting scowl and returned to his seat. Zamaril dropped off the wall and resumed his languid sprawl on the bench. Corrin hadn't said anything. Halun continued to stare. Tiercelin looked amused, like he'd just witnessed a pair of dogs fighting in the street.

Talyn took a deep breath and injected firmness into her voice. "Whether any of *you* like it or not, you are Prince Cuinn Acondor's new guard detail. Whether *he* likes it or not, you will all be very close to him for the rest of your time in the WingGuard. You will meet him, and he will get to know you, and it will be your sole purpose in life to keep him alive. If that's not to your liking, I'm not stopping you from going back to the cells."

Talyn stood away from the exit gate and motioned towards it, sweeping her glance over those gathered. Nobody moved. She gave it a good minute, but they all stayed where they were.

Corrin shifted a little in his spot, finally lifting his eyes to her. "Captain, I don't want to go back to the cells, but I can't stomach being a Falcon." His voice was soft, but Talyn didn't miss the thread of dignity in it. "They were... cruel... to my family. It's not like we even have wings."

Halun nodded vigorously.

"Excuse me?" Tiercelin raised his wings, sending leaves flying.

She flashed them both a warning glance. "Your job is to protect the prince. It doesn't matter what you're called. Now, I'd like to see a demonstration of your individual skill level. Theac, you're the most experienced, so you'll be my second."

Theac merely grunted at her words, clearly unimpressed. But when she selected a wooden training sword from a nearby rack and tossed it at him, he caught it cleanly. He hefted it, then looked at her in question.

Talyn shrugged. "If you beat me, you can have command of the wing."

Theac's eyes widened.

"Oh, the poor man has no idea."

"It's only fair." She smiled, ignoring Sari. She needed to establish her dominance here, and quickly. Already she was barely holding their attention, despite the threat to return them to the cells. It was something she'd seen happen a hundred times over, in any group of warriors she'd ever fought alongside.

Not that she and Sari had ever had to make an effort. From day one as apprentices they'd been acknowledged and accepted as the best in the class. Any warrior that looked inclined to challenge that superiority in the years since had thought differently after seeing them in action. Still, that didn't mean she wasn't capable of asserting herself. "Especially since you have the experience," she added.

Theac nodded and moved into the centre of the yard, the sword swinging loosely from his hand. He appeared suddenly confident, as if control of the situation had shifted towards him. It was amusing how little he thought of female warriors. He was about to get some of his illusions shattered. She might be broken, but she was still Callanan trained and facing a man who was woefully underestimating his opponent.

She picked up a training sword for herself and held the hilt loosely in her hands, swinging it slowly. A condescending smirk flashed over Theac's face. Tiercelin's smirk was even wider, while Zamaril pretended to examine the ground under his bench in apparent boredom. Halun and Corrin eyed them without comment, the boy's eyes interested, but wary.

Theac attacked without warning, moving with a speed that belied his age. The sword swung smoothly in his hands, its weight nothing to his burly arms.

But Talyn was even faster.

She moved aside, a hair's breadth away from the falling sword. Hers swept up behind him, cracking him on the back with the flat of the wooden blade right at the moment his lunge forward had him most off-balance and unable to riposte with any speed. A quick sweep of her right foot into his ankle at the same moment and the ex-Patrolman went crashing headfirst into the leaf-littered stone yard.

She swung the sword once more, bringing its blade to rest against the back of his neck. He dropped his sword with a clatter, grudging respect flashing in his eyes when she removed her weapon and reached down a hand to help him up.

"I've never seen anyone move that fast." He frowned, rubbing his bleeding nose where he'd hit the ground.

"Then Mithranan warriors leave something to be desired. That was a basic first-year Callanan apprentice move," she said sharply.

Theac's face tightened in humiliation, but surprisingly he took her comment with a terse nod and no challenge. That was interesting. Deciding he'd been embarrassed enough, she turned to Corrin. "You said you could handle a knife. Would you mind giving a demonstration?"

He flushed dark red, clearing his throat before bobbing his head. "I'll need a volunteer."

"I'll do it," she said. "Where do you want me?"

"Are you sure?" He went pale. "I mean... I don't want you to get hurt. Someone else could do it."

"I'm sure." Her reflexes were almost certainly fast enough to stop a knife thrown by an untrained boy before it got anywhere near anything vital. She'd taken much bigger risks than this before, and building trust by letting Corrin wave a knife around her was worth it.

She felt another flicker of surprise when he didn't protest any further, just pointed. "Then could you stand just over by that wall, please?"

Talyn nodded and walked to the wall, the warmth of it seeping into her back. Sweat dripped uncomfortably down her spine as she stood, relaxed. The others fanned out, giving Corrin room. He backed up until he was standing halfway across the yard.

"Ready?" She could barely hear his soft voice from that far away.

"Go ahead." She nodded.

Metal flashed, then suddenly a knife was quivering in the wall half in an inch from Talyn's right ear. Before she could register what had happened, Corrin's hand moved again, and a knife landed the same distance from her left ear. Within the next few seconds, six other knives surrounded her body.

Silence filled the yard. Even Zamaril had straightened up and was staring—open mouthed—at Corrin.

Talyn kept her expression even, but her heart pounded. It was her turn to have her assumptions shattered—she hadn't even come close to moving quickly enough to avoid those throws. If he'd been off-target by a mere millimetre... this un-assuming young man had real talent. She'd have to watch him a little more to be sure, but if he had the kernel of magic too, back home he would have been recruited for the Callanan. For the first time she was glad she'd trusted her instincts the previous day. Out of all of them, this boy could become a real asset to her wing.

"What was that you were saying about Corrin earlier, Zamaril?" Tiercelin smirked at the thief.

"That's very impressive, Corrin," Talyn finally said as she collected his blades and carried them over to him. "I doubt even I could have thrown with such accuracy and speed and I've had some training in knife-work."

Corrin went red at the attention, and his gaze dropped back to his boots. Halun looked at her, then walked over to the rack of training weapons. Ignoring the swords, he selected a large club, lifted it as if it had been made with feathers, then swung a few times around his head before putting it back.

"You can use a club." She nodded. "All right, thanks, Halun."

"You know my training," Tiercelin said. "Three months initial training with all the other WingGuard cadets. We learned with swords, and did some basic knife drills. Nothing advanced."

Zamaril crossed his arms defiantly. "Well I can't demonstrate anything. I've never used a weapon, and I've never been in a bar fight. I'm pretty much useless as a guard."

She considered him for a long moment. He was technically right, but confirming that would sink his confidence even further. The silence grew heavier when she didn't respond, the pressure in her chest building. If she lost him now, it would be close to impossible to get him back... and one bad seed in a unit, she'd seen the consequences of that before.

"Think about it, Tal. He's not without skills. We would have run this guy as an informant back in Port Lathilly."

Right, that was true. A crazy thought suddenly occurred to her. "I don't think you're useless, Zamaril, and I'll prove it to you. Does anybody know where Prince Cuinn's rooms in the palace are?"

"He lives in the eastern tower." Tiercelin shrugged, then smirked. "As far away from Mithanis as he can get."

"Lead the way."

RAVINIRE HADN'T BEEN wrong about the barracks being a distance from the central area of the palace. With Tiercelin leading, it was a quarter-turn-long walk involving six different ladders and one precariously swaying rope bridge, to reach a hub of buildings on the eastern hillside.

"Do these hills have names?" She craned her neck—it was hard to tell but she thought the one which the royal palace sat on was the largest of a long line of them that stretched back from the harbour. It was also the highest. The walkway they were currently on looked down over other areas of the citadel but was too far around the hillside to be able to see the ocean or Dock City. Instead only unending lines of forested hills and cloudless blue sky stretched north and east into the horizon.

Tiercelin shook his head. "There are too many to name, and we winged folk navigate by how things look from the sky, not the ground."

The unconscious assumptions continued to startle her. "Why do you even bother with all these ladders and walkways and narrow staircases then? Clearly this citadel is not welcoming to humans."

"Our children don't begin to grow their wings until they're about eight or nine, and aren't strong enough to fly until they reach their early teens." He cast the others a glance. "And humans do live and work here."

"Yeah, as servants," Zamaril muttered.

"*Paid* servants," Tiercelin snapped.

All three humans promptly glanced at Halun, who scowled and looked down. She frowned, but was forestalled from asking what was going on when Tiercelin stopped outside an arched gate set into a waist-high wall. "Here we are."

Without thinking, her mind shifted back into Kingshield mode, the result of hours of drills and lesson-based training. Beyond the gate was a brightly coloured garden that covered a large open space at the base of a circular tower. To their right, a precipitous drop into nothing. To the left, a high marble wall that revealed nothing of what was behind it.

No guard stood at the gate.

"This isn't the main entrance," Tiercelin explained. "But the garden beyond is part of the tower grounds."

"Where's the main entrance?" she asked.

He pointed upwards. From where they stood, the tower looked like it was suspended out into open air. A graceful bridge spanned the gap between what she judged was the second floor of the tower, and the nearest cluster of buildings set closer to the hillside.

"Those buildings the bridge leads to? Those are part of the palace proper," Tiercelin explained. "This is the eastern slope—the queen's rooms are on the northern slope, along with the other princes'."

It was lovely, like everything else in the home of the winged folk. It was also isolated—and if it was separated from the rest of the family's quarters, it was also separated from the security of their WingGuard details.

Her eyes dropped back to the gate. "It's not locked, is it?"

"No, Captain."

"Are there guards on the main door? Or at least at the entry to the bridge?"

"Usually." Tiercelin shot her a sheepish look, then sighed. "Not always. Not really anymore."

Talyn frowned. Her confusion only deepened the more she learned about how things worked in Mithranar. She'd been invited here, ostensibly by the queen, in a formal capacity, even if Ravinire seemed opposed to the whole idea. Yet it was equally clear that nobody much cared about the youngest prince's safety—to the point Ravinire thought it okay to have criminals drafted into his guard unit. Unless it was true that he genuinely believed criminals were a safer option than WingGuard soldiers. In which case she was utterly at a loss as to how that could be.

"Maybe we're talking competing interests? One party seeking to protect the prince, one seeking to harm him?" Sari's voice whispered in her mind.

Perhaps. But if a person or persons out there wanted to harm Cuinn, they'd clearly had opportunity to do so already. So what had changed to warrant the request for her presence? And which side did Ravinire fall on?

"Ravinire seems sincere to me. Terse, rude even, but sincere."

"Maybe, but the fact he wouldn't tell me what's really going on doesn't count in his favour."

"Maybe he doesn't know."

"Captain?" Corrin's quiet voice broke her from her thoughts.

"He's rarely in there during the day anyway." Tiercelin seemed to think her drifting off was annoyance at the lack of guards. She didn't correct him.

"Then where is he?"

The winged man shrugged. "Playing alleya sometimes, eating and drinking with his friends, just normal stuff."

Zamaril smirked. "Yes, Captain, it's very important we keep the pretty winged prince alive. He's critical to the wellbeing of Mithranar, what with all the women and the partying."

She turned an enquiring look on Tiercelin, but he just shrugged again, eyes dropping to the ground as he mumbled, "he likes to have fun, that's all. Nothing wrong with that."

"No, nothing wrong with that while half the Poor Quarter is starving," Theac barked. "Captain, are we going or what? It's damnably hot out here."

Halun pushed past them before she could respond, opening the gate and striding through. Tiercelin was immediately behind him, clearly looking to escape her questioning look. Talyn waited for the rest to go inside before following.

The grass inside the picturesque garden was a vivid green, and brightly coloured flowers adorned the bushes lining the walls. At the northern end of the garden stood the tower, reaching up about four stories high. The waist-high wall encircled the garden, closing it in around the tower—so it could only be accessed by the door set into the base of the tower and the gate they'd just come through.

She had to jump back quickly when Tiercelin suddenly stretched out his wings in front of her, reminding her sharply that any winged person could just *fly* in.

"Zamaril." Talyn looked at the thief. "If there was something in Prince Cuinn's bedroom that you wanted to steal, could you get in there?"

"Of course," Zamaril said confidently.

"Do it."

"What?" His cocky facade dropped as he stared at her.

"We're supposed to protect Prince Cuinn. That means learning how an adversary might get access to his rooms and closing off any vulnerabilities." It had been a spur of the moment idea to try and build rapport with Zamaril, but she was liking the possibilities more and more. Who better to probe potential vulnerabilities than a skilled thief?

Suspicion clouded his face. "How do I know you're not just trying to trap me into doing something that will get me thrown back in jail?"

"You don't have a lot of experience with trust, do you Zamaril?"

His face hardened. "Trust gets you killed."

"If I wanted you in jail, I would never have pulled you out in the first place. I told you I wanted your expertise, and I meant it. Show us how you'd get in there."

After another brief hesitation, Zamaril looked at Tiercelin. "Which floor's the bedroom?"

"Third, I think," Tiercelin replied, looking highly amused by the idea of Zamaril trying to break in.

Zamaril shrugged, then walked to the door at the base of the tower and turned the handle. It swung open without protest and the thief sent a challenging look at Talyn. "I'd walk up the stairs, grab what I wanted, and stroll back out the unlocked door. Probably whistle while I'm at it too, since there seems to be nobody around."

She stifled the smile that wanted to emerge, and merely lifted an eyebrow instead. "Pretend it's locked and barred, and you can't get through."

"Fine." He closed the door then stepped out onto the grass, eyes scanning their surroundings. Within a minute he was crossing to a tree on the edge of the garden and in one quick movement, he gripped a low hanging branch and hauled himself up. He climbed like a cat, quickly and without fear.

Soon he was balanced on a swaying branch a good few meters below a third-floor windowsill. Then, with a flash of elite balance and agility, he leaped upwards to grab the sill and swing himself up onto it.

If she'd been alone, Talyn's mouth would have dropped open in astonishment. What were the odds of coming across two men with

Callanan potential inside her first two days in Mithranar? And both in the same jail cell.

That wasn't coincidence. She was beginning to feel like a puppet in someone else's game. And if she wasn't mistaken, there was more than one game being played.

A grunt of surprise from Theac broke her from her thoughts, and she re-focused on Zamaril as he pulled something from his pocket and worked at the window for a moment. It swung open, and then he was inside.

Talyn and the others waited, staring fixedly up at the window. Several minutes passed, and then he re-appeared at the sill, clutching something in his hands.

"Captain Dynan?"

She spun around as Ravinire dropped lightly into the garden behind them. He had an enquiring expression on his face that hardened to suspicion when he saw Zamaril perched on the prince's window ledge.

"Sir." She saluted respectfully. Only Tiercelin followed suit. The others stared sullenly at the ground.

"May I ask what you're doing?" Ravinire's gaze remained on Zamaril, who had leaped back to the tree and was now shimmying quickly down it.

"I asked Zamaril to demonstrate how easy it would be for someone to obtain entrance to the prince's quarters," she said.

Ravinire's stern look shifted to her. "And what is he carrying?"

She kept her voice casual, light, resisting the urge to fidget under that gaze. "Zamaril was bragging about his skills, and I dared him to accomplish the climb while holding something in his hands."

He looked at her a long moment, then nodded and stepped back. "Prince Cuinn has some time to meet with you later this afternoon. If you will all please wait back at your barracks, I will send a Falcon to take you to him when he's ready."

"Yes, sir."

Ravinire cast a suspicious look over the men behind her, then spread his wings and leapt into the air. Talyn turned to Zamaril, who had dropped to the ground, a smirk curling his lips. Tiercelin was stiff with affront, but at least he hadn't opened his mouth.

"What did you take?" she snapped.

Shrugging insolently, the young man handed her a gold wrist chain.

"Prince Cuinn's, I presume?"

Zamaril nodded, insolence in every line of his body.

"You..." Tiercelin gaped at Zamaril, seemingly lost for words, then turned accusing eyes on her. "You lied to the Falcon!"

"I did. Because I meant it when I said I didn't want to see Zamaril back in the cells." She looked directly at the thief and tossed the chain back to him. "Put that back instantly, and if I catch you stealing from your prince again, Ravinire won't have the opportunity to kick you out because I'll do it first. Am I clear?"

He snorted, took the chain and headed for the unlocked tower door. She let his attitude go. For now.

Once he returned, Talyn waved them all back out the gate. "First rule is never insult your wing mates. Second rule—always keep a clean barracks. Let's go!"

CHAPTER 8

*H*e was on edge, though his voice had sounded utterly relaxed as he spoke the password that allowed him access over the bridge to the palace. Humans weren't rare in the citadel, even less so in the palace. Many were employed as servants, or worked with the Falcons as smiths, cooks and cleaners.

And it wasn't like the WingGuard were a highly skilled elite force of warriors. The Falcon he spoke the password to barely looked at him as he waved the Shadowhawk through. Mostly their incompetence roused only scorn and contempt in him, along with a certain amount of relief—it made his activities that much easier to undertake. But sometimes, nagging behind that, was a shiver of worry. Mithranar's only army would never hold back any serious attempt to take the country.

The Shadowhawk rarely came up to the citadel, but he'd felt it was important enough to risk coming this morning. Navis's information warranted further investigation, but he didn't want to betray his interest to the information broker—it never paid to appear *too* interested in anything—and so he needed to do this himself.

The fact that the Falcon had chosen an unused barracks far from the busiest area of the palace for the new wing that would be Prince

Cuinn's protective detail—one of the human smiths had sent word of its location through the Shadowhawk network—made accessing it much easier. He wouldn't dare risk trying to get closer to the central part of the royal residence in full daylight.

Not only was the barracks unused, it was on the opposite side of the hill from the palace's Falcon barracks. Ravinire was clever. None of this—the foreigner or a wing made up of humans—was going to be taken well in the winged folk world. The Falcon was clearly sensitive to that. Did that mean he'd had involvement in the foreigner's arrival? Or did he just see it as an opportunity? The Shadowhawk shook his head—the man might just be looking to avoid the inconvenience of brawling between WingGuard wings.

He slipped through the walkways and stairs, casual, unnoticed. Another Shadowhawk network member had once provided him detailed hand-drawn maps of the palace. Whoever it was had clearly not only understood how to draft architectural plans but also had a thorough understanding of palace life, because they'd included annotations explaining where the lesser-used routes were and where someone in a servant's uniform would expect to be seen. Such 'gifts' sometimes gave him a chill—wondering why a human would have taken such careful note of such things led his mind to places he'd rather not think about.

Despite his misgivings, he'd memorised the plans, and on the rare occasion he came up here on Shadowhawk business, he used them to get around without being noticed. Today he made it to a deserted walkway that looked down over the barracks assigned to the new wing. Slipping into the shadows of a tree, he went utterly still. There were enough shadows cast by the morning sun that he could easily draw them around his body, making him invisible to anyone giving the tree a passing glance.

A small group of men were waiting in the leaf-strewn yard as he settled into position. Four of them were Dock City humans. He frowned, his unease deepening. What was the queen thinking, approving a guard of humans for her son? And it had to be her call— there was no way Ravinire would have made a move like this on his own. Invite a Kingshield to Mithranar, maybe, but not create a wing of humans. As far as the Shadowhawk knew, there had never been humans in the WingGuard.

Clever, Ravinire was, but not creative, or particularly courageous when it came to flouting the desires of the royal family. This would look like an insult to Cuinn, if not a humiliation for the entire royal family. It made no sense.

Unless it wasn't about Cuinn.

Before he could chase that thought any further, the foreigner walked into the yard. His gaze narrowed in on her, searching for any detail that might help him understand why she was here.

His first instinct was to laugh. The Twin Thrones had sent a woman! Ravinire must be having apoplectic fits. A wing of humans led by a woman to protect a winged prince. Utter insanity.

She was being set up to fail. Or someone was. He shook his head to dismiss the multiple variations of that possibility and re-focused on her. She was tall for a woman, but what first struck him was that she walked with the same easy grace as one the winged folk, even though she was clearly human. Her raven hair was tied back in a no-nonsense braid pinned at her neck, and the sleeveless vest she wore revealed fair-skinned arms wiry with muscle.

It was impossible to tell from this distance what she looked like, but her presence was striking, carrying clearly to any observer. A warrior, most definitely. And something else he couldn't quite name, something dissonant about her, like two parts not quite in sync, or something inside her restrained... no, that wasn't it. His frown deepened. It was a puzzle, and one that might provide the key to why she was here if he worked it out.

This is winged folk business. It's not for you to worry about.

But it was. As much as the winged folk and humans would like to believe otherwise, the lives and wellbeing of both groups in Mithranar were inextricably linked.

He watched silently—nobody passing his hiding spot—as the foreigner spoke to each of the men in turn, although he couldn't hear what they were saying from such a distance. Their body language spoke volumes, though. None of them wanted to be there. When she dispatched the older man with the training sword, he whistled under his breath at the breathtaking ease with which she did it. *Well, you're certainly not just ceremonial. They sent a real warrior.*

Maybe that was exactly what the queen had been hoping for. Or not. Again the sense of unease swept through him. The coming of this woman meant something, he was sure of it. He just needed to work out how whatever it was would affect him and his activities. He couldn't be caught.

Capture meant certain death.

Confident the foreigner would be occupied for a while, he slipped away from his hiding spot and headed for the guest quarters. Dressed as a servant—clothing stolen on one of his other trips to the citadel— he would claim he'd been sent to clean if he was spotted, but the open walkway outside her room was empty.

It was the work of seconds to get inside her locked door, and he closed it quickly behind him, allowing his eyes a moment to adjust to the dimness beyond. The rooms were stark, and even though she'd already been there a day, there was little to suggest anyone lived in them. The cushions on the sofa were untouched, the chair at the desk put neatly away.

The bedroom was the only space that looked lived-in. Slowly and carefully he went through her few belongings, memorising where everything had been and ensuring he returned all of it to exactly the same spot.

There were several changes of clothes—mostly spare uniforms— some blank parchment and quills, and a small sack of coin. And then, buried right at the bottom of her duffel, a heavy object wrapped in velvet cloth. He took it out, unwrapping the cloth to reveal two matching daggers. Their hilts were intricately carved, with tiny emeralds embedded to form a hand grip, and blades the length of his forearm. With those carefully placed emeralds—they'd been designed for one person's hand, their unique grip.

The daggers weren't hers.

No, you don't carefully wrap your own daggers up in velvet and leave them at the bottom of your duffel. She'd been wearing different weapons earlier too, fork-looking blades he didn't recognise. These daggers weren't hers, but they meant something to her. Carefully he put them back. It was interesting, but it didn't shed any light on why she was here or what her intentions might be.

And he'd been here too long.

He would need to find another avenue to get the information he needed. And from looking at the men gathered in the barracks earlier, he had an idea about how exactly to get it.

As quietly as he'd come, he left.

CHAPTER 9

$\mathcal{B}$ack at the barracks, Talyn had put the men to work sweeping the leaves and debris covering the yard. They were predictably displeased by the order, but she sent Theac to find brooms, shovels and sacks, then joined in with the rest of them as they began sweeping.

Tiercelin and Zamaril were particularly amusing to watch—it was clear neither of them had been near a cleaning implement their entire lives—not that she let them know it. Tiercelin was the worst, mouth in a tight line, his lack of effort displaying clearly what he thought of being forced to do menial work.

At least they were quiet. No attitude or bickering for a precious space of time. Talyn warmed to her task—despite the suffocating humidity, she enjoyed the push and pull of her muscles, the quickening of her breath in her chest.

Once she'd filled three sacks with leaves, she paused to see how the rest were doing. Zamaril and Tiercelin had barely filled a sack between them, and Theac was scowling so hard at his broom she thought it might be in danger of breaking. Corrin worked willingly away, though, efficiently clearing his area of the yard.

And Halun. Something seized her when she watched the big man work. He'd done this before, his movements quick and economical, but something in his expression, in the way his shoulders had sagged slightly... it tore at her.

"Halun?" she asked, having no idea what she was going to say, just knowing she had to get that vacant look off his face.

He turned just as a young winged man wearing the Falcon teal and scarlet landed in the yard. The winged man swept a scornful glance over them before looking at Talyn. "The prince is ready for you, Captain. I'm to take you to him."

"Let's go!" she snapped when they didn't immediately stop what they were doing.

Ignoring the sighs and reluctant expressions, she set off after the Falcon, a hard look warning them to fall in line behind her.

The young Falcon led them away from the barracks and around the hillside, eventually walking up a set of marble steps to a wide, open-aired avenue lined by marble columns on each side. At the end of this avenue, more steps rose to the level above. Unlike their drill yard, these steps had been swept clean and gleamed, silver and ethereal, in the afternoon sun.

Talyn's eyes widened as they reached the top of the steps and came upon a turquoise pool laid out at their feet, cool and enticing. It was ringed by the same marble most of the citadel seemed to have been constructed from, with several plush deck chairs lining the edge to her left. To her right, a railing looked south out over Feather Bay, providing a stunning view of the ocean and harbour.

"The royal family's private pool," their escort said tersely. "Nobody is permitted to be here outside members of the family and their personal guard details."

"Understood," Talyn said, her gaze shifting to a figure leaning casually at the railing. Silver-white wings hung loosely from his back, feathers trailing on the ground. He was the only person in sight, and so must be her new charge, Cuinn Acondor. Curiosity kindled despite her uneasiness over this assignment—not only was this her charge, but also apparently a member of the Dumnorix family she'd never met.

She'd only taken a few steps when she realised the others weren't following. A sharp gesture and matching glare had them mutinously trailing after her. Their Falcon guide had vanished without a word.

The prince turned to face them as they approached, a languidness to the movement that spoke of either disdain or simple lack of energy. For the briefest of moments she was struck dumb, just as she had been on first seeing Mithranar, and again when first seeing one of the winged folk.

Silver-blonde hair turned rich gold in the sunlight was swept entirely to the right, falling over his right cheek and jaw and framing an aquiline face that showed no signs of Dumnorix blood and was all winged folk sculpted beauty.

He wore an open silk jacket in midnight blue, so perfectly tailored to fit his broad shoulders and lean frame that she wondered momentarily how he got the thing on. Underneath the jacket was nothing but bare chest. Equally fitted breeches in ivory silk completed his attire. His feet were bare.

Despite all that carefully accented and tailored beauty, his most arresting feature was his eyes. A deep emerald in colour, they shone brightly, hinting at a merry, mischievous nature. It was this that convinced her he possessed a hint of the same blood that ran through her veins. Those vivid eyes in a shade of green she'd never seen before were all Dumnorix. There was no instant recognition on an instinctive level though, like she felt when with her relatives back home.

When he spoke, his voice was melodious and seductive, rich with warmth and life. And full of awareness of how attractive he was.

"I suppose you must be the foreigner." His gaze slid over her. Slowly. "Count me intrigued. I was expecting a scarred, overly-muscled veteran warrior... not this beauty."

She almost laughed at the blatant seduction in his voice, thinking of Tarcos' lean body with its hard muscle and collection of small scars. This peacock was nothing even approaching her type.

"That's right. I'm Talyn Dynan from Calumnia. You must be Prince Cuinn."

"Quite the powers of deduction." Amusement tinged that beautiful voice, and then he lifted his eyebrows, looking behind her. "And who, may I ask, are all of you?"

She cleared her throat. "I'm sure the Falcon has informed you—we're your new protective guard detail."

The amusement moved from his voice to his eyes, veering close to contempt. "He told me they were bringing in a foreigner, then muttered something about a wing of humans. I must admit, I tuned out at that point. Ravinire can get so deathly boring at times."

Her pride flared and she spoke the words before she could bring them back. "I'm not just a foreigner, Your Highness. I'm a guard with the Kingshield of the Twin Thrones."

"What a mouthful." He raised a brow. "And only a lowly guard sent? Interesting."

"The Falcon has assigned me the rank of captain in Mithranar." She reined her voice back to brisk politeness—soldier to her charge—though this man's condescending manner had her prickling with affront.

"I see." His lip curled in deeper amusement. "How long have you been here?"

"I arrived yesterday morning."

"Well, I'm sure you'll be wanting to rest after your long trip. You may leave."

It was a dismissal, and one delivered with a sublime arrogance that echoed everything she'd felt from her interaction with the winged folk so far. But that didn't matter. She didn't have to like him, just protect him.

"With your permission, Your Highness, I'd like to introduce you to my wing first. After all, they will be in charge of keeping you safe."

The amused grin morphed into a smirk. She was surprised he didn't outright laugh. "You want to introduce a prince of Mithranar to a group of humans, Captain? I recall Ravinire blathering something about criminals, too. I admit I am the youngest of the royal family, but even so, there are standards."

"*Sock him in the nose, Tal! What a stuck up, arrogant, sickeningly pretty—*"

Talyn cleared her throat, trying to dislodge Sari's voice, and the amusement that threatened to escape her in a smile. It had always made her laugh when her partner launched into one of her righteously indignant tirades. It didn't help that socking this princeling in the nose was becoming increasingly tempting. But her self-control had always been masterful, and she called upon it now. "They're no longer criminals, they've been pardoned, Your Highness."

"I suppose they have." Cuinn straightened from the railing and cast his eye over the men standing some distance behind Talyn. She fought not to roll her eyes at their stubborn refusal to come closer. "Go on, then. Make it quick, I have somewhere to be."

She gritted her teeth, fighting the realisation that Cuinn's attitude had stolen control of this situation from her, and persisted after a deep breath. "Prince Cuinn, this is Theac Parksin. He recently retired from the City Patrol and will be my second. And these men are Zamaril Lightfinger, Halun Arasan, Tiercelin Stormflight, and Corrin Dariel."

She didn't miss the flickers of surprise across their faces at her knowledge of their full names—she'd insisted on that information from Ravinire before meeting them earlier—but said nothing.

"I've heard of you, Lightfinger." Once again, Cuinn's smile threatened to shift into an outright chuckle, and she was momentarily concerned she'd have to stop the thief launching himself at the prince. "I'm not sure how good a thief you can be if you got yourself caught so easily. And you, Tiercelin, how did you end up in with this unfortunate collection of downtrodden humans? I thought for sure your parents would have made sure you ended up in Azrilan or Mithanis's wing by now."

Tiercelin flushed red with embarrassment; Talyn wasn't sure whether it was because the prince was addressing him, or at his obvious amused contempt. She suspected it was the latter. At least Zamaril's clear satisfaction in the winged man's discomfort distracted him from the insults the prince had just thrown his way. It was impossible to tell what the other three were thinking. Corrin's gaze was firmly on the ground, and both Theac and Halun were scowling.

"I intend to do my best to protect you, Prince Cuinn," Tiercelin said with as much dignity as he could muster. It was a graceful response she wasn't sure she'd have been able to manage in his situation. He'd also chosen not to add to or agree with the prince's insults about the humans in his guard. Her gaze lingered a moment on the winged man's pretty features—maybe there was something in there she could work with.

Cuinn turned his attention back to Talyn, boredom now filling his face and voice. "There. We've been introduced. Happy now?"

Talyn nodded and turned to address the men. "Go. You have the rest of the day off. Be in the yard at dawn tomorrow. The entire barracks are assigned to you, so bring up your belongings and anything else you need. Theac—make sure they're neat about it."

They all scattered without a word, glad to escape Cuinn's presence. Talyn turned back to find the prince regarding her with a raised eyebrow. "Did my not so subtle dismissal escape you, Captain?" he enquired.

"I'm here to protect you," she said. "That means you go about your business as usual, and I follow."

Cuinn laughed. "I truly have no idea why you were brought here, but I'm not in any danger."

"That doesn't change the fact that I've been assigned to protect you."

He laughed again. "Look at me. I'm beautiful, wealthy and popular. I don't have any enemies. Even you can't help but be affected by me, despite your annoyance and how intensely you already dislike me. Leave me, Captain. I cannot express with words how uninterested I am in having you follow me around like a lost puppy."

She hesitated, debating arguing the point. He'd given her a clear order, though, and challenging him wasn't going to get her anywhere except annoying him further. And a charge that was annoyed with his guard was a terrible place to start.

So she turned to walked away, but only got a few steps before her pride had her turning back. He was still watching her. "I understand that you and every other winged person in this country feel nothing more than mild contempt for humans," she said evenly. "But I am a highly trained warrior and I'm *very* good at what I do, Prince Cuinn. Someone invited me here for a reason. You might want to consider that."

Not waiting for him to respond, she turned and stalked away.

It was growing dark when she returned to her room. Exhausted despite having done very little physical activity, she dropped onto the bed and lay there for a long moment.

This was not going to be easy.

And if she was honest with herself, she wasn't sure she was up to it.

Her wandering gaze fell on her duffel, and she frowned. It sat at the foot of the chair in the corner of the room. Only, she swore she'd left it sitting *on* the chair that morning. An old back injury had stiffened overnight and she hadn't wanted to bend all the way to the floor to dig out fresh clothes, so she'd lifted it to the chair.

The back of her neck tingling, she rolled off the bed and crossed to her bag. It was closed, just as she'd left it, and when she opened it up, there were no obvious signs that the contents had been rifled through.

Even so. Her instincts were prickling all through her body.

Someone had been in her room

She strode to her front door, bending down to study the lock. It didn't look as if it had been tampered with.

"But it's a standard, basic lock, Tal. Someone trained could have picked that without leaving any marks. We could have done it."

And they had, multiple times. "Either that or whoever it was had a key."

"Ravinire promised you had the only key."

"That doesn't mean someone didn't make a copy without him knowing. Or he might have been lying."

"No, he's an honest man."

Talyn let out an exasperated huff. "You and your instant instincts about people. We don't know anything about him."

"Point out one instance where my instincts were wrong?"

Before Talyn could reply she was gone. It was always like that. Sari's voice came and went without any rhyme or reason she could detect. And each time it left her in a tumult of despair that the voice wasn't real, that Sari was gone, and sweet relief at the sense of having her partner back. Not to mention the deep, heart-rending fear that maybe something was seriously wrong with her, that she was irrevocably broken.

Sari's voice was even stronger since she'd come to Mithranar, and she wondered if that was because she'd left her Dumnorix family behind. It shook her confidence further. What if she couldn't do this?

She stood, trying to fight back those despairing thoughts. Digging through her duffel, she pulled out the parchment and ink she'd brought and sat down at her desk in the main room.

She had some planning to do. Hopefully filling her mind with the familiar patterns of strategy might help her relax enough to sleep.

Talyn had originally imagined her role in Mithranar would be to train the members of the royal family's guard details in the specifics of close protection, and had expected to have to somehow work her way to training Cuinn's detail specifically. What she'd been confronted with was so utterly different to her expectations she wasn't sure what to do.

"One step at a time, Talyn," she muttered aloud, taking a deep breath.

She was going to be leading a wing. Not something she'd done before, but definitely something she'd trained for. She just needed to rely on that training.

Each Kingshield protection unit was formed of warriors with differing, but specific, skillsets. A talented leader used that to fashion a flexible, adaptive and highly skilled protection detail. If she ignored the fact she was dealing with a group of mostly untrained men, five warriors short of a single ten warrior Kingshield detail, then she had the basics already.

Both Corrin and Zamaril had raw Callanan potential, and Corrin already had a signature weapon. Theac was experienced in fighting *and* command. Halun and Tiercelin would be more difficult to train to the required skill level, but Tiercelin's wings and agility and Halun's brute strength could be an advantage if she focused their training properly.

The small number of them was an issue she couldn't escape. With what she had, it would be impossible for Cuinn to have a continuous guard presence. Ravinire clearly expected her to build a full sixty-strong wing, which was sensible. It would provide six individual details that could rotate through shifts protecting the prince and leave time for training and rest.

"Admiring the difficulty of the problem isn't going to solve it."

Talyn's hands curled on the desk.

"Dammit!" she cursed loudly and pushed out of the chair. She didn't want to be like this. She wanted to be what she had been before. Powerful. Unshakeably confident. In control.

She took a deep, steadying breath. What had her Callanan instructors always said—break the big, complex problems down into smaller steps. Then rely on your training. She and Sari had become so experienced, so skilled and in tune, that even complex situations hadn't been hard anymore. Their confidence had soared, and it got them through everything. Until that one battle.

Focus. She just needed to focus. And break the problem down.

So, her wing wasn't going to be a polished protection detail anytime soon, but maybe she could get them well on the way before her posting finished and she went home to Calumnia.

The first thing to do was to get their measure.

CHAPTER 10

She spent a mostly sleepless night trying not to focus on her fears, and eventually gave up just before dawn. Opening the front door revealed a glowing pink horizon. Mist hugged the treetops of the hillside directly across from the walkway outside. Allowing the simple beauty of her surroundings to calm some of her edginess, she stood at the railing for a few moments, taking slow, deep breaths of the flower-scented air.

A handful of winged folk swooped by overhead, dropping almost close enough for her to touch before disappearing around the side of the hill. She craned her neck, fascinated to watch them in flight, but they didn't return.

By the time she'd eaten—there'd been a large supply of fresh bread, cheese, fruit and dried food left for her in a cupboard, though she supposed she'd be eating at the barracks mess once it ran out—and changed into her sleeveless uniform, the sun had risen fully into the sky, moving from warm to hot on her bare shoulders. Amazingly, she managed to find her way to the barracks without help.

They were all there, waiting, sitting well apart from each other once again, and with expressions ranging from mutinous to bored.

"Theac?" She waved him over.

"Captain?"

"I want you to run them through basic warm ups and then beginner sword drills. Nothing complicated. I just want to see what they look like."

He scratched his head, looking like he wanted to protest, but in the end, nodded and turned away from her.

Theac drilled them for an hour while Talyn stretched and ran through her Callanan agility exercises. Part of her attention focused on her movements, the remainder on the progress of her men.

It was quickly apparent that Tiercelin was the only one who had any knowledge whatsoever of how to use a sword. He burst out laughing when Zamaril wrapped his hand around the hilt of his new sword as gingerly as if he were picking up a dangerous snake, then proceeded to drop it as soon as Theac tapped the blade with his own.

The thief flushed scarlet in mortification, and bent to pick it back up, holding it in a white-knuckled grip this time. Halun waved his training sword about as if it were a fifty-pound club, while Corrin merely looked terrified he might hurt someone with his.

Worse, they were slow to follow orders—in some cases because they didn't understand Theac's instructions and in others because they quite obviously didn't want to do what he was asking them to. Theac barked non-stop. It was clear that he was angry about more than just the lack of skill and discipline being demonstrated.

When he finally called a halt, Talyn joined them, running a critical eye over the group. Tiercelin was breathing easily and Theac was mastering his fatigue manfully despite being dangerously red in the face. Corrin looked pale, his arms trembling, and once again his gaze was firmly on his shoes. Zamaril was flushed and had a sour look plastered over his face. Halun sweated profusely and sucked in air with big gulps, presumably well used to heavy work, but not stamina training.

They all held their blades warily, without a trace of the proper stances and footwork that she was accustomed to seeing at drill. Tiercelin was a little better than the rest, but from what she'd observed, seemed to forgo discipline for showiness.

As she faced them, she was momentarily at a loss.

Since her childhood, from riding with the Aimsir to her Callanan apprenticeship to the Kingshield, she had trained amongst the best warriors in her country. She had absolutely no experience with raw recruits who were essentially forced conscripts—something that wouldn't even happen in the Twin Thrones.

The silence became drawn out, and it took her a few moments to realise they were picking up her sense of hopelessness. Corrin's shoulders drooped while Zamaril's tired expression turned sneering. "I told you we were worthless. Maybe you should just send us back to the cells now and be done with it."

His defeatist attitude stung Talyn's temper. "If you talk like that, of course you're going to be useless. None of the skilled warriors I know lack confidence." *Except me. But I'm going to get it back. I have to get it back.*

"We're not skilled warriors," Zamaril countered.

"If you think we're useless, then why should we think differently?" Corrin said in a small voice. "We can tell from the way you and Theac look at us."

Halun merely dropped his sword and crossed his arms over his chest, glare firmly in place.

"Don't be so sure." Talyn took a breath. "All the fine warriors I know didn't start out that way. Neither did I, when it comes down to it. We just have to start from the beginning and work hard."

Theac grunted, but the others just looked at their shoes. Talyn gritted her teeth and forced back irritation. *One step at a time.* "How are the barracks? Comfortable enough for you?"

"They'll do." Theac grunted.

"Actually, I couldn't find my money pouch this morning." Tiercelin threw a dark glance at Zamaril. "I don't suppose anybody knows where it is?"

"Are you insinuating I took it?" Zamaril snapped.

"Well I don't know. You *are* our resident thief," Tiercelin said.

"You probably lost it, you flea-bitten feathered moron!"

"How dare you call *me* a moron!" Tiercelin flushed an angry red. "Remember your place, human!"

Letting out an inarticulate shout of anger, Zamaril threw himself at Tiercelin. The winged man was taken by surprise and fell backwards with the force of Zamaril's charge. They hit the ground and rolled over and over, throwing punches that mostly didn't land and wrestling for the upper hand. The warrior part of Talyn frowned when Tiercelin didn't even try to use his wings to help him fight, allowing the much smaller and wirier Zamaril to get the upper hand.

She let them at it for a few moments, then when they staggered to their feet, still wrestling, she moved. Swooping down to pick up Halun's dropped training sword, she cracked Zamaril hard on the back with it, then gripped the collar of his shirt, trying to pull them apart.

When he ignored her tugging and they continued to brawl—a careless elbow nearly catching her in her jaw—she kicked Zamaril hard in the back of his right knee, forcing the leg to fold under him. Then, as he dropped, she stepped around, drove her elbow into Tiercelin's solar plexus and sent him staggering back. Before he could right himself, she drew her sai, spinning it so the morning sunlight glinted brightly on the blade.

"Either of you keep going and I start removing important body parts!" she snapped.

Tiercelin froze into instant stillness while Zamaril stumbled to his feet, glowering and rubbing the back of his knee.

"Theac!" she bellowed, and the veteran reluctantly stepped forward to stand between the two men. Blood flowed from Zamaril's nose and both he and Tiercelin sported darkening bruises on their cheekbones. Their chests heaved and sweat soaked through their clothes, making a pitiful sight.

"Zamaril, did you take the money?" Talyn asked him.

"No," he said, tugging up the hem of his threadbare shirt to swipe at his bleeding nose. "I didn't take anything."

"Do you promise to never steal from anybody in this wing?" She lifted a hand as he opened his mouth. "And before you answer you better damn well mean it. I told you yesterday, these men are your comrades. We don't insult each other and we don't steal from each other. Trust is imperative."

"I don't trust them," he muttered.

"Zamaril!" she shouted. "If you don't start showing some sliver of cooperation, so help me I will send you straight back to that cell. I won't tolerate any further insubordination from you. Am I clear?"

"All right," he said sulkily. "I promise I won't steal from anyone in this wing. You have my word."

"Tiercelin." Talyn rounded on him. "You do not go around making accusations about fellow members of your wing without solid proof. Am I clear?"

"Whatever." He brushed the dirt off his shoulders, flaring his wings to shed them of leaves too.

She levelled him with a look. "You don't have to be here either. I'm just as happy to have zero winged folk in my wing, so feel free to fly off right now if you can't follow my orders and be a part of this team. Am I *clear*?"

He stiffened, his pretty face flinching at whatever must be written in her expression, but he gave her a sharp nod. "Yes, Captain."

There'd been a hint of fear in his eyes at her words, and she wondered at the source of it. The question of why he was the only Falcon here nagged at her. She dismissed the curiosity for now, keeping her voice cold as she widened her gaze to address them all. "I will not tolerate infighting in this wing. We will be relying on each other for our lives. Theac, do you agree?"

"This isn't a wing," he said darkly, glowering at her. "This is a flea-bitten rabble."

She stepped up to him, lowering her voice so that only he could hear. In the heat of her anger and frustration, she'd recaptured a flash of who she'd once been, utterly implacable in the face of attitude. Combined with her natural Dumnorix charisma, it was difficult to stand up to, and she used it on him ruthlessly. "You are my second. That means you back me up in front of the wing, and you help when

109

I'm trying to break up a fight. If you aren't prepared to be a second, you can leave. Now."

He stared mutinously at her, jaw set.

"Make your choice," she said evenly.

"I'll stay." He jerked his head.

"Don't make me do this again," she warned. "I won't give you a choice next time. I may be a woman, but I'm not soft."

"Understood," he growled.

Talyn stepped back, taking a breath to calm herself before turning back to the group. Anger could be used, but it needed to be controlled too. "Zamaril, Tiercelin, if it happens again, you'll both be out. That goes for the rest of you if you try and pull the same thing. Being here is an opportunity for all of you. It may not be one that you want, or that you like, but it is a damn sight better than rotting in those cells, so start acting like it!"

They nodded, feet shuffling, eyes on the ground. She almost allowed herself to roll her eyes. Was this truly what command was like? It felt more like what she imagined parenting small children would be.

"Captain, can I ask you a question?" Corrin asked hesitantly.

She let out a breath, using it to calm herself. "You can ask me anything."

"Would you tell us about the badge on your chest?" He pointed.

Taken aback, she glanced down, reaching up to trace her fingers over the little stars. "The crossed swords is the Dumnorix sigil. The Kingshield, Callanan and army all wear this to reflect that. The colour matches the eye-colour of the current monarch. The Dumnorix family have quite striking and brightly coloured eyes—like starlight— hence this emblem is stitched from stars."

"Your king has amber eyes?" Tiercelin asked, sounding as curious as Corrin now.

"Yes, that's right."

Zamaril was next, frowning in confusion. "Why did you join the Kingshield?" he asked. "You have the skills of a great warrior, why waste them protecting a king or a prince?"

"The Dumnorix are worth protecting. They devote their lives to looking after *all* their people," she said simply, realising the words sounded trite, but utterly unwilling to explain the real reason she'd joined the Kingshield. "It is an honour to protect and serve their family."

Zamaril let out a scornful laugh. His raking glance suggested he knew she was lying through her teeth.

"An admirable king who protects his people," Theac muttered angrily. "A hopeful thought indeed. I think you live in some sort of dreamworld, Captain."

Having had a stomach full of black looks and bitterness, Talyn decided to end the conversation there. "Training is over for this morning. You will spend the remainder of the day finishing sweeping and clearing this yard. If I see one leaf or speck of dust on this ground tomorrow morning, I will make you clean it again." She tried to quell her frustration with them, but it was a losing battle. "Dismissed."

"I didn't do anything wrong." Corrin frowned, glaring in Zamaril's direction.

Halun growled, presumably in agreement, crossing his brawny arms over his chest.

"What happens to the wing affects the entire wing," she said. "You'll all clean together. Perhaps next time Zamaril and Tiercelin won't be in such a hurry to insult each other. Now get to it."

Looking insolent and irritated, they shuffled off towards the barracks. Talyn doubted that the yard would be cleaned very well, but at least they were doing as she asked.

Sort of.

"You!" she snapped at Theac as he turned to follow the others.

He turned and raised an eyebrow, not even bothering to address her by her rank.

She sighed. "Theac, we need to instil confidence and a sense of teamwork in them. They will look to you because of your experience and because I'm a woman and they don't trust me yet."

"I never asked them to."

"If you'd like to make this difficult for me, then fine. But I warn you Theac, I will succeed here."

Theac spread his arms, a bitter grin crossing his face. "I'm not going to stop you from trying, and I'll do my job. Just don't expect any more than that, *Captain.*"

"Get out of here," she snapped.

He turned and stalked away. Talyn let out a breath—threatening people to make them obey her wasn't her ideal choice, but she wasn't averse to it if necessary.

"That was expertly handled. I don't know why you keep doubting yourself."

"Get out of my head," she snarled, before stalking out of the yard.

A FALCON SENT by Ravinire was waiting for Talyn as she arrived back at her room. She followed him to the WingGuard commander's quarters via another confusing route that took her not far north of Cuinn's tower. If she remembered Tiercelin's explanation from the day before correctly, that would place her almost adjacent to the queen's rooms. She tried her best to memorise the route, but wasn't sure she'd succeeded.

The Falcon barracks were sprawling and busy. Two wings drilled in a large yard not unlike her own, while another wing filled the sky above practising aerial manoeuvres. Their musical voices drifted in the warm midday air.

Ravinire's quarters took up half of the top floor of the barracks building, while the other half held a series of offices, presumably occupied by his staff. The working space was much less cluttered than her experience of Callanan Tower and the Kingshield offices at home.

Here, the space seemed designed around the fact that all of its occupants had wings that could easily topple anything fragile and would be cramped with too much furniture around. Instead there were only a handful of tables and none of the chairs had backs. Parchment was kept inside boxes so piles couldn't be carelessly swept away by an unfurling wing, and the ceiling was high.

She liked it. It gave the otherwise busy working area a sense of breathing space, especially given how hot the air was.

Her Falcon guide rapped sharply on a half open door, then pushed it open when a voice inside told them to enter. Talyn stepped in to find a pair of suspicious brown eyes staring at her from a winged man sitting behind a desk—the desk was the only furniture in the room and the chair was more like a stool.

"The Falcon is waiting for you," he said, tone bordering on rude.

She ignored the tone and the look, simply giving a friendly nod before crossing the small space and opening the only other door. A large office lay beyond, floor to ceiling glass directly behind Ravinire's desk offering a view over three hillside buildings she was fairly confident were the queen's quarters.

There was another door to her immediate left—firmly closed. Otherwise the room was sparse apart from the desk and two backless chairs sitting before it. Two boxes of parchment sat at his right and left hands.

"Good morning, Captain Dynan." Ravinire looked up. "Please, take a seat."

She did as asked, her posture stiffer than usual without the back of a chair to lean against. "Good morning, sir."

"As you've now had a day to settle in, I would like to discuss my expectations from you for the year you are with us." He gave her a wry look. "As you've already pointed out, the crown paid dearly for the benefit of your presence here, and I'd like to make sure that investment isn't wasted."

"Yes, sir." Good, some firm boundaries and expectations. Maybe they would help her feel less like she was floundering.

"For a start, five men is not a wing. You cannot protect Prince Cuinn at all times with only half a single detail."

"I agree, sir. However, unless you can provide me with some trained fighters, I don't have enough resources to train more than five men at one time."

"The WingGuard has no additional resources for you, Captain," he said. "I can provide more pardonables."

"No sir." She shook her head. "I can't effectively train more than five raw recruits at a time, particularly those that have no desire to be soldiers and are only doing this because the alternative facing them is jail."

He said nothing for a moment, his expression unreadable as his gaze studied her. It almost seemed he was searching for something. She kept her expression equally bland, and it was impossible to tell whether he found what he was looking for. "I will accept that for now," he said. "However, both Theac and Tiercelin are trained fighters. Use them to expedite your training requirements. If you aren't able to build an effective protection wing, then there's no purpose in you being here."

"There it is, Tal! He doesn't want you here, and he's looking for a reason to get rid of you. Or convince whoever asked for you to get rid of you. Fail at this and he has his reason."

Talyn took a breath. Sari was correct. What he was asking was impossible, yet she read clearly the implicit warning in his words. She either did as he asked, or she was going to be sent back home, izerdia or no. "Yes, sir. I'll do my best."

"I thought you liked him?" she muttered.

"I just said he was honest."

"Helpful." Talyn returned her attention to Ravinire as he spoke again. "Good. Now, how did your meeting with Prince Cuinn go?"

"Not well, sir. He insists he doesn't need a protective detail and refused to allow me to remain as his guard in the interim before the men can be trained up." She spoke honestly. "I would appreciate any advice you could give me on how best to handle that."

"Prince Cuinn is a… difficult subject," Ravinire agreed. "Should it become necessary, I will talk to the queen. For now, given you don't have enough for a detail anyway, I think it better you devote your time to training up the men. We'll revisit once you have a functioning detail."

"Thank you, sir." She shifted. He'd already shut her down once, but she was going to try again. "Is there anything I should know about the security environment here, particularly as it pertains to Prince Cuinn? I want to do everything I can to fulfil my duties."

"I'm sure you have worked out for yourself there are certain tensions between the Dock City population and the citadel, but those tensions have always been there. I don't truly believe the humans pose a specific threat to Prince Cuinn, or anyone in the royal family," Ravinire said. "Should the WingGuard be made aware of any such threats, I will of course let you know."

"Yes, sir." She hesitated. She was already pushing him, but she needed to know *something,* so she summoned as courteous a tone as she could manage. "May I ask the reason a Kingshield liaison was requested at this particular time?"

He watched her again, the moment dragging out, until she felt the need to clarify. "Instead of being placed with your WingGuard to assist in training them in the specifics of personal protection, I've been asked to create a new wing for the queen's youngest son. I would have thought it more logical to assign me to the queen's unit, or even the eldest prince's, to help improve their skills. Given that, I assume there's a particular danger that has developed recently where Prince Cuinn is concerned and that's what prompted your queen to reach out to the Twin Thrones."

It was a shot in the dark, but his face gave her no indication whether it had landed. "You'll find that what you might consider logical for the Twin Thrones is quite different to what makes sense in Mithranar." He finally looked away, shifting his attention to the papers on his desk. "I've already answered your questions. If and when there is a threat to Prince Cuinn, you will be advised. Dismissed, Captain."

HER THOUGHTS RAN BUSILY as she departed the WingGuard barracks, left to her own devices to find her way back. Ravinire had told her the previous day he'd been wanting Cuinn to have a protective detail for some time, yet she had the distinct impression this whole thing was more about setting her an impossible task so he could have good reason to send her packing or convince whoever wanted her here to send her home.

"Maybe it's not that nefarious. Perhaps he's put you in the youngest prince's guard to test you, see whether you're any good. Maybe even to see if he can trust you before he lets you train his soldiers."

That made sense. He clearly hadn't been the one behind the request to bring her here. And she tended to agree with Sari's assessment that he was fair and honest leader. If she proved herself useful, then good, he'd use her expertise. If not, he could send her home at the end of the year, no harm, no foul. Experiment over.

"Maybe it's both. He could be looking for excuses to get rid of me while also testing to see how good I am."

"Agreed. The more interesting question is why the Callanan are so interested in this Shadowhawk character that they asked Ceannar to send you here."

Maybe that was one question she *could* answer. Some dedicated investigation should yield results there. Talyn stopped walking suddenly, staring around her and realising she was lost. *Dammit.*

She briefly considered flagging down one of the passing winged folk, but given their reaction to her arrival, she was loathe to own up to being lost. No, she would find her own way, no matter how long it took or how many ladders she had to clamber up or down.

And she'd use it as an opportunity to start learning her way around this damn labyrinth of a hill city.

IT TOOK HER A FULL-TURN, but she made it out of the citadel and down into Dock City. Dusk was falling, the air still thick and warm, but now outlined in a hazy orange glow. She'd considered checking on her wing before leaving the citadel—but after their interaction earlier she wasn't sure she could face another helping of bad attitude. Half of her was afraid she'd find them utterly disobeying her order to clean. That would force her into carrying out her threat to send them back, and then she'd have no wing. Ravinire would most certainly see that as a failure.

Fear clawed at her chest, and she tried to fight it down. She hadn't failed yet.

At least in walking through Dock City she wasn't subjected to the regular looks of derision or contempt she got in the citadel. In fact, a man closing up his store for the day was more than happy to point her in the direction of the City Patrol station in the Market Quarter.

The building was almost identical to the headquarters in the Wealthy Quarter, just smaller. Two Patrolmen sat at the front desk. These two wore crisp uniforms and seemed to be paying attention to their surroundings, which was an improvement on the two she'd met when choosing her detail the previous day.

"Can we help you?" the one on the left asked politely.

"My name is Talyn Dynan. I'm looking for Watch Officer Tye. Is he here?"

The Patrolman rose from his seat. "He's back in his office. I'll go and get him for you."

Dark-skinned with neatly-cut black curls, Tye had brown eyes that were full of curiosity as he appeared through a door to the left. He also barely reached her shoulder. "Kingshield Dynan," he greeted her, an edge of puzzlement to his polite tone. "What can I do for you?"

"I wanted to ask about the thieves I helped catch the other day. What happened to them?"

"Two are already out. They'll be on work-crew duty for two weeks to clear the slate. The one who threw the knife at you has gone to the city jail. He'll be there for several months I expect." A small smile. "Normally the Shadowhawk gets his people out before that can happen, but in this case, I expect he took exception to the knife throwing."

At the flash of confusion on Talyn's face, Tye continued. "He won't like that one of his people used a weapon to attack you. Beats me how he hears about these details, but there you go."

Interesting. She needed to know more. "Do you have time for me to buy you a drink? I'm going to be here in Mithranar for a while, and there's clearly a lot for me to learn. If I'm going to do my job properly, I want to learn as quick as I can."

He gave her knowing look. "I don't suppose the winged lot up in their pretty citadel have been too welcoming of a human?" He looked around, as if assuring himself all was quiet. "I'm on duty tonight, but I have some time for a break. If we go to the inn just around the corner, the lads will come and get me if there's any trouble."

The inn was clearly a hotspot for off—and on—duty Patrolmen, and most of its patrons had a wave or a shouted greeting for Tye as they entered. Music was playing in the background, just a man and woman playing a merry tune on flute and fiddle.

"If you don't mind me asking, what *is* your job here?" he asked as drinks were placed in front of them—Tye ordering a cold juice rather than ale.

"The Acondor family requested a Kingshield liaison to assist in training the WingGuard in close protection skills. We provide personal protection in the Twin Thrones. The Falcon has asked me to develop a wing for Prince Cuinn's protection."

Tye frowned. "I don't pretend to understand winged folk thinking, but I suppose it makes sense they'd eventually get around to creating a wing for Prince Cuinn. Though why they're asking a foreign warrior to do it escapes me. The winged folk aren't ones for respecting those without wings."

"As has been impressed on me strongly so far," she muttered.

He flashed a warm smile. "I bet. Can I ask what the Twin Thrones gets out of this?"

Talyn eyed him in satisfaction. The man wasn't a dullard. That would make him an even better informant. "A very pricy shipment of izerdia."

"I see. You must be very good at what you do." He tipped his glass towards her in genuine acknowledgement. "Go ahead and ask your questions, Captain."

"First question." Talyn kept her voice casual but interested. "The Shadowhawk is a criminal, yet from what I've seen so far, you all like him. The Falcon said something to me about half the City Patrol being in his pocket."

"Like's not the right word." Tye sipped his drink. "And half is a massive exaggeration. You've been here what, two days? So you've already had a taste of what things are like here. Between the humans and winged folk, I mean."

"You could say that."

"It's more than just sentiment. Mithranar is not a resource-rich country, and apart from our izerdia, the copper mines, and wood we export, we are reliant for most things on trade from other places. The winged folk look after themselves first, then the humans, and because of their opulent lifestyle, they don't spend any more than they absolutely have to." Tye's face turned sober. "It means we—the humans— don't always get the food or other essentials we need. The Shadowhawk's activities address that problem. There are times when the supplies he and his network steals are the only thing stopping parts of the Dock City population from starving."

Talyn considered him a moment. "So the City Patrol *is* sympathetic to him?"

"The City Patrol is a lot of things." Tye gave a bitter laugh. "The winged folk don't much care for how we police ourselves, as long as what happens down here doesn't affect them up there. Some of us are sympathetic to the Shadowhawk, yes. Some of us take bribes or other incentives from the Falcons to help catch the Shadowhawk, or for other reasons. Some care about enforcing the law, others not so much."

And you're one of the ones who cares. "You're certainly the most helpful Patrolman I've met so far."

"I heard the Falcon asked you to take on pardonables for your new wing." Tye traced a finger over the grooves worn deep into the wooden tabletop. "I'm glad you picked Parksin."

"He's not."

Another quicksilver smile flashed over Tye's face. "He trained me —he was Patrol Captain of the Poor Quarter when I first started. And I won't lie, there's good reason he was thrown out. But none of it was because he was one of the Patrolmen I talked about who like to take bribes."

There was a message in there, but she was hesitant to probe

further. Tye had already told her a lot and she didn't want to push him too far. He could be a useful source if she handled this carefully. So instead she offered an appreciative nod as he drained his juice. "Thank you for taking the time to talk to me, Watch Officer. It's been extremely helpful, but I don't want to hold you up if you're on duty. Can I walk you back?"

"Andres, please." He rose as she did. "And I'm happy to answer any questions you have as you settle in, Captain. Mithranar is a strange enough place for those of us who have lived here our whole lives."

"I may take you up on that." They walked back out into the street. Immediately a wave of warm night air enveloped them. Sweat prickled on her skin.

"Until next time, then." He offered that quick smile again as they stopped outside the Patrol building, then turned and took the steps two at a time.

She turned back to survey the busy street, and a sigh escaped her. It was going to be a long walk back up that blasted wall.

CHAPTER 11

When Talyn appeared in the training yard early the next morning, it had been cleaned and swept, but nobody was there except for Theac and Corrin. Theac glowered as he sharpened a new axe. The boy sat disconsolately on a stone bench, and in a startlingly unsurprising development, was staring at his shoes.

"Where are they?" she asked Theac.

"I looked for them," he said grudgingly. "Couldn't find them."

She stared at him, but he was unbothered, his gaze dropping back to the axe. Corrin's eyes flickered up to glance between them, uncertain, before returning to his shoes. For the first time she noticed how threadbare they were—his toe poked through a hole in the right one.

"Both of you," she snapped. "Get up and follow along as best you can."

Without another word, she settled into a series of stretches before beginning a warm up. The familiar movements of *sabai*—the Callanan form of unarmed combat—calmed her mood and focused her mind.

She was just finishing up, Corrin and Theac stumbling awkwardly behind her, when Tiercelin spiralled down out of the air. She said nothing, simply raised her eyebrow at him.

"Apologies Captain, but I had to attend a family dinner last night and it ran rather late." He offered a smile. "I'm sure you understand."

"No, I don't," she said, "If I order you to be here at a certain time, I expect you to be here."

"Zamaril and Halun aren't here either." He seemed astonished that she was angry with him.

"I don't care where everybody else is," she said. "And sleeping in is not a sufficient excuse for being late to drill."

Before he could reply, the door to the barracks opened and Halun and Zamaril appeared. The thief slouched in, then sprawled along one of the stone benches. Halun looked at him, then shrugged and sat down beside him.

"Where have you two been?" She rounded on them.

Zamaril yawned widely. "Sleeping. Cleaning out the yard yesterday was tiring."

Talyn glanced at Theac, whose glower had only become more firmly settled over his features. She took a few deep breaths. She was Talyn Dynan, Callanan warrior and member of the Dumnorix family. This rabble of poor-attitude and reluctance was *not* going beat her.

"Theac, the inside of the barracks needs cleaning," she said, voice light but firm. "See that it gets done by nightfall."

"Yes, Captain," he muttered, heaving himself to his feet.

"And if you can't display enough leadership ability to get the wing to appear for drill on time, you're out." She strode to the gate, casting her eye over all of them. "Be here on time tomorrow, or don't bother coming at all."

As they walked away, some of her confidence faded, and she seriously contemplated the fact she might need to go to Ravinire the next day and tell him she'd had to send them all back to the cells. The unfairness of what he was expecting rose up in a choke-hold of frustration, but it was only covering her deeply buried fear that she *couldn't* do this. That the person she'd been before, who would have succeeded no matter how unreasonable Ravinire's task, had gone forever.

"No," she said the word aloud to give it greater emphasis. "I won't give up."

"*I'm with you, Tal.*"

Her eyes closed at the whisper of thought through her mind. "*But you're not. I'm here alone.*"

TRYING to keep a firm grip on her determination, Talyn spent the rest of the morning and early afternoon exploring the palace until she felt she could find her way around to the places she needed to without help. She also discovered the way to the main entrance to Cuinn's tower—the bridge leading over to his front door was, of course, unguarded. He wasn't there, so she kept exploring.

The palace was a hive of activity. Winged folk either glided or flew past Talyn as she strolled the walkways. The only adult she saw walking had part of her left wing bandaged.

Their musical voices added an air of liveliness to the bright day. None of them acknowledged her though, beyond the occasional frown thrown her way at the sight of a human. Talyn saw only a handful of other humans on her walk, and judging by their similar clothes and manner, she guessed they were servants.

The sharp contrast between the beauty of the citadel and the lack of warmth in its residents was hard to adjust to, leaving her strangely torn between the alluring loveliness and music of the citadel and the distinct feeling that she was not welcome or wanted.

On her way back to her room, legs burning from all the climbing, she diverged from the path past her wing's barracks. Now more familiar with the layout of the palace, it was obvious how far they were from the main living areas of the royal family, and from the other WingGuard barracks. Most likely a deliberate move on Ravinire's part. A smart one too, given what she'd experienced so far.

Nobody was about in the yard, and she swore to herself that if she found them inside doing nothing, she'd send them all back to jail, Theac included. Tiercelin could go back to his family dinners and another wing of the Falcons. Maybe Ravinire could be convinced to give her proper soldiers, or allow her to simply be Cuinn's only guard for the rest of her posting. Or he'd just send her home because she'd failed his ridiculous test.

And then they would all know she'd failed. How broken she was. Before she could slide all the way down into the vicious cycle of fear and despair, a snatch of music caught her attention. It was a soft, sad tune. Haunting enough to draw her out of her emotion and back into the day.

Curious, she followed the drifting notes around to a small gate set in the wall of the barracks. It led into a pretty garden adjacent to the barracks' mess hall.

Corrin was in there alone, his back to her, seated on a stone bench. His hands cradled a small flute, which he was playing with deft fingers, his head bowed over the instrument, long hair hiding his face.

The surge of irritation at the sight of him not following orders broke through the spell his music had set over her. "You've got ten seconds to explain to me why you're not cleaning as ordered, or I'll walk you back to the cells myself."

He started, and almost dropped the instrument. But when he turned to face her, she was shocked to see tears glistening on his cheeks. In a flash her anger was gone, and she wavered, unsettled by how his tears tore at her own wounds.

"Is everything all right? Did something happen?" She crossed to sit beside him on the bench, concerned. As with the others in her wing, she was uncertain what to make of Corrin. Callanan potential notwithstanding, he was young and timid and didn't fit the mould of a warrior in any sense of the word.

He swallowed and shook his head. "No, nothing's happened, Captain."

"Then why aren't you cleaning the barracks?" she asked sharply.

"I finished the section Theac assigned me." He sniffed, reaching up to scrub his face with a dirty sleeve. "And playing music always helps me feel better."

Corrin was no Zamaril, so she decided to accept he was telling the truth. And because he was still so stiff around her and she truly wanted to know what had upset him, she smiled. "You play beautifully. How long have you been learning?"

"Since I was a boy." A sad smile flicked over his face. "My father taught me. Learning an instrument isn't uncommon here, but Da used to say I had the talent to be even better than him."

"He's not alive anymore, is he?" she asked softly. One thing she would always recognise—the grief of loss. It was written all over him.

"No." He looked away from her.

"Why were you crying, Corrin?" She kept her voice gentle.

"It's nothing." His jaw clenched.

She was silent a moment, searching for what to say. If she wanted her wing to succeed, she needed to try and win this boy over, to earn his trust. "Corrin, being your captain doesn't just mean I'm the person who yells orders at you. It makes me responsible for you, and that means having your back and looking out for you. If you're in trouble of some kind, it's my job to help you get out of it."

His gaze shifted and he stared at her for a long moment—he looked so painfully young with his green eyes wet from tears and his thin shoulders literally sagging under the weight they bore. She watched as his strength faltered and he twisted back away to stare at the ground.

"I don't know what to do," he said raggedly, his breath hitching.

"About what?" she asked firmly.

"It's just..." His shoulders sagged further, then suddenly the words poured out of him in a torrent. "It's my mam, and my sisters. They're all alone now that I'm up here. Da died in prison. The Falcons caught him stealing from one of their warehouses. We're a poor family, and he didn't make enough from his music to feed us last winter, so he took to stealing what we needed. He wasn't a criminal... he just... we didn't have enough to eat, and my baby sister was so sick with a cough. The Falcons didn't care about a human thief. They put him in a prison cell that was damp from the monsoon season. He caught a fever and died."

Talyn's heart lurched with misery for the young man and the awful position he was in. "Corrin, I—"

"Ever since he died we had to fend for ourselves. I'm only seventeen, but I was the oldest, my sisters are only babies... I had to take care of them." His voice broke. "I worked playing music on the street corners, at the inns, almost twenty full-turns a day, but it wasn't enough, not after what we had to pay for medicine for my sister. They wouldn't take me on at the docks because I'm not strong enough, and I had no trade skills to get an apprenticeship. So I had to take to stealing too, to feed my family. But of course I got caught and now I'm here and my mam and sisters are all alone. I don't know what to do. I'm trapped up here, and if I leave, I'll get put back in jail. I'm so scared that they won't survive without me."

Talyn sat there, momentarily at a loss on how to respond or what to do. Corrin's distress was deep and powerful, and she'd never been good at comforting people. Neither had Sari. They hadn't needed to be.

But she *could* imagine how awful it would be to be in Corrin's plight—she'd made sure Sari's husband and young son were settled before leaving for Ryathl, and part of her wages ever since had gone to both of them. It would tear her apart to know they were struggling and she couldn't help.

She reached out and settled her hand on his shoulder. "Corrin, I'm sorry, I had no idea."

"It's not your fault. I wouldn't have lasted long in the cells. You probably saved my life." He tried to smile through watery tears. "Though I have no idea why you chose me."

"I had an instinct about you, Corrin," she replied absently, her gaze distant as her mind thought furiously. The urge to do something was almost a compulsion. Corrin was her responsibility now and she had to look after him. That was the Dumnorix in her.

"I want to help." She turned back to him. "But I need your permission to tell the others."

"No," he said instantly. "They won't care, and they'll just think I'm weak. Zamaril already calls me a baby."

"Can Zamaril throw a knife as well as you can?" she asked him.

He paused. "No."

She gave him a look. "Then perhaps you shouldn't bother so much about what he calls you. You can be important to this wing, Corrin, but first you need to start believing it."

"It's not easy." His tears had stopped and he wiped his face with a sleeve. "I'm not even full grown, and after everything that's happened... it's hard to believe that things will ever get better."

"I know that to you, I'm a stranger and a foreigner." She met his gaze. "But I ask you to give me your trust even though you have no reason to. Do that, and from now on we do this together."

He stared at his feet for a long moment. She sensed his deep reluctance to do as she asked, but along with it, a growing acceptance that he had little choice. Eventually he sniffed, then nodded. "All right."

"Good." She injected a little ice into her voice. "And so help me, if you keep staring at your shoes in my presence I'm going to chop both your feet off at the ankles. If you're going to be a warrior, Corrin Dariel, straighten your shoulders and meet the world like the man you want to be."

He swallowed, lifted his gaze to hers. "Yes, Captain."

SHE LEFT Corrin to his music and went in search of the others in the barracks. They were huge, standing three stories high and clearly meant for a full wing of Falcons. After a long hunt to track each of them down—they'd all chosen to work as far from each other as possible—she ordered them to a ground floor common room that exited directly out into the yard.

It was the friendliest place she'd seen in the building, with a fireplace dominating one wall—seriously, who *ever* needed a fire in Mithranar?—thick carpeting and several comfortable looking chairs and sofas. Tables were scattered throughout the space for work or study, and a doorway on the far wall led directly to the kitchen and mess. She suspected it had been designed for human servants working for the wing living at the barracks.

None of her wing had been cleaning with any effort to do a decent job. All jumped to attention with alacrity when she appeared, looking wary. She said nothing, simply telling them to come downstairs. This made them look even warier, but they complied without a word.

She ran a slow, deliberate gaze over the dust an inch thick that covered all the surfaces, then raised an eyebrow at Theac.

He shrugged. "This room was next on my list."

"I see."

Zamaril and Tiercelin sat opposite each other around a low central table, both sprawled lazily on comfortable lounges. Halun sat in between, idly carving a piece of wood and ignoring the glaring going on.

"I'm here to talk to you about Corrin," she said without preamble, choosing one of the chairs left vacant.

Zamaril gave an exaggerated sigh. "Aren't you going to tell us off for shirking our duties first? Maybe make us scrub the tiles with our bare hands?"

"Where is he?" Theac asked, shooting a glower in Zamaril's direction.

"You know, the more often you glare like that, the less scary it is," Tiercelin pointed out.

Theac levelled another look in his direction. Tiercelin grinned. Halun carefully placed his wood carving on the table, then gave Talyn his full attention. She gave an inward sigh of relief—at least one of them seemed to care.

"I ran into him outside. He was upset." Talyn explained to them what Corrin had told her about his situation.

"Poor lad." Theac whistled, his face softening with genuine sympathy for the first time since Talyn had met him. "He's got no way of caring properly for his mother and sisters. I saw plenty of families like that, back when I was in the Patrol. It rarely turned out well for them."

"I'm going to tell you the same thing I just told Corrin." Talyn leant forward. "Whether any of us are happy about the situation or not, we've been lumped together. As your captain, I am responsible for you. I want to help Corrin. I don't know yet how things work here, which is why I need your help. Any ideas?"

Tiercelin shrugged. "Most humans are poor. It's their lot. Corrin's lucky he was able to get out of that when you chose him to be pardoned."

Talyn stilled her flare of anger at Tiercelin's arrogant and unthinking words. Yelling at him would do no good. When Zamaril opened his mouth, she shot him a glare so fierce that he closed it with a snap and sank back into the cushions of the couch.

"Tiercelin, do you have sisters?" she asked.

"A younger one." He nodded. "And two older brothers."

"Then I want you to imagine your sister didn't have enough to eat. Imagine she lived in a small house that wasn't warm enough in winter, and didn't keep out the rain. That she was in constant danger of being attacked, robbed, or raped because of the area she lived in. Imagine your mother being in the same situation. Now, imagine if Corrin sat where you are now and told you that you were lucky because you'd left your mother and sister behind in that situation."

Tiercelin made no reply, but he shifted on the couch as if suddenly uncomfortable. The cockiness faded from his expression and he wouldn't meet her eyes. Zamaril's sneer was back. Theac looked suddenly old and weary, like this was a battle he'd fought many times before and lost. Halun's fists were clenched in his lap but he wouldn't meet anyone's gaze either.

That was all right. Once step at a time.

"Look." Talyn took a breath. "Corrin said something to me before that made me think. He told me that given what has happened to him, he finds it almost impossible to believe that things could ever get better. That's something you all share with him, right?" *And it's something I share with all of them too. They just don't know it.*

Theac and Halun looked discomfited, and even Zamaril had lost his smirk.

"Yeah, maybe," Tiercelin said softly, surprisingly.

Talyn looked at them. "Things won't get any better if you don't try. I know that's easy to say, and I know that none of you want to be here. What I'm telling you is that being here is your chance to turn things around. Together, we can work towards making it better. I think you've got a better chance doing that here than in the cells, am I correct?"

Silence.

"I'm in your corner. I'll support you all the way, but you have to give me something back."

"You're a woman from the Twin Thrones. What can you do for us?" Zamaril muttered.

"I think you'd be surprised at what I can do. You have me for a year. At least give me a chance." And if she could succeed, if she could make things better for them, then maybe there was hope things could be better for her too. She wanted that so desperately she could taste it. She met their eyes one at a time. "Let's start with Corrin."

There was another long silence, and Talyn hoped it was borne of thoughtfulness, not apathy. She let the silence go, not wanting to push any further than she already had. Eventually, Theac shifted in his chair and looked up.

"My sister and her husband live in Market Quarter. He's a merchant of some means," Theac said. "Their two daughters have a tutor come to their house every day. I might be able to arrange for Corrin's sisters to join the lessons. After all, the tutor is already paid for, and my sister is a kind woman. With an education, his sisters may have a better future."

"Are you sure your sister wouldn't mind?" Talyn asked, a flare of hope rushing through her.

Theac glowered. "I probably have some apologising to do, but now that I'm back in uniform she'll help me out."

"Theac, thank you," Talyn said with relief. "Now, I'm receiving wages from the Kingshield back home, and the WingGuard. I don't need both, given my food and board here is all provided. I'll send a portion of my WingGuard wages to Corrin's family."

Another silence filled the room. None of them said anything, but she didn't miss the surreptitious looks of surprise Halun and Zamaril shot each other. Or the sharp glance from Theac.

Then an unfamiliar, surprisingly soft, voice broke out. "I know many people on the docks. I'll spread the word around that Corrin's mam and sisters are to be left alone, or they'll have me to deal with. I also have some friends who could keep an eye on his family, make sure they're okay."

The entire room shifted to stare at Halun. His voice held none of the musical Mithranan accent, or the lengthier drawl of Talyn's home. It was shorter, clipped, but his words were clear and well-enunciated. Somehow, somewhere, he'd received a fine education.

"He speaks!" Zamaril announced into the silence.

Halun glared at the thief and promptly subsided back into silence. Talyn ignored it, her heart leaping. His offer would be a true help for Corrin. "Thank you, Halun."

He gave her a little nod, then turned to settle a long look on Tiercelin. Theac did the same. Talyn tried not to show how anxiously she awaited the winged man's response.

Tiercelin's eyebrows shot up in surprise, as if asking whether he, a *winged folk,* was supposed to help. When the stares didn't waver, he gave a sigh of resignation and rolled his eyes. "My family owns a number of apartment blocks in Dock City. I suppose I could arrange for an apartment in the Market Quarter to be kept empty. Corrin's family can move there. It won't be big, but it will be warm, and dry and secure."

This time Talyn couldn't hide her smile, but Tiercelin looked away, again refusing to meet her eyes. "If my parents find out about this, I'll be in serious trouble," he muttered.

Footsteps sounded before she could pursue that any further, and they all turned as Corrin opened the door from the yard, hesitating in surprise at the sight of them all gathered inside.

"Come in, have a seat." She waved him to an empty chair. Only then did she realise Zamaril had gone. Disappointment filled her. She had hoped he was a better man than that. "We've been talking about what you told me."

The boy went red. "I wish you hadn't told them, Captain. I don't like people knowing our business."

She met his gaze. "I asked you to trust me, remember?"

He nodded reluctantly. His eyes dropped to the floor, then quickly back up again. She smothered a smile. "Yes, Captain."

"Good, because I think we have a plan." Talyn outlined what they had worked out to help his family. Corrin's eyes became progressively lighter as she spoke, and when she finished, he held a trembling hand over his heart, as if unable to believe what she was telling him. He opened his mouth to stutter his thanks, but was forestalled by a loud scratching sound, then Zamaril appearing through the open door to the kitchens, dragging a heavy sack behind him.

He dragged the sack over to where they were sitting and opened the tie. Immediately a whole pile of turquoise and white clothing spilled out, falling at Corrin's feet.

Zamaril rubbed his hands together in smug satisfaction. "I figured with new living arrangements, school lessons and better food, your mam and sisters might need proper clothing, Corrin. After all, monsoon and then winter is not all that far away. There are some waterproof coats in there—I hope they like teal and white. There weren't many colour options."

They all gaped at him for a moment, then,

"Where did you get all that from?" Theac demanded.

"There's a storeroom in the basement full of spare WingGuard uniforms. It's bulging with clothes and things that nobody ever uses— at least, from what I could tell the place hasn't been touched for months." Zamaril hesitated, his gaze darting to Talyn's, challenge written in them. "When you were all offering your help, I remembered what the captain said about us all having our own talents. It was easy, picking the lock to the room and getting this stuff out."

"You *stole* them?" Tiercelin squeaked, looking horrified.

"I did." Zamaril held Talyn's gaze. "You only made me promise not to steal from my wing mates."

She couldn't help herself. A half-exasperated chuckle escaped her. Zamaril relaxed slightly. Tiercelin sank into the chair, hands covering his face.

"You certainly have a unique skill, Zamaril," she said eventually.

"And I don't see any problem with Corrin's family making use of good clothes that were only sitting around doing nothing."

"Those clothes belong to the WingGuard," Tiercelin argued. "We'd be hung if they found out Zamaril had stolen them. I'm under obligation to report him."

"Then we'd best make sure they don't find out," Theac said pointedly.

"I didn't see anything, especially since you and I were taking a walk around the citadel this afternoon, Tiercelin," Talyn said firmly.

"You're like no other Falcon I've ever met," Tiercelin said, shaking his head.

"That's because I'm not WingGuard. I'm Kingshield."

"I thank you from the bottom of my heart for all your help," Corrin said earnestly.

"It was nothing," Tiercelin said languidly, sprawling out on the couch and closing his eyes as if to sleep.

"Yeah." Zamaril headed for the door. "Don't read too much into it, kid."

Theac stood, muttered something about going to visit his sister and left the room. Halun heaved himself to his feet. "Do you feel like a walk to the docks, Corrin? We can introduce your family to some friends of mine, make sure they know who they're keeping an eye on."

Corrin nodded, almost tearing up again. She thought it was only his astonishment at Halun speaking aloud that stopped him from breaking down. "I'd like that, Halun."

The big man turned to her, lifting a questioning eyebrow. So he could talk, but clearly preferred not to. Another mystery. Were none of her new wing exactly what they appeared to be?

"Go," she said. "Cleaning can be finished tomorrow."

Moments later she found herself alone in the common room. And for the first time in two years there was a lightening of the weight of despair in her chest. Tears sprung to her eyes at the realisation, and she sank into a chair, trying not to cry.

The men she'd picked were rough, ill-mannered and lacked confidence, but they had good instincts. Maybe there was hope after all.

CHAPTER 12

*A*s the first light of day glimmered on the horizon the following morning, Talyn arrived at the barracks to find all of her wing assembled in the training yard. Corrin stood straight, face set in a determined expression, long hair tied neatly back from his face.

It was a start.

She stopped before them. "I am going to demand a lot from you. Most of the time you will curse my name and wish you had never joined this wing," she said clearly, not allowing any trace of her under-lying doubt to enter her voice or bearing. "But I will make you into warriors. Better yet, I will forge you into a formidable team."

She was silent for a beat. Theac glowered into the distance, but the others, even Zamaril, looked alert rather than bored. It wasn't resounding enthusiasm, but it was better than nothing.

"Tiercelin," she continued. "Could you please show us the quickest way to the wall walk down into Dock City?"

The winged man gave a jolt of surprise, but turned and began leading them out of the yard willingly enough. As it turned out, the barracks was only a quarter-turn walk through three narrow walkways, two alarmingly swaying bridges and down four ladders to the top of the wall walk.

The sun was already warm in the air, and Feather Bay gleamed a calm blue. There were a high number of ships docked in the harbour, and workers swarmed around the berths, beginning to load and unload ships now that it was growing light enough.

"The first thing we'll work on is your stamina," Talyn lectured as they paused at the top. "Good conditioning will allow you to last longer in a fight and give you that extra bit of strength to put into a final thrust. It will make you a better, more agile fighter."

Without waiting for reply, Talyn set off down the path at a fast, swinging stride. It took almost a full quarter-turn to reach the bottom, and by that time they'd all worked up a sweat. She eyed their clothing, making a mental note to request proper uniforms from Ravinire. Like most Mithranans she'd met so far, they wore loose pants, sandals, and shirts that were either sleeveless or rolled to the elbows. Tiercelin was bare-chested, his dark skin gleaming in the sunlight.

"That wasn't as hard as I expected," Zamaril said, panting, sweat soaking his shirt to his chest.

"That was just the warm up," Talyn said. "Now we are all going to run back to the barracks. For today it can be a light jog—we'll increase the speed over time."

Once again, she didn't give them time to say anything, instead moving straight into a slow jog back up the road. Behind her, Theac snapped at Zamaril to stop standing around and get moving. A smile threatened to escape her.

As she ran, she glanced down the precipitous drop to her right, noticing that a few of the people moving along the street at the base of the wall had stopped to stare up at them in curiosity. None of the stares held dislike or contempt. It was a refreshing change.

She gave the men credit—they made it almost halfway up the road before slowing to an exhausted halt. By then Halun was dangerously red in the face and Zamaril was staggering precariously close to the edge. The other three were bent over, gasping desperately for air. She cajoled them a little further, then allowed them to walk the rest of the way.

Back at the training yard, all five immediately slumped to the benches lining the yard, sweating and exhausted. Talyn directed a look at Theac. He nodded and heaved himself back up with a grunt.

"Right. On your feet!" he bellowed. "I don't give a flea's shit how tired you all are. If you're not all up in five seconds and standing in a straight line, there'll be no breakfast!"

With a smattering of grunts, groans and muttered complaints, they staggered into line before Talyn. Theac stood with them, back straight and shoulders up, looking of all of them like a proper soldier.

"Along with being fit, you also need to be strong," she said crisply. "Following your run every morning, we'll spend another hour doing strength exercises. After that, you'll have a short break for breakfast, then you'll be back here for sword drills. Two full-turns of that, then I'll take over your instruction in *sabai,* a form of unarmed combat that the Callanan use. Then lunch for a half-turn, before another full-turn of individual training with Theac or myself in your respective specialist weapons. The remainder of the day you'll have to yourselves. Of course, when Prince Cuinn decides he needs a guard, those duties will fit in around your training schedule. Anybody want to leave yet?"

Silence. Then,

"Oh, it doesn't really sound all that bad." Tiercelin grinned, full of arrogance.

Zamaril snorted, amused despite himself.

"Excellent. You can start off with fifty push-ups in that case. Zamaril, you too. The rest of you can do forty." Talyn clapped her hands. "Get to it. Come on!"

"Talyn?"

"Hmm."

"You're going to teach them sabai?*"*

"Two of them already have Callanan potential, and all of them live in a

winged world. They'll need an advantage to be able to stand their ground if Prince Cuinn is ever attacked."

"I don't disagree. But you're not technically allowed to train Callanan. And by that, I mean the First Blade will have a fit if she finds out."

Talyn smiled thinly. "She's not my commander anymore. Besides, I'm not training Callanan... technically. I'm training Kingshield."

"You mean you're training WingGuard."

"Have you seen those winged soldiers? No, if Prince Cuinn is going to be protected properly, I'm training Kingshield, not Falcons," she said. "Not that I plan on mentioning that to Ravinire."

A trickle of laughter, then a hesitation. *"I'm glad you're not ignoring me anymore."*

Talyn shifted uncomfortably. She wasn't at all sure that humouring a voice in her head was the healthiest thing, but she simply couldn't stay away from holding onto something of her partner, even if it was just in her imagination.

As if understanding her conflicting emotions, Sari faded away quietly and left her to her thoughts.

"I'D LIKE to do some training sessions down in the forest around the foothills," Talyn said to Theac as they put away the training weapons late the next afternoon. "Supposing there *is* any flat land down there. They need to learn how to fight outside a drill yard."

"That won't be possible," he said shortly.

"Why?"

His scowl deepened, and he put away the last sword before walking away and making a gesture for her to follow. Swallowing her irritation at his abrupt manner, she followed him until he came to a stop at the far end of the yard, a few steps back from the sheer drop to the treetops of the forest miles below. Straight ahead of them were more rolling hills leading as far as she could see.

"Is there any habitation outside the citadel and Dock City?" she asked curiously.

"Not much," he said. "Almost the entire peninsula of Mithranar is hilly—it reaches back about seventy miles or so, then there's Mairland, which is a bit of flat land before the foothills of the SkyReach. Only there and in Dock City have we built on land."

"The SkyReach?"

He turned and pointed north. "It's a mountain range that cuts off the northern third of Mithranar. If you think we're up high here, wait until you see the royals' summer palace amongst those peaks."

"Right." She nodded and turned back to him. "Fascinating geography lesson notwithstanding, none of this tells me why we can't go and train down in the forest," she said.

"Nobody goes down there unless they have to," he said. "The wall is there for a reason, Captain. There's one tunnel that goes underneath, and it's only ever traversed during daylight hours—if those trees didn't hold the izerdia sap, nobody would ever go down there."

"Izerdia." The substance that had paid for her presence in Mithranar. While she knew it was the core basis for any type of explosive material, she didn't know much about how it was gathered.

"You can't make explosive powder *without* izerdia," Theac said, taking her response as a question. "And our trees are the only ones that produce it—something to do with the unusually warm climate on the peninsula. Only the most desperate humans voluntarily sign up to go into the forest each day to extract the sap, and the rest of the workers are conscripts—usually working off a sentence after being arrested." A dark look filled his face. "And of course the winged folk *never* bribe the City Patrol captains to fill quotas of criminals so enough people are going into the forest each day."

There was bitterness there, deep, corrosive bitterness, and she was loathe to bring more of it out. "What's so bad about the forest then?"

"Mithranar is a beautiful country. You've seen the citadel, and I've heard there's more wondrous splendour in the north." Theac settled more comfortably, thrusting his hands into his pockets. Her shoulders relaxed as that bitterness vanished from his face. "It's also bloody dangerous. The winged folk were the first and only ones to settle here because their magic allowed them to survive. It protected them from what lives below us."

Her eyebrows lifted even higher. He smirked. "The forest is full of creatures, Captain Dynan, some of them vicious, meat-eating, and/or poisonous. Even living way up here, folk still occasionally go missing. And workers on the izerdia details? There's rarely a shift that doesn't lose a worker. That's why the great wall was built, to keep Dock City safe when humans began settling here."

She leaned over the edge, staring down. All she could see was an unending sea of green treetops waving in the afternoon breeze. The canopy was too thick to see anything beyond but dim shadow.

"Trust me, they're there." Theac spat, aiming it over the side. "You would not want to go wandering around down there without a full wing at your back. Tawncats alone are as big as a mountain wolf and will rip your throat out before you even know what's coming. Then there are the snakes so venomous you could die just looking at one." He hesitated. "There are rumours that some of them, tawncats in particular, are more intelligent than most animals, though that could just be a myth."

Frowning, she went back over what he'd said. Above-average intelligence in such vicious hunting creatures might explain the need for such a magnificent wall and a hill city. But her interest caught on his mention of magic, recalling her conversation with Cynia and Leviana before leaving Ryathl. "Tell me more about winged folk magic."

He shrugged, the scowl returning to his face. "Most of them possess one of three forms of magic—some can use the body's energies to heal far quicker than medicines and human healers. Others have magic in their voice, they can incite emotion when they speak or sing—you've never heard music until you've heard them sing." He shifted, looking uncomfortable to be praising one of the winged folk. "Then there are those who mostly end up as Falcons—they have an ability to focus their energy into single bursts of power."

Talyn straightened. "That sounds similar to what the Callanan can do—summon shields of pure energy. It's an ability unique to the Callanan."

"Your Callanan must have winged folk blood then." Theac frowned. "Come to think of it, something's been nagging me about you since we met. At certain angles, you almost look like you have the features of the winged folk too."

"I don't think so." Talyn dismissed that with a laugh. Her parents were both firmly human, and certainly none of the Callanan had wings—someone would have noticed that. "None of us can fly. Are there any other magical abilities?"

"In the old tales, like the ones about intelligent creatures, there was another ability called glamour. It had something to do with the ability to cast illusions. But none of the winged folk have been born with it in decades, and there is some suggestion that maybe it never existed." Theac shrugged. "And magic isn't such a wonderful thing. We humans don't have any magic, and it's just another thing they use to keep themselves superior."

"Does the royal family have magic?" Perhaps if Cuinn did, he might be able to protect himself better than she'd assumed after their meeting.

Theac scowled. "They're the most powerful of them all. Prince Mithanis alone puts the fear of a tawncat into anyone thinking twice about trying to take a bite out of Mithranar."

"You mean Montagn?" Again, Cynia's supposition came to mind.

"Aye. The queen's father took the threat from Montagn a little more seriously than his predecessors and married her to a Montagni prince. Princes Mithanis and Azrilan are both half-Montagni, and that familial link helps keep the ahara at bay."

"A wise strategic move," she murmured. "Who is Prince Cuinn's father?"

"Nobody knows." Theac's voice grew short. "Or gives a shit. Are we done here, Captain? Drill is over and I'd like a cold drink."

As he turned away, Talyn had a sudden thought. "Wait. You said most winged folk have magic. Does that include Tiercelin?"

"You'd have to ask him." He shrugged, clearly not caring one way or the other.

"All right. Thanks for today, Theac. We'll forgo those training sessions in the forest for now. I'll see you tomorrow morning?"

"Aye." He nodded and walked off.

AFTER STOPPING the first Falcon she spotted on her way to the palace's exit, Talyn went looking for Tiercelin. Not bothering to offer his name or acknowledge hers, the Falcon had brusquely told her the location of an inn popular amongst the WingGuard. He couldn't have been more eager to keep moving, only reinforcing the sense she was an unwelcome outsider amongst the Falcons. She almost had to smile —if only they knew how little their casual indifference mattered against the constant aching grief she carried inside.

Still, something told her he wouldn't have helped at all if she hadn't mentioned Tiercelin's name specifically. She wondered exactly how Tiercelin's family fit into the winged folk hierarchy. Clearly noble, to be on speaking terms with Cuinn, and he'd said something about his father sitting on the Queencouncil, whatever that meant. The Falcon's grudging assistance indicated they could be more than just noble. Which made it even stranger that he hadn't made it into any other Falcon wings.

The inn was outside the palace, and she paused on the bridge spanning the rushing waterfall that separated the palace from the rest of the citadel, gazing down with awe and a touch of apprehension. The spray was delightful against her hot skin and she lingered to enjoy its cool touch.

How odd to have such a dangerous land underneath a city of beauty and light. Despite Theac's warnings, if Sari had still been alive, little would have stopped them going to investigate what was really down there.

She moved on when the two Falcons on guard at the bridge entrance started throwing her annoyed glances, lengthening her stride and meeting their looks as she passed with cool indifference.

Laughter drifted through the thick afternoon air as she made her way along a busy thoroughfare and caught sight of a crowd of people sitting at tables and chairs outside the inn she was looking for. It was late afternoon and the residents of the city were probably finishing up work for the day and going out to drink and socialise.

She had yet to establish whether the noble winged folk did actual work. Or if they didn't, what they did with themselves during the day.

"I can't think of anything more boring." A quick mental shudder from Sari.

"Too right," Talyn muttered. What was life without purpose?

As she paused in the entrance, a quick scan of the inn found Tiercelin sitting at a long table by the wall with a group of off-duty Falcons. Part of her noticed once again how different the architecture of an inn built for winged folk was—wider and longer with higher ceilings and large spaces left around each table to accommodate wings. The rest of her was monitoring the tension that began filling the room the moment she stepped inside. Humans weren't welcome here, and Prince Cuinn's guard or no, she was very much human.

Her right hand dropped to her sai, her body falling into the instinctive watchfulness of years of walking into places where Callanan weren't welcome. The space at her right shoulder where Sari always stood was suddenly gaping and stark and she had to fight not to keep looking over her shoulder.

She was in an inn in Mithranar. Nobody was going to attack her here.

A deep breath and she centred herself. Then, ignoring the hostile looks directed her way, she headed towards Tiercelin. He nodded amiably when Talyn asked to speak with him outside, though he endured a deal of ribbing from his companions as he rose and followed her. By the time they exited the inn and crossed the walkway to lean against the railing on its opposite side, the winged man's ears were red.

"How can I help you, Captain?" he asked politely.

"Thank you for coming out to talk to me," she said, not indifferent to the embarrassment he must be feeling. "I know you're off duty."

He seemed surprised by her sincerity, but his shoulders straightened a little. "That's all right."

"I came to see you because I'm curious," she said. "I was just talking to Theac about the different magical abilities winged folk possess. He thought you must have the ability to focus your energy into a ball of power, to attack, or you wouldn't have been accepted into the Falcons." She frowned. "Why didn't you mention it when I asked about your individual skills?"

Tiercelin flushed a deeper shade of red and his shoulders sagged again. He shot a surreptitious look back inside the bar. "I have some healing magic," he mumbled so softly she could barely hear him. "Nothing useful really."

"So you *can't* do what Theac described?"

If possible, he turned redder. It confused her—why were her questions making him so uncomfortable? Wary of pushing him too far, she stayed silent, letting him come out with it on his own.

"Most winged folk only have one ability, and everyone's strength and skill in using it is different. A rare few of us have two abilities. Nobody has more than that." He cleared his throat, voice still barely audible. "They accepted me into the WingGuard, because the healers think I have the potential for the warrior magic as well as my healing magic, but I wasn't so good at that."

Ah. She suddenly knew where this was heading, and kept her voice as non-judgemental as possible. "Have you ever done it?"

He squirmed. "Not exactly."

"That's why you haven't been placed in one of the other wings," she said. "You didn't want anyone to find out you couldn't do it."

"My parents would have been horrified if I was kicked out because I failed at warrior magic," he said hopelessly. "I've always been the lesser son compared to my older brothers. I'd only be confirming I was useless if I failed."

She paused before replying. There were so many issues with what he'd said, she wasn't sure which angle to attack first. Winged, noble and privileged he might be, but Tiercelin's self-confidence was as poor as Zamaril's. "First, Tiercelin, healing is one of the most useful magics I can think of. You have the power to make people feel better, to take their pain away. That is no small thing."

He shook his head but said nothing.

"Tiercelin?" She waited until he reluctantly lifted his head to meet her gaze. "You said yourself you wouldn't have been let into the Wing-Guard unless you had the ability for warrior magic, even if you haven't learned how to access it. I can help you with that."

"Really?" His face lit up, then he frowned. "How can you teach me? You're just a human."

"Thanks," Talyn said dryly.

He stiffened. "I'm sorry, I mean—"

She raised her hand, though her voice was sharp. "I don't need your validation to know my own self-worth as a human, Tiercelin."

He cleared his throat. "What I meant was, how can a human with no magic teach me how to use mine?"

"I *do* have magic," she said. "A very specific kind. Back home, we have an elite cadre of warriors called the Callanan. I was one of them before I joined the Kingshield. Callanan all have the power to form an energy shield for protection—it sounds a lot like the warrior magic Theac described earlier, only we use it for defence, not attack."

"Can you show me?" Tiercelin's ingrained arrogance vanished like it had never existed at all in the face of his eagerness. He shuffled his feet like an excited boy.

Talyn nodded and stepped back a little. Nobody was coming along the walkway, and they were momentarily alone, so she held out her palm and concentrated for a moment. With a hiss of air, a bright sapphire shield appeared in the air, luminous and shot through with cobalt sparks. The drain on her strength was immediate and strong, like a sharp tugging in her chest. One of the reasons Callanan warriors kept themselves so physically fit was the energy drain that resulted from summoning a shield—it fed directly from their body's strength. Most Callanan only used the shield in short bursts when desperate. Talyn had always been the strongest of her class, even more so than Sari, able to maintain a shield for much longer.

After a moment, she let it dissolve. "Now, I don't know about firing off bursts of energy, but I can certainly show you how to summon a shield." She smiled at him. "I bet that's something none of your Falcon friends can do."

A look of fascination spread across the winged man's face. "But that must mean you have winged folk magic in Calumnia. How is that possible when you're human?"

"I'm not sure. Maybe the magic isn't specific to winged folk?" She raised an eyebrow, her tone suggesting maybe the *winged folk* weren't so special after all.

"But you said only a specific few possess it?" He frowned in thought.

"The ability to make a shield of energy, yes," she said, "but we have SkyRiders who possess a special level of balance and fearlessness that allow them to ride the skies on our mountain eagles. There has to be magic in that. The same with our Aimsir riders. Or the abilities that the Firthlander Shadows are rumoured to have. I've even heard the Montagni berserkers are impervious to wounds when they're in the heat of battle."

His eyes widened further. "More types of magic in the world," he murmured.

"Yes," she said pointedly. "There is a wider world outside you winged folk and your lovely citadel. And more people with magic too... *humans* with magic, Tiercelin."

"Maybe," he said, his face clearing. "But the magic you Callanan have is winged folk magic, I'd put bags of gold on it. So how do I do that shield?"

Talyn laughed. "I said I could teach you, but it will take more than one lesson. If you don't mind staying back after training every day, we can work on it then. Deal?"

"Deal." Tiercelin nodded with a bright smile. His grey wings flared in his excitement. After a moment though, he sobered. "It's probably best we do it in private, though. I wouldn't suggest making it public knowledge you can do that, Captain."

"Why?"

"Even if I tried to explain, you wouldn't understand. Just trust me."

His smile came back. "And accept my true thanks."

"I'm happy to help," she said. "Go back to your friends. I'll see you bright and early for training tomorrow."

"I'll be there," he promised, before ducking back into the bar, still smiling broadly.

CHAPTER 13

*H*e stood watching the izerdia workers return from the forest, climbing one by one up the ladder from the tunnel and out into the street. Six Patrolmen stood at the top of the ladder, one of them marking off names. Each worker carried a ceramic pot under their arm. Two Falcons were there too, taking the pot before the workers were allowed to leave and go to their homes, or to line up to be taken back to the cells if they were working off a sentence.

Whenever he had the time, whenever he was in Dock City at sunset, he made a point of watching the workers return. And each time, he marked their haggard appearance, the twitchiness in their shoulders, the look of fear still fading from their eyes. And he counted the ones that had to be helped up the ladder by their fellow workers— either hurt while climbing trees for the izerdia or attacked by one of the forest dwelling creatures.

Anger burned, hot and strong, enough to turn his hands into white-knuckled fists at his sides. All the WingGuard had to do was send a Falcon detail beyond the wall to guard the workers—with proper armed guards they could do their work without fear of attack. The Falcons had wings, they didn't have to fear like the humans did. Yet they still refused.

It was shameful. Arrogant beyond belief. And he hated it.

Once the last worker dragged himself to the top of the ladder, it took two Patrolmen to lift the heavy, barred gate and swing it down over the opening. Once it settled into place, they chained and locked it closed.

Even though there were heavily barred gates at the other end of the tunnel too, this entrance wouldn't be opened again until full daylight.

By then the Falcons were gone, winging their way back up to the citadel with the day's collection of izerdia carefully stacked into a cushioned sack they carried between them. The Shadowhawk's gaze tracked them as they flew. It was never stored in the same place—the stuff was too volatile, and the winged folk would never risk an accidental explosion in their beautiful citadel.

And it was sold in a trickle, the queen's treasury and trade councilors carefully releasing to market to ensure they fetched the highest price possible and that demand remained high. The profit it made went right back into the winged folk coffers.

He'd considered stealing it before. Izerdia was Mithranar's most valuable trading commodity—the winged folk, and the royal family in particular, wouldn't have the wealth they did without the prices izerdia commanded and their monopoly of the market. If he took that away, he could cripple them. The output from the copper mines in the north and the valuable wood trade wouldn't be enough to prop up their lifestyle.

But izerdia was dangerous. And the humans were angry, knowing full well they never benefited from the profits of the sap that they risked their lives to collect. There was no guarantee he'd be able to keep the stuff controlled if he stole it. There was no way to ensure it wouldn't be used for purposes other than selling.

Still.

He pushed off the wall he'd been leaning against, dismissing thoughts of izerdia and what might be done with it. Night was falling over the city now, and he had somewhere to be.

. . .

AFTER CROSSING the bridge into the Poor Quarter, he turned off the main street and moved quickly into the warren of dim back alleys that made up the quarter. Once he was alone in the darkness, he tugged the mask from his pocket and slid it down over his face. Then he unbuttoned his shirt and pulled out the thin cloak that had been lying, folded flat, against his skin. It was damp with sweat, and he made a face as he shook it out then swung it around his shoulders.

With a final look around to ensure he was still alone in the alley and nobody had seen him, he set off again. A quarter-turn's walk brought him around and back to the eastern side of the bridge—he'd taken a convoluted enough path that he was confident he hadn't been followed. It also meant he was slightly late. It was deliberate, so he could take stock of his contact and the surroundings as he approached.

The man leaned against a wall, boots crossed at the ankle, watchful air hovering around him like the cloak the Shadowhawk wore.

"You're late."

The Shadowhawk didn't reply, eyes scanning everything around his contact. Nothing he saw or sensed alarmed him—everything looked and sounded as it should for this time of night in the Poor Quarter.

For the moment the street was empty, but it wasn't guaranteed to remain that way. This particular block was gang territory and even though he had a tentative arrangement with all of the gangs in the Poor Quarter—he'd leave them alone if they did the same in return—he'd rather not deal with any of their thugs.

He jerked his head for the man to follow as he turned off the street into a narrow alley between two buildings. The rotting scent of sewerage mixed with decaying *something* hit his nose, and he muttered a curse as his stomach threatened to rebel.

"Don't tell me the Shadowhawk is too precious to get down in the gutters with the poor folk." The man's mocking voice rang out.

He ignored the jibe. "What do you have for me, Zamaril?"

Zamaril shrugged. "What do you want? I said I'd keep an eye out to make sure she wasn't going to be a problem for you. So far all she's done is make us clean and run."

"That's all you've got?" the Shadowhawk said, disbelief edging his voice. "The best thief in Dock City, and all you can tell me is she makes you clean and run?"

There was a moment's silence, then, "She's not like the Wing-Guard," he said begrudgingly. "But she was brought here for a purpose, though she says she's only here for a year, until next Onemonth. And choosing human criminals for Prince Cuinn's guard? It's pure insanity. There's something going on."

"Right." Impatience threaded his voice. "Which is why I asked you to find out what that is."

"I'm not one of your network patsies, Shadowhawk," Zamaril snarled. "This is a favour, and one I'm doing only because you're a thorn in the side of those miserable Falcons."

"I'm aware of that." He tried to keep his frustration in check. "But if I get caught, if her arrival here interferes with my work, then the humans lose out."

Zamaril nodded. "I'll keep an eye and an ear out. She's not... she's very *earnest*." A note of bewilderment flashed in his voice. "If there's an ulterior motive in bringing her here, I'm not sure she's aware of what it is."

"Has *she* told you why she's here?"

"We haven't asked, and she hasn't offered." He gave a languid shrug.

He cursed under his breath. "Zamaril, for a thief you make a terrible spy. Ask the flea-bitten question, will you? Judging from what I know of you, she's not going to be surprised with you flinging a question like that at her. At least that might tell us why she's here *now*."

Zamaril's face tightened at the Shadowhawk's tone, but he nodded. "I'll ask. She's big on honesty and trust, or so she claims, so she'll find it hard to wriggle out of an answer."

"So you think she's an innocent?"

"Oh no." The thief's head came up. "The way she talks, the way she behaves? She's no simple Kingshield guard, I'd bet a large bag of jewels on it. She might not be aware of whatever alternative motives are at play, but there's a lot going on behind that cool exterior of hers. I'd risk a smaller bag of jewels that the Twin Thrones is sniffing around here for some reason of their own too."

Interesting. Maybe his assumption that Mithranar had initiated the request for a Kingshield was wrong. "Find out what she knows, or thinks she knows, but focus on the Falcon's purpose in all this. I still think he, or one of the royals, must have asked for her. Whatever the Twin Thrones political motives are, they're unlikely to have anything to do with the Shadowhawk."

"Fine." He pushed off the wall. "This alley stinks, so I'm out. I'll let you know next time I've got something to tell you."

"Thank you for your help, Zamaril."

"I'm not doing it for you."

The Shadowhawk waited until the thief's soft footfalls had vanished entirely from hearing before he moved. He walked another convoluted route through the back streets of the Poor Quarter, then crossed the Rush over one of the makeshift wooden bridges used by the fisherfolk accessing their boats down near where the river flowed into the bay.

It was closing in on midnight when he carefully approached the back of the *Fish and Fly*, a dive frequented by sailors that conveniently backed onto a dark and stinking alley. Here, behind a loose brick in the worst-smelling section of the alley, his Dock Quarter contact left messages.

One waited for him, as expected, though he cursed under his breath as he read its contents. One of the shipments they'd been waiting on, fresh supplies of seeds for planting ahead of the monsoon season, had arrived three days earlier. It had taken him too long to come for the message.

"Dammit!" he swore again.

He crumpled the note in his hands and replaced the brick before wrapping himself in shadows and walking away. The seed shipment would be long gone, spirited up to the citadel by now.

Which meant a long night of scribing out notes awaited him.

CHAPTER 14

Several days later, Talyn mentioned at the end of the afternoon's training that she was heading down into Dock City to explore. In the two weeks she'd been in Mithranar, she'd focused on using her free time to learn the layout of the palace and the citadel around it. Despite her suspicions about her room being searched, and a desire to investigate the Shadowhawk, understanding her surroundings would be crucial to protecting Prince Cuinn, and that had been her first priority.

Now though, it was time to broaden her horizons. The world of humans was where she would find a trail to begin hunting the Shadowhawk. Her conversation with Andres Tye had been the first step, giving her better context about the Shadowhawk and what he did. None of that had explained why the Callanan would have any interest in him, so it was time to do some more digging.

Corrin asked to accompany her, explaining that he'd been planning to go and visit his mother and sisters anyway. They strolled down the wall companionably, Corrin asking her endless questions about the Kingshield and Callanan.

"Your warriors sound amazing." He sighed. "We humans see little of the WingGuard in action. They are there for the winged folk, not for us."

"I admit I'm surprised by the separation in your society," Talyn said. Shocked was a better word, but she was wary of stirring up what were obviously complex relationships between the two societies. "The ruling Dumnorix family who sit the Twin Thrones see it as their duty to protect and care for all of the people of Calumnia and Conmor. The Warlord of Firthland is a little fiercer but essentially very much of the same view. I'm not suggesting they're perfect, but it's vastly different to what I've seen here."

"That kind of world is hard to imagine. We humans have something to contribute too, you know?" Corrin said fiercely. "We're not useless."

She glanced at him, startled. In a matter of weeks, he'd come a long way from the painfully shy and sobbing boy she'd first encountered in jail. He always looked her in the eyes now and walked with straightened shoulders that showed how tall he actually was—and likely with more growing to do if his skinny frame was anything to go by.

Or maybe the hopeless boy she'd first met had never been a true reflection of who he was. The nagging tickle of unease returned in force—he and Zamaril had been deliberately placed in that cell, she was close to certain of it. Laid out like bait in a trap. A trap for her? Or was something else playing out that she was utterly unaware of?

"And were Halun and Theac part of that same plan?" Sari's presence roused in her mind.

"I don't know. If those other prisoners hadn't been attacking Halun when I walked in, there's no guarantee I would have taken particular notice of either of them, let alone picked them."

Corrin slowed suddenly, pausing by a torn piece of parchment hanging from a town noticeboard situated at a busy crossroads. Like the one she'd seen on arrival, it was nailed to the wood by an arrow and signed with the lightning symbol. It talked about a shipment of vegetable plant seeds from Montagn that had arrived three days earlier and been delivered straight to the citadel.

"We can barely grow enough down here to feed ourselves—Mithranar is almost entirely reliant on importing food because of the lack of proper farming land," Corrin explained without her having to ask. "Soon it will be planting time—before the rains come in Seven-month—for those with enough space in their gardens or property. Without the seeds to grow basics like wheat and vegetables, the bakers and other food merchants in the city won't have the supplies to produce enough to meet demand later in the year, so instead they will have to import it. That means it gets too expensive for the poorer families to afford."

She'd seen the large gardens up in the citadel, mostly tended by humans, that held not only beautiful flowering plants and trees but rows of wheat, grains, fruit and vegetables. She was no expert on farming and had no idea whether the neat gardens she'd seen would produce enough for both the winged folk at the citadel and Dock City. But judging from what she'd experienced so far in Mithranar, and what Corrin was implying now, she doubted that produce was shared.

"What about meat?"

Corrin gave her a look. "No land for keeping animals either, Captain. All we eat down here is fish caught in Feather Bay and out beyond the headlands. What little meat gets imported from Montagn fresh enough to eat goes straight to the citadel."

She frowned again at the discrepancy with what was so familiar to her. While she'd never taken much interest or notice of her family's political activities—she had no right to, even if she had been inter-ested—she was aware of how hard her uncle pushed the Calumnian and Conmoran lords on the proper distribution of food from the farming regions out to the more rugged areas—ensuring they weren't hoarding for themselves or their districts. Leviana had mentioned more than once how it annoyed her father.

But the complexities of Mithranar society weren't the reason she was here. She had a job to do.

"Who is the Shadowhawk?" she asked softly, brushing sweaty tendrils of hair from her forehead. Down in Dock City, where the closely packed streets blocked out any breeze from the ocean, it was several degrees hotter than the citadel. She resolved to make her future trips down later in the day once the sun had set.

Corrin shrugged. "Nobody knows. But the Shadowhawk is the only one who tries to help us. The WingGuard hunt him constantly, so he and his network are limited in what they can steal. The Falcons will rip down that notice as soon as someone tells them about it."

"Why the lightning? What does it mean?" Maybe that might help her learn who he was.

"Nobody knows."

Or not. She tried another tack. "He's human?"

"Nobody else would fight for us," Corrin said sadly. "Not even his network knows who he is, though. Those who've caught a glimpse—he always wears a hood and mask—swear he's human."

That concurred with what Andres had implied, that the Shadowhawk wasn't working alone. He had help. That was good news—his associates would provide options for her to track and find him. Sari stirred again, her anticipation leaking through Talyn. They'd been here many times before. And they'd always found what they hunted. Doubt twisted up through her, familiar and unwelcome. Could she do any of this without Sari?

Talyn shoved away the voice before it could speak, ignoring the sudden shaking of her hands. She had to try, even though the prospect of failure was unbearable. Because if she didn't try, she would never truly live again.

"Are you all right, Captain?" Corrin asked softly.

She spun to meet his concerned green gaze, startled that he'd noticed her reaction. "I'm just curious about the Shadowhawk." She brushed him off. "How often does he post these?"

"Whenever he learns something that we need to know about, like the shipment of seeds."

"Isn't it too late by then?"

Corrin nodded. "Mostly. But sometimes when these notices go out widely enough, the Falcons will send some of the supplies down to us. The idea of a riot worries them—the human population is much larger than that of the winged folk. Anything that might affect the izerdia extraction worries them even more."

"Is that all he does, put the notices up?" A test question, to see whether Corrin would tell her the truth.

Corrin's gaze flicked away. "He acts sometimes."

"What does that mean?" She pushed gently.

"Sometimes, when he learns of a shipment ahead of time, he'll steal the supplies before they can be offloaded. His network hides them, then distributes them once the furore dies down."

"If that's true, then I don't understand how the Falcons haven't caught him. Surely they know when their ships are coming in and could lay a trap?"

Agreeing with Sari, Talyn asked, "Isn't it odd for a human to have such good access to information on the Falcons and their activities? He wouldn't have avoided capture all this time without it."

Corrin shrugged. "I guess so. I never really thought about it."

He genuinely didn't seem to know any more than that, so she tried testing him on something else. "What happens when he encounters Falcons or City Patrol when he's trying to 'liberate' supplies for Dock City?" she asked carefully.

Corrin shrugged, deliberately causal. "He doesn't kill, Captain."

"Never?"

"Not once that I'm aware of." He hesitated. "He has a deliberate policy against using violence—everyone knows it. Sometimes the Falcons get hurt, though mostly it's accidental. But when the Falcons catch his network members, they are executed immediately or put to work for a year on the izerdia teams, which in itself is a death sentence."

She sighed. Corrin's account matched Andres' and it confused her —while clearly a criminal, the Shadowhawk's intentions, at least on the surface, appeared good, and very specific to Mithranar. Not to mention he eschewed violence but had somehow managed to rob multiple ships without being caught. Why did the Callanan care?

She had to admit, it made her curious about him. And she hadn't been curious in a very long time.

Glancing away from the note, she caught the look on Corrin's face as he too looked at it. She touched his arm. "I wouldn't support the Shadowhawk out loud, Corrin, not where you are now."

His gaze flashed to hers. "You don't think what he does is right, Captain?"

"I don't know enough about him, or your country, to make that judgement. I counsel you for your own safety. You said yourself the WingGuard hunt the Shadowhawk and execute those they catch. If you were to be heard praising him up at the palace, you could be returned to the cells, and I have a feeling I wouldn't be able to do much to stop it."

He gave her a terse nod. "I understand."

"Come on, let's keep walking. I want to see where the waterfall flows down into the river. Do you have time to show me how to get there?"

"It's on my way," he said happily. "And it's called the Rush. The river, I mean."

They stopped for two tin cups of what Corrin promised would be the best thing she'd ever drunk. He called it kahvi, and it consisted of a warm dark liquid stirred with a dash of honey and pinch of unfamiliar spice.

"I told you." He beamed when he caught the look on her face after her first sip. "It's a human drink—they won't touch it up at the citadel."

"It *is* delicious," she agreed.

She'd devoured the whole cup by the time they reached the flowing river which carried the sparkling water from the waterfall out into Feather Bay. The road they were on led to a wide stone bridge arching high over the Rush, but Corrin tugged on her arm when she went to cross it.

"I'm happy to continue on my own if you want to head to your mother's," she said, wondering if it lay in a different direction.

"It's not that. You don't want to go over there, Captain," he said uncomfortably.

She frowned. "Why?"

"That's the Poor Quarter. It's where most of the city's criminals live, and there are three different gangs with territory in there. The Patrolmen based there always go out in small groups after dark." He shrugged. "Even in daylight you're likely to lose whatever money you're carrying."

"That whole area." She waved to the unending sea of roofs spreading away from the east bank of the river out towards the forested eastern headland.

Corrin nodded. "In population and size it's almost a quarter of Dock City."

"Is that where the Shadowhawk lives?"

"I have no idea. Probably. It would be the best place for him to hide, to stay anonymous." He hesitated. "The city used to end here at the Rush. See the stone levies built up high along the west bank in case of flood? We get serious rainfall during the monsoon season."

That's why the bridge was so high—so it would remain above the water level if the Rush flooded. "Right, but not on the eastern bank?"

"The city can't afford the cost of building a levee over there. And of course the winged folk won't pay for it." He shook off his obvious anger. "I'd best be going—if I'm late for dinner Mam will kill me. Are you all right to find your way back?"

"I am, thanks, Corrin."

"I'll see you for drill at dawn."

With that he was off, his tall gangly frame weaving easily through the crowded streets.

Talyn lingered a few moments longer. It looked harmless enough, the Poor Quarter, though admittedly rundown and obviously poor. The people crossing the bridge in either direction didn't look like they were about to rob her of anything valuable in her possession.

But she knew from experience that appearances were deceiving.

It wasn't just a lack of confidence in her old skills that had her turning away from the bridge rather than braving the streets of the Poor Quarter, though. She hadn't struggled with her Callanan work— arresting and removing criminals from the streets had left her with warm satisfaction. She'd been doing her duty, making the cities and towns safer for the citizens of the Twin Thrones, *her* people, to live in.

But here... it was different.

CHAPTER 15

*T*alyn awoke to the sound of loud banging. Instinct took over, the sudden noise sending her into a quick roll off the bed to land in a fighting crouch on the floor, one hand shooting out to grab the sai resting on her bedside table.

Once her sleep-groggy mind processed it was someone knocking at her door, not an invasion of her room, she relaxed and stood straight. Keeping the sai in one hand, she pulled on a robe over the loose shirt she slept in and went to open the door. Her eyes widened in surprise at the sight of Halun's bulk filling up the entryway. "Halun, it's after midnight, what are you doing here?"

"I need you to come with me, Captain." He was standing straight and tall, hands clasped loosely at the small of his back in the way she'd been teaching them only the day before. Something about that made her smile, despite the odd tone of his voice.

"Why, is there something wrong? Is someone hurt?"

"It's about Theac. He's not hurt, but..." He shifted his weight from foot to foot, ruining his stance in his agitation. Talking so much was clearly making him uncomfortable. "I think it's better if you just come with me, Captain."

It was on the tip of her tongue to demand that he tell her what was going on or leave. She was tired and out of sorts and the last thing she wanted to do was go traipsing through the citadel without knowing why. But instinct checked her. Building trust with these men was already a close to impossible task and dismissing Halun now would make it harder. He'd come to her for help, and like with Corrin, she needed to show him she'd be there.

Of course, if it turned out Tiercelin and Zamaril had gotten into another squabble in the barracks they couldn't sort out themselves, she would be having a very sharp conversation with all three of them later.

"All right, Halun. Give me a moment to dress."

Relief crumpled his shoulders, making her instantly glad of her decision. Sighing inwardly, she left him standing there and returned to her room to drag on her uniform and buckle on her sais. Back at the door, she gestured for Halun to lead the way and locked it carefully after her.

The citadel was quiet at such a late hour, but the darkness was illuminated by artfully arranged lamps and fairy lights that provided plenty of illumination to see where they were going. It was beautiful.

"Where are we going?" she asked.

"Dock City."

"Dock City?" She halted mid-stride. "What's going on?"

"I think it would be best if you saw for yourself, Captain," he said cryptically.

"Halun..." She hesitated. Another leap of faith. One of these was going to be the wrong call. "All right, fine, lead the way."

His strides quickened, the big man clearly catching her irritation. The night air was much cooler than during the day but still carried the scent of flowers. They walked down the wall path in silence. Despite the hour, she was almost glad of the opportunity to see the citadel in this light—it was just as stunning as it appeared on a bright sunny day.

Dock City was busier than the citadel had been. She supposed that when you had to work for a living, you didn't always have the luxury of sleeping through the whole night. Her stomach grumbled as they passed a baker's shop and the delicious scent of baking bread wafted out into the street. It must be closer to dawn than she'd thought.

She shot Halun a sharp look when the Market Quarter patrol headquarters appeared ahead, but he quickened his pace to avoid her questions, and took the front steps in one massive stride. Talyn followed him, trepidation curling in her gut.

The smug voice of a Patrolman greeted them. "We just about gave up on you, Halun. Thought you weren't coming back."

Two Patrolmen sat at the front desk, and from the money and chips scattered across the table, it looked like she and Halun had interrupted a game of cards. The man that had spoken had a cigar wedged into the corner of his mouth. He was familiar too—the older Patrolman who'd been there when she'd chased down the thieves on her first day. Rolf? The acrid smoke drifting through the room had her eyes watering.

Disliking his tone, and their slack behaviour, she levelled a stare at Rolf. "Halun, it's time to tell me what's going on."

Before he could reply, the door to the back opened and Andres Tye appeared. Unlike the two on the front desk, his uniform was crisp and neat. A flicker of surprise crossed his face at the sight of her. "You came."

"Halun asked me to," she said testily. "Can someone please tell me what's going on?"

"Come with me, Captain." Andres led her and Halun across the entrance foyer to a barred door. Beyond was a long hallway of cells similar to what she'd seen in the main headquarters. He waved them through, then closed the door behind them, shutting off the curious stares of Rolf and the other Patrolman.

"What am I..." But her words slid to a halt as she caught sight of Theac sitting in the first cell. He was cross legged on a pile of dirty straw and singing at the top of his voice. Even from outside the bars, the stink of alcohol on him was clear.

"Halun?" she asked softly.

The big man was staring at his feet, all traces of his crisp warrior stance gone. "He asked me down to the city for a drink after training finished yesterday. Only, he drank a lot, Captain. We were picked up a full-turn ago because he was causing a ruckus outside the inn."

"Halun asked me not to do anything until he'd fetched you," Andres said quietly, casting a sad glance into the cell.

She ignored Andres, gaze firm on Halun. "Were any of the others with you?"

"No. Corrin and Tiercelin are with their families and Zamaril doesn't like spending time with any of us outside of training." He hesitated, seemingly torn between embarrassment and reluctance to keep speaking. "I didn't know he would drink so much."

The drunken warbling reached a high pitch, almost drowning out Halun's last words. The sound was unbearable.

"Theac!" Talyn snapped.

The singing cut off and Theac peered drunkenly through the bars at her. When he recognised her, his face fell, and he looked away.

"Rolf and the other Patrolman wanted to keep him locked up in here. Apparently he's done this before, a lot. It's why he was kicked out in the first place," Halun said. The big man was folding in on himself, clearly upset and uncomfortable. It struck an odd note. He was so big, so physically fearsome, yet right now he had all the demeanour of a man who'd participated in something wrong and was shamed by it.

Disappointment settled in her stomach. "Did you know?"

He hesitated, then, "I heard things."

Stifling a sigh, she turned to Andres. "What happens now?"

"He'll be sentenced to a week or two of izerdia extraction if Patrol Captain Finnus—he heads up Market Quarter—is in a good mood. A few months in the city jail if not." Andres hesitated. "I haven't yet informed the captain that he's here."

His message was clear. Talyn closed her eyes, stifling the urge to reach up and rub her suddenly aching temples. "Halun, get him back up to the barracks. I'll sort it out with the Patrol."

Halun hesitated. "He's out of the wing, isn't he?"

"You know the answer to that. I can't afford to have an unreliable drunk guarding the prince."

She turned to go, but Halun still hesitated. "Then why even bother to take him back?"

"Halun, you have your orders."

"I know, Captain. Only—"

"I'm losing patience," Talyn snapped. The situation wasn't the big man's fault, but she was furious with Theac, and with herself for choosing him in the first place. How could she have gotten it so wrong? Crushing doubt cascaded over her, and the only way to fight and keep her head above it was to focus on her anger. "Just do what I say. Dammit, Halun. Now!"

She was astonished when he dug in, shoulders straightening again. He had to know he was risking his own position, but the words spilled out of him in a rush, more than she'd ever heard from him. "I've heard about Theac, before. He was a good captain, fair and kind. But he was strong too. There were no gangs in the Poor Quarter in the years he ran the Patrol there. Corrin's family would never have had to worry back in those days. He ensured his men helped people." The last part was mumbled so incoherently that even Talyn's sharp hearing barely picked up the words.

She kept her face and voice resolute. "You have your orders, Halun. Take him back to the barracks. Do as I say, or you're out too. Am I clear?"

"Yes, Captain."

Andres said nothing as he unlocked the cell and stood aside while Halun went in, hefted Theac to his feet, and proceeded to drag him out. Rolf was opening his mouth in protest when she and Andres followed them into the entrance foyer.

"Orders from the WingGuard," Andres said crisply. "He's one of theirs now so it's up to them to deal with him."

"But Watch Officer, he—"

"Theac is ours," Talyn said coolly, capturing Rolf's stare with unyielding steel and holding it until he looked away. "We'll take it from here."

Andres accompanied her to the exit. "You could face trouble with the Falcon for this," he murmured in a low voice. "I can't guarantee one of my Patrolmen won't tattle to the WingGuard."

"I'll deal with it," she said. "Thanks for helping Halun, and for helping Theac too."

"I owed Parksin one," Andres said. "But I can't keep stepping in. I'll be on thin ice with Finnus after this."

"Theac is a grown man. He can look after himself." Her voice was short, made so by anger and weariness.

"I know." Andres nodded, looked away. "I heard what you did for Corrin Dariel's family. You should be careful, Captain."

"Why?" she frowned.

"Because WingGuard don't do things to help humans."

"I'm not WingGuard."

He lifted his hands in the air as if in surrender. "Just a friendly warning. I'm sorry you had to get dragged down here tonight."

"I'll be back soon," she said, voice softening. "Buy you another drink in thanks."

BY THE TIME Talyn got back to her rooms, she was wound up and unable to sleep. She went to a cabinet and pulled out a bottle of something Corrin had convinced her to buy down in Dock City; it was alcoholic, strong and flavoured with coconut. She poured a half glass, then went and slumped down into the chair by her empty fireplace. Taking a long swallow, she allowed her head to drop back against the cushions, enjoying the searing path the alcohol burned down the back of her throat.

She was angry. Despite its many frustrations, coming to Mithranar had so far been good for her—the challenge of trying to put together a functioning wing had kept her from thinking about home or what had happened. It was a fresh start of sorts, without everything around her constantly reminding her of Sari.

But tonight, faced with what she was going to have to do in a few hours, she just wanted to go back. Back to a time when she was a Callanan, fighting alongside her partner, revelling in the thrill of the chase. She didn't want this. She didn't want anything but that.

The tears spilled silently down her cheeks.

IN THE DEATHLY QUIET hour before dawn, Talyn opened the door to Theac's room without knocking. As her second, he had a tiny but private room adjacent to the dormitory where the others slept. He was sitting on the edge of his cot, face pale and drawn in the moonlight shining through the window. She doubted he'd had any sleep either. Yet despite his haggard appearance, he was awake, and had shaved and dressed. Clearly he'd been waiting for her.

"Big night last night?" she asked.

"Something like that," he grunted.

"I hear this sort of thing is a habit with you, Theac. In fact, I heard your drunken behaviour is the reason you got kicked out of the City Patrol. Is that true?"

He nodded.

"Give me one good reason I shouldn't kick you out of this wing too?" Her voice became hard as ice.

His jaw clenched. "It won't happen again, Captain."

"No, I need something better than that. I need a second who I can rely on *all* the time, not just when he's sober. You disappointed me, and I don't want to give you another chance. I wouldn't even be standing here if Halun hadn't intervened on your behalf. The man who's barely spoken two words since I met him, who is so withdrawn he seems afraid of his own voice, he *spoke* for you last night, Theac. He says you were a good man once, a good leader." She paused. "But in a protective detail, a drunk could cause the deaths of his charge and his wing mates. And if that happened, that's on *me*. Do you understand?"

Theac's jaw clenched and he turned away, wincing slightly as the movement probably tore through an aching head. When he turned back, his scowl had faded to hopelessness. "I need this, Captain. I truly want to straighten myself up."

"Then what was last night about?"

167

"Pushing the boundaries until I screwed things up so completely you'd have no choice but to kick me out," he muttered.

She kept her voice sharp. "What's to stop that happening again?"

His shoulders sagged, and despair added to the hopelessness on his face. "Rock bottom is not a nice place to be, Captain."

"Theac..."

He looked up to meet her eyes, his bloodshot gaze filled with resolution. "I promise you here and now that it will not happen again. If it does, I'll walk away before you have to tell me to, and I'll hand myself back over to the City Patrol."

She wavered, still uncertain. "You say that you need this position, but you haven't been too interested so far. In fact, you've been downright obstinate."

He turned away, jaw clenching. "Like I said, Captain, I was self-destructing."

"Why?" She pushed. "What changed?"

He took a deep, shuddering breath, but his gaze didn't leave hers. "Life can be pretty awful for the human folk in Dock City; I should know, I grew up with practically nothing. I've seen horrors that no child should ever..." He broke off. "I wanted to at least try and keep people safe from being robbed or raped or killed for their coins. I wanted to make sure the Falcons had as little excuse as possible for treating us even more badly than they already did."

"So why did you start drinking?"

"I've been running from the demons of my childhood ever since I was old enough to escape them, and it eventually caught up to me. Every crime started to get to me until the only way I could escape the pain was to drink."

"I see." Talyn turned towards the door. His words—the utter grim *aching* of them—had gotten to her, and she didn't want him to see that. The brokenness he talked about—she knew it all too well. And just like with Corrin and Zamaril, she wanted the same hope Theac was asking for. In the end, she took a deep breath and turned back to him. "All right, you stay for now."

Theac looked stunned, and as her words sank in, he forced himself to his feet. "Thank you, Captain. You won't regret it."

"It isn't me you should thank." She stopped in the doorway. "Halun stood up for you last night and risked himself to do it. Don't make him regret his words, and don't make me regret my weakness, because that's what it is, me giving you a second chance. Weakness."

He nodded, again unafraid to meet her eyes. Angry with herself, Talyn turned and stalked out for the door.

"Talon."

"What?" she snapped, turning at the doorway.

He held her gaze. "In the WingGuard, a talon is the commander of an individual detail within a wing. We've only got half a detail, but if I'm your second, then it's Talon Parksin."

She slammed the door behind her.

TALYN WENT STRAIGHT BACK to her rooms so that she could change clothes and splash some cold water on her face before returning to the barracks for dawn drill. She'd had no sleep apart from the restless hour or two before Halun had woken her, and was emotionally and physically wrung out.

"I wouldn't have let him back in."

"I know."

"The Kingshield would have sent him packing last night."

"I know."

"Tal... I love you, but you're not coping and it's causing you to make rash decisions. Theac isn't you and giving a drunk a second chance doesn't mean you'll suddenly heal from what you're feeling."

"Maybe if you left me alone I might be able to forget and move on!" she sent the words screaming through her mind, shoving as hard as she could. Sari vanished, whether because of her words, or how hard she pushed, it was impossible to know.

She patted a towel over her face and stared at herself in the mirror, mentally preparing herself for the day of pushing and cajoling and gritting her teeth through their poor attitude.

. . .

STILL TRYING to find some way to summon motivation for the day, Talyn dropped down the ladder to the walkway leading into the drill yard and pushed open the creaky grate. Once through, she stopped in astonishment.

Instead of finding them sitting disconsolately around the yard as she had every single morning so far, Theac was pacing a straight, crisp line, barking orders as he harried the other four through a series of stretches. His eyes were still bloodshot, and he had to be feeling terribly hung-over, but his back was straight, and his voice boomed in the parade ground bellow she'd heard in the cells that first day.

"Captain!" He came over to greet her, carrying a steaming mug in his hand. "I brought this for you from the mess in case you'd run out of time this morning. It's kahvi."

Talyn took the cup. "Thanks."

"They're almost done with the warm-ups," he continued. "We'll be ready for the wall run in a few minutes."

"Good," she said. "Talon Parksin."

"Zamaril!" Theac bellowed, striding away from her. "It's called stretching, not having a nap!"

She wasn't sure whether to laugh or start crying as she stood there clutching her mug of kahvi. Had she just made the right call in a complex situation, or made another horrible mistake?

"Oh Sari, I wish you were here."

CHAPTER 16

$\mathcal{M}$idnight deepened into the early hours of the morning and the Shadowhawk quickened his stride, moving deeper into the narrowest and darkest alleyways of Dock City. A long, formless grey cloak swirled around his ankles, the hood pulled well down over his masked face.

The quick strides and intimate knowledge of the layout of these streets usually kept him safe from the cutthroats and pickpockets who looked for far easier marks. The cloak marked him as someone who wanted to remain anonymous, and in this part of town, those who wanted to remain anonymous would usually kill for the privilege, so it paid to steer clear of them.

And if it came to it, he could always draw the shadows around him and disappear.

His gaze marked the three lines etched in white chalk on the wooden side wall of a shoemaker's shop. The third line had been drawn carefully under the first two—acknowledging his agreement to meet.

Good.

After walking three more blocks, then circling the area twice to ensure he wasn't being watched or followed, he stopped at a door set three steps down from the street.

It swung open noiselessly and he stepped into the darkness beyond. As soon as it closed behind him, flint sparked and light flared from a small lamp. He glanced around, relaxing slightly at the sight of the covered windows.

"It's taken you a while." Saniya's voice was edgy, but that was nothing new. "It's my third request for a meet."

"When you rely on chalk markings in unsavoury places, it can take me a while to notice them." He pushed back his hood, revealing the mask. "Why did you want to meet?" They never did this without reason. Apart from Navis, Saniya was the only living person to speak to him face to face so frequently.

While he'd been the one to seek out Navis after carefully researching those that peddled information in Dock City, it had been Saniya who had approached *him*. She'd offered logistical assistance in return for access and information. The people she worked for—he'd never met any of them—could also quickly move and hide those in danger of arrest by the WingGuard or Patrol, and did so willingly.

He suspected the group had started out as smugglers and seen him as an opportunity to expand their business. Guilt never failed to rise its ugly head at the understanding he was likely helping a criminal organisation, but he couldn't deny that since Saniya had approached him, his ability to distribute stolen food and other necessary goods had increased markedly.

"A Wall Quarter Patrolman found one of the storehouses where we were keeping the wheat. They cleared it out before we could move it."

Anger leapt in his chest. "How did they find it?"

"We don't know. You need to tell your people to be more careful. I can't have them carelessly—"

"They don't carelessly do anything," he hissed. "They risk their lives each and every time they help me and they know it. Some of them have died, and if you think they've forgotten that—"

"Even so." She was unbothered by his anger. "They need to do better."

His mouth curled. "And what is it you're so afraid of, Saniya? That your gang might be caught and rolled up by the Patrol, or better yet, the Falcons?"

She snarled, reaching his side in a second, dark blue eyes cold and flat. "I'm afraid of the same thing you are, Shadowhawk. Exposure. Endanger my people and I'll hang you out to dry."

"You're mistaken in the level of control you imagine I have over my network. I work alone. They help me when they can, but it's too dangerous—for them and me—to have direct contact."

"Just tell them to be more careful." She stepped back.

"I don't take orders from you, and neither do my people," he said evenly. "You're useful to me, but I won't put lives at risk by working with you. How am I to know that your people didn't make a mistake? Or that one of them isn't taking bribes from the Falcons?"

"We don't take bribes and we don't make mistakes," she said coolly. "So quit acting like you're not just as much of a criminal as I am. Like you said, our alliance works because we suit each other's purposes, but it can break quickly if you become a vulnerability we can't afford."

"You say that," he murmured, voice taking on an edge. "But I've seen the look in your eyes when you talk about the winged folk or the Falcons. You're not just in this for the money."

Her mouth thinned. "You know nothing about me."

"I know more than you think." Like the fact he'd just hit home with his words. For the first time he began to wonder why it had been *her* to approach him, not another member of her group, or even the group's leader. "And I won't accept you continuing to talk to me like I'm an incompetent inferior of yours."

Her jaw tightened. "I know more than *you* think too, Shadowhawk. Like this poor street criminal act you've mastered... no poor street criminal has the level of access to winged folk and Falcon activities that you must to have stayed un-caught all this time."

He held her glance for a moment, not giving away anything by reacting to her words, then moved on. "My notices about the shipment of seeds have been up for over a week. If the Falcons ignore them much longer we'll need to consider other ways of getting some."

She paused at the door, voice grudging. "We could use some of those seeds."

The Shadowhawk nodded. "We give the Falcons a few more days, then we'll meet and work out how best to get the supplies we need."

The closing door was the only affirmation he got.

He was halfway back to his apartment when the *feeling* in the night air changed around him. In a single movement, he stepped off the street and pressed up against the shadows of the nearest wall. Before he had time to sweep the area with his gaze, or even begin to draw the shadows around himself, a woman screamed and came running out of the alley to his right.

She was scantily dressed, hair long and tangled—a streetgirl. But those who worked this part of Dock City didn't scare easily. This one had terror filling her eyes and voice, so much so she didn't notice him as she ran past in a panicked sprint.

Not allowing himself to stop and debate the sense of what he was doing, he edged around into the mouth of the alley. Darkness filled it, the upper stories of the buildings to either side leaning over so as to eclipse any moonlight above.

A whisper of movement rasped over his senses, and he was about to back away—the smart thing to do—when he caught sight of the fallen body. Eyes up, he strode quickly towards it, kneeling down and placing two fingers at the person's throat. No pulse.

His hand came away sticky with blood. His stomach tightened.

Another whisper of movement came from further down the alley. Fear curled down his spine—unfamiliar and unsettling. The darkness rarely made him afraid.

Instinctively he drew the shadows more closely around him, hiding, then took a breath and a step in the direction of the movement. His eyes stared into inky darkness. Beyond the thud of his heartbeat and the soft murmur of his breath, he swore he could feel another presence in the darkness.

Whoever it was stood there, still, waiting. The Shadowhawk

fought through the fear binding his limbs like stone and took another step forward.

Another flash of movement. Eyes sliding through the dark. The glint of copper, and then running footsteps.

The sense of danger he'd felt was gone just as suddenly.

The Shadowhawk shifted, moving so that the little light from the street beyond fell on the body. A man, middle-aged and finely dressed. The Shadowhawk's eyes narrowed—someone from the Wealthy Quarter enjoying an illicit night out.

A murder like this wasn't entirely uncommon in the Poor Quarter, yet...

His gaze caught on a scrap of parchment curled in the dead man's hand. He pulled it out, careful not to rip it. It was a tiny piece, the size of what you'd place in a capsule to deliver a message by bird. A single word was etched in black ink.

Vengeance

Footsteps sounded in the distance—several people at least, and then snatches of the hysterical voice of the streetgirl who'd run screaming. She'd probably gone for the protection of the gang she worked for. He couldn't afford them seeing him and assuming he was the killer.

The Shadowhawk pressed the paper back into the dead hand, then rose and moved swiftly in the opposite direction, drawing the night to him as he ran.

CHAPTER 17

*T*alyn pushed her new wing hard. It would take months of dedicated training before they were capable fighters, and in the meantime, strength, speed and stamina would be the only advantages they had. Her main hope, however, was that they would become united by their shared exhaustion and physical misery. The added side benefit was that they were often too tired to fight or snap at each other.

A winged boy appeared at her room early in the evening eight days after she'd fished Theac out of jail. It had been an especially hot day and she was contemplating whether she could be bothered walking down to Dock City to see if Andres was free. Mid-Twomonth was looming and she'd been so caught up with the effort required to keep her wing together and listening to her that she'd yet to make any further progress on her investigation into the Shadowhawk. Anxiety curled in her gut.

"You haven't even been here a month yet," Sari reminded her.

"A month used to be plenty of time for us to solve a problem like this."

"Stop it. We were intimately familiar with Port Lathilly and its

surrounds. You're in a different country with wildly different customs and expectations. It's going to take time, Talyn."

Despite Sari's reassurances, she'd made the decision to go and visit Andres when the knock came at her door. The boy didn't look any older than ten or eleven and beamed up at her with a toothy smile. Someone had attempted to run a comb through the unruly mop of curls on his head, but it had been in vain. A pair of bright emerald wings rustled at his back, half unfurled as if he were ready to leap into flight at any moment.

"Can I help you?" she asked.

"Prince Cuinn Acondor would like to see you, Captain." He bobbed his head. "I'm to bring you as soon as you're ready."

"Give me a moment."

Talyn ducked back inside to pull on a fresh shirt rather than the one she'd sweated through drill in, then re-plait her damp hair. Once done, she re-opened the door.

"Let's go."

By now she was confident of her way around the palace, but she let the boy take her to the bridge that led across to Cuinn's tower. The front door was, of course, unguarded. The boy knocked, and they waited patiently for an answer. "What's your name?" she asked him.

"I'm Willir Wingswept," he announced proudly. "I'm Prince Cuinn's page."

He looked inordinately proud of himself, and Talyn couldn't help but smile. "That's a high honour for someone so young. How old are you?"

"Just turned thirteen, Captain." He brightened at her words. "Nobody else thinks it's an honour. The other pages sneer at me— they say Prince Cuinn isn't important enough."

"Everyone is important in their own way, Willir," she said seriously. "You should remember that."

He laughed. "What they've been saying about you is right. You're not like most winged folk."

She shuddered to think what 'they' had been saying. "I'm not winged folk at all," she said.

"Maybe." His thin shoulders straightened. "But I like you."

She was still fighting back a smile when Cuinn's musical voice sounded from inside, inviting her in. Assuming a serious expression, Willir opened the door and gestured for her to enter. "I'll see you again soon?" he asked hopefully.

"Count on it." She shook his hand solemnly, and he flashed her a grin before running off and launching into flight.

It was cool inside despite the heat of the day and the arched windows letting in the orange glow of the setting sun. The sky-blue carpet was soft under her boots, the furniture sparse but tasteful—a table by the lounge, a small desk and a case filled with stacks of parchment and the occasional book. A spiral stairway in the far corner joined other floors in the tower. Mostly for show, she presumed.

The one oddity was a small flute sitting on the desk. Apart from a quill and inkpot, nothing else rested on its bare surface. There was no chair near it.

A door abruptly opened on the other side of the room and Cuinn appeared. Again, everything about him was carefully styled to enhance his natural beauty—the sleeveless satin shirt in midnight blue with the top buttons artfully undone, atop fitted breeches in ivory that ended in casually bare feet. His blonde hair was wet and stuck up in messy spikes—a casualty of the rough dry he was giving it with a towel.

"Sorry." He sounded anything but as he offered a lazy smile, eyes running over her from head to toe. "I just came back from a rather energetic game of alleya, and I thought I should freshen up before meeting you."

"That's fine," she said. She had no clue what alleya was, and deliberately looked away to keep her irritation at his entire manner from being completely obvious. She frowned at the realisation that there were no bolts or latches on the window.

"You're angry."

"What?" She turned at the sound of his voice.

"You're angry." He motioned to her. "I can sense it. Did I do something to annoy you?"

178

For a moment she was utterly confused. Her voice and expression had remained neutral since she'd stepped into the room—a soldier speaking with her charge—but then she remembered Theac telling her about the magic of the winged folk. "You can read my emotions? I thought you could only project them."

"It's rare, but the more powerful ones—like me—can do both." He winked. "I normally don't pry, but I couldn't help but sense your anger just then. It was coming off you in waves."

His gaze narrowed, voice turning distant before trailing off entirely. The expression on his face turned inwards, and sudden terror seized her. The idea that this prince might see what was inside her, the broken parts and suffocating grief...

"Stop!"

Her voice ripped through the room, laden with Dumnorix command and a hint of desperation. Cuinn recoiled as if stung, dragging himself out of his daze, green eyes snapping to hers. His mouth opened but she spoke before he could register what happened, and this time she managed a cool, but firm tone.

"I would prefer my emotions remain private, Your Highness," she said. "And if you're wondering why I'm annoyed, you might consider that I don't appreciate being looked up and down like I'm a particularly attractive piece of meat every time I'm in your presence."

He laughed. The bastard actually *laughed*. The amusement lit up his face as he dropped into the nearest sofa, wings spread wide to either side of him. "I can't help it if you're a beautiful woman, Captain Dynan." He cocked his head to one side. "In fact, one of your parents at least must have been winged folk? You have the look of one of us about you."

"My parents are not relevant, Your Highness. What is relevant is that I was sent here to do a job, and you have not allowed me to do it." She took a breath, fighting bitterly to drag the conversation back on track. "I'm hoping that's why you've asked to see me this afternoon."

The amusement faded, boredom sweeping in in its place. "Bringing you to Mithranar wasn't my idea. And I've told you already that I don't want or need any sort of protection. Do you think I enjoy being laughed at by my brothers and my friends about having a misfit human guard made up of criminals?"

"I think you're deliberately choosing to believe you don't need protection because it's easier," she said, keeping her tone neutral. "And if you think for one second that *I* have anything to do with whatever ulterior motives are at play here… well, let me say this. I've been training to be a warrior since childhood, Prince Cuinn, and I take what I do very seriously. I have dedicated my life to it."

"How very stirring," he said, rolling his eyes and heaving a massive sigh.

"I understand you have two elder brothers." She forced patience into her tone and expression, pushing down her annoyance. "But things happen. What if one of them took ill, or—"

His chuckle cut her off. "I'm never going to be in line for the throne of Mithranar, Captain." At her raised eyebrows, he gave a languid shrug. "For a start, I'm illegitimate."

"Oh." She kept her mouth closed with an effort. She hadn't expected that. Ceannar had said Cuinn's Dumnorix blood came from a different branch of the family tree, but she'd just assumed as a prince he would be legitimate. She still didn't feel that instinctive kinship with him that she did with Ariar and Aethain, although that might be because her irritation with his entire manner was overpowering it.

"We're not too fussy about that sort of thing here, and when my mother took a lover after her husband's death, it was hard to be discreet when she fell pregnant in any case." Another shrug, his attention almost entirely taken by an invisible piece of lint on the hem of his shirt. "But the winged folk nobles would never accept me as king, and not only because of that. Trust me on this, Captain."

Once again he'd veered the conversation off track, and she struggled to bring it back, some of her frustration finally escaping into the sharp edge in her tone. "Despite that, you might also consider those you just called misfits will be responsible for keeping you alive. They are, each and every one of them, worthwhile men and they are sweating and working every day to learn how to be warriors. They have my respect, and they should have yours too."

"As inspirational as that little speech was, those misfits would be lucky if—collectively—they could keep a cat alive." He stretched out lazily. "And I realise you haven't been here long, but if you use that disapproving tone with anyone else in my family you'll likely be flogged. Not a pleasant experience, so I don't recommend it."

She faltered. "You're serious."

"Me being serious happens very rarely, but in this case yes, I am," he said. "Mithranar is beautiful, Captain Dynan, but that beauty hides a lot of ugliness. You may have had the freedom to express your views to your superior officers back home, but don't do it here." He shifted, the boredom coming back to his face. "That advice applies for the dinner being held in three days' time."

"Dinner?" she said blankly, stumped by the sudden turn in conversation.

"Yes, my mother is holding one of her regular dinner parties. I have been instructed to make sure my wing is there." He waved a hand. "I'll need at least two of you, or whatever you think best. Try to make them look marginally presentable if you can. I'd rather not have a ragtag bunch of petty criminals show up as my guard. Please ask them to avoid tripping over their shoelaces or doing something equally embarrassing."

"I can do that," Talyn said stiffly.

"Excellent." He reached forward to pour from a carafe of wine on the table. "That will be all, Captain. Your irritation with me is quickly reaching painful levels."

"*Lucky I'm not there. I would punch him.*"

"*I don't get it,*" she said in utter mystification as she left Cuinn's tower without another word. "*Flogging? This place is just...*"

"*A nightmare?*"

"*Something like that.*" She lifted a hand to her suddenly aching temples. She'd taken so much for granted, growing up in the Twin Thrones without any real knowledge of the outside world apart from the lessons taught in her schooling and then at Callanan Tower. She'd known Mithranar had a queen, that the winged folk had magic, and that they were the world's only producer of izerdia.

But that there was a place in the world where people thought they were superior because they had wings and magic, where the ruling family thought it was acceptable to flog people for disagreeing with them, or to hoard food for themselves… that she hadn't known.

And her father. He'd never said a word about any of this, despite how much of a shock it must have been for a human from Dock City to settle in the Twin Thrones, married to a Dumnorix with their views on ruling.

Why?

TALYN TOLD her wing about the dinner following the wall run the next morning. After almost a month of training, they were beginning to show improvement. Running up the wall was still a gasping, exhausting experience, but they could make the full distance at a run now. Once she'd finished, they glanced at each other or at their shoes.

Theac glowered at Zamaril. "We already know," he grunted.

"You do? How?" She frowned at him.

"Our resident thief was listening at the window when you spoke to the prince yesterday," Tiercelin looked torn between horror and amusement at the audacity of such a thing.

"Six thrices, I'll murder him!"

"I see." She tried to keep her voice even. Usually that was easy for her—she'd never found it difficult to maintain a cool calm no matter the situation, which was why she and Sari had always worked so well together. But leading this wing was like wrangling a group of wild cats. Sari chuckled gleefully inside her head.

"I wanted to know what he was saying to you," Zamaril spoke with his usual cockiness, but he was shifting his weight from foot to foot. "And I wanted to know whether you meant all that fleashit you've been giving us about trust and respect."

"What he did was wrong," Corrin said unexpectedly, giving Zamaril a disappointed look. "I'm glad Halun walloped his ear for it."

Talyn shot a startled glance at the thief, noticing his reddened left ear for the first time. He scowled, gaze dropping to the ground. She then swung her gaze to Halun, who stood with his arms crossed, looking thoroughly unapologetic.

"You did say we had to trust each other," Tiercelin pointed out, cocking his head as if trying to remember. "At least *six* times that I recall, though there was probably more. I don't always pay attention when you start lecturing. Spying isn't trust."

She swallowed a sigh that almost wanted to be a laugh. "I agree, and I meant what I said. But we also need to avoid hitting each other, where possible. Next time, Halun, talk to Theac or myself if you have a concern."

"Zamaril told us what you said to Prince Cuinn," Corrin said, directing a pointed look at the thief. "And we'd like to say thank you."

"All of us," Theac said, elbowing Zamaril sharply in the ribs.

The thief scowled. "I still don't get it. You want us to trust you, but I can't even figure out what you're doing here in the first place. A Kingshield helping out the WingGuard, it doesn't make any sense."

She settled a thoughtful gaze on him. This thief was smart, an intelligence born of a life where he'd had only himself to rely on for survival, and he'd been pushing her every single second since joining the wing. The pushing she could take, but she was starting to wonder whether there was more to it.

"It's not a secret," she said evenly. "Your royal family requested a Kingshield guard to assist in training the Falcons. King Aethain agreed on the condition that my services were paid for with a rather large shipment of izerdia."

"So why are you here instead of training Falcons?" This was from Corrin, who sounded genuinely curious.

"I don't know. I'm a soldier just like you. I came here as ordered, and when I arrived, the Falcon told me I'd be building a new wing for Prince Cuinn's protection. So that's what I'm doing."

"For how long?" Zamaril challenged. They all glanced at each other at his question, and she didn't shy away from the truth. She would take his challenges and throw them back every time until he learned to trust or he walked away. Now she pinned him with her gaze until he began looking uncomfortable. "I've already told you. A year. Now, have I answered your questions sufficiently, or would you like to interrogate me further?"

The thief scowled again. "No, Captain." He hesitated. "And yes, I appreciate what you said too."

"I meant every word," she said, then gave Zamaril the fiercest look she could. "If I *ever* hear about you following me around or eavesdropping on my conversations again, I will be furious, understand?"

His face tightened. "Yes, Captain."

Theac cleared his throat. "What do you require from us for this dinner?"

"First, no wearing of shoelaces." Tiercelin grinned.

Talyn allowed them their chuckles before turning back to business. "We'll all be participating. I don't expect any problems, so it will be a learning experience. You've all been undertaking basic weapons skills and building up your strength and conditioning, but you also need to start learning about the practice of guarding someone."

They had all been focusing intently on her words, but as she got to the end, their attention started to wander. Even Corrin's eyes shifted to gaze at some point over her shoulder. She turned, forced to bite down a surge of irritation at the sight of Cuinn standing there with another winged man.

"You're angry again," he said as he approached, faint reproof in his voice.

"Not at all, Your Highness," she said smoothly. "What can we do for you?"

"I've come to speak to my guards." He gave her an amused grin, indicating he knew full well how annoyed she was, before moving past to stand in front of the men. She shifted, positioning herself so that if he said something insulting, she could stop Zamaril from doing anything stupid. The prince's companion stayed back.

"You're a sorry looking lot," Cuinn noted, eyeing them over with a disdainful air. He stood with one hand in his pocket, the other languidly reaching up to sweep his hair back from his face. "But we're stuck with each other for now, and I'd like to make sure you reflect positively on me tomorrow night. After that, we can happily go back to ignoring each other."

"Yes, Your Highness." Theac managed to force his head into a polite nod. The other four muttered an assent. Muted sullenness was written all over their faces— even Tiercelin's. Clearly Zamaril had related every part of the conversation he'd overheard.

Cuinn glanced at Talyn, a hint of laughter on his face. "They all look very enthusiastic about protecting my life, don't they? I shall definitely sleep better at night."

He was completely right, but he was genuinely *amused* by it rather than concerned. Either he was oddly confident that his life would never be in danger, or he was a fool. She was beginning to suspect the latter.

Before she could respond, he swung back to them. "You will all need proper uniforms—it's horrifying to think you've been wandering around up here in those rags." Cuinn paused. "I imagine none of you really want to be Falcons, and the feeling is mutual, I'm sure. Choose a name and colours for yourselves, and Aine here will take your measurements. Your uniforms will be ready by this evening."

"We are representing you, Your Highness." Theac ventured gruffly. "Wouldn't you prefer to choose our colours?"

"I really don't care, as long as it's something sensible." Cuinn's voice was bored now, and he turned to go, but Zamaril's voice stopped him.

"I have an idea for a name, Your Highness."

Talyn stifled a smile—only Zamaril would have the nerve to speak so confidently to the prince. He stood with his arms crossed and smug expression in place, daring Cuinn to disapprove of him. The prince merely raised his eyebrows.

"You're right. We don't want to be Falcons. I think we should be called Wolves."

Tiercelin gasped in shock, while Halun and Corrin simply turned to gape at Zamaril in horror.

"Shut your mouth before I shut it for you, Zamaril!" Theac barked.

Talyn wondered what she was missing. She suspected if she'd known, she'd be putting Zamaril on dishes duty for months. The moment froze as everyone waited for Cuinn's reaction.

He only laughed. "Fine. Wolves it is. I'll also make sure you get a full set of uniforms with spares, including proper boots and shoes. Extra weapons, too."

"There are six of us, Prince Cuinn," Talyn objected. "The Falcon has already provided the weapons we need."

He turned and smiled at her. "I'll not have my wing lack anything every other wing of the WingGuard has. I'd be even more of a laughingstock if that were the case."

"And we wouldn't want that," she said dryly.

His smile widened. "Indeed not. I'll see you all tomorrow night."

They watched as Cuinn lifted off with one mighty sweep of his silver wings. Talyn, still fascinated by the sight of a human flying, turned abruptly as Theac coughed to gain her attention.

She turned back. "Tell me what all that was about." She gave Zamaril a dangerous stare. He flashed her an insolent look before dropping his gaze from hers.

Theac glowered. "The Falcons don't go down into Dock City very often, but when they do, they hate it. They say it's like going into a den of mangy, starving wolves—on account of us being so dirty and noisy."

She wasn't sure whether to laugh or be horrified. "Zamaril! Do you *want* to get thrown back in the cells?"

"Did you think of me at *all* while coming up with that stupid name?" Tiercelin spread his wings for effect. There was indignance in his voice, but a hint of real distress too. She didn't think the others picked up on it, but it was clear as day to her. "I'll never hear the end of it when my family finds out."

"You've probably not noticed, what with how your pretty nose is stuck up in the air most of the time, but your kind are outnumbered in this wing," Zamaril remarked.

"My kind?" Tiercelin took a step towards the thief, insult hardening his handsome face.

"Enough!" Theac stepped in between them before Talyn could, placing a restraining hand on Tiercelin's chest. "Tiercelin, I'm sure you can understand why humans think the way they do about winged folk, and Zamaril, you'd better pipe down or you'll be cleaning shit from the privies for the next month. Am I clear?"

The moment froze, Talyn finding herself freezing along with it. That Theac had stepped in before she could was a stunning development, but Zamaril simply wouldn't let his attitude go, and Tiercelin was nothing if not arrogant and proud.

In the end, Tiercelin was the bigger man. Her shoulders relaxed as he nodded and stepped away from Theac's restraining hand, speaking stiffly. "I *am* outnumbered in this wing, and it's only fair that our name be chosen by a group vote."

Zamaril nodded sullenly. "I vote for the Wolves."

"As long as we're not Falcons, I don't care what it is," Theac said.

Corrin's gaze flickered to Tiercelin, but he said quietly, "I don't want to be a Falcon. I vote for being called Wolves too."

Halun simply gave a firm nod.

Tiercelin spread his hands and shrugged. "Fine. I'm already a joke anyway. Why not add to the hilarity?"

"All right, the Wolves it is." Talyn sighed. She wasn't sure allowing the name was a good idea. Deliberately irritating a group of people that already didn't want them wasn't smart, but she'd been seeking a way to give her wing an identity, something that could bring them together, and this might be it. "On one condition. I hear even a whisper of you giving Tiercelin a bad time about the name, and you'll be Falcons, no matter how much you hate it. He's shown his respect for you by allowing you to choose the name in a vote. You show him the same respect. Am I clear?"

"Yes, Captain!" Theac and Corrin spoke at the same time, sharp and loud. Halun reached out and shoved Zamaril so hard he almost fell. Then gave her a satisfied nod.

She stifled another smile. "I'll leave you to work out what colours you'd like to wear. Please decide in time for Aine to get the uniforms ready for the dinner." The poor winged man was still lingering awkwardly just out of earshot. "Theac, if they bicker, you get deciding vote."

"Yes, Captain."

"Zamaril, a moment please?"

He reluctantly followed her away from the group. "Captain, if you're going to ride me about suggesting the name—"

"It's not that." She looked him hard in the eyes. "You realise Tiercelin was the better man back there, I hope? Your behaviour and attitude were poor and you should be shamed by it."

His lip curled. "I don't live by your stupid rules of fairness and trust. I'll do as I'm ordered so I can stay alive and not go back to the cells, but I've lived with only myself to rely on for my entire life and you've shown me absolutely no good reason why that should change."

"And what good reason have I shown you to *not* trust me? Trust us?" she asked quietly. "You've been following me around and spying on me, after all."

His face tightened.

"You're afraid, and I get that," she continued. "Being alone can feel safer. It means you don't have to fear losing something. Trust me, I know."

"How do you know?" he asked quietly.

She couldn't do it. She couldn't share with him… it was too hard, too raw. When he realised she wasn't willing to tell him, his face hardened. "Right there," he said. "That's my good reason."

He was gone before she could say or do anything. Her hands clenched at her sides as she fought tears.

A LETTER from Tarcos arrived that afternoon, waiting on her doorstep when she returned to her room. The sight of it—of word from home, from someone she cared about—was welcome after the fight with Zamaril, easing some of the tight clutch of despair in her chest.

She sank into her soft couch, ripping the seal open and unfolding the letter within.

TALYN,

I GOT YOUR LETTER YESTERDAY. IT CERTAINLY SOUNDS LIKE YOU'VE BEEN GIVEN A CHALLENGE, BUT I'M SURE YOU'LL GET YOUR NEW UNIT UP AND RUNNING IN NO TIME. I HAVE GREAT FAITH IN YOU. YOU SHOULD TOO.

I'VE GOT SOME NEWS OF MY OWN. MY UNCLE HAS GIVEN ME PERMISSION TO JOIN PRINCE ARIAR'S AIMSIR BATTALION IN THE NORTH TO GAIN SOME FIGHTING AND COMMAND EXPERIENCE. APPARENTLY THE BRIGAND ENCAMPMENTS THROUGHOUT THE MOUNTAINS HAVE BEEN GROWING THESE PAST MONTHS, AND KING AETHAIN IS KEEN TO INCREASE HIS FORCES IN THE AREA. I THINK THE FACT I'LL BE TAKING MY PERSONAL BEARMAN DETACHMENT HELPED SWAY THE KING IN MY FAVOUR ONCE MY UNCLE AGREED. DON'T WORRY THOUGH, I'LL BE BACK IN RYATHL BY THE TIME YOU RETURN.

LEVIANA AND CYNIA ASKED ME TO PASS ALONG THEIR GREETINGS. THEY'VE JUST BEEN GIVEN A NEW ASSIGNMENT SOMEWHERE OUT WEST— THEY WOULDN'T TELL ME WHERE, OF COURSE—AND THEY ASKED ME TO TELL YOU THEY MISS YOU AND CAN'T WAIT TILL YOU GET BACK.

I'D BETTER GO, LORD MARKIM HAS INVITED ME TO DINE WITH HIM THIS EVENING. A FRIEND OF OURS HAS RECOMMENDED A TROUBADOUR GROUP PLAYING IN RYATHL UNTIL THREEMONTH, AND MARKIM HAS INVITED THEM FOR A PRIVATE SHOW AT HIS RESIDENCE.

THERE'S NOT MUCH ELSE TO SAY, ASIDE FROM I MISS YOU, TAL, AND I WISH YOU WERE HERE. I'M COUNTING THE DAYS UNTIL YOU GET BACK.

YOURS,

TARCOS

After reading it, she carefully put the letter down and sank further into the cushions. Tarcos was joining Ariar's Aimsir battalion in the Ayrlemyre Mountains—brigand numbers were on the rise again.

Tears pricked her eyes despite her best efforts to hold them back. She had to stop this. Tarcos was thrilled, and she needed to be happy for him. She *was* happy for him. Fighting with Ariar would give him valuable experience—experience he'd need if he wished to become his uncle's heir. It's what he wanted, had wanted for a long time now.

But working against the brigands, reducing their numbers, keeping the roads across the mountains safe for travellers and merchants alike—that had once been her job. Hers and Sari's. They'd had other assignments too, of course, one memorable one involving infiltrating a gang of violent smugglers in Port Lathilly. But more often than not they worked against the ragtag, yet well-organised, well-supplied and heavily armed criminals that used the rugged and isolated Ayrlemyre range to grow and thrive.

She'd loved it. Loved the life, the challenge, the hunt *and* the fighting. Better yet, they'd been *good* at it. More than good. The effect she and Sari—in concert with the local Aimsir and other Callanan posted there—had on brigand activities had been noticeable. Now their numbers were growing again. And there was FireFlare. She missed her Aimsir mare constantly, the bond between horse and rider so strong that the mare wouldn't let anyone else touch her while Talyn was away.

She wanted that life back so badly she ached. And at the same time, she never wanted to go anywhere near it ever again. Because it had been *her* fault that... Tears threatened, and she bit her lip, almost hard enough to draw blood, refusing to let them fall.

She needed a distraction.

Forcing herself up and out of her chair, Talyn went to the desk and yanked open the drawer. Inside she kept scrawled notes of her observations on the Shadowhawk. They wouldn't make sense to anyone but her and Sari—they'd developed their own shorthand after years working together—but they mostly revolved around the two notices she'd seen since her arrival in Mithranar and what she'd learned from her conversation with Andres.

After spreading the notes across the desktop, she studied them, forcing her brain to think, to focus on something other than Tarcos's letter and her run-in with Zamaril and how both made her feel.

Corrin had said the Shadowhawk's notes sometimes forced the WingGuard into sharing the winged folk supplies for fear of a riot or other trouble with izerdia extraction. And sure enough, she'd heard the Wolves talking over lunch the previous day. Corrin's mother had told him that some of the recent shipment of seeds was beginning to be distributed throughout the Wealthy Quarter.

But from what she'd seen of the WingGuard so far, they wouldn't take kindly to being forced into action by the Shadowhawk. Her mind snagged on that, turning it over.

"No, they'd want some sort of retribution. Or at least a way to lash out." Sari agreed.

"But they haven't been able to catch the Shadowhawk," Talyn answered absently. "So, they'd go after his network, perhaps?"

"Or anyone, really. After your experience of them so far, I can't see them being particularly discerning."

"You're right. And remember what Andres said about the man I caught on my first day? The one linked to the Shadowhawk? He said the man had gone to jail, but that usually the Shadowhawk would have intercepted him before that." Talyn shoved the parchment back into her drawer and reached for her cloak.

This wasn't going to be as hard as she'd thought.

ANDRES TYE WAS on duty when she walked into the Market Quarter Patrol headquarters, standing by the main desk chatting with Lidrin— the young Patrolman she'd met on her first day.

"Captain Dynan." Once again Tye looked surprised to see her. "I hope there's nothing wrong?"

"No," she assured him, glancing at Lidrin with an apologetic smile. He beamed back at her. "Do you have a moment to chat?"

Tye glanced ruefully towards the door leading to a back room. "I'm in the middle of questioning one of our less-scrupulous jewel sellers, but I could use a break. Let's step outside. It's stupidly warm in here."

It wasn't that much cooler on the landing outside, but at least there was a faint, sluggish breeze moving through the streets. Tye settled himself against the railing, able from there to keep a watchful eye through to the foyer, as well as see anyone coming up from the street.

"I came because I wanted to thank you for what you did for Theac." It was her pretence for coming to talk to Andres about the

Shadowhawk, but as the words came out, she realised she meant them. "From what I've gathered about the Patrol so far, not many others would have given me the opportunity to help him."

"I heard you kept him in your wing." His words were without emotion, giving no indication of what he thought of that.

"I did. Everyone deserves a second chance."

"It's a risk. Keeping a drunk on in a protective unit." Tye shifted. "The Falcon would have tossed him out on his ear if he knew."

"A good thing he doesn't." She kept her voice as toneless as his.

"Not yet. Most of the Patrol knows about it by now. My men." A slight tightening of his mouth. "Don't always keep their mouths shut. Some of them are in the pocket of the Falcons."

He was warning her. Her estimation for this Patrolman rose incrementally, along with more questions. "Why are you in the Patrol, Andres?"

"To help where I can." He crossed his arms, clearly not interested in divulging any more. "My turn. What really brings you down here tonight, Captain?"

She weighed her words, decided against pretending she didn't have another reason for coming. "Corrin told me the Shadowhawk's notices resulted in some of the recent shipment of seeds being distributed throughout the city."

"True." Andres nodded. "It all went to merchants in the Wealthy Quarter, but still, it's better than none coming down at all."

"That wouldn't have pleased the Falcons, I imagine? Being forced into action like that."

Tye pushed off the railing, taking two steps back toward the open door and pausing there. "No, they weren't. But I don't see what this has to do with your job here, Captain."

"Who did they arrest?" she asked softly.

He let out a breath, looked away, then gave her a grim look when he glanced back. "Two dock workers are currently sitting in the Dock Quarter cells. I know the watch officer over there, and just between you and me? He has no clue why they were arrested."

She nodded, hiding the flare of triumph that went through her at his words. "How long have they been there?"

"Since yesterday afternoon."

Then the Shadowhawk should have heard about it by now. She flashed Andres a smile. "Good luck with your criminal jeweller."

His chuckle followed her back out into the street.

CHAPTER 18

"She's hiding something."

The thief delivered these words flatly, back resting against the wooden wall of the brothel, arms firmly crossed over his chest. The Shadowhawk studied him—he'd approached Zamaril to be his informant because he'd never had any contact with any of the other men Talyn Dynan had chosen for her wing, and Zamaril had occasionally helped him in the past. Never at his request or command, and only when it suited him, but still.

"Like what?" he eventually asked.

Zamaril shrugged. "She keeps going on about trust and being wing mates, but she's closed up like a steel drum holding a year's worth of gold coin. And she talks about her Kingshield like it's some wonderful, amazing thing, which has to be absolute rubbish. Either that or she's a fool."

"Just because things are the way they are here doesn't mean that's the way they are everywhere else," he murmured.

Zamaril spat. "Since when were you a philosopher? And what does that even mean? Things are the same everywhere—those that have money and power prey on those that don't. That's the way the world works."

"That's the way the world you've grown up in works," the Shadowhawk pointed out, then turned to the original topic. "A shipment of izerdia seems a steep but reasonable price for a Kingshield guard. And at least now we know the request for her came from here." Now he just had to work out who, and why, and whether it affected him in any way.

"Whatever." Zamaril was clearly bored with the conversation. "She's not the only reason I asked to meet anyway. Halun told me this afternoon that two dock workers he knows were arrested yesterday—on Doljen's orders."

Doljen. The Patrol Captain commanding the Dock Quarter patrol. One of the captains that regularly accepted bribes from the WingGuard.

"What for?" he asked, voice dangerously quiet.

"Halun says nobody knows. Says both men keep their noses clean—they were yanked out of their homes without any reason."

"The notices about the seed shipments." Anger rose quick and hot, hands curling into fists at his sides.

"Probably."

Zamaril's hand whipped out to grab his arm as he went to shove past. "You're too predictable, Shadowhawk. One day even that moronic bunch of feathered incompetents is going to manage to ambush you successfully."

"If you want to be helpful, just stick to what I asked you to do," he snarled, then pulled the darkness down over him like a shroud and disappeared into the street.

The Shadowhawk stalked through Dock City. Anger simmered in his veins, adding an edge to the night around him. The Falcons had once again had their petty revenge. Arrested yesterday—a day after he'd stumbled over the dead body in the alleyway.

The anger flashed white hot, his mouth curling into a snarl. It was easier to feel that, to *focus* on that, than the guilt that loomed beneath it, turning his gut sour. The men weren't amongst his network of helpers—he would have heard already if that was the case. He doubted they were Saniya's people either, or she'd have reached out with an urgent message. There had been no chalk marks in the usual places when he'd checked on his way to meet Zamaril.

No, they'd only been arrested so that the Falcons could have a scapegoat. And it had taken him more than a day to learn of it. Too damn long.

Despite the emotion churning inside him, he moved silently through the pre-dawn darkness, the hood of his usual cloak pulled well down over his face, long strides eating up the ground. He'd discovered the roof entrance to the Dock Quarter Patrol headquarters over a year ago and so far, despite the three occasions he'd broken prisoners out in that time, neither the Patrol nor the Falcons had been able to discover how he got in and out so easily.

His lip curled in a brief sneer at the thought of their uselessness.

Once inside, he found the watch officer inside his office. This one was as open to bribes as his captain, but he didn't care where the bribes came from. And he already knew what the Shadowhawk had come for. A greasy smile spread over the man's face as he made a curling gesture with his fingers. The Shadowhawk swallowed down his anger and tossed a small bag of coins on the desk without a word.

"Last cell on the left." The watch officer took the sack and tucked it into his tunic. "I kept them well away from the others to make it easier for you."

He didn't bother with thanks.

The two men were asleep in their cell. Even in the dim light cast by flickering torches out in the corridor, it was obvious their faces were swollen, skin dark with bruising. The Shadowhawk's eyes slid closed as fury burned through him, white hot, and he had to fight down the desire to go back and start throwing his fists at the Patrolmen guards on the front desk—they might be slack and uninterested, but this may not have been their handiwork. And even if it was... he didn't use violence. No matter how angry he was, he just couldn't.

He used his key on the lock—another thing they didn't know he had—and cautiously swung the cell door open.

The first prisoner woke at the sound, terror flashing over his face before he realised it wasn't a Falcon or Patrolman in the cell with him. The Shadowhawk raised a finger to his masked lips and the man nodded. Together, they tried to rouse the second man.

When he finally woke, his eyes were glassy, and he had trouble standing. The first prisoner wrapped an arm around him for support as the Shadowhawk led them out through the cell door and locked it behind him. They passed nobody as he hustled them as quickly as possible towards the roof exit.

Both men struggled to climb the ladder set into the wall. Guilt and shame sickened him at the sight of their struggles. These men were hurt because of him, because the Falcons had wanted to retaliate. He hated himself for it, but he couldn't stop either. He had to do *something*.

"Stay low," he murmured once they were on the roof. "Can't afford anyone seeing us creeping around up here."

The first prisoner nodded, already in a crouch. The second was barely conscious. The Shadowhawk wrapped an arm around the second man's waist, angling his body carefully so they didn't get too close, and then he and the other prisoner lifted him to his feet.

Forced to move in an awkward crouch, with the weight of an insensible man between them, they made painfully slow progress across a series of roofs before negotiating another ladder down to street level.

Relief slackened his shoulders when they reached the darkness of the narrow alley. All around them was quiet. Dawn was still at least a full-turn away. The watch officer he bribed was on shift until then, so they still had some time before the alarm was raised.

He and the first prisoner propped the second man against the alley wall. The Shadowhawk reached into his cloak, tugging out the small flask he kept hidden in his tunic. Carefully, he tipped some of its contents into the first prisoner's mouth. The second man squatted nearby. He said nothing, gaze fixed on the Shadowhawk.

A second later, the unconscious man coughed, spat. His eyes blinked open, still foggy, but awake. The Shadowhawk offered him another swallow of the spirits before tucking the flask away. "We've got a short walk ahead. Can you make it? I'd rather not look suspicious by having to carry you."

He coughed again, blinking. "I can do it."

The words were slightly slurred, but he was already clambering to his feet, leaning heavily on the wall for balance. "Thanks for getting us out."

The other prisoner spoke then. "We wouldn't have been in there if not for you."

"I know," the Shadowhawk said quietly. "Come on, we need to go."

He led the men—the injured prisoner stumbling every few steps—through more back streets until reaching a run-down house at the end of a dank alley. He'd used it before. Those inside provided food and shelter for the homeless in the area and any others in desperate need.

Its owner also knew how to contact Saniya.

Once the two men were well enough to move, they'd be funnelled to Saniya's network. The Shadowhawk didn't know where they went from there, or how, all he knew was that they disappeared from the city for good. It was safer for everyone that way. He rapped sharply on the door, pressed a bag of coin into each man's hand, and left before they could say anything.

His strides quickened as he moved down the alley—he didn't want thanks or any other conversation, especially blame. The less anyone saw or knew of him the safer they'd be. Already their lives were ruined because of him. They'd have to live in hiding indefinitely, unable to return to their work or their normal lives until the Wing-Guard forgot about them, if ever.

His hands curled in his pockets. He hated what they did so much, hated how they'd forced him into this.

Thoughts busy, he took one step out into a main thoroughfare and froze. The night air prickled around him—where a moment earlier it had been cool and sharp now it felt heavier. He stared around him.

Two fishermen walked towards the docks, chatting busily about the fog descending on the street and what it would mean for the day's catch. From the opposite end of the street a merchant drove a cart laden with bottles of fresh milk and eggs toward him. Light shone from inside a shop on the other side of the street—a baker's, if he remembered correctly.

But there was something *else*.

Slowly, carefully, he studied the pre-dawn darkness shrouding the area. His neck prickled as if something was out there. It was nothing like the breath of darkness he'd felt the other night, before finding that body, but even so...

Eventually his gaze lingered on a shadowy corner in the overhang of a dark and closed millinery. The cart passed by. Nothing moved. No sound was audible.

He shook his head. He was becoming paranoid. Who would be watching him? If the Falcons or Patrol had managed to track him from the prison, they'd be descending on him already, swords drawn.

Even so, he was unsettled. He walked quickly back to the apartment, taking a deliberately long and complex route and locking the door securely behind him.

TWO FULL-TURNS LATER, once dawn had broken over the horizon, he walked the streets without hood, cloak or mask. Despite the unsettling experience earlier, he wanted to make sure the two prisoners had escaped cleanly and that any Falcon search didn't come close to finding the house he'd left them at.

As he passed the street leading down to the start of the wall walk, on his way to the Dock Quarter Patrol headquarters, he paused at the sight of Prince Cuinn's new wing making their morning run down the wall. He'd heard talk of it, but never seen it in action.

The foreigner led them, running easily, and the new guards trailed behind her, looking almost comfortable at the swift pace she was setting. The feeling of unease returned. Whatever Captain Dynan had been brought here to do, it remained a mystery. She must suspect by now that she'd been set up to fail, but she was still here, and seemed set on doing her job.

His fear that she would bring extra attention to him so far hadn't materialised. Even so, his gaze as he watched her remained wary. He shifted back into the shadows of a shopfront as they reached the bottom of the wall and ran past, the ex-Patrol captain barking orders for them to move faster.

Her gaze scanned her surroundings watchfully, but she didn't seem to be overly suspicious—just the habit of an experienced warrior. Sharp sapphire eyes swept over him as he pressed against the wall of the shop, just one of the many other unremarkable humans on the street, and he took a breath, holding it, until her gaze continued past.

Then they were gone, circling the block before heading back up the wall. Despite himself, his gaze lingered long after they'd vanished from sight, worried and uncertain. After a moment, he shook himself out of his daze and began moving again. His focus was the two men he'd helped the night before—making sure they stayed safe. The foreigner and her new guard had nothing to do with him.

He would make sure of it.

CHAPTER 19

On the afternoon before the dinner, a knock came at Talyn's door just as she was getting out of a cold bath. Afternoon drill had been particularly exhausting in the thick Mithranan humidity. By the time she'd thrown on a robe and gone to answer the door, whoever it was had gone, leaving behind a bulky package wrapped in paper resting against the outside of the door.

She picked it up and kicked the door shut behind her. Her fingers made quick work of the ties, and the paper fell open to reveal three sets of clothing.

The new uniforms.

Curious despite herself, she spread them out on her bed—a training uniform, general duties attire and a formal set. Her wing— the Wolves, now—had chosen charcoal grey and white for their colours. She liked the choice.

The uniforms were beautiful, made by a skilled hand and from the finest cloth. Designed for the humid environment, the training uniform consisted only of a sleeveless cotton shirt in light grey and pants made from the same cotton in darker grey; loose, but only falling to just below the knees where the fabric gathered in around the calves. Right at the bottom of the package were a pair of black leather sandals—hardy and well made, but light.

A dry chuckle escaped her. Her wing would be nice and cool in these, but good luck to them when they fell hard during training or their sparring partner got through their guard. Bruises and cuts would be a regular occurrence.

The general use—for when they were on duty—and formal sets were less weather-appropriate. These included a sleeveless charcoal leather vest that fell halfway to the knees with a split down the front for ease of movement. Underneath the vest was a long-sleeved white cotton shirt. The breeches were fitted, but made from soft white cotton. The formal set had silver embroidery stitched into the outside of the legs and around the edges of the tunic. In the same package was a beautifully tooled weapons' belt. A pair of matching boots in charcoal complemented the set, made from supple leather that laced to mid-calf.

Neither of the tunics, or the shirt of the training uniform, had a sigil—the chests of each were bare. She'd seen the Acondor sigil on the Falcons plenty of times now, golden wings sprouting from a golden crown, but was unsurprised the Wolves had chosen not to wear it. However, a small image of a snarling wolf had been stitched out in dark blue thread on the bottom left corner of each tunic.

Shaking her head, Talyn folded all the clothes back up and put them away in the bottom of her chest. Instead, she unpacked her formal Kingshield uniform from the bag sitting on the chair by the end of her bed.

She polished her boots and laced them up over the black breeches, firmly ignoring how the layers instantly made her uncomfortably hot. Next she polished her sais until they shone. Finally, she braided her long black hair neatly then traced her fingers gently over the starred emblem in bright amber on her chest.

Then she went to find her wing.

THE WOLVES WERE STANDING in a neat row in the drill yard, awkward in their finery. Even the gruff Theac looked ill at ease, fingering his shirt cuffs and glaring at anybody who so much as glanced at him. Cuinn's tailor had done well though—the uniforms fitted each of them perfectly, from Halun's huge frame to Corrin's too-skinny one.

Talyn greeted them with a smile. "You look great."

Zamaril gave her a sour look. "This is the most ridiculous thing I've ever worn. How am I supposed to remain inconspicuous in this?"

"You're not a thief any more, Zamaril. You need to stand out—make it obvious that the prince has protection. It suits you."

"Tiercelin's the only one who looks good in this absurd get up," he snapped.

"You're just jealous because we look good in clothes," Tiercelin retorted airily.

Talyn couldn't help but agree. The winged folk's seemingly universal ethereal beauty made them stand apart from the humans. Their arrogance stemmed from that, and from their magic, she supposed. Tiercelin did look gorgeous, the grey and white uniform complementing his brown skin and grey wings perfectly.

"I think you look very impressive, Captain," Corrin said in his quiet voice.

Halun grunted, yanking at his collar.

"Can we get going, Captain?" Theac asked. "I feel like a prize fool standing around in this get up."

She shook her head. "No. The Falcon wanted us to wait here for him."

"Of course he does," Zamaril said. "Humans aren't competent enough to make their own way to places. They need guides."

"Zamaril," Theac warned.

They fell into awkward silence. Studying them, she quickly realised the other reason they were standing so uncomfortably. They'd begun basic weapons training, centred mainly around sword skills, but none of them were accustomed to carrying weapons yet.

Theac didn't seem to notice the axe hanging down his back—he preferred that to a sword in a fight, he'd told her, and she allowed it—but the other four kept shifting to adjust the weight of the swords at their waists. She was glad to see Corrin also had two knives sheathed in his belt.

"When people are watching, you're going to have to stop shifting about like you've got ants crawling up the insides of your legs," she commented. "You'll get used to the weight of those swords quickly."

Tiercelin flushed red and instantly stilled himself. Corrin looked startled, as if he hadn't even realised what he was doing. Both Zamaril and Halun glared at the ground.

They all jumped simultaneously when the gate creaked open. Booted footsteps sounded on the stone, and then Ravinire appeared, resplendent in WingGuard teal and scarlet, golden sigil gleaming on his chest.

"I've come to escort you," he said briskly, looking them over with grudging approval. "Are you ready, Captain?"

"Yes, sir," Talyn said, smiling approval at the way the Wolves immediately fell into an orderly line behind Theac. At least they'd learned to form a straight line in the past month, if nothing else. Ravinire's eyebrows lifted in what looked like surprise but he said nothing as he led them away.

Night was falling. As the light faded, glowing lamps blinked into existence along the walkways and bridges, and small coloured lights adorned the trees of the scattered gardens.

It would be an amazing sight for any ship entering the bay. The artistic way the lights had been designed and placed gave the night a magical glow. It was utterly unlike Dock City at night, where darkness and unease seemed to fill any space and the few lights struggled in a losing battle against it.

The building they were heading for was lit up more than the rest. Ravinire took them through a side entrance that emerged onto an upper balcony looking down over the room below.

It was large, almost the size of their training yard, and luxuriously appointed. Sofas, lounges, chairs and rugs sparsely covered the floor, which was carpeted in a plush lilac. After a quick count, she estimated at least a hundred guests, probably more, reclining on backless couches or clustered in small groups talking.

Food covered the tables along the edges of the room and human servants carried platters of drinks around. Others moved discreetly in and out, replacing whatever was eaten from the tables. The winged folk in the room didn't even seem to notice they were there.

"You never noticed the servants at the Ryathl palace when you spent time with your family there either," Sari pointed out.

"Yes, but that was..." She struggled to find the word. Different, yes. But that didn't capture it entirely. Part of it was that when she was with her family, she was completely focused on putting forward a smiling, confident front, so they would think she was fine. Paying attention to anything else was out of the question. And the rest... well, it was just *different* in Mithranar. Still... *"Maybe I should have."*

She focused her attention back on her surroundings. Arched floor to ceiling windows allowed light from the setting sun to shine through, and several were open, so that the evening breeze filled the room, redolent with the scent of flowers and wine.

"It's just started." Ravinire spoke at her shoulder. "Prince Cuinn will be arriving any moment. He'll need an escort in."

"I know how to run a guard detail, sir," Talyn said firmly. "You can leave us to it."

Ravinire nodded, stepping off the balcony and floating down into the room. Talyn turned to see all five members of her wing looking at her expectantly. She stifled a smile. Focused attention was a definite improvement on the sneers and attitude from her first few weeks with them. A knot of tension she hadn't realised was there uncoiled slightly.

"Tiercelin, do you know the entrance Prince Cuinn will use?"

"Yes. I've been to plenty of these things before." He made a face. "They're so boring. We're not going to have to stand and watch all night are we?"

She gave him a hard look. "You and Theac will escort the prince inside. Once he's inside, your job is to stand guard by the main entrance with the other Falcons for the evening. Keep your back straight, don't fidget, and don't leave your post for any reason unless the prince comes under attack." She looked at her second. "You know what to do, Theac."

"Aye." He bowed his head, then he and Tiercelin exited through the door they had just come through. The winged man gave a long-suffering sigh as he left.

Talyn turned to the other three. "We'll be monitoring the area to make sure it remains secure. Zamaril?"

The thief had been pulling at the stiff collar around his neck, but when Talyn spoke he dropped his hands and looked at her. "What?" he snapped, surly.

"You can drop the attitude for a start," she said tartly. "I want you to think like a thief—go outside and study the building, discover the most likely place for any assassin to get in, then report back to me."

"How should I know where an assassin would come in?"

"Pretend you wanted to break in here and steal something valuable in the middle of the dinner." She kept her voice sharp. "I'm getting sick of doing this dance with you, Zamaril."

"I'll do it," he muttered. "Where will I find you when I'm done?"

"I'll be here."

Zamaril slipped out the door, and Talyn turned her attention below, studying the guests. The attention of the entire room shifted to the main doorway when a slim winged woman entered. That, more than the richness of her clothing and the size of her retinue, told Talyn this must be the queen of Mithranar.

Sarana Acondor was a daunting figure, tall and beautiful, her long blonde hair turning silver with age. From so high up, Talyn couldn't see her in much more detail, but those closest to her kept darting glances her way, as if awaiting an order and ready to carry it out instantly. The queen held them in the palm of her hand, yet seemed utterly unaware of it at the same time.

A winged man crossed the room to greet the queen. He was tall also, with a powerful build, dark hair and ebony wings that glimmered bronze in the glow of dusk. People moved out of the way when he walked, some of them not even seeming to realise what they were doing.

"The prince of night," Corrin murmured as he came to her side. Halun stepped up on her other side, a silent but solid presence. His gaze mirrored hers—scanning the room below.

She turned, lifting a questioning eyebrow at Corrin.

"It's what they call Prince Mithanis. The queen's eldest son," he clarified, then straightened slightly and pointed. "And the second son, Prince Azrilan. The prince of games."

The prince of games was slighter, not as tall, but just as dark-haired as his eldest brother. His charcoal wings rustled as he too crossed the room to greet his mother, though he was careful to let Mithanis speak first, and his gaze constantly flicked to his elder brother, just like the queen's attendants did with her.

"Games?" Talyn asked, half-distracted by the interplay between the royal family. It was nothing like she was accustomed to. There was no natural ease there, no slight relaxing at being in each other's presence. Instead there was watchfulness and a hint of unease.

"He's a master at any game you could think of, but particularly cards. It's his favourite pastime." Corrin shrugged. "At least, that's what I've heard. He probably gets it from his father—the Montagni love gambling."

These winged folk do like their ostentation and fancy titles, don't they?

"And the prince of song," Corrin murmured.

Halun straightened a little beside her. Her eyes shifted to where Cuinn was walking through the door, flanked by Theac and Tiercelin, and surrounded by a gaggle of pretty winged women. Almost as one, his mother and two brothers turned at his entrance, their gaze focusing on him from across the room. Cuinn seemed unaware of their regard.

He left his two guards by the door and entered the room with the women. As always he was impeccably dressed—tonight in an open ivory jacket over a deep violet shirt and pants, tailored to perfectly fit every inch of him. The sandals on his bare feet flashed with some kind of jewellery, as did the cuffs of his shirt.

One of his companions, a slim blonde woman with green wings, slipped her arm through his. He flashed her a lazy smile. Talyn scanned the room to see how the attendees responded to Cuinn's entrance. Maybe here she could get a clue of whether he truly faced any danger.

There was nothing of note. The women, and not a few of the men, in the room watched him with varying degrees of interest, some more overtly than others, but there were others—those she recognised from the way they carried themselves as probably amongst the high nobility—who completely ignored the youngest prince. Their attention was almost fully occupied by the queen and the eldest prince.

There was nothing there that made her uneasy or raised her suspicions. Ravinire claimed there were no specific threats from outside the citadel. She'd not yet identified any—to Cuinn, at least—from the inside. On the surface, it seemed as if the crown's request for her presence simply to improve the skill of their WingGuard was all there was to it.

Except instead of having her train the WingGuard, she'd been tasked to build a new wing for Prince Cuinn's protection. Was Ravinire just testing her skill before letting her train his soldiers? Or was there more to it?

"I think there's more to it," Sari murmured.

"I agree." If that was all there was to it, then how did two Callanan potentials end up in a cell together the day she was choosing soldiers for her wing? She refused to believe that was coincidence. And there was still the question of why they'd requested a Kingshield now. Ravinire hadn't provided a satisfactory answer on that score. She turned to Corrin. Maybe she could start with the rest of the royals. "Why such names for the princes?" she asked.

He shrugged. "Prince Mithanis is the most powerful winged folk born in generations. He's got warrior and song magic, and he's known for being a skilled and vicious fighter. Because of that, along with his dark wings and hair, well, I suppose people just thought 'prince of night' stuck, and he's never dissuaded it. Prince Azrilan loves to play, as I said. And Prince Cuinn, well, he only has song magic, but it's powerful. I've heard that hearing him sing is a once in a lifetime experience."

"Sure, that makes sense. But why the names at all?"

"Well, the queen is an only child, so was her father. But now we have three princes, only one of whom can become king. Giving them nicknames increased the theatrics of it all, I suppose. Something to entertain them."

A loud grunt from Halun on her other side gave her a solid idea of what he thought of that.

She frowned. "Doesn't Prince Mithanis become king?"

"That's not how it works here." Corrin shook his head. "The ruling monarch chooses their heir, along with input from the five most powerful noble families—they form what's called the Queen-council."

Talyn turned back to the room below, eyes falling on Cuinn. Maybe that was the answer she'd been looking for—she'd just assumed there was only a slim chance he'd ever ascend the throne because he was the third born. His revelation that he was illegitimate had only deepened that assumption.

"Of course, nobody truly expects it to be anyone but Prince Mithanis." Corrin dispelled her new theory a second after it had formed. "He's far and away the most powerful of the three, and that's traditionally what decides things. From the gossip I've heard in Dock City, the noble families are too afraid of Prince Mithanis to even think about advising the queen to pick Prince Azrilan. And none of them would consider Prince Cuinn."

"Why?"

"I'm not entirely certain, Captain." Corrin cocked his head. "We humans aren't really privy to the details of royal court machinations, but ask anyone and they'll tell you the same thing. Maybe it's because nobody knows who his father is—the queen has always refused to name him, and so the assumption is that he wasn't from a strong family; he might not even have been noble. Or maybe it's just because he does nothing but drink and party." A hint of contempt edged Corrin's voice.

Theory ruined, Talyn dismissed her thoughts. It was time to turn her focus back to this event and ensuring Cuinn's security. She was about to send Halun looking for Zamaril—he should have been back by now—when there was movement in the corner of the room.

A small group of winged folk were gathering on a raised platform. One of them held a guitar in his hands, and the other a flute. The queen crossed to her youngest son, taking his arm and murmuring in his ear.

Cuinn nodded and disentangled himself from the three women who were sharing a couch with him. As soon as people saw him move towards the musicians, all eyes turned that way. Talyn did a sweep of the guards. They were all looking with anticipation at the same thing, including Tiercelin. Theac was at his side, scowl firmly in place.

"Why is everyone so interested in Prince Cuinn all of a sudden?" she asked Corrin and Halun.

"I don't know." Zamaril chose that moment to re-appear. "But I overheard the Falcons outside talking. It seems like everyone wants to be assigned guard duty for these events when Prince Cuinn is attending."

"Did you survey the area?" she asked.

He nodded. "There are four possible entrances aside from the main one. I'd only use two of them—the others are too open and it would be easy to be spotted trying to sneak in."

"Take Halun and Corrin." She glanced at them. "You'll keep watch on one entrance each. When you've shown them, come back here, Zamaril. I want your eyes. You know what to look out for."

"What if someone tries to get in the entrance I'm guarding?" Corrin looked startled by her order.

"Call me," Halun said unexpectedly. "I'll help you."

She gave the young man a reassuring look. "Yell for all you're worth, then remember those knives on your belt and what you can do with them."

"Aye, Captain." Looking only marginally reassured, Corrin followed Halun and Zamaril out.

The musicians started playing then, breaking into a merry, rollicking tune that had Talyn pushing away the impulse to tap her fingers against the railing. The music spread throughout the open space, cheerful and bright. The chatter of conversation elsewhere in the room faded slowly, and almost everyone edged a little closer to the corner.

Once he knew he had the full attention of the room, Cuinn stepped up to the platform and sat behind a beautifully carved and painted harpsichord. His fingers ran lightly over the keys and then he glanced back to the musicians.

Without a word being exchanged between them, the music they were playing changed, moving into a deep, haunting melody. There was almost a collective intake of breath throughout the room as the audience clearly recognised the music. A hush of anticipation fell over the space.

A little smile crossed Cuinn's face, and his fingers began moving on the harpsichord, the instrument's clear sound joining that of the fiddle and flute behind him in perfect harmony.

Then he opened his mouth to sing.

Talyn had never heard such a voice. She was so entranced by the richness and beauty of it that it took her a few moments to begin paying attention to the lyrics of the song.

Long ago in the dusk we came
Mithranar through the cold and rain
Forest dark, horrors untold
The night is full and will test your soul
The night favours only the bold

Cuinn sang of the history of the winged folk, of their arrival in Mithranar. How they'd faced the terrors of the forest, how they'd needed to band together and fight for their right to live in their new home. And as he sang his magic swept through the notes of the music —haunting and melancholy at the words describing their desperate struggle for survival, then soaring into pride and joy as the song spoke of the construction of the citadel, of its beauty and splendour.

We remember all those we lost

Feathers bright they will not be forgot
Our citadel shines golden and true
For all time. For all time

The prince of song.

This was his magic. It unfolded like a flower as he sang, enveloping everyone in the room. She felt every single emotional beat of the song, as if each emotion were hers alone, her struggle, her triumph, her pride and fear.

As one, dear heart, as one
We fly as one
The wind will guide us home
To glory under the sun
All glory under the sun

Every single guest stood entranced. Most had tears in their eyes, others were holding tightly to each other. All the guards had forgotten their duties, the entirety of their attention on the prince sitting at the harpsichord, eyes closed as he made the most beautiful music Talyn had ever heard. Even Theac was staring, the scowl on his face softened to something like wonder.

Cuinn's voice soared into the pinnacle of the song, until its very essence vibrated through the air, almost too powerful to be endured. As it reached its peak, hovering in beautiful melody, something inside Talyn eased. For the very first time in two years her despair ebbed away and the constricting weight of grief on her chest was gone.

She took a single, deep breath, shoulders straightening and tears welling in her eyes.

In that moment she felt whole again.

Then, slowly and gently, the music faded away and the song was over. A collective sigh echoed through the room. The tendrils of her depression came sinking back through her as he let go of the magic holding them all.

"They say he's the most powerful song mage ever born," Zamaril muttered. "Still… I had no idea."

She started as she realised Zamaril was standing beside her, mouth open, face entranced. She'd been so engrossed in the song, she hadn't been paying any attention to her surroundings, let alone the room. She flushed hotly and scrubbed at her still wet eyes.

Below, Cuinn's gaze shifted, a slight frown on his face. A moment later it landed on her, high above him. The expression in his eyes seemed to indicate concern, rather than the amused contempt that was usually written there, as if he could feel her emotion.

Which he probably could.

Instantly she straightened up, slamming her emotions down deep and quickly tugging back her cool mask and well-practiced self-control. A moment later his gaze shifted away from her, face breaking into a smile as one of his companions came over to murmur something in his ear.

"He's not going to sing another one." The disappointment in Zamaril's voice was acute, and Talyn felt an echo of it herself as Cuinn stood up from behind the harpsichord, offered a languid wave to the musicians, then returned to the women he'd been entertaining.

"Go and check on Halun and Corrin, make sure they've seen nothing of concern," she barked at the thief, the sharpness of her voice covering up her guilt and frustration.

Several assassins could have entered the room and gotten all the way to Cuinn without any of them noticing during that song. And once they'd gotten that close, she'd never have reached him in time to save him.

Despair slid through her. Her focus had slipped because she'd been overwhelmed. By the aching grief that was still so acute.

She took in a deep, shuddering breath. Cuinn was still alive, nothing had happened.

Tomorrow she'd speak to the Wolves about losing their focus next time Cuinn sang at one of these events. She'd come up with a strategy to manage how his magic affected them.

One step at a time.

CHAPTER 20

*E*ventually it was over. Talyn dismissed the Wolves after assigning Tiercelin and Corrin to escort Cuinn back to his rooms. If she had her way, he would have guards surrounding his tower all night, but they simply didn't have enough men for that yet, and besides, the prince didn't want it. She wondered when Ravinire was going to push the point with Cuinn... if he ever would.

If Ravinire was testing her, well, she'd yet to prove anything to him.

As she walked along an open walkway in the direction of her room, still unsettled by what Cuinn's magic had done to her, she caught a flicker of shadow out of the corner of her eye and stopped. A shiver ran down her back. Subconsciously, her right hand reached for the hilt of one of the sais at her back.

A deep breath.

For the first time since she'd arrived at the citadel, the darkness of night held a hint of menace. She wasn't sure if it was her imagination, or if it was simple instinct, but a warning thrill of danger brushed across her senses.

Her heart jumped as footsteps sounded coming towards her. Fast.

Movement flickered again in her peripheral vision, and this time she swung quickly enough to catch the outline of a figure moving across a rooftop in the distance. It vanished almost as quickly as she spotted it, but she was confident she hadn't been imagining things. The footsteps came closer, and suddenly Theac's stories about wild, unnatural creatures in the forest below came into her mind.

Fear tingled. She forced it away and calmed her mind in a quick, well-practiced move.

Her sais were halfway out of their sheaths when the owner of the footsteps appeared.

Theac.

He stumbled to a halt at the sight of her, of the sais glinting in the nearby light of a lamp, what must be the readiness in her stance to attack. It didn't take him long to steady though, gaze shifting from her sais to her face. "I was hoping to catch up with you. I'm uneasy, Captain."

"Me too. I..." she began, then, too far away to make out clearly, she saw two more figures, hanging from the railing of a walkway under the same roof. As her eyes strained to try and make out more detail, they clambered over the rail and disappeared into the shadows wherever the walkway led. A quick scan of her mental map of the citadel—they were heading in the direction of the main Falcon barracks.

Which was near the quarters of the queen and her two elder sons.

"Get back to the barracks!" She spun, voice urgent. "Wake the others. Arm yourselves and get to Prince Cuinn's quarters right away!"

"What is it?" Theac's hand reached for his axe.

"Just go," she barked. "And be quick!"

Her second didn't need telling twice. He turned and ran for the barracks. Talyn moved in the opposite direction, breaking into a run, heading straight for Cuinn's tower. As she did so, alarm bells began pealing throughout the palace.

Her heart thudded in her chest, anxiety twisting inside her. It took her wind away, made her legs burn with the effort of running. She couldn't fail again, not the first time she'd tried since—

The breath rasped in her throat as she forced her body into a sprint, pushing herself faster, faster. Within moments, she burst out of a pair of double doors and onto the swaying bridge leading across to Cuinn's tower. Someone was already there, a darkly cloaked figure, face covered by a hood.

"*Reckless, Tal.*" Sari's voice whispered through her mind. And she was. In her panic, she'd come sprinting into potential danger without even taking stock of her surroundings. The figure on the bridge stiffened as she appeared, and a flash of metal glinted silver in the moonlight.

More than a year since she'd been in a fight, and yet her body responded as if it were only yesterday.

Extended at a full run, she had no time to stop or swerve. Instead, she dived out over the railing of the bridge just as a knife hissed through the air where her head had been a moment earlier. She rolled in the air, free falling a few meters before reaching out to grab the railing of the nearest balcony.

Her arms and shoulders jarred, but she let go before the force was too strong, and falling again, she twisted out wide, flipping gracefully and angling her body towards a balcony lower down. She landed in a crouch, one palm slapping into the ground for balance.

Then she went still.

Her heart raced, body tingling and alive with adrenalin. A moment later she was on her feet, swinging onto the railing, and then *leaping* for the balcony above. Her fingers just caught the edge of it, and she brought her legs up, catapulting herself up and over before rolling into the shadows.

She looked up. The bridge to Cuinn's rooms wasn't far above now, the cloaked figure still there but now moving, peering over the railing, presumably looking for her. She remained still, hidden in the darkness of the balcony, until whoever it was straightened and moved back from the edge.

After waiting another full minute to ensure he didn't reappear, she climbed onto the railing and *leapt* upwards, using every bit of Callanan ability she had. It was just far enough. Her fingers scrabbled for a moment, then gripped the drainpipe on the outside of Cuinn's tower she'd been aiming for.

Taking a moment to catch her breath, she then shimmied up the drainpipe, moving ever closer to the underside of the bridge. Once she judged she was close enough, she braced her legs against the wall, pushed off hard and leapt up again, twisting mid-air.

Her jump took her above the height of the bridge and her searching gaze quickly found the cloaked figure on the bridge. Mid-flight, she pulled out her sai. It swung as she came down, slamming its hilt into the hooded head as her feet dropped. He crumpled without a sound.

She dropped to her knees, adrenalin and the unaccustomed energy she'd just used in those leaps making her momentarily lightheaded.

"*Cuinn.*" Sari's voice prompted her to push through the weakness.

Ignoring her trembling muscles, she shifted over to the prone body, giving him a good shake to make sure he was unconscious. Then, she took a deep, steadying breath, sheathed her sai, and ran for the tower door.

She shouldered it open without thought, only just catching the glint of a blade as it flew for her head. Desperately, she ducked aside so that the thrown knife flew past her face and out over the side of the bridge. "Shit!" she swore, freezing momentarily as a sharp burst of fear went through her.

"*Calm down, Talyn!*" Sari's voice was sharp.

Someone echoed her curse, and then came the bright flare of flint igniting. Tiercelin stood with the prince in a corner of the room.

"I'm sorry," Corrin stuttered in horror, pale face illuminated by the lamp he'd just lit. "I thought someone was coming to attack the prince."

She was jittery, too much adrenalin, too much strength drained from her muscles. Her mind wasn't as clear as it needed to be. Barging in like that had been stupid.

Focus. She'd trained for this.

"Don't be sorry." Talyn forced her voice to crispness and crossed the room to the windows. "You have excellent reflexes—that was my fault. Help me get these drapes closed. If there are any archers outside, I don't want them having a clean shot into this room."

"You think there are archers outside?" Tiercelin's voice shot up an octave in alarm, yet he didn't hesitate in moving towards the windows.

"We have to prepare for the possibility," she said. "Have you seen anyone out there?"

"No. We escorted the prince back here, and just as we were about to leave the alarms sounded, so we stayed," Corrin answered. He was taking a good look out each window as he closed the curtains. The fingers of his left hand tapped nervously against the knife in his belt. "The garden below is empty."

"Somebody *was* out there." She glanced back at the door. "Whoever it was tried to kill me on my way in. Theac's gone for Halun and Zamaril." Now that the interior of the room was invisible to anybody outside, Talyn turned to the prince. "Are you all right, Your Highness?"

"I'm fine," he said, silver-white wings rustling in what she thought might be irritation. "But I'd like to know what's going on. What do you mean someone out there tried to kill you?"

"I was going back to my room when I saw at least three strangers in dark clothes scrambling across a nearby rooftop. I came straight here, only to literally run into a man standing out there on the bridge. He's unconscious now, but I've no idea how many other intruders there might be or what they're after."

The prince lifted an eyebrow. "How exactly did he get unconscious?"

"He attacked me," she said flatly. "That rarely ends well for people."

"Were the men you saw heading this way, Captain?" Corrin asked.

"No." She shook her head. "But that doesn't mean there aren't others."

"So now we're being invaded I suppose?" Cuinn dropped onto his sofa with an exaggerated sigh. "Dear me, Captain, but you sound awfully paranoid. You probably just saw some winged folk too drunk to use their wings properly trying to get back to their rooms. There was a party tonight, remember?"

"With respect, Your Highness, if that's the case, then why are the alarm bells ringing?"

Talyn shot a surprised glance at Tiercelin. His words had been deferential, but firm.

Cuinn scowled. "Ravinire's as overly paranoid as your captain seems to be. Nobody is coming to kill me."

"Do you want me to go out and look around?" Corrin asked bravely. Both he and Tiercelin ignored the prince and looked to her. She wasn't sure whether that was a testament to growing trust in her, or a reflection of their attitude towards Cuinn. She suspected it was the latter.

"No." In the past she'd be out there, hunting, chasing the danger rather than let it come to her. But she was Kingshield now. It was her responsibility to stay and protect. She wasn't sure she liked the change. "Our job is the prince's safety. We'll stay here with him till Theac gets here with Halun and Zamaril. Then we can secure the area."

"Maybe we should go up to the bedroom," Corrin suggested hesitantly. "It's on the next level, but there's only one window in there and a single interior door to guard."

"How exactly do you know what my bedroom looks like, human?" Cuinn questioned.

"Good thought." Talyn nodded. Her turn to ignore the prince. "I—"

A knock at the door cut her off.

They all froze until Theac's voice barked out. "It's me."

She gestured silently for Tiercelin and Corrin to take the prince upstairs, and waited till they were gone before going to the door and answering it. Theac stood there, axe drawn. It was hard to read his expression in the darkness, but his voice was calm when he spoke. "Who's that?" He gestured to the unconscious man.

"Don't know. Attacked me with a knife though," she said quietly. "Come in."

Halun and Zamaril followed him inside. The big man had left his sword behind, instead clenching a wooden club. He seemed as steady as Theac. In contrast Zamaril was pale, no trace of his usual smirk on his face. Despite that, he held the sword in his hand steadily, exactly as he'd been taught. The beginnings of pride flickered in her.

"I ran into the Falcon on the way," Theac said. "He wasn't sure what had triggered the alarms, but he told us to stay with Prince Cuinn. He'll assign some Falcons to secure the outside of the tower and let us know as soon as it's safe."

"Good." She thought for a moment, mind running through King-shield procedure. "There are four floors and three entrances to this tower, so let's make sure we cover each one until the WingGuard get here," she said. "Zamaril, there's a roof entrance on the top floor, that's your job. Halun, you tie up our unconscious man on the bridge so he doesn't try anything if he wakes up, then leave him there and guard this front door from the inside. Theac, you watch the windows and garden entrance on the lower level. I will stay close to the prince up in the bedroom."

She had to hope that Ravinire would hurry securing the tower. She could only rely on herself and Theac to fight effectively if they were attacked. The others were still far too new in their training. Danger prickled under her skin, threatening to send her self-doubt into crip-pling paralysis. She'd been caught out unawares and barely avoided being killed.

She wasn't in fighting sharpness. She'd been lulled by the lack of obvious danger in Mithranar and a year away from battle. It took a few moments for her to realise the others had left and she was standing alone in the too-hot room. She swallowed, hating that her grip on her sai was slick with sweat.

"*Reacting is never a good way to face a threat,*" Sari's voice echoed. "*But dwelling on that won't help and you're doing fine so far. Stick with Prince Cuinn until more Falcons arrive.*"

Taking a firm grip on reason, Talyn climbed the stairs to the bedroom and sent Tiercelin and Corrin back down to join Theac and Halun on the lower floors.

She automatically scanned the room, noting with approval that her two Wolves had drawn the drapes close together over the windows and lit only a single lamp. Cuinn sat in a chair by one window, sprawled out comfortably, bored expression firmly in place. He was drinking from a tumbler half full of dark-coloured spirits. A massive bed sat in the centre of the room, covered in a thick doona. At its foot was an ornate chest, and an archway to her right led to a narrow space full of clothing. Near the window was a smaller version of the harpsichord he'd played earlier in the night.

Despite the size of the bed, the instrument and the chest, there was still plenty of open space in the palatial area. She thought her entire guest room might fit in it.

"Like what you see?" Cuinn inquired.

"I'd like for you to go and stand in that clothing closet for a moment," she said. "While I take a quick look out the window."

Surprisingly, he did as she asked without comment, though he did heave an overly dramatic sigh as he passed her. She padded over to the drapes and pulled them a fraction away from the glass. The alarms had stopped ringing a few moments earlier, and now an eerie silence filled the night.

Outside, the dim outline of the garden below was visible. She tensed as a shadow flickered, but then realised it was only a tree branch moving in the breeze. She stared till her eyes were straining but saw nothing to concern her.

"Anything?" Cuinn's voice in her ear made her almost jump through the roof. She swore before she could stop herself, then forced her body to calm.

"No," she said tightly. "Could you please stay away from the window?"

"Your man guarding the roof, what's his name? The thief?" Cuinn frowned. "He's terrified. I can feel it from here."

"Zamaril?"

"Yes." Cuinn's face was a mask of concentration, half hidden by the hair that fell like a curtain over the right side of his face. "He's spent his whole life hiding in the shadows, you see, running and hiding from danger. That's how a thief lives. Now he has to sit up there and confront the danger. He can't run and hide, like he's used to. That scares him to the core."

"You can understand his emotions, as well as read them?" Talyn stared at him, astonished despite herself and the situation. "That's an amazing gift."

"Far from a gift, Captain, his emotions are irritating." He sighed and dropped back into the chair, picking up his drink. "Could you do something about it, please?"

At least he said please. She nodded and checked the windows again. Nothing out there. "If you want me to deal with Zamaril, then you need to move into the closet. I'm not leaving you alone in here sitting right by the unlocked windows anyone could climb through."

"Fine." Taking the drink with him, he tucked his wings behind him and stepped into the closet.

Ensuring he was out of sight from both the windows and anyone glancing in from the hallway, she went to leave.

"You may want to tamp down on that annoyance of yours too." His voice drifted from the closet. "It's giving me a headache."

Biting back her scowl, she headed out of the room and up the stairs.

ZAMARIL WAS SITTING on the top floor, back against the wall, eyes trained on the entrance—a trapdoor through from the roof. A thick bolt had been slid across the opening from the inside. Nothing short of a battering ram was going to get through, but even so he was pale, face covered in a sheen of sweat.

"Everything all quiet up here?" she asked.

Zamaril started violently at her words, then relaxed a little when he saw who it was. He gave her a jerky nod.

"How are you doing?" she asked, moving to sit cross-legged beside him. Zamaril may be rude and smug at the best of times, but in his face she saw an echo of the panic that had descended upon her only moments earlier. It wasn't something she could ignore in someone else.

"I'm terrified." His voice shook, words laced with bitterness. "How am I supposed to be a Wolf when I'm scared all the time? This isn't me. I don't know why you picked me."

Talyn rested her head back against the wall, keeping her voice light. "My mother taught me something once. She's a warrior too, one of the Callanan," she said, a smile coming to her face at the thought of her mother. "She told me that courage isn't about not being scared. Courage is about being absolutely terrified, and still going forward."

He scoffed.

"Really," she insisted.

"You don't look scared." He looked away.

"That's just because I've had a lot more experience in managing my fear." She hesitated, eyes firmly fixed on the bolted trapdoor, but not really seeing it. Instead her gaze was filled with the memory of a thick forest and a body on the ground, green cloak tangled underneath it. "You asked me before how I knew what true fear was like. Every time I've fought before, I had..." Even now she couldn't say it aloud. Had to clear her throat before she could continue. "But things changed, and tonight is the first time I've faced a fight alone. I was scared. I'm *still* scared. I'm not even certain I can ever be what I was before. But right now it's my job to keep Prince Cuinn safe, so I pushed my fear away and I focused on my job."

A heavy silence sat between them. Then Zamaril shifted slightly, his shoulders straightening against the wall. "What happened?" he asked softly. Stripped of its cockiness and contempt, the thief's voice was a pleasant drawl.

She stared at her hands. "Maybe one day I'll be strong enough to tell you the story."

He nodded, accepting that, and she stood. "What matters to me is that you're here, Zamaril, and haven't run off, despite how scared you are."

He gave another short nod, gaze returning to the entrance. Talyn climbed back down the spiral stairs, nodding at Tiercelin and Halun who stood by the front door.

"Tiercelin, go and keep Zamaril company. He's getting bored. I think Halun can handle anybody trying to get through the front door."

The winged man rolled his eyes—he and Zamaril remained extremely reluctant wing mates—but Talyn gripped his arm as he turned to go. "Don't forget he's part of your wing. If twenty assassins come through that door, he'll be fighting at your shoulder, whether you like him or not."

Tiercelin sighed, nodded, and headed up the stairs.

CUINN WAS LEANING against the archway to the closet when Talyn returned. His head came up the moment she appeared. "This is ridiculous," he began. "Ravinire should have us secured by now. It's not good enough that I'm expected to sit around in the dark like this."

She went back over to the window, glanced outside. The garden remained dark and empty, the night sky clear. "I'm sure the Falcon is working as quickly as possible."

He snorted, brushing past her as he returned to his chair. "Well, at least you did something about Zamaril. His panic has dropped from overwhelming to manageable." He paused. "What did you say? He was very scared."

"I told him that courage wasn't about not being scared, it was about being scared and doing something anyway."

Cuinn flashed her a grin. The son of a bitch looked *amused.* "Would it surprise you to know that I'm not afraid right now?"

"No. You've convinced yourself that there's no reason anyone would come after you. Therefore, you don't believe you're in any danger."

"You're clever, Captain Dynan."

To that, she said nothing, turning her back on his snort of laughter and taking another look out the window. Still nothing. She wished Ravinire would hurry up.

"Why did your Kingshield send you here?"

She stared at him, window forgotten. He sounded genuinely curious, which meant he didn't know. "Somebody here requested it. Your mother, I assume."

"Don't look at me." He shrugged. "I had nothing to do with it."

"You don't find that odd?"

He grinned again, clearly having worked out how much it annoyed her. "I have very little to do with the workings of Mithranar, Captain. I prefer to be bored as infrequently as possible."

Refusing to be baited, Talyn went to the doorway, checking that the hall outside was clear. Where was Ravinire? Returning her attention to Cuinn, she leaned against the doorframe, a pose that looked casual but gave her a view of both the hallway and the windows, and injected curiosity into her voice. Maybe she could take this opportunity to learn more about the prince. "I heard you have a different father to your brothers. Who was yours?"

A lazy grin spread over his face. "No idea."

She lifted an eyebrow. "Hasn't your mother told you?"

"I've never cared much either way about my father." He shrugged. "And as far as I know, she never told anyone who he was. He died when I was young, apparently."

Increasing interest tore her attention away from the hallway. Cuinn's father had been a Dumnorix. Why had he died so young?

"The better question is why the queen kept his identity a secret?"

"It might just have been because she took him as her lover without marrying him."

"That doesn't seem to be much of a big deal here." Sari sounded dubious.

Good point. "How did he die?" she asked Cuinn.

"I think she said something about a fever. I wasn't paying a lot of attention at the time."

That didn't sound right. "A fever? And your magical healers couldn't help him?"

The prince let out a long-suffering sigh, his head falling back against the chair. "I assume it was a bad fever. Either way, he was never in my life. What does it matter who he was or how he died?"

A knock at the front entrance below interrupted before she could push further. "Stay where you are," she said, leaving the room.

It was Ravinire. Halun was opening the door to him and four of his Falcons as Talyn came down the stairs. Without a word to her, the Falcons dispersed throughout the tower.

"The situation has been contained," Ravinire said. "Three intruders were trying to get into one of our barracks storerooms—we're not sure why. We interrupted them in the attempt, but they all escaped. The palace is now secure, and we've doubled the Falcon guard. If you and your wing want to get some rest, my men will stay here to watch the tower until morning."

Talyn nodded, concealing her doubt. Three intruders went to all the effort of infiltrating the palace just to break into a barracks storeroom? That seemed unlikely. "Are you sure it was just the three intruders?"

"A thorough search of the area found nobody else."

"What about the man outside?"

Ravinire raised his eyebrows. "There's nobody out there."

She couldn't help the glance behind him through the open door— the bridge was empty. "I was attacked attempting to enter the tower earlier. I managed to contain the threat, but we had no spare resources to watch him. Last we saw, he was unconscious on the bridge outside." She hesitated. "That makes at least four intruders, sir."

For the first time since she'd met him, Ravinire's impassive demeanour shifted, something like unease flickering across his face. "Are you saying one of these intruders tried to enter Prince Cuinn's rooms?"

"I'm not sure, actually, sir," she said. "When I arrived, he appeared to be keeping a lookout, not trying to get in. As soon as I dispatched him and entered Prince Cuinn's tower, there were no further attempts to gain entrance that we could tell."

"All right, we'll do another search of the area around this tower." He rubbed his forehead, the only sign her information disconcerted him. His voice was brisk and unconcerned. "Get some rest, Captain."

She hesitated. Ravinire looked impatient to be gone, but she had a lot more questions for him. "Can we speak further in the morning, sir?"

"I'll send a messenger for you when I have the time." He nodded. "Good job tonight, Captain."

Ravinire departed. Theac, Corrin, Tiercelin and Zamaril appeared from above and below and she quickly relayed Ravinire's news. "You did excellent work this evening," she told them. "Go on back to the barracks and get some sleep. Tomorrow morning we'll review tonight's events and identify areas where we can do better next time."

Tiercelin's wings rustled. "I might just go up and let Prince Cuinn know what's happening, if that's okay, Captain?"

"Sure." She waved him on. It saved her from having to talk to the prince again. "Theac, can I have a moment?"

The Wolves dispersed without further comment. Now that the adrenalin had faded, they looked tired and worn. Corrin's hands were shaking, and Zamaril's gaze hadn't left the ground, even as he walked away. Halun tailed behind, silent as always.

Talyn fell into step beside Theac as they followed the others over the bridge, relaying to him what she'd told Ravinire.

He frowned. "So you don't think he was trying to get in?"

"That's not the impression I got. When I ran out onto the bridge, he was facing towards me, not the tower door. Obviously he was ready to fight, because he threw that knife at me pretty quick, but I don't think he was trying to get in."

"Almost like he was *watching* the door? That doesn't make sense, Captain," Theac muttered. "None of what happened tonight makes any sense. Three intruders break into the palace and go straight for a barracks storeroom while one hangs out on the bridge leading to Prince Cuinn's tower?"

"I agree." She sighed. "Hopefully the Falcon will have some more information for me tomorrow."

They reached the junction where Theac needed to turn off to head to the barracks. He stopped and cleared his throat. "I thought they did well enough tonight, Captain."

"Agreed," she said. "Zamaril was terrified, though. Prince Cuinn sent me up there to try and calm him down, his emotions were that strong. Despite his terror he stuck around, and I didn't expect that."

"If he runs, he's got nowhere to go," Theac pointed out.

"I'm not forcing anyone to be here," she said sharply.

"I know that's not your intention, Captain, but we've got nowhere else to go. That pretty much gives us no choice but to be here."

"Maybe." She nodded. "But I'm not the reason none of you have another choice."

"That doesn't mean a thing," he said. "You're a fair captain, and skilled too, and I'll never forget that you gave me another chance. For me, it's not so bad, I've always been a soldier. But for Halun, Zamaril and Corrin? They're young, they should have other opportunities, dreams, but instead they're human in Mithranar. That gives them the choice of starving on the streets, resorting to crime, or being a warrior in this unit."

She huffed, trying to keep the incredulity from her voice. "You can't tell me that all humans here have no choice apart from starving on the streets or resorting to crime?"

"No," he said thoughtfully. "There are plenty who do well for themselves, own their own businesses or have a trade. But a good many don't, and for them, life can be miserable."

"You're speaking from experience." It wasn't a question.

"I was lucky. I got into the City Patrol," Was all he said.

"All right, Theac, you've made your point." Her voice had an edge. She was exhausted and wrung out from her own emotional battles of the evening, and the last thing she wanted was to be blamed for things that weren't her fault. "Is there anything else you'd like to make me aware of?"

He had the grace to look chastened and dropped his gaze to his feet. "It's just… seems to me you're a good sort, Captain. Not your fault you don't understand how things work here. I just thought you should know, that's all."

Now she was the one to feel chastened. He hadn't been blaming her, just trying to help her understand the men in her wing a little better. He'd been doing what she wanted from him from day one—to be her second. "Thank you, Theac," she told him quietly. "For your trust."

He nodded. "You'd best go get some rest. It's been a long night."

She watched him go, then turned to trudge back towards her guest room. Now that it was all over her muscles ached in protest, and the calf she'd twinged running through the streets of Dock City on her first day hadn't much liked her Callanan acrobatics under the tower bridge.

"He's still alive."

Talyn scoffed at Sari's attempt to be encouraging but she didn't reply as she unlocked her door and went inside, heading straight for the soft bed.

She didn't have the heart for it tonight.

CHAPTER 21

*T*wo days passed without Ravinire sending for Talyn as she'd requested. Annoyed, she went to his office in the barracks to see him on the third day. Impatient for information, she'd already spoken to Zamaril.

"They weren't thieves." He'd scoffed the moment she suggested it.

"How do you know?"

"Thieves don't work together in harmonious groups. And even if they did, I don't know many thieves in Dock City with the skills to break unseen into the palace," he said. "Not to mention that no thief with that level of skill is going to try and break into a barracks storeroom. They'd go for the treasury offices or the royal quarters where the family keeps their expensive jewellery."

It was a convincing argument.

"Right, not thieves," she'd said dryly.

He flashed a smirk at her, the cockiness in his voice a complete mirror to the terror that had been there the night before. "I could ask around discreetly, talk to a few of my old contacts, find out if maybe there's a new crew operating?"

She'd matched his smirk with a raised eyebrow. "Told you you'd be useful in the Wolves, Zamaril."

She was reflecting on the sour look he'd given her when a young Falcon showed her through to Ravinire's office. As soon as she stepped inside it was clear that he had no time for her.

"Captain," Ravinire greeted her distractedly as she walked in. "How can I help you?"

Talyn watched him shuffling through three piles of parchment, a slight frown creasing his eyebrows as he failed to find what he was looking for. "I asked to see you to discuss further what happened the other night. I don't mean to be rude sir, but it's been three days."

Ravinire finally looked up, irritation deepening the frown. "I spoke to Prince Cuinn the morning after. If he hasn't relayed our conversation to you, that's not my concern."

"As overall commander of the WingGuard, the physical safety of the royal family is your responsibility sir, is that correct?" Talyn kept her voice polite.

"And the integrity of our borders, yes." Ravinire went back to rifling through parchment. His tone was distant, his focus clearly not on their conversation.

"Then you are responsible for Prince Cuinn's safety. You and I both know that Prince Cuinn does not take his guard seriously."

"That's his prerogative," Ravinire said, a hint of impatience colouring his tone now.

"So what exactly am I doing here?" She paused deliberately, leaving the edge in her voice. "Sir?"

Ravinire finally pushed aside the piles and looked up. "There's little to tell. Nobody got a good look at the intruders. They managed to infiltrate the palace but didn't get close to the queen or any of the princes."

"Do you know for certain how many there were?"

"We're fairly confident there were none but the three we interrupted trying to break into the storeroom."

"Plus the one that threw a knife at me," she said pointedly. "There's only the single bridge over to the palace and your WingGuard passwords are changed regularly. The intruders I saw were human, as was the man who attacked me. How did they get in?"

Ravinire ran a hand through his short-cropped hair. "The Falcons on guard were lax. We haven't faced a serious threat from anywhere for decades. The sentries weren't paying close enough attention."

She nodded, accepting that, as utterly incomprehensible as it was. "What was in the storeroom they were trying to get into?"

"Straw dummies—we use them often in training drills."

"Straw dummies?"

Talyn let a beat of silence fill the space between her and the Falcon, not missing the way his eyes had flicked downwards or his sudden slight shift in the chair. "Three human intruders skilled enough to get into the palace unseen tried to steal some straw dummies?" she clarified.

"It's what we store in that room, Captain," he said flatly.

"Sure. And what else did they store in that room?"

"Exactly." She considered. *"Or* used *to store in there?"*

She surveyed him, trying to decide how far to push. "Sir, my understanding is that there would be few thieves in Dock City skilful enough to accomplish what these intruders did, and that even if there were, it would be extremely unlikely for them to work as a group."

"You are well informed," he said. "And right."

"Then who else would have motive and ability to break into the palace?" She paused, deciding to be direct. "And why? We both know they weren't after straw dummies."

Ravinire spoke reluctantly. "I am equally confused, Captain."

He'd told her everything he knew, or at least everything he was willing to tell her. Not that that reassured her. For the overall commander of Mithranar's army, he knew disturbingly little about a blatant breach of palace security. "If you're interested in my thoughts, I got the distinct impression that the other night was a reconnaissance of sorts."

His gaze narrowed. "You think the intruders were testing how easy it would be to get in?"

"As you say, they went for a storeroom rather than anywhere valuable, and disappeared—successfully, I might add—the moment the alarms were sounded." Talyn shrugged. "But whoever they are, they've now learned how far they could get into the palace unseen, and how you responded when they were discovered."

"Even so, the guard is now doubled and those watching the bridge will not be so lax again."

"Good. But someone got to Prince Cuinn's tower too, and so far I've had no luck in being allowed to surround him with a guard detail."

"You're doing well with your wing," Ravinire said grudgingly, and with enough surprise it was clear he hadn't expected such progress. Testing her indeed. "But that doesn't make them a sufficient detail yet. I will continue to do my best with the Falcons until they are up to scratch."

"Yes, sir." She rose. He was done and she was reluctant to push further. "If you'd like any help with the investigation into the intruders, I'd be happy to assist."

Ravinire stared at the window to his left. "Good day, Captain."

The dismissal was clear, so she saluted and left without another word.

FRUSTRATION TOYED WITH FEAR, the warring emotions tightening her chest. She had the skills to find out what had happened and who had been behind it, but either Ravinire didn't trust her enough to use her help, or he didn't recognise what she was. And the worst part was, a tiny part of her was *glad* he hadn't taken her offer... if he didn't ask, she couldn't fail.

Both emotions continued to twist through her as she walked back to her room. With five untrained guards and a commander unwilling to engage her help or even tell her everything he knew, she was essentially operating blind.

An armed man had gotten to Cuinn's tower unseen. He could do it again and she wouldn't even know. She couldn't protect Cuinn properly like that.

The shadows of falling dusk slid over the open walkway outside her room, and her steps slowed. Standing there, she took a deep breath. She and Sari had operated successfully with little information before and she did have some details.

The intruders had been human.

With the focus and work required to prepare the Wolves for the dinner, the progress she'd made in her other mission had been pushed to the back of her mind. But now she wondered. Perhaps that could be another source of answers.

Ducking into her room, she changed into civilian clothing, waited till darkness had properly fallen, then went out again.

CHAPTER 22

*T*he Shadowhawk strolled through the evening streets, hands deep in his pockets, shoulders hunched forward. Even when moving through Dock City without the mask, his instinct was always to blend in, to stay unnoticed.

The bridge across the Rush from the Poor Quarter was busy—full of those who had managed to find work in the other quarters of the city heading home for the night, many of them haggard and dirty. The jobs available were usually only those others didn't want to do.

Not to mention the izerdia workers struggling home after surviving another day extracting the priceless sap from the forest trees. Apart from the conscripts serving sentences for whatever minor crime a corrupt Patrolman had trumped up, the volunteers were generally all from the Poor Quarter—those that had no option other than resorting to crime to survive.

And anyone who'd had business in the Poor Quarter during the day was getting out before night fell and it became a dangerous place to be. The Shadowhawk often headed to his apartment from the Poor Quarter. It provided a route that was less noticeable and had the added benefit of giving anyone who got it into their heads to follow him the impression that the famous criminal lived in a nest of criminals.

Out of habit, he took a circuitous route through the Market Quarter to ensure he wasn't followed before finally pushing open the wooden door to the tall, narrow building housing his apartment in the Dock Quarter. The staircase creaked under his boots, but none of the other occupants were around to notice him as he reached his door and unlocked it. It gave the usual groan as he pushed it open, then took the usual complicated jiggling to get it to close properly.

He took one step into the room before freezing, his heart thudding so hard in his chest he thought it might burst.

Someone was standing on the other side of the room, leaning casually against the wall.

It wasn't Navis.

Silence filled the space, thickened, turned so heavy it constricted his chest. His fingers curled, searching his pocket uselessly for his mask. It was too late for that. The person shifted and metal glinted through the faint moonlight coming in through a gap in the sheets over the windows.

"Not the nicest place for the lair of a famous criminal."

For a moment he was struck utterly dumb. He knew that voice, recognised the face as soon as she stepped away from the wall. How had she found him?

"You've been dealing with inept WingGuard and even more incompetent City Patrol." She laughed softly. "I'm Callanan. It took me a matter of weeks to find you."

He summoned his voice, kept it a balance of indignant and firm. "I have no idea what you're talking about. Who are you, and why are you in my apartment?"

She regarded him with a cool sapphire gaze. "If you'd like to play that game, I'll call the City Patrol now and you can have this conversation with them." She stepped closer. "I know you're the Shadowhawk. Denying it will only waste both of our time."

His eyes closed as he took a deep, slow breath, using that time to anchor himself and take a firm grip on who he was. Then his eyes snapped open and his gaze met hers unflinchingly. "If that's what you believe, why haven't you turned me over to the City Patrol already?" He moved slowly towards the table by the wall. Underneath it he kept hidden a—

"I already found the dagger," she said. "And the ones under your mattress. Nice pair of knives in the privy too, though I have to say, they're certainly the most pungent weapons I've ever encountered. Not to mention the stash of unique arrows in the floorboards."

"You might be Callanan," he said, giving up on searching for weapons. Part of him was panicking, recognising too late how badly he'd underestimated her, how badly he'd overestimated himself. He'd relaxed too quickly, dismissed her as a concern when there'd been no immediate consequences to her arrival. Still, the rest of him was slowly regaining control. He'd dealt with worse than this before and survived. "But there's a reason I've stayed alive and uncaptured so long. Some might call your coming here alone foolish."

"Some would," she said, an odd bitterness to her voice. "But I don't much care about foolish these days."

"Why are you here instead of the Patrol?" His initial burst of fear was fading rapidly. If she'd intended having him arrested, she wouldn't have come alone. And he knew more than she thought he did. His confidence rapidly reasserted itself.

"I have questions, I need answers, and the City Patrol aren't going to get them for me."

He barked a laugh. "I can't possibly imagine what you think I know that could help you."

"There was a break in at the citadel three nights ago. Four humans. Was it you?"

The question was blunt, shot at him without preamble or hesitation. Genuine astonishment filled his voice, the words spilling out before he could consider them. "Why would I break into the citadel?"

She took a step closer, eyes raking his face. It wouldn't help her. He was a master at hiding his expression, hiding *himself*. Something flickered over her face—realisation of that maybe?—and she shifted away. "If you don't help me, I *will* go to the City Patrol. Or perhaps if I present you gift-wrapped to the Falcon, he'll start trusting me enough to tell me what I need to know."

"As long as you don't give me to the Dock Quarter Patrol. They couldn't get information out of a chatty drunk," he said.

A half smile flashed over her face. His own lips curled up in response. "I don't have to give you anything, Captain Dynan. You're not going to turn me over to the City Patrol, and once you leave this place tonight you'll never find me here again."

"Is that so?" Her tone had been nothing but even since he arrived, leaking no trace of what she was thinking. It appeared well practiced, like she'd done this many times before. But at the same time, he caught a hint of discomfort about her—she kept glancing briefly to her side, as if expecting someone to be there. "You mean you'll go to your real bolt hole?"

For a moment utter panic filled him at the thought she might have followed him long enough to discover... but no, this conversation would be going differently if she had. So he said nothing and she gave him another pointed look. "You don't live here. This place is for appearances only. An extra layer of protection? Or something else going on?" She wandered closer. "Either way, I can find out if I put my mind to it."

He needed to change the subject, slide away from her attack and regain control. "You claim to know a lot about me, but I know more than you think too." He walked over to the wall, deliberately turning his back on her. Reaching up to slide a rotting plank away from its spot, he pulled out the dagger inside and turned back to her. She didn't move. Her expression didn't change. "How would the humans you're trying to train feel to find out you're royalty? Might ruin the precious trust you're trying to build there, no?"

"I have no idea what you're—"

"Save it, Captain." He considered the knife in his hand. "I hear things about you too. Like the way you speak to Prince Cuinn, the way you address your wing so confidently. I hear that you walk around in all that splendour up at the citadel without a hint of discomfort, almost as if you're used to such wealth and power. And now? Seeing you in person, the casual arrogance of your stance. I was guessing at royalty. I thought at least nobility, but that reaction confirms my guess was right."

Despite the faintest of flinches the first time he'd said *royalty*, she really was masterful at hiding her reactions. The silence between them deepened. She wasn't going to give him anything. For the moment he buried his astonishment at how right he'd been—for now he needed to focus on maintaining the upper hand in this conversation.

His voice dropped to a murmur. "What *are* the Acondors up to, bringing a Dumnorix to Mithranar to protect their useless playboy prince?"

Her eyes flashed, and she glanced sideways again, as if searching for someone standing there. He stared. "They don't know? Why are you really here, then? To spy?"

"Who broke into the citadel?" The cool tone was back, her equilibrium restored as if it had never vanished.

Their gazes locked, neither willing to back down. In the end he gave her a faint smile. "I had nothing to do with what happened the other night. That's for free, Captain. Now, you leave me alone from here on out or the Falcon learns who you are. Clear?"

"I won't be threatened by a criminal, and I certainly won't be leveraged by one." She shrugged, glancing around. "Move away from this place and I'll find you again if I need to."

"You're bluffing."

A matching cool smile curled her mouth. "You want me to believe you're going to walk up to the citadel and tell them what you know? And expect Ravinire to believe you?" A beat passed before she continued. "You need to stop forgetting I'm not City Patrol or WingGuard, Shadowhawk. I'll best you each time. There was a time I did nothing *but* hunt criminals like you."

"Then why not turn me over?"

"I'm Kingshield now. All I care about is that you're not a threat to my charge. Steer clear of Prince Cuinn and you and I don't have a problem."

Without waiting for him to respond she turned and strode for the window, swinging herself up and through with an easy agility he'd never seen before. A cool breeze drifted through the gap she'd left in the sheet covering it.

A long moment passed. Then, slowly, he turned and placed the dagger back in its hiding spot in the wall. She'd left his other weapons in a pile on the bed in the other room. When he reached down to pick one up, it took him a moment to realise his hand was shaking.

She'd found him. Easily. Now she was a threat to him—a serious one. But he wasn't as afraid as his brain told him he should be. He wasn't sure what he felt.

They'd sent a real warrior. And not just a warrior. She was smart, fearless and knew how to hunt. A protector of the highest calibre.

For the WingGuard.

Why?

CHAPTER 23

*T*iercelin frowned in concentration. He stood on the edge of the drop, grey wings half-furled and rigid, palm out in front of him. A hiss sounded in the air and, for the briefest of moments, a silver light flashed in front of him. It vanished in the next second.

"I did it!" he whooped, flinging his wings out, almost smacking Talyn in the head and knocking her off the edge.

She stepped nimbly aside and nodded in approval. "I told you that you could do it. It just takes hard work and practice."

His expression of delight turned to one of astonishment as he regarded her. "How can you do that?"

"Do what?"

He gestured to her feet. She glanced down and saw nothing but treetops—in avoiding his outflung wings, she'd stepped right to the edge of the precipice, a drop easily far enough to kill her if she fell.

"I've never seen a human who can walk so close to the edge without fear," he continued.

"No offence, Tiercelin, but I don't think you winged folk take the opportunity to notice much at all about your human countrymen. Besides, I'm Callanan. Agility is in our makeup."

He shook his head. "You must have *some* winged folk blood in you, to balance so casually on the ledge. We're born with that instinct. Humans aren't."

"I don't know what to tell you. My father is Mithranan, but he's human, and all Callanan could do what I'm doing right now."

"Then your Callanan have some winged folk heritage. It makes sense—it would explain how you have our warrior magic too." He frowned in thought, eyes intent on her face. "Even so, there's something else about you, Captain. It niggles at me."

She shrugged. As much as Tiercelin protested that all he wanted was to be a successful Falcon and master his warrior magic, she was beginning to suspect he had the heart of a scholar. So much fascinated him. "Maybe your winged folk lived in Calumnia or Conmor generations ago, and their bloodline pops up every now and then in those we recruit for the Callanan." She wondered what he would think if she pointed out that Corrin—and probably Zamaril—had that blood too.

"Wouldn't that be fascinating?" He sounded entranced by the idea. "Do you have records back home that you could use to trace the ancestry of your Callanan?"

"We do, but I'm not sure they'd go far enough back. And while that idea is the easiest explanation, it doesn't make complete sense. If winged folk heritage was the source of Callanan magic, then why do we have only a single ability? Why no magical ability to sense and impart emotion, or to heal? And your magic doesn't explain all the other magic in the world."

"A good question. Perhaps the winged folk magic has become so diluted that's the only way it comes out now?" His brow furrowed in thought, but after a few moments he looked up, giving her a sheepish look. "Speaking of magic, Captain, I thought it might be a good idea if I went back to lessons with the winged healers. We all get taught our magic to a basic standard during our schooling as youths, but I never developed it any further. Our wing doesn't have its own healer, after all."

She had to fight the urge to smile. "I think that's a great idea, Tiercelin."

Halun approached, interrupting the slight awkwardness that had descended. He clapped Tiercelin on the back in a friendly manner, and the birdman tottered forward, almost going off the edge. Halun's expression remained serious, but she didn't miss the twinkle of amusement in his brown eyes. Tiercelin scowled, but there was no anger in it.

"I'm surprised to see you still here, Halun," she said.

He shifted uncomfortably. "I like to watch the pretty man here practice his tricks."

Tiercelin preened. "You are welcome to watch anytime."

Halun scowled, and Talyn's gaze was caught by the dark green tattoo on his cheek. She'd wondered about it multiple times since first meeting him, but hadn't gotten around to asking about it. "Why did you get that? Does it mean something?" she asked.

His entire body went rigid at her question, eyes dropping to the ground. Was that *shame* on his face? She was sick at the thought she'd caused such a response and searched desperately for something to say to take it back.

"Captain, I thought this extra lesson was for *me*, not a chance for idle chat with the humans." Tiercelin's voice hit the perfect note of high-born haughtiness, not unlike it had many times since the Wolves had come together. Halun mumbled something—an apology, she thought—and walked quickly away.

She glanced around to see Tiercelin watching him go, something approaching sympathy on his face. Had the winged man just deliberately intervened to let Halun escape gracefully? Before she could ask, he swung back to catch her looking at him.

"It's the Montagni slave mark," he explained. "We've noticed it's a touchy subject for the big human. I wouldn't bring it up again."

Her annoyance at Tiercelin's high-handed manner vanished, shock taking its place. "You don't actually mean he was a slave?"

Tiercelin shrugged. "Sure. Before he came to Mithranar—escaped here, I suspect. A slave from birth, from the stretching on the tattoo." He sobered. "You think your king is powerful on his Twin Thrones, but he's nothing compared to the power and might wielded by the Montagni ahara."

"I know about Montagn, Tiercelin," she said, a tad impatiently. "We might be much farther south, but we are aware of the rest of the world in the Twin Thrones."

He grinned down at her. "Didn't know they had slaves, did you?"

"I did," she admitted. "I just didn't realise Halun... how many of them are there in the Montagni empire?"

"Thousands," Tiercelin said. "They're either born into slavery, or bonded to it when they commit a crime, or cross the wrong person."

Talyn grimaced. "I don't understand why anyone would want to enslave another human being?"

"Free labour," Tiercelin said simply. "The kingdom would collapse without the slave labour that holds it up."

"The idea is monstrous." Sari was suddenly loud and strong in her head. Talyn winced, but she didn't disagree. Her own disgust welled up and churned with Sari's, close to overwhelming.

At the look of horror that had to be written all over her face, Tiercelin gave a little shrug. "It's part of the reason Montagn is so powerful. We've considered adopting the same practices here in Mithranar once or twice before."

"What?" she snapped.

That scholarly look was back on his face. "It's true. Previous monarchs have considered enslaving part of the human population, especially to help with increasing izerdia extraction. After all, they are inferior to us."

He'd gone too far, and she fixed him with a hard, uncompromising look. "You don't actually believe that."

Interestingly, Tiercelin didn't look away from her stare, and there was honesty in his voice when he said, "We can fly, we can use magic. In some areas, we *are* superior to the humans, Captain."

"Yet I think you'll find that in other areas, human folk are superior to winged folk, Tiercelin," Talyn said firmly. "And you have some flawed assumptions. *I* am human, yet I have your magic. And one day, so will Corrin and Zamaril."

He laughed, clearly amused at the thought and not believing her for a second. "If you say so."

"I think we're done here." Voice hard, she went to walk away.

He called her back. "No matter what I think about winged folk compared to humans, I don't believe in slavery, Captain."

She nodded, turning back to face him. "That's a start."

"They mock me, you know, all the time," he said quietly. "My family thinks less of me for answering to you, for having humans as wing mates."

She didn't reply, waiting for him to continue. He hesitated, clearly searching for the right words. "When you first told me that you could teach me to use my warrior magic, I was excited because I figured that as soon as I learned, I could transfer out of the Wolves and be a Falcon again."

"I would be surprised if you hadn't thought that. In your position, I probably would have too," she said, meaning it. Tiercelin was winged, and his friends and family were winged. It wouldn't be easy to be thought less of by those you loved most. It was why she kept her grief and self-doubt so deeply hidden. If she truly was broken, if she could never be again what she once was, she was desperately afraid of her family, her brother and sister warriors, knowing it.

"I'm not like them, not entirely," he said. "But I am one of them. I am out of place here."

Talyn took a breath. "Tiercelin, it seems to me that you belong in a place where the people around you respect you for who you are, respect your choices, and offer you friendship not based on material things, but on your worth as a person. I understand if you want to transfer out of the Wolves, and I won't try to stop you. But the way you describe your friends and family? That doesn't sound like a place where you belong."

He couldn't entirely hide the hurt in his eyes. "I'd best go. I'll see you later, Captain."

And with a rustling of wings he was gone, leaping high into the air and out of sight.

· · ·

SHE WAS STILL MUSING on the idea of slaves as she returned to her rooms that evening. Her mind flashed back to the conversation she'd had with Leviana and Cynia before leaving Ryathl—their news that the Callanan were going to establish a liaison post in Montagn, and their surprise that the Twin Thrones would look to establish any kind of official link with Montagn that could be perceived as tacit support for slavery.

"No more odd than the Callanan suddenly developing an interest in a criminal in Mithranar."

She threw herself onto her bed, considering that. "You think they're connected? From what I've learned so far, the Shadowhawk doesn't appear in any way tied to the Twin Thrones. He's a criminal, nothing more, and talking to him directly didn't give me any reason to think otherwise."

"Even so. It's two odd things happening at the same time." A pause, then, *"and despite how unassuming he looked, the Shadowhawk is more than he appears. You saw that too."*

Unease and guilt flickered in her at the memory of that interaction. Sari was right again. On the surface, the Shadowhawk had seemed nothing more than a street criminal with his lank brown hair and quick, shifting gaze, and he'd most definitely underestimated her, but she'd made the same mistake. She shuddered at how quickly and accurately he'd sized her up and guessed her identity. And now he had something on her.

"How am I even talking to you?" Bitter grief swelled up. She so desperately wanted this back, the way she and Sari had worked together, planned together, thought together. But this voice that remained, her grief, it only served to give tantalising glimpses of things that could never be.

Sari's voice didn't answer. She was gone as abruptly as she had come. Talyn wrenched her mind back to Montagn and the Callanan. She wondered if Leviana and Cynia had ended up applying to go—she couldn't decide if it was a good idea or not. Leviana was likely to take one look at a poor slave and start a war right there to free them all.

That coaxed a small smile to her face. There'd been a time when she'd have dived right into that fight too, filled with confidence and strength and a skill that was unmatched amongst her peers. She still wasn't able to accept that time was gone.

At some point she fell asleep, her mind still tangling with slaves in Montagn, criminals in Mithranar and how they all tied in with the Callanan.

SHE WOKE SUDDENLY, eyes snapping open. The room was still and silent around her, the blue light of early dawn through the window providing enough dim light to reassure her the room was empty.

Still. There had been something.

Wide awake now despite how deeply she'd been asleep, she sat up and pushed back the covers, swinging her legs out of bed. Her bare soles had just touched the floor when she saw it.

A torn piece of parchment lying on the table by her bed. On it was a single letter—an S—bisected by a jagged lightning bolt. Weighting it down was a carved wooden arrow, fletched in black feathers. Her heart thudded. He'd been in her room while she slept. Close enough to slit her throat if he'd chosen. The parchment was a threat, proof that he could get to her whenever he wanted.

A little smile curled her face.

No, this was no simple street criminal, no matter how perfectly he pulled off that look. The Shadowhawk wasn't going to be easy prey at all.

CHAPTER 24

*T*alyn took the Shadowhawk's warning to heart—at least in the short term. She was confident she could find him again if needed, but he had leverage over her, and his threat had been clear.

Their brief encounter hadn't done much to answer her questions. The surprise in his voice when she'd questioned him about the break in she'd judged to be genuine, yet he'd promptly then demonstrated his ability to get in and out of a guestroom in the palace without detection.

Answers, no. A better sense of who the Shadowhawk was? Most definitely. A master at hiding, yet one that had grown complacent pitting himself against the lazy Patrol and incompetent WingGuard. And despite that, despite every snippet she'd gathered about him indicating he worked alone, he had a network of good sources.

To have deduced what he had about her... he was clever. And much more than what he seemed.

No, ultimately there was no value in pushing the issue and going after him again—she'd written to the Callanan and told them what she'd discovered, and until they wrote back with more instructions, it would be wiser to leave it.

So she placed her full focus on the Wolves and shaping them into a decent protective guard.

So far it was working.

Inch by gruelling inch, they were beginning to meld into a unit. As the weeks passed, Twomonth becoming Threemonth and then Fourmonth, their strength and stamina improved, and they began to handle their weapons with a semblance of skill.

One particularly hot afternoon, Talyn sparred with Zamaril, the wood of their training swords clacking loudly across the yard. Sweat ran down both their faces. Half her attention was focused on inwardly cursing how damn humid it was. It was like sparring in soup.

Then, with a quick flick of his wrist, Zamaril was suddenly inside her guard. He stopped, stunned, and Talyn recovered quickly, smacking him on the shoulder with the flat of her blade. Irritated at her lapse, the hit was harder than she'd intended.

"Next time you get through an opponent's guard like that, don't stop and gape like a fish," she said as he scowled and rubbed his shoulder.

"You let me beat you," he challenged.

"I have too much pride for that. You got through on your own."

His return scowl was half-hearted, and she caught the glimmerings of pride in his pale blue eyes. Of them all, Zamaril was the hardest to train. He had no confidence in himself aside from his skills as a thief and refused to let go of the idea that he was useless to them. Talyn made a point of acknowledging his every achievement, doggedly trying to instil some self-esteem into the man.

"Good work today. Off you go and do some more practice with Theac."

She'd been keeping a close eye on Zamaril and Corrin to see whether their suspected Callanan potential would emerge. The thief, because he'd spent years being light on his feet and honing the natural athleticism and agility of his body, had shown particular talent for the dancing movements of swordplay. The fact he'd just gotten through her guard, after two months training, gave her hope. She might be rusty, but she was still a fully trained and experienced warrior.

Halun, brawny hulk that he was, had the physique and strength for the heavy battle-axe. Theac had begun lessons with him, and he had shown definite aptitude for the weapon. Talyn's second was delighted —as hard as he tried to hide it. Axmen had been few and far between in the City Patrol.

Corrin's talent had already been clear—knife work. He was also a quick learner with a sword and was beginning to display the athleticism Zamaril already had in spades, something that would likely improve in leaps and bounds once he stopped growing and settled into his gangly frame.

Tiercelin, while not possessing the natural aptitude of Zamaril and Corrin, or the experience of Theac, nonetheless had the superior vision of the winged folk. So she'd tested him with a bow.

She'd been surprised to learn there weren't any archers in Mithranar. An archer gave their wing a long-distance capability, an advantage given how severely under-resourced they were. Theac had looked askance when Talyn had asked why the Falcons didn't carry bows.

"Why would they need that?"

It had seemed obvious to her. "Their single advantage in battle is their ability to fly. As soon as they're on the ground fighting with the swords they carry, they're no different than any other soldier."

A surprised flicker had crossed his face. "That's why you've got Tiercelin using those wings of his against us in sparring."

"If he doesn't learn to use them, he'll only find them a hindrance and a vulnerability in a real fight."

"You keep saying you made me your second because I'm the only experienced one here." Theac cleared his throat. "But truth is, Captain, I've only ever been in one-on-one fights, the occasional brawl. Nothing like a battle you'd see in war."

It meant she was the only one who could teach Tiercelin. The bow wasn't her favourite weapon, but she'd developed the marksmanship skills that all Aimsir possessed during her youth. The weapon the Aimsir used, however, was a smaller recurve bow, and she hadn't used one in years. Because of Tiercelin's well-developed upper body musculature necessary to support his wings, he was better suited to the longbow, which had longer range and more power.

Zamaril now engaged with Theac, she put aside her training sword and wandered over to where Tiercelin was patiently stringing his new longbow.

"Halun's been helping me out." Tiercelin looked up at her approach. "The arrows we've been using felt a little unbalanced. He carved me these new ones last night. What do you think?"

Talyn took one and balanced it in her hand. "It certainly feels about right. Keep working with Halun, he's very talented."

"Thanks, Captain." The tone of respect he used warmed her.

"Captain!" The sharp note in Theac's voice had her turning quickly.

Brightly coloured wings fluttered in the sky as a group of winged folk descended into the yard. Talyn gestured sharply, and the Wolves stopped what they were doing to come and stand behind her in a straight line.

She counted seven winged men, five of whom were Falcons. Their teal jerkins had scarlet slashes across their shoulders, which Ravinire's Falcons, the queen's detail, didn't—these were from a different wing.

"Prince Cuinn's brothers," Theac murmured, his voice pitched so only Talyn could hear it. Her gaze went instantly to the two not wearing uniforms, and not just because of Theac's words. They stood out from the rest in the way Cuinn often did.

The one on the left was taller than her charge, and broader across the shoulders, his musculature evident underneath his fitted jerkin. Dark wings hung from his back, a beautiful ebony shimmer sparkling through where the feathers caught sunlight. He was the first to step forward, and the coiled strength and power in his movement marked him clearly as the elder brother—Mithanis Acondor.

So this was the prince of night.

"You must be the Calumnian warrior." A hint of mockery dripped from a voice that was otherwise smooth as silk. Odd, that one brother's voice could be so full of laughter and music while the other's held a hint of menace that sent an odd flash of uneasiness through her.

"Prince Mithanis." She bowed politely. "I am Captain Talyn Dynan."

The other brother—she struggled a moment to recall his name, Azrilan?—smiled broadly, putting her in mind of a cat after eating its prey. A little shorter than Mithanis and leaner, he was darkly handsome with his pale skin and charcoal wings and eyes. When he spoke, he didn't exude the same malice as Mithanis, just the edge of unconscious arrogance that she heard every time one of the winged folk spoke to her. "This is our dearest brother's new wing?"

"It would seem so." Mithanis ran his gaze over them. Despite the slight smile on his face, there was no warmth in his black eyes. "What did they call themselves again? Rabbits? Frogs?"

"Dear me, Mithanis, I think it was Wolves." Azrilan's voice was light, teasing, as if genuinely amused rather than intending insult. There were flashes of Cuinn in him, and she could see the close relation.

Halun growled under his breath behind her, and she shot him a quelling look. Anger wasn't going to serve them here. She kept her tone unchallenging and polite. "Was there something you wanted, Your Highness?"

A little smile curled up Mithanis' mouth, his eyes catching hers in a long look that told her nothing of what he was thinking. There was power there, though, and it made her instinctively wary. "We come bearing good news, Captain. Being a foreigner, you may not be aware of our annual Monsoon Festival. It's a big event in the citadel, and people come from everywhere to attend."

"A last hurrah before the rainy season, you might say," Azrilan drawled.

Rainy season?

"You're right," she said. "I haven't heard of it." This wasn't going anywhere good—she could tell from the shifting feet behind her and the dancing amusement on Azrilan's face as he watched their interaction. "It sounds like fun."

"It is," Mithanis assured her. "The festival runs for an entire day, and contains displays of skill, exhibitions if you like, from different

Falcon wings. There are also stalls and markets, and parties of all types. The main event is an alleya game traditionally played between two wings of the WingGuard. This year I have decided to invite your wing to participate."

Everything about his tone and appearance suggested she was supposed to take this invite as an honour, even though it most certainly would not be. She summoned a pleased look. "Thank you, Prince Mithanis. Who would we be participating against?"

"My wing." Azrilan smiled, teeth flashing with merriment. "It should be fun, Captain. Your men will put up a good fight, I'm sure."

"We appreciate the honour of your invitation, and of course we would love to participate," she said evenly.

"I'm glad to hear it." Mithanis swept a final look over them. "And I'll be sure to pass the news on to Cuinn."

Murmuring with each other, Mithanis and Azrilan and their guards leaped back into the air, winging swiftly away. Talyn watched them go, mastering her unease, before turning to look at the Wolves. None of them would meet her gaze. Not even Theac. Unease trickled through her.

"Do any of you know how to play alleya?" she asked with a smile, trying to lighten the mood.

"Of course," Corrin mumbled. For the first time in months the young man was looking down at his feet. Her unease deepened. "All children play it growing up, winged or human."

"Then why all the glum faces?" The princes' attitudes had been far from pleasant, but that wasn't unexpected, nor unusual. There was something she was missing here. The level of dejection and horror in those standing before her spoke of genuine distress.

"I joined this wing to escape being imprisoned for the rest of my life!" Zamaril burst out. "Not to be humiliated by the entire race of winged folk."

He turned on his heel and stalked off before Talyn could say a word, muttering curses the whole way. She fixed Theac with a glare. "Tell me what is going on. Now."

"Those feathered bastards are doing this to make fun of us," Theac growled, his glare returning. Talyn's mouth fell open as he, too, turned around and walked off in disgust. Halun followed him, arms crossed belligerently over his chest.

"Will one of you please tell me what's so upsetting about this?" She looked pleadingly at Tiercelin and Corrin. Corrin was still staring at his boots, hands thrust in his pockets, shoulders hunched. Tiercelin simply looked miserable.

"Humans and winged folk both play alleya, like Corrin said," Tiercelin said eventually. "But the winged folk are faster, more agile, and more athletic than humans. We're also stronger, on account of our wings. Not to mention the Falcons' warrior magic. The princes invited us to play against Prince Azrilan's wing for a reason. They want to humiliate the human folk, and their brother. It's a political game. We'll be routed if we play, and then we—and by extension Prince Cuinn—will become the laughingstock of the citadel."

Talyn's inclination to dismiss Tiercelin's words as exaggeration was swallowed by the depth of her wing's reactions. "I see," she said quietly. "Very well, you're dismissed for the afternoon."

He and Corrin walked off in silence.

CHAPTER 25

*N*avis entered the apartment soundlessly as always, dressed simply, manner deliberately innocuous so that any eyes falling on him would simply pass by without question. It was exactly the same thing the Shadowhawk did, and for similar reasons. He worked alone and his entire livelihood relied on not being noticed.

"It's been months, Navis," he snapped, annoyed by his calm façade and trying to push him into some sort of reaction. "I asked you to get information on her and you—"

"Don't work for you," Navis replied smoothly. "I bring you information when and if I get it. That's how it works."

Suspicion rose in a hot tide. He needed Navis's information, relied on it to do the work he did. But there was always the underlying unease that only grew with every encounter they had. Navis knew too much, could undo him with a single word to the City Patrol or the WingGuard. Maybe it would be better to cut ties completely, go it entirely on his own.

As if sensing his thoughts, Navis came straight out with the information he'd brought. "Talyn Dynan is Calumnian born and—"

"You've told me that already."

"She's a warrior." Navis kept talking through the interruption.

"Joined the Aimsir at an unusually young age, then went to Callanan Tower at an equally unusual age. By most accounts she was the best of her class. They sent their best, Shadowhawk."

That confirmed everything he'd learned from their brief meeting. She hadn't been bragging, and he'd been a fool to keep acting the way he always had since her arrival and not expect her to catch him. "There's more, though, Navis. I can feel it."

A test. Did he know she was royal, were his sources that good? And if he did, would Navis tell him?

The quality of the informant's silence was odd, like maybe he was surprised. No, that wasn't it. Agreement, maybe? When he spoke, the Shadowhawk sensed frustration. "From what I could gather, there is some confusion about why she joined the Kingshield. She was too good, too successful, to leave the Callanan. I couldn't learn any more than that. The Callanan and Kingshield both are incredibly protective of their own—they don't talk to outsiders."

"Do the queen or her sons know everything you just told me about her?"

"As far as I can tell, no. They asked for a Kingshield but don't seem to have taken much particular interest in the one that was sent." The frustration in the man's voice deepened.

The Shadowhawk shook his head. "And the break in at the citadel? You know the WingGuard are blaming me for that? I've asked around my network, but it wasn't any of them. I'm sure of it."

"I have nothing to tell you on that."

The suspicion was back. "You're an information peddler, Navis, yet you have no information on such an unusual event?"

"Not yet, I don't." Firm grey eyes lifted to meet his. He must have seen something in the Shadowhawk's face because he looked around suddenly. "You're in a new location. Why?"

"She found me."

"Who?" A hint of panic filled the informant's voice, and the Shadowhawk frowned. What had caused sudden emotion out of the deliberately opaque informant?

"The Kingshield."

"And she let you go?"

He barked out a laugh. "Such a high opinion you have of my self-preservation skills, Navis."

"I told you what she was. If she found you once, she can do it again. All it takes is her talking to the Falcon and you're done."

"But she didn't... and I'm not without leverage of my own. She understands that I can get to her too," he mused, thinking. "And it gave me the opportunity to learn about her. If there's an ulterior motive in her posting, she doesn't seem aware of it. She seemed very focused on her job to protect the prince."

"The upcoming alleya match bears that out," Navis said with a shrug, his equanimity seemingly restored. "If she were aligned with Mithanis in any way, he would never have set her up to fail so miserably."

He started pacing again. "The only one with power to act in Mithranar outside Mithanis is the queen. She either requested the Kingshield or approved Ravinire requesting it."

"You have an interestingly thorough understanding of winged folk society," Navis said, ignoring the Shadowhawk's sudden stiffening. "I agree, but the question then becomes why is she acting now, and without Mithanis' approval?"

"Montagn continues to breathe down her neck." The Shadowhawk considered. "Maybe she thinks having an official liaison from the Twin Thrones here might help keep them at a distance."

"By suggesting a stronger alliance than actually exists?" Navis sounded sceptical. "There are more compelling reasons Montagn would think twice before attempting to take Mithranar, not the least of which is that Mithanis is the most likely to become the chosen heir. His Montagni blood makes him one of their own, and his magic is a powerful deterrent. Which is why undermining his future rule isn't necessarily the best idea."

Anger flared, hot and bright, making him snarl. "So we all just stand by and let his family continue to treat the humans like cattle in a penned yard?"

The silence that followed his outburst was patient, like the man knew it was guilt and doubt that had made him lash out, not anger directed at him. When Navis spoke again, it was to change the subject. "I have something else for you too."

"What is it?"

"Payment first," Navis said evenly.

The Shadowhawk drew the bag from his tunic and passed the man a single gold coin.

Navis took it. "There's a shipment of flour arriving in two days. The WingGuard plan to use it to ambush you. I think that earns me a second gold piece."

He gave a sharp nod and passed Navis a second coin before tucking the bag securely back inside his tunic. If the flour was needed, there would be other ways of going about it, but Navis's warning would keep him and his network members from getting caught.

He needed to be more careful now.

When the door closed behind Navis, the Shadowhawk continued pacing. Deep weariness flooded him, a bone tiredness that warned he needed sleep or there would be consequences. And he couldn't afford to get so tired that he couldn't....

He swore and slumped into a chair—there were so many possibilities and he didn't know which was the right way to turn. There was nobody he could trust.

His thoughts snagged on Navis's reference to the alleya game. Humans couldn't match the athleticism of the winged folk or their magic. The Wolves would be utterly humiliated, and then it would all be over; as a laughingstock, they could never be a serious protection detail.

Abruptly, he sat up straight. Could *that* be the true purpose? Leave Cuinn humiliated and without proper protection? A counter move against the queen, or whoever had requested the Kingshield?

The captain's face floated into his mind and he closed his eyes. She seemed strong, fair and dedicated to her task. But she'd found him so easily, and something told him she hadn't just done that to find out what he had to do with the break in at the palace. The way she'd studied him and his surroundings, her careful questions... and then there was Zamaril, who was certain she wasn't just here as a King-shield liaison. The thief had solid instincts.

If she betrayed him to the Falcon or the City Patrol, he would die, there was no doubt about that. But she hadn't. Whatever her reasons were, right now they didn't include him being caught. And whatever her purpose, it didn't include caring about the wider concerns of humans in Mithranar. There was little she could or would do to help him.

Steeling himself, he rose from his chair and moved towards the doorway. Midnight was rapidly approaching, he had things to do, and already he'd been away too long.

MIDNIGHT HAD COME AND GONE, but the run-down bar in the Poor Quarter was full of patrons. The Shadowhawk leaned at the corner of the long bar top sipping at a half-full glass of watery ale. Sticky rings marked the dark wooden surface, left by a substance he was very careful not to touch, or wonder too much about. He was already breathing through his mouth at the urine-edged scent of ale hovering like a cloud in the humid air.

He'd only come to leave a request for Saniya to meet—making a white chalk mark under the edge of the far end of the bar. But leaving as soon as he'd arrived would look odd in a place like this, so he'd lingered, sipping at ale and hiding his impatience to be gone.

Even that was difficult. Weariness weighed down every inch of him. The anxious tug in his gut—he needed to be elsewhere, had already been gone too long—didn't help.

He'd almost finished his ale when that whisper brushed over him again. The inn was loud, the poor acoustics making the hum of conversation close to deafening, yet it had been clear as day.

Just like the night he'd found that body.

He frowned, trying to isolate the feeling. It wasn't dissimilar to the sensation of drawing the shadows around himself—an instinctive ability he'd had since childhood. Not once had he ever come across anyone else who could do it, not even amongst the best of the thieves and criminals in the city.

Maybe that had changed. It whispered across his senses again, an edginess carrying a hint of darkness. Both warning and threat.

His head came up, scanning the room in quick glance. There wasn't much light, only what was cast by a handful of lanterns hanging from the cracked and unpainted walls. It showed people packed wall to wall, most drinking, all talking. Few were on their own like him.

The whisper brushed over him again, and his hand reached for the knife concealed at his back of its own accord. A low hiss sounded through the room. It cut through the noisy chatter.

Then another hiss. From a different part of the room.

A flash of copper. The Shadowhawk began to push through the crowd towards it. Unnamed disquiet filled him. Another flash of copper—a mask, just like the one he'd seen that night.

His hand curled around the cool hilt of his blade. He never used the knife, it was a last resort only, but the sheer weight of the danger in the room made it impossible not to reach for the reassurance of a weapon. A warning thrummed at the back of his mind, urging him to get out now, to walk away and not look back. It told him he was walking into something deadly.

But he'd never been able to walk away.

A scream cut over the noise then. It was followed quickly by a shout of mingled shock and anger. People began crowding around an area in the corner of the room while others pushed their way towards the exits. The Shadowhawk was shoved from all directions as he kept trying to get to where he'd seen the mask.

A man brushed by him, sending all his senses screaming into awareness. Non-descript clothing. Tall, wiry, and wearing a copper mask that covered the top half of his face. The metal gleamed under the hood of a cloak pulled well down over his head.

He turned, a hand half-raised to grab him, but hesitation cost him, and the crowd of fleeing bodies closed around the masked man, quickly carrying him out of the Shadowhawk's reach.

Cursing, he kept moving, pushing through the last line of patrons until reaching a cleared space on the filthy floorboards. A body lay there in a spreading pool of blood. Another man. Well-dressed. Clearly not a resident of the Poor Quarter. His throat had been slashed from ear to ear. A piece of torn-off parchment lay on his chest. Another marker.

Vengeance.

The inn was emptying out quickly now. The City Patrol might even be called, especially since it looked like a wealthier human who'd been killed.

Again, he hesitated. He wanted to take a closer look, but he wasn't wearing his mask tonight and didn't want to stand out. Someone might remember the man who took an unusual interest in a dead body. Nor did he want to be here when the City Patrol arrived.

He had to leave.

Spinning, he strode for the back exit, not realising until he got to the door that his hand was still clenched, white-knuckled, around the hilt of the knife at his back. Forcing himself to let go, he tried to shake the residue of fear and threat by focussing on the details of what had happened.

It hadn't been a single killer this time. He'd seen at least two masks, working in tandem. And it hadn't been a random kill. And this felt different, very different, from the killings he'd seen in Dock City before. Deaths weren't an uncommon occurrence when people were poor and lived in areas infested by competing criminal gangs. It was one of the reasons he did what he did—an often useless attempt to get enough food and basic supplies to people so they didn't need to rely on crime to survive.

No, this felt targeted and specific. And no criminal gang he'd heard of left notes behind to mark their kills. Usually they just dumped bodies and left them there to be discovered or not.

Uneasiness trickled down his spine. Who wanted vengeance? And for what?

Worse, if a new gang had formed to start a killing spree, it would draw even more attention from the City Patrol into areas the Shadowhawk preferred they stay clear of. And if they couldn't handle the problem, the Falcons would get involved.

He was already dealing with having to be extra careful after Talyn Dynan had found him, and now this. It would make what he did even harder, at the very least he'd have to curtail some of his activities.

Which meant less people he could help. Frustration boiled over, but once it was gone there was only the bone-deep weariness he'd felt earlier.

He had to get back.

CHAPTER 26

*T*hings were not going well.

As quick as a flash, the morale that Talyn had slowly and painstakingly been nurturing amongst the Wolves vanished as if it had never been. They began dragging their feet during the morning run and strength exercises. Weapons training was half-hearted at best, and nobody seemed to care. Theac tried to whip them into shape, but not even his heart was in it.

She pushed them as strongly as she knew how, but all this won her was a grudging few hours of activity. She despaired. She'd been so close to winning them over... and now it was all gone. They had been improving. They'd begun to have some pride in themselves.

Now that fledging pride had been ripped out from under them, and their spirits and self-esteem were worse than when she'd first met them. They saw the coming Monsoon Festival only as a chance for the winged folk to ridicule and humiliate them.

Talyn struggled to see a way out of it. No matter how she approached them—barking orders, gently cajoling or simple reasoning—she couldn't get them to respond to her. Days passed, and their progress halted entirely.

She was at a complete loss.

With all her attempts to re-ignite the morale of the Wolves failing, and Cuinn refusing to take a protective guard seriously, she'd effectively become useless.

Worse, she *felt* useless. And like a failure.

Without the wing to focus on, to keep her grief and depression at bay, she struggled. Proper sleep returned to being almost impossible, and she spent long hours of the night wide awake and trying not to dwell on the past. It didn't help that she was in such an unfamiliar environment.

Back home, warriors took pride in themselves and what they did, and nobody had to cajole them into it. At home, the king and his family—*her* family—didn't treat their people like they were there for their own amusement. She struggled to understand, to deal with how things were in Mithranar.

More than once she considered writing a letter to the First Shield, to explain the situation and request reassignment back home. Each time the flicker of hope that thought roused died quickly. Ceannar already doubted her, and she couldn't afford the Kingshield thinking she was broken—she couldn't have them find out how lost she was. And even if she had a good excuse, to fail on her first posting... no, that would raise doubts and questions beyond just Ceannar.

Sometimes in her darkest moments, she wondered if that would be such a bad thing. Maybe she should just accept she was no longer able to be a warrior and leave the Kingshield, leave it all behind.

But what else was there for her? A blank space yawned, a space that terrified her to the very core of her being. Because even though she didn't know how to get back to what she'd been, she was warrior born.

There was nothing else for her.

Two weeks after Mithanis delivered the alleya invitation, she was called to Ravinire's office late in the afternoon. It was the first time she'd seen him since their discussion about the palace break in.

"Captain." Ravinire rose from behind his desk to greet her. "Please take a seat."

"Sir." She took the chair before his desk, curious despite herself.

"You've been here almost three months today, Captain," he said briskly. "You remember the task I gave you?"

She shifted, crossed her legs. "Yes, sir. You wanted an active wing ready to perform guard duty."

"You presented well at the queen's dinner, and your wing handled the intrusion into the citadel better than I had expected," he said. "You can be assured I don't intend to hold the fact that Prince Cuinn refuses to have a permanent guard against you."

This was odd. Was Ravinire *praising* her? She tried not to frown in confusion. "Thank you, sir."

"From what I can see, your men are on their way to becoming professional guards," he continued briskly. "I thought we should discuss deployment and resources a little further."

"Sir..." She hesitated, then made a quick decision to be frank. He was her commanding officer, after all. "While I would be appreciative of more specific direction from you, you should be aware that their training has stalled. I am doing my best, but they are refusing to cooperate beyond the most basic instruction."

Ravinire's mouth tightened. "The alleya game."

"Yes, sir."

He sat back in his chair, gaze steady on hers. "If your wing is refusing to cooperate with your command, Captain, I'm sure you're aware of your options."

"I am, sir, but I am reluctant to see four good men dispatched back to the Dock City cells because of their unwillingness to be publicly humiliated."

"Your frankness is unwise, Captain." The words were delivered sharply and before she'd even finished speaking, but she got the distinct impression it was more from a desire for her to stop speaking than genuine anger at her words.

"Sir." She bowed her head.

"I am willing for you to see things through until after the game," he said eventually. "If you cannot turn the situation around afterwards, then they will go back to the cells. Is that clear?"

She straightened, unable to hide her relief. "Thank you, sir."

He nodded, face and tone turning back to business. "I spoke to the queen, who has counselled a patient approach where Prince Cuinn is concerned. From now on, it has been agreed that your wing will form a guard detail every time that there is an official occasion such as a dinner or ceremony. You'll also guard Prince Cuinn any time he leaves the citadel."

"And the rest of the time?" She raised an eyebrow.

"As I said, a patient approach has been agreed. We will build beyond that, but for now you'll need to stick within those parameters."

"Thank you, sir." It was a positive development, and it brought about a slight easing of the tight ball of anxiety that seemed to sit constantly in her chest. If she'd won this much in three months, maybe there was hope she could achieve a full-time guard before the end of her posting. At least then she'd go home with a member of the Dumnorix family properly secured—after all, that was the sole aim of the Kingshield.

"Good." He picked up a sheaf of parchment and passed it across to her. "Those are resource request forms—anything your wing needs, fill one out and give it to my clerk outside. If I approve the request, he will see that you get what you need."

"Yes, sir." She couldn't help adding, "And he would be the Falcon sitting outside that gives me a contempt-filled look every time I walk in here?"

"His name is Firas GrassWing." Ravinire cleared his throat. "I meet weekly with all wing captains, and I expect you to be at those meetings from now on. I'll require a progress report on the week, and we'll discuss any security concerns that exist. Any questions?"

"No, sir." She squelched the urge to ask if she should expect similar treatment from his captains as she received from his clerk.

He smiled slightly. "Dismissed."

"Thank you, sir."

. . .

DUSK HAD FALLEN by the time she left Ravinire, and her wandering feet took her past the royal pool. It was deserted, so she took the opportunity to stand at the railing and watch the fiery sunset over Feather Bay. Despite the beauty of the sight, looking down on it from the palace left her unsettled, uncomfortable with the way the winged folk used everything—even their home and architecture—to look down on those in Dock City.

Leaving the palace, she made the long walk down into the city, where the bustle of human life made her feel much closer to home. The night markets were on—a once a fortnight event Corrin had encouraged her to attend—in the Market Quarter, but she was in no mood for the crowds already thronging the streets.

Instead she turned in the opposite direction. She had no particular location in mind, but when she passed a well-lit inn close to the boundary of the Dock Quarter, the music and conversation of its patrons spilling out into the street, she turned and went inside.

Talyn rarely turned to alcohol to numb her despair—it never made her feel better for more than a snatch of hours and would usually make her depression worse after that—but tonight she wanted to watch from the outside as those around her, normal people, enjoyed their evenings the way she once had.

Hardly anyone glanced her way as she ordered at the bar, then snagged a small table in the corner, her back to the wall, facing the crowded room. The spirits were fiery on her tongue as she tossed back two quick shots before sipping more slowly through the others she'd bought.

It wasn't a large place, but clearly popular. Light music drifted through the room from a handful of musicians near the door. The inn wasn't far from the docks, and many of tonight's patrons looked to be sailors and dockworkers. Talyn worked her way slowly through the drinks, ordered another when a server came by, content to simply sit and watch and do her best not to remember.

A couple of men—and one woman with striking platinum hair—

tried approaching her, but a quick well-practiced look had them stumbling away without even speaking. Even if there had been no Tarcos, she wasn't interested in that sort of company tonight.

Her father had probably once frequented an inn just like this—he might have even come to this one before. It made her wonder again what his life had been like here, what his experience of the winged folk contempt for humans had been. Had that been why he'd left to captain his own ship? She still didn't understand why he'd never mentioned it.

"Maybe it's why he fell in love with your mother so quickly. It must have been quite the experience to meet a princess who actually cared about her people," Sari mused.

"Maybe. I wish I'd gotten a chance to speak to him about my posting before I left."

Sari's disapproval was clear enough that Talyn pushed her away before she could say anything. Talyn hadn't gone home after Sari's death, had lingered, lost, in Port Lathilly for a few weeks, seeing nobody, before abruptly leaving to go to Ryathl. There she'd handed in her resignation at Callanan Tower before signing up for the Kingshield.

Seeing her parents had seemed an impossible task. She loved them dearly, but they would know at once how badly wounded she truly was, and she hadn't been able to handle anyone knowing that. So she'd sought the comfort of her relatives instead, those who didn't know her as well, but took her in without question.

Talyn cleared her throat, dragging herself out of her musings with a long swallow of the ale that had just been placed at her elbow. She forced her attention back to the present, to the lives carrying on around her.

When another man tried approaching her, sliding onto the low stool opposite her before she even knew he was coming, her hand was on her sai before he'd settled into place.

"I found *you* this time," he observed. "It wasn't hard."

The Shadowhawk.

Her heart pounded with a mix of shock and self-disgust at her failure to notice his approach. "You followed me," she said flatly.

He gave a low chuckle. "Not to harm you, so you can take your hand off your weapon."

A high collar and the shadows of the corner of the room hid most of his features, but she remembered the tangled brown hair and stubbled jaw. A man who looked no different than any street criminal who'd seen too many years of hard living—except he didn't look *that* old. Mid-thirties at best. It was an odd dissonance. She lifted her hand away from the sai and took a sip of her drink, deliberately slow. "So this is just a social call?"

"I don't do those. I wanted to check in." He shifted closer as someone passed by behind his chair—interesting. "You're a sword hanging over my neck, Captain Dynan."

"And you've ably demonstrated that I should be careful about lowering that sword." Was he really here to ensure she'd been appropriately warned off by his threat? No, she sensed some other purpose. The Callanan First Blade hadn't yet responded to her letter with further instructions, but old habits had her leaning into this conversation, using it to wring every piece of information she could out of it.

"Something tells me that were I really to sneak into your room at night intending harm, you'd have one of those oversized forks buried in my throat before I even realised what was happening."

Once, yes. Now... she wasn't so sure. Her edge was gone. She made no response, taking another sip of fiery spirit, wanting to draw him out. The more he spoke, the more she could learn.

"Is that a hint of doubt, Captain Dynan?" he murmured, reading her silence far too accurately for comfort. "From what I hear, you're a born warrior. The best of the best."

"While you're a born criminal?" She lifted an eyebrow.

"Such a blunt and uncompromising term," he murmured. "I do what I can to help those that need it, and I don't let arbitrary and unjust laws stop me."

"Where I come from, that's called being a criminal, no matter how pretty your intentions."

His mouth curled up. "Why did you leave the Callanan?"

She took a slow breath to hide how his question got under her guard, and shifted back on her stool, resting casually against the wall behind. "You have some sort of skin rash or extra sensitivity to contact?"

"What?" he blurted, thoroughly taken aback by her question.

She smiled inwardly. "I can't help but notice how you shy away the moment anyone passes near the table. You did it the night we met too, kept shifting your feet to keep me from getting too close."

He laughed softly. "It's a hazard of living in the Poor Quarter, I'm afraid. I get twitchy when people get too close."

A good answer and given naturally. Still, she didn't quite buy it. "Why are you here?"

"I heard about the alleya game. It tells me something about you, Captain Dynan. It tells me you're not here in Mithranar at the prince of night's behest."

And why is that an important distinction? "I'm here at the behest of my commanding officer and nobody else."

He laughed softly. "And you're too smart to believe something that simplistic. You've been here long enough now to see how things work."

"Perhaps. Why do you care about the alleya game?"

"I told you, I do what I can to help the humans." His voice turned dark, intense. It had an edge of almost-madness to it. "The game is an opportunity to humiliate your wing and by extension, the human population."

She searched his face, looking for the emotion that went with that bitter voice and failing to find it. He was a master at hiding himself. "Why?"

"Why what?"

"Why care so much about the humans?"

"Someone has to."

A glib response. He wasn't going to give her anything she could use against him. She stayed silent, waiting him out. Eventually he sat back. "If you're as good as I hear... the game might go differently than they expect."

She couldn't help the smile that rose up in her at his words. He was the first person in Mithranar to even consider that fact, and it told her something about him too. He was smart. And he knew more about her than he should. Where was he getting that information from?

"It might," she acknowledged. "I've never heard of the game before, but I have certain abilities."

"I'd like to see that." A smile flashed, genuine and bright, but then faded as quickly as it had come. "You win the game for them, and a target will be on *your* back, Captain. The elder princes won't take a loss from humans lightly and the youngest has no power or desire to help you."

Surprise flashed through her and she sat forward, once again trying and failing to read his shadowy features. "Did you come here tonight to *warn* me?"

"I've heard about you, Captain. I've heard how you treat your men with respect, how you treat them like they're worth something. You stand *with* them."

"Don't drag me into your crusade," she said, ignoring the passion in his words that tugged at her. Their voices had dropped, and they were both leaning over the table now, faces inches apart. "I'm King-shield and Calumnian and I am *only* here to protect Prince Cuinn."

"You could have fooled me." His eyes searched hers. "And you could have had me killed or arrested anytime since you found me. Why haven't you?"

"Because I don't take action that has significant consequences unless I'm certain of where I stand." *Not anymore. Never again.* "You are a criminal. You're also the reason Dock City residents now have some of the seeds they need to grow their produce," she said. "But don't mistake me, if you become a threat to Cuinn, you won't live longer than it takes for me to bury this sai in your neck."

"Something happened to you." He was unfazed by her threat. "Something that led the finest Callanan of her generation to leave and join the Kingshield to be a lowly guard. A Dumnorix princess, to boot. And now you're here and I don't know why."

Neither do I. The words were on the tip of her tongue, and she was shocked at herself for how close she came to saying them aloud. Instead she countered, pushing back at him. "Why the lightning? You think it looks cool? Strikes fear into the heart of your enemies?"

He laughed softly, without mirth. "Quite the opposite. It represents how fleeting my help is, Captain. What I do is bright, vivid, breaking the hopelessness the humans feel for an instant. And then it's gone as quick as it came, and the darkness returns."

She had nothing to say to that.

He nodded, sat back, and stood up. "Think about what I said. I don't want to see your wing humiliated any more than you do. But you're of more use to them alive and safe."

"You truly believe the princes would do something to me?" Incredulity filled her voice. "I'm an official liaison of the Twin Thrones."

"Accidents happen, particularly when Kingshield are so far from home." His face hardened. "And yes, Captain, I truly believe Prince Mithanis would come for you. He doesn't take insult well, and he's an angry and powerful man. You were right before. You're an outsider. You don't yet understand how things work here."

She stayed at the table once he was gone, steadily drinking her way through her remaining glasses. The spirits didn't give her the numbness she'd been seeking. Her chat with the Shadowhawk had left her oddly energised. He was more than a criminal and it was clear he truly believed in what he was doing. How he'd described his symbol...

But there was *nothing*, not even a trace, of why the Callanan were so interested in him they asked the Kingshield to breach their self-imposed mandate of only protecting the Dumnorix.

"That's my second question. The first is why Cuinn's existence is so secretive Ceannar was pretending like he was doing the First Blade a favour by sending you here. Why not just tell everyone he found another Dumnorix? Send a whole battalion of Kingshield here who could spy for the Callanan in their spare time?"

She tried to ignore Sari, turning the Shadowhawk's warning over in her mind. While she didn't quite believe anyone would come after her if her presence meant the Wolves won the alleya game, it certainly wouldn't help her standing. And if the royal family were to find out she was Dumnorix—that wouldn't be a good look at all.

And yet...

"Maybe the answer to your first question has something to do with what the Shadowhawk just implied. Maybe Ceannar is trying to keep it secret from those here?"

Before Sari could reply, she dismissed the topic in her head. Her defensive words to the Shadowhawk had been spot on. She'd done as the Callanan had asked. No doubt the extra information she'd given them on his identity would lessen their interest in him. Now her only job was to keep Cuinn safe for the remainder of her posting, no matter where or from whom any threats came.

She toyed with her final glass. She'd spoken to Cuinn in anger when she'd told him that a leader had to be worthy of those that followed, but she'd meant every word. And by letting the Wolves get the best of her, by *letting* them give up, she was essentially giving up on them.

Her fingers curled around the warm glass and she tossed the spirits back before slamming the glass down on the surface and rising to her feet.

She was a Dumnorix. More than that, she was a warrior. She would get this wing into shape if it was the last thing she did. And maybe in the process she could fix herself.

SHE ROSE EARLY SO that she could visit a small drink stand she'd found not far from the palace entrance and order a large cup of kahvi, not missing the grimace of distaste tossed her way by the winged woman also there ordering a drink. It took her a moment to remember Corrin's words about kahvi being a humans-only drink, and by then the woman had moved on, so Talyn shrugged it off and headed down to the barracks.

The Wolves were already there, going through warm-ups with their typical level of apathy.

Keeping face and voice calm, she stretched while they completed their warm-up and then joined them on the run down the wall and back. Once they were back at the barracks she allowed them a few moments of hunched-over panting.

"Right!" she ordered. "Stop what you're doing and get over here."

They trudged listlessly over to where she stood. All were sweating and red-faced. She buried her frustration at their apathy and kept her voice firm but not unkind. "We're having a different training session today. It's hot, and we're going to go and get a cool drink. Tiercelin, take us somewhere nice please, out of the palace and where we won't run into any Falcons."

Barely a murmur. Not even the prospect of escape from their usual arduous training roused any interest in the Wolves.

That was fine.

Tiercelin led them out of the barracks and through the citadel to an open-aired café that stretched out from a larger building clinging to the hillside. For her own peace of mind, she didn't dwell on how exactly the thing was held up.

Something about the decided way in which Tiercelin led them told her he'd come to this place before. Possibly as a refuge from life at the palace. While pretty as everything else in the citadel, the cafe didn't look fine or exclusive enough to be a spot nobles would choose to dine at.

Not that she minded. It was nice to be away from the gloriously dressed nobles or WingGuard she always saw around the palace. The sight of Tiercelin prompted the almost instant appearance of the café's winged owner—another indication of the status of Tiercelin's family—and they exchanged a few words before the owner led them outside to a table along the railed edge of the platform.

A brightly coloured shade cloth shielded them from the heat of the sun, and all around drifted snatches of birdsong from treetops directly below. Given the early hour, there weren't many patrons, and they had privacy.

For a moment Talyn simply sat there, neck slightly craned as she looked upwards to the tiers of buildings and walkways in the hillside above her—the group of winged folk flying between balconies, a hint of music from somewhere to the east. Sun gleamed on the creamy marble and picked out the hints of rich colour in the wings of those drifting by.

"Pretty, isn't it?" Theac's surly voice broke the silence.

She lowered her gaze, giving him a shrug rather than biting on his attempt to bait her. "It certainly is, Theac."

A human waiter soon followed them out, carrying a tray of cold drinks. Talyn took hers gratefully, sipping the sweet, cold liquid with pleasure. It wasn't as good as kahvi but tasted fruity and sweet. Zamaril stared at his like it was poison, but the other three humans reached for theirs with varying degrees of reluctance.

"So what?" she said. "Kahvi is a humans-only drink, while whatever this is, it's just for the winged folk?"

Tiercelin rolled his eyes. "It's not like it's a rule."

"We don't generally have enough fruit down in Dock City for frivolous drinks like this," Corrin said quietly.

Right. She wasn't interested in another debate of the unfairness of human versus winged folk in Mithranar, and it wasn't why she'd brought them here. Before any of the others could chime in, she changed the subject. "When is the alleya match being held?"

"Late Sixmonth." Tiercelin offered when nobody else seemed willing to respond.

"Well, you're all going to get your backsides whipped, aren't you?"

Five pairs of eyes shot to her, glaring in mute indignation. She fought back a smile, instead summoning the sharpest tone she could manage. "Don't look at me like that! Of course you're going to get beaten, you've been doing nothing for the past two weeks but whine like babies."

"We're going to lose because the winged folk want us to lose. How are humans ever going to beat Falcons in a game of alleya? They can *fly!*" Zamaril spoke bitterly, but she counted that as an improvement.

He hadn't said a word to her in three days. "They have magic, Captain."

"You're making a lot of assumptions there." Talyn sat back in her chair, deliberately keeping a relaxed, casual posture. "But before I go into that, can one of you explain to me what exactly alleya is?"

Corrin's head came up. "You've never played it?"

"I've never even *heard* of it."

"There are five players from each team on the field at one time. You can use any open space, but the festival game is held in the great amphitheatre in the middle of the citadel," Tiercelin began. "There's a goal at each end, and the aim is to get a round ball into your goal. Your team gets one point for each goal."

She frowned. "That sounds simple."

Halun and Tiercelin rolled their eyes at each other before Tiercelin continued. "It's not. Each player is allowed a weapon, blunted of course, and essentially you can use any method to stop the other team's players from scoring, including magic. You can't stray outside the bounds of the field, you can't attack an opponent's head, and you can't inflict serious injury. Those are really the only rules."

She sat up in her chair, staring at them in surprise. "You're telling me this game is basically a mock-battle, with the added wrinkle of getting a ball into a net?"

"When the Falcons play." Theac glowered. "Down in Dock City we use brooms and buckets and throwing slings—it's more of a fun scrap than a battle."

"And what happens if you break any of those rules?" she asked.

"The ball goes to the other team." Corrin scratched at an imaginary speck on the tabletop.

She paused for a moment, then, "How many winged folk do you know who have learned *sabai*?"

Silence.

"You've been learning it for the past three months. That is going to be your advantage over Prince Azrilan's Falcons. They can fly and use magic. *You* know Callanan unarmed combat."

"It's not quite as simple as that," Theac chided. "We're barely past the basics."

"Maybe, but at the very least you can put up a good fight—I know you have the ability to do that. We have roughly six weeks till end of Sixmonth, right?"

She waited for their grudging nods before continuing. "From now on we'll drop sword drills in the morning three times a week and spend it learning *sabai* instead." Talyn looked at them all in the eye. "I can make you good enough to surprise them at the very least. But to do that, I need you to trust me, and I need you to buy in. Will you give me that?"

"You keep asking us to trust you, Captain," Zamaril said. "But you don't understand what you're asking of us. You don't know what it's like to be human in Mithranar."

"No," she said evenly. "I don't. But I also think you're using the bad circumstances you find yourselves in as an excuse to not even try. And I won't accept that."

A brief moment of silence, then,

"She asked me to trust her, and I did. And look what happened for my mam and sisters," Corrin said, fixing his green eyes on Zamaril. "You say you're the best thief in Dock City? Well, prove it. You'll be nothing but a laughingstock if we back out of this game because we're scared."

Talyn stared at Corrin in astonishment, but he didn't notice. His determined gaze was fixed on the thief. For his part, Zamaril looked lost—as if he wanted to take the hope Corrin was offering but didn't believe in himself enough to do it.

"Boy's got a point," Theac added gruffly, his gaze fixing on hers. "But so has Zamaril. You're offering us something you don't fully understand, and if you're wrong, we'll never be Prince Cuinn's guard. A humiliated group of humans won't be respected or feared by anyone meaning the prince harm. You know that, Captain."

She did. But what else was there to do? Mithanis had placed them in an impossible situation, a check-mate move. "And if that happens, you go back to the cells. I understand." But it would also mean that *she'd* failed. Without a wing, she'd be on the first ship back home. "But I don't see how not trying helps you any. At least my way you give yourselves a chance, albeit a small one."

"I'm not afraid of Falcons," Halun spoke up unexpectedly in his quiet, cultured voice. "But that doesn't mean I think we can win. And no offence, Captain, but pretty words won't help."

"I'm not promising you a victory," she said steadily. "I'm promising you a way to do this without being utterly humiliated. You give the Falcons a good fight and lose, they can't laugh at you."

"I think you'd be surprised," Tiercelin said darkly, but then lifted his gaze to all of them. "But that doesn't matter. And I played a lot of alleya when I was young—we're not entirely without winged folk here."

"Zamaril, please. Remember what I told you about courage." Talyn pleaded with the thief. His face was hard, and he had completely withdrawn back into himself. Finally he nodded, but he refused to meet her gaze.

"Back to training, then." Theac rose to his feet, looking at Talyn with raised eyebrows. "Perhaps we can do an extra session on *sabai* this afternoon?"

SHE DELIBERATELY LAGGED behind the others as they headed back to the barracks, giving Theac a look so that he matched her slowing pace.

"Can you give me any insight as to why Prince Mithanis has done this?" she asked in an undertone. It still nagged at her what the Shadowhawk had said about the eldest prince, about her not being in Mithranar at his behest.

"He wants you gone and he wants us filthy humans out of his palace," Theac muttered.

"Right, but why?" Talyn pressed. "We're no threat to him, and it would be easy for him just to ignore us. If I understood his motivations, I might be able to figure out a way to get us out of this."

Theac gave her a look. "I'm a human from Dock City. I don't know why you think I have any insight into the motivations of the prince of night." He huffed a breath at her pointed glance. "Fine. I'm betting it's got to do with the queen's heir. Mithanis wants it to be him—that's no secret. This game gives him an easy opportunity to thoroughly humiliate his youngest brother, and in the process remove any potential competition. The winged nobles will never put their weight behind such a weak prince, and neither will the queen."

"I thought Prince Cuinn was already essentially out of the running."

"He is. But that doesn't mean Prince Mithanis won't take any opportunity to re-emphasise how unworthy a candidate Prince Cuinn is."

"And Prince Azrilan?"

"I truly don't know that one, Captain. He's always stuck close to Mithanis, the very picture of brotherly devotion."

This was getting off track. She stopped dead, leaving the others to walk on. "Theac, there was a time when I could face five Falcons and take them down without breaking a sweat. You and I both know they're ceremonial—all style over substance. And don't forget I have magic too. If I play, we win. You're too experienced not to know that already. So why are you just as downbeat as the rest of them?"

"*You haven't actually seen the Falcons use their magic. Don't underestimate them,*" Sari warned.

"*Magic is simply another weapon, Sari, and I've seen them in drill. They don't fight with any purpose, any heart. And their skill isn't any more than basic competence. It won't be any different with their magic.*"

Theac's sharp words took her away from any response Sari made. "Because if you walk out there and single-handedly destroy five Falcons, you will do to Prince Azrilan what he and Prince Mithanis are trying to do to Prince Cuinn. What then do you think our chances of remaining here will be?"

His words echoed that of the Shadowhawk. Interesting. Both men knew Mithranan society far better than she ever would, but even so she struggled to truly believe what they were saying.

She stepped back from him, letting out a long breath. "Theac, my one and only goal here is to build a protective guard capable of keeping Prince Cuinn safe before I leave. This alleya game is an opportunity. I can train you all up well enough in six weeks so that you can give a good accounting of yourselves without my help, and at the same time forge them into an even stronger team. With me there, we ensure a victory, even if we have to make it appear like a difficult one to save everyone's face."

"And you seem to think that telling us this, that offering us hope via inspiring words is going to change anything for us, Captain." Frustration tinged his voice. "We've lived here our entire lives. We've dealt with winged folk contempt our entire lives. Nothing has ever changed that, so why is it so difficult for you to understand that it's impossible for us to believe what you're saying? Our reality proves you wrong."

He strode ahead before she could respond, his words hitting her like a punch to the stomach.

"*He's right.*"

"*I goddamn know that!*" Talyn seethed. "*But if I can't change anything, why am I even here?*"

"*I didn't say you couldn't change anything. You bloody Dumnorix can't help yourselves. It's just that you'll have to show them, not tell them.*"

The crippling doubt hit her again. It was so much easier to say the words than have faith she could carry them out. And her conversation with the Wolves just now had made something terrifyingly clear—she needed to succeed here to prove to herself she wasn't done, that she could go back to what she was, but now she realised it wasn't just her life, it was theirs. Steer them wrong, fail them, and they would go back to the cells in which she'd found them, their lives over too. The weight of that burden was stifling.

"*You're as bad as they are!*" Sari said in a huff before vanishing from her mind completely.

CHAPTER 27

*S*he still had to cajole the Wolves through training each day. They did try harder, but Theac had been right. They were so demoralized it was impossible for them to see any hope of a good outcome.

Despite that, despite her own crippling doubt, she was determined to make the most of the six weeks they had. She introduced *sabai* techniques that were advanced for beginners, things she hadn't begun learning until the second and third years of her Callanan apprenticeship. Predictably they struggled, particularly Theac and Halun, but the increased quickness and agility gained from perfecting the moves was going to be needed against the winged folk, and so she pushed them— making them repeat the moves over and over, a hundred times, two hundred times, until they could get it right.

Every evening they retired to the barracks with sore, aching muscles, and needed lengthy stretching the next morning to work out the stiffness. Still, it was not without reward. She saw the improvement in them, even though they thought it made no difference.

Talyn worked just as hard alongside them in the heat, trying to show them that she was with them all the way. Every time she sensed an improvement in their attitude or morale, she pushed at the crack, trying to widen it. Most times she failed, but there were times when she didn't, and through it all, she refused to stop trying.

And somehow, it was helping her too. As horribly frustrating as it was sometimes, the sheer effort and focus she had to put in meant she wasn't thinking about Sari every other second or dwelling on her fear of being permanently broken.

She didn't know how long the distraction would last, but she welcomed it with open arms nonetheless.

TALYN SHUT the door to her rooms behind her, a heavy sigh escaping her as she sprawled along the plush couch. It was evening, and she was exhausted. After another difficult training session with the Wolves, she'd spent the remainder of the afternoon working off her frustrations in solo practice. As a result, her muscles ached with the pleasant weariness she always felt after a workout.

She sighed again and rose from the couch, loping into her small kitchenette to pour a glass of water from the jug she'd brought up that morning. She sipped it while she busied herself tidying the room and folding her meagre pile of clean washing.

Darkness was beginning to fall by the time she finished, and she decided to have a bath and clean up before grabbing a quick meal in the barracks and then curling up in bed with a book—she'd found a library in one of her many wanderings around the palace. Hopefully it would keep her engaged until she grew sleepy enough to fall asleep without her mind turning to darker thoughts.

Her bedroom was dim and stuffy from the day's heat. She went to open one of the windows and swore aloud at the sudden twitching of the shadows in the corner. Before the realisation had even fully processed she was leaping back towards the door, hand dropping to her sais.

The Shadowhawk was her first thought—he'd gotten in again, dammit—but then the shadows moved forward, materialising into a much older man with his hands held up in the air. "I'm not here to attack you," he said in a whisper-smooth voice. "Just to talk with you."

Talyn eyed him. He was tall and lean, wearing simple, innocuous clothing. She could just make out a pair of expressionless grey eyes under the hood. Most obvious was the fact he was human, not winged. Although she could barely make out his features despite the light from lanterns outside shining through the window.

"Normally people knock on my front door when they want to speak to me," she said coldly, keeping the open door at her back and not moving her hand from her sai.

"I'm not normal people. I've been waiting here for an hour."

The dry impatience in his tone took her aback. "Sorry to hold you up," she said. "Are you one of the Shadowhawk's people? I thought he'd already made his point about how easily he can get to me."

"My name is Savin."

"Is that supposed to mean something to me?"

The gaze pierced her. A chill shuddered down her back. This man had a dangerous, predatory air about him. Yet she didn't feel threatened. Odd. "Nobody has mentioned my name to you before?"

"*So we've got a Shadowhawk, a royal family who can't make up its mind whether their youngest prince should be protected, a prince of night, and now a shifty man named Savin? The puzzle just keeps getting more complicated, doesn't it?*"

Talyn ignored Sari's gleeful summary, keeping her focus firmly on Savin. His tone irked her. "No. I just asked you the question to hear the sound of my own voice."

"I don't appreciate sarcasm."

She huffed a laugh. "*I* don't appreciate people creeping around in my bedroom, especially when I didn't let them in here in the first place."

He studied her for a long moment, and she had to fight the urge to squirm as if she were a naughty child. "I'm here because I've been instructed to introduce myself to you."

"By who?"

"That's not relevant."

Talyn had had enough of the secrecy and mysteriousness. If this man meant her ill, he would have attacked already. Dropping her hand, she walked to one of her lamps and lit it, before motioning him out of the room. "You said you wanted to talk. So talk. Who are you?"

"I work to protect the royal family through the gathering and exploitation of information."

"So you're a spy?" She'd wondered if the Falcons had a more secretive wing. And though she was surprised they would stoop to recruiting humans, it made sense given how large the human population in Mithranar seemed to be.

"That's a crude way of putting it, and the word doesn't encompass all of my activities, but yes. My role is to guard the Acondors' wellbeing. Since you are the captain of Prince Cuinn's newly formed wing, I was instructed to make contact with you so that we can form a working relationship. There will be occasions when you have information I need, and vice versa."

"I've been here three months." The question was implicit in her voice, *why now?*

He chose to ignore it. "You have."

Fine. We'll play it that way. "Who is your ultimate loyalty to? Prince Cuinn or the queen? Or the Falcon?" she challenged.

A beat of silence. "I have an interest in the youngest prince."

"That doesn't answer my question. As Kingshield, my *only* interest is Prince Cuinn. I couldn't care figs for the queen, her other sons or anybody else in this country. If it came to a choice between saving Prince Cuinn or his mother, or even my king, my oath demands I save Prince Cuinn. I won't be sharing information with anybody who will be relaying it to a third party."

"I understand." Savin nodded gravely. "Believe it or not, I appreciate your loyalty."

Talyn relaxed slightly and leaned against the wall. "You do, huh? Tell me more about this spying, Savin."

A smile crossed Savin's face, but it was far from warm. "What you know is the same as the other WingGuard captains in the protective flight. It's all you need to know."

"Very mysterious," Talyn said dryly. "The curiosity is killing me."

"I came here tonight, not only to make contact, but to discuss the Shadowhawk."

Talyn's head came up in a flash. It had only been a few days earlier the Shadowhawk had followed her to a bar. It seemed more than a coincidence that this man who'd crept into her bedroom uninvited now wanted to discuss the Shadowhawk with her. "The criminal who champions the cause of the humans? What could you possibly want to talk about with me?"

"I believe he was behind the break in at the palace. I know his sympathies lie with the humans, and his network is based in the human community, primarily in Dock City. Yet I don't know who he is, and I haven't managed to identify anyone close to him."

She laughed softly. "You must think me a fool."

He shifted, the darkness blending and rippling around him. "I'm sorry?"

"You say you're here because you protect the royal family and I'm in charge of Prince Cuinn's protection—yet it's taken you three months to come and talk to me. Then you say you want to chat about the Shadowhawk because you think he broke into the citadel. *Two* months ago. You're not here for either of those reasons, and if you thought I would believe your rubbish pretences, then you must think me a fool."

There was a long silence, then, "Well, if I did think you a fool, I certainly don't any longer. Yet what I told you is true—I am concerned with Prince Cuinn's welfare, and I am concerned that the Shadowhawk might have been behind the break in."

"Are you telling me you think the Shadowhawk is a threat to Cuinn?" She frowned, seeing an opportunity to learn more about this man the Callanan was so interested in. Not to mention the easy way someone had gotten so close to Cuinn that night left her profoundly uneasy. "What has this Shadowhawk actually done besides steal some supplies from the winged folk? What's he after?"

"It started some time ago—around ten years before Prince Cuinn was born. Things would go awry. Shipments of delicacies meant for the nobles disappearing, troubles for the WingGuard when they went into the city, muttered unrest, that sort of thing. At the time, it was all blamed on a shadowy figure who named himself the Shadowhawk."

Her eyebrows lifted in surprise. "This has been going on since before Prince Cuinn was born?" *And why is he telling me all this?*

"No, that's when it started. When the princes were all still boys, the activities stopped, and the name of Shadowhawk faded away. For a long time he stayed dead, then it all started again some three years ago. We don't know if it is the same person. He'd be older now, but it's definitely possible."

"If it is the same man, why did he stop for almost thirty years?"

He stared at her, expression unchanging. *What does he want?*

"Okay, you don't know that either. What makes you so certain the Shadowhawk was behind the break in?"

"I'm not certain of anything at the moment, Captain." He glanced around. "I think we're done here."

Just as he reached the door, she had a flash of inspiration. It was almost like she could hear Sari's voice in her head, urging her on. This man was a problem—he'd accessed her quarters with ease for the primary purpose, she was now certain, of learning what she knew. She had no clue as to his motives, or his true position in relation to Cuinn. Until she learned that, she needed to keep him on the hook. "Wait!"

He turned, almost a complete shadow in the darkness of her room.

"If you are who you say you are, you will keep me apprised of any information that relates to Prince Cuinn's safety," she said. "But don't expect it to be a two-way street. I don't know you, and creeping into my rooms with false reasons for why you've come doesn't leave me inclined to trust you."

The silence became drawn out as Savin made no reply. She almost thought she caught a flicker of approval in his eyes, but in the shadows, it was impossible to tell.

Eventually, he spoke. "I'll contact you soon to set up a way of meeting covertly when I have information for you. I will agree to do so, if you agree to keep our contact a secret."

She nodded agreement. "I'll be waiting."

Savin paused at the door. "You're not at all what I expected, Captain Dynan."

"No, what did you expect?"

"In all honesty, I had absolutely no idea."

As he walked out, Talyn caught an expression on his face that made her suddenly think she'd just been very cleverly manipulated into something he'd wanted all along.

"Who are you, Savin?" she murmured into the darkness, "and what is it that you really want?"

He wasn't to be trusted, but he was a way of gaining the information the Callanan had sent her here to get. And a way to help protect Cuinn. Information was power.

She'd have to handle him very carefully.

CHAPTER 28

"*O*nce the rains hit, we're all pretty much housebound until they end, human and winged folk alike. Nobody goes out unless they have to. Nothing lighter than a drizzle for days on end. It's the reason I never became a fisherman," Andres Tye told her as they shared a cup of kahvi one particularly humid afternoon. She'd asked him about it, not failing to notice that the upcoming Monsoon Festival was becoming a topic of conversation almost everywhere she went. "The festival is a way to celebrate the end of summer and ready ourselves for the rains."

"How long do the rains last?" She shifted, trying to ignore the uncomfortable trickle of sweat down her back.

"Usually six weeks or so." He flashed a knowing smile. "And it only gets more humid from now until finally it breaks, and we get the rain."

"Delightful." She made a face, then took another sip of her kahvi. The warm liquid slid down her throat, sweet and potent at the same time. "I'm not sure how much more of this ridiculous sweatiness I can take."

"At least wait until the festival before escaping back home. It's the only time of the year that both humans and winged folk enjoy together—we're allowed free reign throughout the citadel to attend the events of the day, though the seating at the stadium for the exhibition game will be strictly separated."

She sighed at his mention of the game. As each day passed, she had to fight harder and harder to get the Wolves to put any effort in. She continued to remind herself that they were nothing like the elite, hardened warriors of her homeland. Except for Theac, they were inexperienced civilians who'd been dragged into military duty, mostly unwillingly.

And deep down she understood their true distress. Theac's words to her had struck home. The alleya match would be a very public opportunity for the winged folk to once again assert their superiority, and her Wolves would be the ones to suffer it on behalf of all the humans. But if she believed Theac and the Shadowhawk, winning the game unexpectedly would have equally bad consequences for the Wolves.

Talyn hadn't grown up as a human in Mithranar, yet even she was equally astonished and infuriated that the princes had orchestrated the whole thing. She couldn't even begin to understand their motivations for it.

"Will many from Dock City go?" she asked. "The general expectation seems to be that the Wolves will be trounced."

"I honestly don't know." Tye considered his cup thoughtfully. "People like the idea of the Wolves—your wall run each morning gets more spectators each day. But... probably not. Few will want a front row seat to a display of humans being trounced by winged folk at a game we all enjoy."

"I don't blame them," she said softly.

And she meant it.

When Talyn took a walk late one evening a few days later, part of a habitual routine she'd established to ensure she knew her way around every inch of the palace, the sound of sparring caught her attention. Following the grunts and clangs of metal on metal, she exited a closed corridor and emerged onto an open-aired balcony. Below, a unit of

Falcons lined the perimeter of a drill yard, watching two combatants sparring.

The two elder princes.

Interested, she stopped to watch the fight from above, eyes widening in surprise. It felt like forever since she'd witnessed the calibre of fighting skill that had been so commonplace back home—but Mithanis and Azrilan could make a case for joining the Callanan.

They fought with real blades, displaying a skill that could only have been achieved from years of practice. And interestingly, both used their wings as natural extensions of their bodies, dancing all over the court, in the air and on the ground. Sometimes they were so quick that their moves were a blur. It was how all the WingGuard should be taught to fight.

Mithanis was clearly the superior fighter. Azrilan was only barely holding his own, despite his skill, and Mithanis gave him no quarter. He demonstrated his superiority with every lunge and counter, drumming the point home over and over, while Azrilan just took the beating.

She felt sorry for the prince of games.

A slight sound came from Talyn's left, and she glanced back, peering into the shadows. Nothing moved. Frowning, she went over to investigate further, almost taking a step back in startlement when Savin stepped out from behind a pillar. Her trained senses usually noticed someone approach before they came into view, but he'd completely surprised her. It was another blow to her confidence.

"Prince Cuinn's young page, Willir, you know him?" Savin asked without preamble.

"We've met." Annoyance at herself made her voice come out sharper than she'd intended.

Savin barely noticed, glancing in both directions to make sure they were alone before continuing. "If I need to get a message to you, I'll send it through him disguised as a note from Prince Cuinn."

She nodded. "And if I need to get a message to you?"

"Leave an empty cup sitting on your bedroom windowsill. I'll come as soon as I'm able."

"Sounds easy enough." Talyn cocked her head in the direction of the sparring. "Can Prince Cuinn fight like that?" She'd certainly be far less worried about assassins getting to him if he could.

"Prince Cuinn prefers pursuits that require less... dedication and practice."

"So that's a no." She shook her head. How was it that Cuinn was the Dumnorix? Although, watching Azrilan, she had a glimmer of understanding of why Cuinn was so determined to avoid anything but parties and women. Maybe it was his brother's overwhelming need to be the dominant one he was trying to stay away from. It certainly didn't look fun for Azrilan.

Savin didn't linger any longer, nodding his head before vanishing into the growing shadows of the evening.

Talyn returned to peer down into the drill yard, but the princes had finished sparring, and were already winging away, their Falcon guards close behind. Senses even more alert since Savin's surprise appearance, this time she caught the approach from someone above in time to crane her neck upwards. The winged man was framed against the setting sun, and despite squinting she couldn't make out his features.

"Good evening, Captain." Cuinn's voice was musical on the night air as he spiralled down to land lightly in front of her. "What brings you here?"

"Prince Cuinn," she greeted him politely. "I just happened across your brothers sparring. They're very good."

Cuinn chuckled. "Yes, though I can't say I understand what fascinates them so much about poking a sword at each other."

"There are some good uses to which a sword can be put," Talyn noted.

"Here we go, you're annoyed with me again." He sighed, rolling his eyes dramatically. "I know, I know... you and your men are willing to die to protect me. You take your job seriously and all that. I was just expressing my boredom with the sport of swordplay, Captain, nothing more. I much prefer a good game of alleya."

She frowned. "I assume your brothers told you about inviting the

Wolves to play against Prince Azrilan's wing at the Monsoon Festival?"

"Your men aren't actually going to play, are they?" His eyes widened in astonishment. "They'll be humiliated."

"That's what they seem to think, too." She eyed him. "I'm told the invitation is an attempt to humiliate not just the Wolves, but you as well."

He laughed. "Someone has filled you in on the way succession works in Mithranar, I take it? Don't fear, Captain, I have little interest in being king. About as little interest as I have in having a guard detail, actually. If your men are determined to be humiliated, then I won't protest."

"Why does that not surprise me?" she said bitterly. This was the one man who should be supporting the Wolves, yet he was laughing at them along with everyone else.

Cuinn regarded her oddly. "Does part of your Kingshield training include learning to insult those you are supposed to protect?"

"No." Talyn shook her head. His lack of rancour only served to irritate her further. "That's all me, I'm afraid. I tend to get insulting when I don't like someone."

Sari laughed in delight inside her head, an echo of what had once always been there. It made her hesitate—she was letting her annoyance with Cuinn breach her self-imposed restraint.

He waggled his eyebrows at her, leaning in closer. "And with that attitude, I'm supposed to feel safe with you commanding my protection wing?"

"I wouldn't have thought so. You don't exactly allow us to spend any time guarding you."

"Well." He shifted closer again, voice dropping to a seductive murmur. "I might consider allowing some close protection at night, Captain Dynan. You *are* stunningly attractive for a human."

"Nice try," she said dryly, utterly unaffected by him. "But if your magic can read my irritation with you, you can certainly sense how uninterested I am in that particular scenario for a whole host of reasons, not the least of which is that you're a little *too* pretty for my taste."

He shrugged languidly, leaning back. "Your loss, Captain."

"You're attempting to be funny, I suppose," she said dryly.

"Sarcasm," he noted. "Yet you *are* amused. I can feel it."

"Oh really?" She arched her eyebrows. "And what are you feeling now?"

He laughed, the amusement in his voice rich and musical as he stepped back and spread his silver wings wide. "Good night, Captain."

He was awful. He had no respect for her, the Wolves, or *any* of the WingGuard. A prince at almost thirty years old and he was literally doing nothing with his life. It was difficult for her to comprehend. She was even further from the throne than he was, yet as far back as she could remember she'd had the unquenchable desire to do something that mattered. To make a difference.

Yet in a way she was almost relieved to have been given a charge so unlikeable. She'd left the Callanan because she couldn't contemplate ever having another partner, nor did she want to continue being a Callanan warrior without Sari. She didn't want to care that deeply about a comrade ever again, and being Kingshield meant having a distance from your charge—it was necessary to do a proper job. Trust, rapport, yes. But losing objectivity was dangerous.

Even so... she couldn't help but wonder how certain the First Shield was that Cuinn *was* Dumnorix.

There was nothing of them in him, not in his physical appearance or his behaviour. In fact, the only person she'd met so far in Mithranar with any similarity to her family had been the Shadowhawk—with his passionate intensity and the hint of instability she'd caught in his eyes, an instability one would expect in a Dumnorix child grown up without other Dumnorix relatives around them.

A chill swept through her. The thought had been half-joking, but what if... why *were* the Callanan so interested in a Mithranan criminal with no ties to the Twin Thrones?

She shook her head at her own foolishness. If they suspected the

Shadowhawk of having Dumnorix blood, she wouldn't have been sent here to protect Cuinn. The Kingshield wouldn't leave him unprotected.

"Tal... this is what you do," Sari breathed through her mind. *"This is why we were so good. You put pieces together nobody else sees."*

"Well these pieces don't make sense. If the Callanan suspected the Shadowhawk was Dumnorix they would have gone straight to the Kingshield. And there is absolutely no way either Ceannar or the Callanan would have me focused on protecting Prince Cuinn if they believed the Shadowhawk was Dumnorix." She was certain of that with every fibre of her being.

"Even so. There's something there."

"I doubt it. We were so good because we were a team," Talyn said bitterly. *"I'm not the same anymore."*

Sari offered no response to that and Talyn pushed all thoughts of her partner away. Her job was to protect Cuinn and find information on the Shadowhawk. She'd done the second and hadn't yet given up on the first.

That was all she had to do.

CHAPTER 29

hree nights before the Monsoon Festival, a nightmare involving Sari had Talyn waking at dawn, throat hoarse from screaming, sheets tangled around her sweat-slicked body. Unable to lie there a single moment longer, she forced herself out of bed, ignoring the trembling of her muscles and how hard it was to dress while fighting the heavy weight of awakened grief with every breath.

Dammit, she couldn't keep doing this. She had to get past it somehow.

It didn't help that all she would be greeted with down at the barracks were long faces and scowls. Her mind was so busy with these thoughts that it wasn't until she was fully dressed and crossing to her front door—hoping the fresh air would help—that she realised how stuffy the room was, how thick the air had become. Opening the door, she was greeted with duller than usual morning sunlight and a wash of humid air.

A glance upwards from the railing of the walkway outside her room quickly explained the dimmer light. Heavy black clouds scudded across the horizon from the east, so low-flying they obscured the tops of the hills beyond the ones closest.

Even as Talyn watched, climbing up to balance on the railing for a better view, the clouds swept in over the citadel. Within moments a light, hissing rain was falling.

By the time she made her way down to the barracks to begin the day, the rain was coming down in thick, steady sheets. The clouds had settled in fully over the hills, shrouding the citadel in mist and giving it the appearance of a city floating in the sky—Dock City and Feather Bay were completely obscured.

Tiercelin and Theac stood under the veranda running along the front of the barracks, staring dismally out into the rain sweeping across the training yard, shoulders hunched. Tiercelin's wings were damp and bedraggled, hanging forlornly from his back.

Talyn dashed through the iron gate and sprinted across the yard towards them. Even in that short amount of time she was soaked through, although unlike the Wolves she revelled in the faint crispness to the air, the easing of the endless heat.

"I thought the monsoon season didn't start for another few weeks," she said.

"It shouldn't." Theac had a pensive expression as he stared at the curtain of falling water. "Sometimes the rains start early, but it's rare."

"I'm sure it will be fine." Tiercelin was staring out at it too. "Just a quick rain before the proper monsoon arrives."

"I hope so," Theac muttered.

Before Talyn could ask him what he meant, he'd turned to head inside, where Halun had started a fire in the common room and Zamaril and Corrin were sitting near it, finishing off breakfast. Talyn pulled at her soaked vest, then gave a shrug and went to stand closer to the warmth of the fire in a vain attempt to dry it.

"You know it's not actually cold enough for a fire, right?" she told them.

No reply. She heaved an inwards sigh.

"I suppose training's out for today." Tiercelin followed them in.

"I suppose you've not noticed the indoor training hall in this very barracks." She raised an eyebrow.

"No." He sighed. "Just thought I'd try."

She smiled. "We'll skip the run though—I don't want any of us slipping in the rain and falling off the edge of the wall path."

"Come on, you lazy sheep." Theac clapped his hands. "Get yourselves organised. This weather doesn't change the fact you've got a game of alleya in two days' time."

"Captain?" Corrin spoke quietly, stopping everyone as they began shuffling for the door. Theac sent a scowl in Corrin's direction, but he ignored it.

"Yes?" Talyn turned away from the fire.

"I'm going down to Mam's for dinner tonight. She asked me to invite you all to join us. You've done so much for her and my sisters, she wants to do something to say thank you." A sweet smiled warmed his face. "She is a wonderful cook, so I can promise you a good meal."

A distraction from another lonely night trapped with her thoughts and memories. Talyn jumped at it. "That sounds great, Corrin. Count me in."

"Me too."

When Talyn stared at Tiercelin in astonishment—since when had *he* been so eager to spend the evening with humans?—the winged man shrugged. "I'm heartily sick of the rotten mush our mess cook keeps making. A home-cooked meal sounds good."

"That's a lovely thought, lad. I would very much like to join your family for dinner." Theac's grizzled face softened a touch.

"I would like to come too," Halun said softly. "Your mother wouldn't mind having me in her house? I wouldn't want to scare your sisters."

Corrin smiled in genuine pleasure. "We'd love to have you, Halun, and I don't think you're scary. Well, not anymore, anyway."

Talyn shot a look at the thief. "Zamaril would love to come too, I'm sure."

He scowled at her but nodded in Corrin's direction. "Sure, why not."

Corrin beamed. "Mam's putting on a special meal. I promise you won't be disappointed."

Talyn straightened. "All right, everyone, that's enough stalling. Into the training hall, quick smart."

THE WEATHER DIDN'T IMPROVE all day. If anything, it got worse. The rain grew heavier, and the temperature dropped so that by nightfall it was approaching cool, a fact that wouldn't have bothered Talyn at all if she hadn't been slowly getting accustomed to the sticky, humid heat in Mithranar.

After training was over for the day—even though they refused to see it, let alone acknowledge it, she saw genuine improvement in the Wolves, and just hoped they wouldn't let lack of confidence overwhelm that—she dug through her duffel for something to wear down into Dock City.

Her hand hovered, trembling slightly, over the Callanan cloak stored near the bottom of the bag. She didn't even know why she'd brought it, but when she'd been packing, some part of her had been unable to leave it behind.

It was dyed the moss-green of the Callanan and designed for wear in all conditions. The outside was oilskin, waterproof in snow and light rain, while the interior was thick, warm wool that generated and held body heat. It was tailored specifically for her, and when she lifted it out of her bag, it smelled like home. Carefully, she turned back the shoulder, revealing the twin amber swords etched from stars on the inside lining above the heart.

Nestled beneath it were Sari's twin daggers, still wrapped as they had been ever since Roan had given them to her at the funeral.

A glance at the rain sheeting down her window decided her. She shrugged the cloak on over her shoulders, ruthlessly pushing aside the wash of emotion that wanted to go along with it.

She managed to get out of the palace and through the citadel to the top of the wall walk by travelling most of the way along covered walkways. The Wolves waited for her there, huddled under a balcony.

"Sorry I'm late," she apologised. "Shall we go?"

Corrin nodded enthusiastically, but the others were all staring dubiously out at the rain, varying degrees of worry on their faces.

"What is it?" she asked.

"Just hoping the rain might have let up by now, that's all," Theac said.

"There's a lot coming down," Zamaril added, serious for once. "And it seems to have settled in."

"I see." She frowned, puzzled. "If you'd prefer not to head down in this weather, we can—"

"It will be fine." Tiercelin cut her off. "Come on, I'm starved."

Talyn pulled her hood over her head and followed Corrin. They walked quickly, rain pelting down around them, careful where they stepped on the steep path down the wall. Once at the bottom they quickened their pace to an almost run. Talyn was soaked through from the knees down, and water dripped from the edge of her hood, running in rivulets down her face.

The wind whipped around them, not quite cold, but with an edge that had taken away the air's humidity. She huddled deeper into her cloak as Corrin led the way into the Market Quarter. After twisting and turning through a number of dark streets he came to a stop outside a two-story brick building.

Water ran, waterfall-like, from the eaves of the buildings around them and splashed into growing puddles in the side of the street. Talyn glanced around to check her surroundings from habit, but nobody was out in this weather.

Corrin walked up to a doorway set into the brick and pushed it open, then led them up an internal staircase. At the top was a narrow corridor interspersed with doorways. Corrin stopped at the first one on the left and knocked loudly.

"It's me, Mam."

A woman's voice called out in greeting, and then running feet approached the door. Someone fiddled with the lock and the door swung open.

"Corrin!" A small girl ran out, a huge grin on her face.

"Elsie!" Corrin swung the girl into his arms and peppered her face with kisses. "You're growing so big!"

"Corrin!" Another girl came pelting down the narrow hall. She was older than the other by a couple of years but had the same dark curly hair and grey eyes. "You haven't come to visit us for ages."

"I'm sorry Janna, I've been really busy. You know we have the alleya game coming up." Corrin put Elsie down and bent to kiss Janna.

Her eyes shone. "Our tutor said we could have the day off lessons so Mam can take us to watch. Elsie and me have been bragging to our friends all week. Nobody else has a brother playing in the game."

"Elsie and *I*, Janna, not Elsie and me." A middle-aged woman appeared in the hall. She had a friendly face and dark hair tied in a bun at the back of her head. "And where are your manners, girls? You don't leave guests standing in the hall like that. They must be soaking wet and cold."

The girls scrambled out of the way, and Corrin's mother came forward to welcome them in. She didn't even blink at Tiercelin's presence, giving him the same warm hug she gave all of them and completely ignoring that his wings were dripping all over her entryway.

"I'm Errana. I'm so glad you could all come. I've been wanting to do something to properly thank you since everything you did for us. I can't tell you how grateful we are. The girls are enjoying their schooling so much, and now I can feed and dress them properly. Even Corrin has a proper job and a future now." Tears pricked Errana's eyes, the gratitude and relief shining from her face. Talyn's heart lurched.

"It was a pleasure to help, ma'am," Theac said, unaccountably verbose. "Corrin is a valued member of our wing. We're a team, we help each other out."

Talyn gave him a pointed look at those words, lifting an eyebrow. He scowled, eyes dropping to his boots. They'd hardly been living up to that mantra recently.

"The day he was recruited to your wing was the luckiest day of

Corrin's life." Errana was beaming at Talyn now and she managed a warm smile in return.

"Theac wasn't wrong, Errana. I'm Corrin's captain, and that means I look out for him. It's nothing special, it's just the way things work where I come from."

"Then you come from a much better place than Dock City, Captain." Errana reached out to squeeze her arm. "Now come on through. You all must be hungry."

Talyn followed, turning back only when she noticed Tiercelin hadn't followed. He was standing still in the hall, eyes on Errana, something odd in his expression.

"You okay?" she asked.

He gave himself a little shake and nodded, his expression returning to normal. "Let's go eat."

ERRANA HAD PUT TOGETHER a wonderful meal despite the family's limited circumstances. The food was hot and delicious, and Talyn found herself relaxing in the warm, friendly house, with the distant hum of rain beating down outside. It was exactly the distraction she'd needed. Janna and Elsie sat on either side of Talyn and pestered her with questions about being a female warrior until Corrin tactfully removed them.

After they were full to bursting, Errana and the girls cleared away the dishes despite the Wolves' attempts to help, and then Errana bought in steaming mugs of kahvi.

As they sat around chatting, Corrin went to retrieve his fiddle. The Wolves—even Zamaril—smiled for the first time in weeks as he played a merry, dancing tune for them. When it grew late, Errana ushered the small girls off to bed.

Talyn was beginning to feel distinctly sleepy from a combination of the warm room and relaxation when a loud thumping came at the door. Everyone jumped. In pure instinct, Talyn leapt to her feet, hands reaching for her sais. Theac waved Errana away from the door and went to answer it, an intimidating scowl on his face.

"What is it?" he barked at whoever was standing outside. There were some inaudible words spoken, then, "Well, you'd better come in then."

A young man stumbled into the room, pale and soaked through. He gulped to find a room full of eyes staring at him. Theac's scowl probably wasn't helping.

"What is it, Arrol?" Errana asked gently, then glanced at Talyn and Theac. "He's my neighbour."

Arrol swallowed. "I've come to warn you. The rainfall is wreaking havoc on the Rush—if it doesn't stop soon, the banks are going to flood. The Poor Quarter will be in trouble first, but so will the rest of the city if it keeps up."

Errana went white. "Are we in danger up here?"

"I don't know." He hopped from foot to foot. "If the rain gets heavier, I think we might be. I have to go, there are others to warn."

The Wolves stared at each other as Arrol raced back out the door. Errana's hand lifted to her mouth in shock. Theac unconsciously stepped towards her but didn't seem to know what to do to reassure her.

"This is what happened last time," Zamaril muttered.

The Wolves turned as one to look at Talyn, clearly waiting for her cue.

Her heart thumped. And then she froze. They were looking at her like she had the solution to everything and she wasn't that Talyn anymore, the one who had an answer to every challenge, no matter how difficult.

The silence fell heavy over the room, and the Wolves' confidence began to waver. She saw the slumping of Zamaril's shoulders, the disappointment in Corrin's. She felt sick.

"*One step at a time, Tal. You need to understand the problem before you can attack it.*" Sari's voice steadied her panic.

She shook herself, clearing her throat so her voice came out firmly. "You said last time? Has this happened before?"

"There's usually a bit of flooding during monsoon season—the banks of the Rush can't handle the amount of rain we get. But it's never good when the rains come early. Last time it was really bad, back when I was a youngster in the City Patrol, maybe fifteen years ago now," Theac said. "Dock City flooded. Hundreds died."

One step. One step. "If floods happen most monsoon seasons, then there must be procedures in place to deal with it?" The towns in the foothills of the Ayrlemyre Mountains were all well-practiced in how to respond in case of avalanche after the spring melt.

"Not really." He cleared his throat. "Most years the flooding is mild and everyone just looks out for themselves, sandbagging their homes and the like. But if we get another bad one... the Poor Quarter will be the first underwater, and they don't have the resources to put anything in place."

"Where do people get the sandbags from?" Like a rusty key in a lock her mind was beginning to work again, to shake off the stiffness of a year away from a battle. She welcomed it.

"The city has a couple of storehouses of them in case of another bad flood. At least, they did back when I was patrol captain."

"They're still there." Zamaril spoke up unexpectedly, then gave them a sheepish look. "They're a good place to hide when you're being chased by the Patrol."

She frowned, thinking over what would likely happen if a similar disaster occurred in Ryathl. "If we're facing another bad flood, then there needs to be a structured approach to managing it if we want to save lives and homes. Theac, go down to the Market Quarter Patrol headquarters as quickly as you can and talk to Andres Tye. He can deploy his men and send word to the other watch officers on duty across the city. If they all work together, they can sandbag the city in strategic locations to stop the progress of the flood."

Theac reached up and pulled on his cloak, promising, "I'll be quick."

"What about us?" Corrin asked.

Talyn hesitated. To her, the answer was clear. But here in Mithranar... the relationship between the WingGuard and Dock City was so volatile, and she didn't understand it well enough to be sure of the right thing to do. But by the time she and Wolves got themselves back up to the citadel, found Ravinire, and asked him for orders, too much time would be wasted.

And the human Wolves were scared, clearly worried for their friends and family. Tiercelin's expression indicated wariness—as if sensing he was about to be drawn into something he didn't want to be. Instinct told her to help, an instinct she'd once had absolute faith in. Until she'd lost Sari. She swallowed, hating herself for being so indecisive.

"Go with your instincts, Tal. They've never led us wrong before."

"They led us to your death!"

"That doesn't make you useless. Enough of this, Talyn!"

"Captain?" Corrin stepped towards her. "Are you all right?"

She was horrified to realise that tears had risen to her eyes. Dammit, why was this so hard? But Sari had been right. If she kept wavering like this, she'd never get herself back. So she took a deep breath, and fought her fear. She looked around—everyone's eyes were on her, even Theac, who still hovered by the door.

She met his eyes. "Ask Andres if he could use our help."

Theac almost smiled, then saluted. "Aye, Captain."

"You're going to let us help?" Astonishment filled Zamaril's voice as the door slammed behind Theac. "What about Prince Cuinn?"

"The citadel is hundreds of metres in the air, Zamaril." She spoke briskly to cover her uncertainty. "They're hardly in danger of flooding."

Corrin nodded, looking at his mother. "Mam, we'll help pack up some things for you and the girls until Talon Parksin gets back. It may not come to it, but you'll need to be ready to leave quickly."

"All right." Colour was returning to Errana's face. "There's a spare bag in the hall closet—it should be big enough for our things, but not too big that I can't carry it."

The four Wolves worked alongside Talyn and Errana to pack the family's meagre belongings. They'd just finished, Errana offering to make some hot tea, when Theac re-appeared at the door, dripping wet.

"How did it go?" Talyn asked immediately.

"Over half the City Patrol has been called up into the citadel. Most of the rest haven't called in to their shifts—Tye's doing his best to drag them onto duty, but they're all protecting their homes."

"Who called them up to the citadel?" she asked in astonishment. "It's never going to flood, they're too far above sea level."

"Prince Mithanis." Theac scowled. "Poor winged folk don't want to get their feet wet."

"It's not that," Zamaril said bitterly. "They're afraid the humans might start fleeing up to the citadel to escape the flood. They don't want to be overrun."

Talyn gaped at him, momentarily at a complete and utter loss. Without a large group of helpers, she had no idea how the city was going to contain a flooding river. The mood in the room had dropped, and Corrin's shoulders were slumped as he spoke. "At least we can make sure you and the girls are safe, Mam."

Talyn stared at them, only half paying attention, as they fell into a discussion about whether they should leave immediately or wait to see if the street looked like it was going to be flooded. Corrin wondered whether the WingGuard would mind if his family sheltered at the Wolf barracks. Zamaril offered to sneak them in so nobody would know. Theac barked at him to stop being a fool. Halun and Tiercelin stayed quiet.

She told herself to listen to them, to help Corrin's family and then shelter up at the citadel. What exactly could she do anyway? She knew little about Dock City, and even less about how to deal with a flood.

But no, she'd already decided to go with her instincts, and it was time to commit.

"Theac?" She spoke before thinking, and everyone in the room turned to her.

"Captain?" He frowned.

"Talk to me. You know this city better than I do. What is the worst case scenario if the rain doesn't stop and the river continues to flood? If it's a bad one like fifteen years ago."

"I don't know exactly. As I said, it's only happened once before, on a day like this when the rains came early and we had a heavy and continuous downpour three days straight. We lost all the slums and a third of the city went under water, most of the Poor Quarter and good chunks of the Market and Dock Quarters."

She chewed on her lip, thinking. "Errana, can I have a quill and parchment please?"

Not questioning her odd request, Errana left the room briefly and returned holding a small piece of parchment along with quill and ink. Talyn took it with a smile of thanks, her gaze turning to the winged Wolf. "Tiercelin, can you fly in this weather?"

"Of course," he said promptly, indignant at the idea he might not be up to it.

Talyn wrote busily. "Take this to the Falcon as quickly as you can and then come straight back and find us."

"You think he'll help?" Zamaril sneered.

"He certainly won't if we don't ask." She finished writing and checked it over briefly before handing it to Tiercelin. "Keep that dry."

Tiercelin tucked it inside his tunic and turned swiftly to run back down the stairs and out into the night, surprising her with his lack of complaint. Talyn turned to face the others.

"Who can tell me where the weakest points in the city are, the lowest areas, where it will flood first?"

For a moment there was a thick silence in the room, and even Errana looked surprised. Zamaril was stripped of all smugness as he stared at her. "You're going to help?"

"*We* are going to help. Quickly now, where do we go first?"

Halun heaved his bulk out of the chair, tone and posture more authoritative than she'd ever seen him. "The Poor Quarter. The western area along the edge of the Rush is in a shallow depression of land—it will fill up like a lake once the banks burst. I know the quickest way to get there."

"All right. Lead the way." She glanced at Errana. "When Tiercelin comes back, please tell him where we've gone."

By the door, Talyn shrugged on her Callanan cloak and pulled the hood down snugly over her head. A jolt of pure energy fizzed through her, and her eyes closed momentarily. She'd forgotten what this was like—heading into an impossible situation with only her wits and strength to guide her. She ignored how terrifying that was without Sari at her side and instead focused on the rush of it. "Let's go."

Zamaril stopped her arm as she was about to follow the others out. "The game is in two days. One of us could easily sprain an ankle or injure something, and even if we don't, we'll be exhausted."

She would have laughed if he hadn't looked so serious. "Lives and homes are far more important than a game, Zamaril. We'll worry about alleya later."

Confusion flitted across his face for a moment, then for the first time since she'd known him, he spoke with genuine warmth. "Thank you."

CHAPTER 30

*R*aindrops stung Talyn's face as she stepped outside. Wind gripped her cloak, ripping the hood from her head. Rain immediately soaked her hair. In quick, practiced movement she pulled it back and tied it neatly before tugging the hood back over her face.

Halun moved into a run as he led the Wolves east towards the Rush. They settled into a distance-eating jog, their hard-won conditioning allowing them to keep up the pace easily.

Her feet splashed through puddles and mud as they moved through a series of darkened back streets for what felt like an interminable period. Eventually they emerged onto an area of high ground that lined the river. A steep stone levee dropped from their feet down to the swiftly-flowing water below—there was nothing like it on the opposite side where ramshackle and rundown homes and shops ran almost all the way to the banks.

The Poor Quarter.

Small fishing boats, surely the lifeblood of many of the quarter's residents, rocked wildly against their moorings. The rainfall had swollen the waterfall cascading over the wall to their left, turning the Rush into something chaotic and powerful. Dismay clutched at her at the sight of it already flooding its western banks and inching towards the buildings.

Directly below it lapped against the levee, still a good distance down. The wide bridge connecting the Poor and Market Quarters remained well above water level.

"Theac?" she shouted over the sound of rushing water and rain. "You said something about sandbags earlier. Where's the best place to start?"

"The storehouses are back in the Dock and Wall Quarters," he bellowed. "Too far away for us to be able to carry enough of them here to be effective."

"It's too late to save the slums, but what if we sandbag Wharf Street?" Corrin suggested. "That's the road leading from the bridge into the residential area of the Market Quarter, and from here that's the path the river will take if it floods the levee."

"The water isn't flooding the levee anytime soon," Zamaril disagreed, the wind catching his words and making them hard to understand. "There's still time to help the Poor Quarter."

"The residents know the river is flooding, there's time for them to make their own way out," Theac barked.

"We can't be sure of that. It's late—half of them will be asleep already. And what about those too young or old to move quickly, or too far from the river to notice how high it's rising?"

"The Poor Quarter is a third the size of the city." Talyn was ruthlessly practical. "Five of us cannot make enough of an impact."

"We don't need to." Halun shook his head. "The eastern half of the Poor Quarter, right up to where it hits the eastern headland of Feather Bay—that's all on higher ground. We just need to worry about this western section where the land is so low. That's a much smaller area to cover, Captain."

Talyn caught movement in the corner of her eye and pointed it out to the others. It resolved into a flying Tiercelin, buffeted by the wind. He struggled his way over, eventually landing beside them.

"I found the Falcon. He agreed to send some of the Patrol back to the city." Tiercelin's musical voice was barely audible. "They're on their way down the wall road as we speak. He also told me that since we're technically off duty, we are free to do as we please."

That was better than nothing. Talyn thought quickly, weighing Theac, Halun and Zamaril's words. "The City Patrol can start sand-bagging Wharf Street while we help the people here. Tiercelin, can you fly those instructions to Tye?"

While Andres was only a watch officer, she trusted him to want to do the right thing. If he couldn't convince his senior officers, she judged he was also resourceful enough to work out a way around them. At least, she hoped he was.

"Why would he listen to me?" He baulked.

"Tell them the request is from me," she said. "Do your best, Tiercelin, then come back here."

Tiercelin nodded sharply and leapt into the air, fighting his way back towards the city. She turned to the others. "The rest of you—can you swim?"

"We're Dock City humans," Zamaril said scornfully. "Of course we can swim."

"How do you want to approach it?" Theac asked, looking out over the steadily rising river to the Poor Quarter homes and shops.

"Follow me."

She ran for the bridge. Already people were moving out of the slums, and they had to duck and weave, forcing the pace. Once they reached the other side of the bridge, she moved off the road and away from the foot traffic, the Wolves gathering around her.

Raising her voice to be heard, she issued her commands. "Until the waters rise too high, we'll work on foot. We aim to warn those who can get out on their own, and help anyone sick or unable to walk unaided, starting with those closest to the riverbank and working backwards through the area Halun described. Theac, is there a central place in the city to send everyone? Some place on high ground where it will be warm and dry?"

"The town hall," he said. "It's big enough to fit hundreds of people and it's in the highest section of the city, near the wall. There are stores of food and blankets there."

"Perfect. For those you're able to warn, tell them to head for the Town Hall. Yell if you get into difficulty and need help. Any questions?"

There weren't any. The urgency of the situation had wiped away their disgruntlement and poor attitudes, revealing four men who were accustomed to difficulty and hardship and knew how to keep a straight head in a crisis. She hadn't seen that in them before.

Her initial instincts had been right about each of them. No matter how little they wanted it, they might one day make excellent protective guards. She forced an encouraging smile to her face. "Let's go."

Halun launched into movement, his big strides quickly carrying him away from them. Corrin and Theac weren't far behind. Zamaril moved to follow them, but Talyn reached out to take his arm. "You know this area, correct?"

He nodded, meeting her gaze unflinchingly. "I grew up here."

"Even with a smaller area to cover, five of us isn't enough to help everyone, not once those banks completely burst. If you grew up here, you know where to find those in the Shadowhawk's network." She figured they were also accustomed to working under pressure and would likely know the area and its residents even better than Zamaril. And when lives were on the line, she would use any resource available to her.

"Some of them." Not even an attempt to prevaricate, not in a crisis, despite the risk to himself admitting it caused. Her estimation of the thief went up.

"Find them. Tell them to start running, warning as many homes as they can farther back in the quarter. You were right before, a lot of them will be sheltering inside, unaware the banks are about to burst. Everyone in the western slums needs to get out, or at least move into the eastern half of the quarter where ground is higher."

He nodded. "I can do that."

"Good, go. Tell them to hurry, Zamaril!" Talyn moved to follow the Wolves, but Zamaril's voice stopped her.

"Captain?"

"What is it?"

"Thank you. There are even folks in Dock City who wouldn't bother with the slums."

"Nobody is more deserving of help than anyone else, Zamaril. Now go."

The Wolves were already a good distance ahead. She ran after them down the incline sloping away from the bridge and onto the main street running along the river's edge. Here water already covered the ground, lapping at the bottoms of her boots and turning the surface into a muddy bog.

People clogged the road, moving out of their homes and shops in a steady trickle. Theac was checking through the houses right on the river, so she turned right, into a narrower street.

The surface under her feet was muddy and uneven, a sewer running down each side. The homes were built from wood, most constructed unevenly from whatever materials had been available at the time. Not all had complete roofing.

She reached the end of the street and banged loudly on the door of the last house. When nobody answered, she pushed open the unlocked door and glanced inside. It was empty, its occupants already gone.

In the next house along, an old woman sat huddled in her bed, staring fearfully out the window.

"Is anybody else here?" Talyn asked gently.

She shook her head vigorously, looking up at Talyn with worried eyes. "I can't walk very well anymore. I thought it safer to stay in here where it's dry."

"It's not safe to stay, the river is flooding." Talyn held out her hand. "Come with me, I'll help get you somewhere safe."

The woman stared at her for a long moment before pushing off her threadbare blanket and stretching out her arm. Talyn grasped the fragile hand and helped the woman to her feet. Once she was steady, Talyn took the blanket from the bed and wrapped it around her thin shoulders. With Talyn taking most of her weight, they inched their way back up the street towards the bridge.

Tiercelin was just landing. He was soaked and shivering, but his shoulders straightened when he caught sight of Talyn. "The City Patrol are headed to Wharf Street." He hesitated. "I couldn't find Tye, so I just went straight to the group the Falcon sent down from the citadel."

"Good work," she approved. "This lady can't walk unaided. Can you fly her to Town Hall?"

The woman shook her head, every inch of her turning stiff with reluctance at the sight of one of the winged folk. She huddled closer to Talyn.

"It's all right," Talyn murmured. "He won't hurt you."

"Where is he taking me?" The woman's trembling voice was barely audible above the wind and rain.

"Somewhere safe and dry. It's going to be okay." Talyn shot a look towards Tiercelin. *Help me out here!*

"What about my house?" She started sobbing, a frail, wretched sound.

"It's going to be all right." Tiercelin stepped forward to gently take her hand. "You'll see. I'm going to take you somewhere warm and safe." He smiled then, flooding the woman with his winged folk beauty even in his bedraggled state. "All right, now, you just have to hold tight onto me. That's right. Don't let go."

Talyn stayed only long enough to see Tiercelin grip the woman tightly and launch into the air before turning around. On her way back along the street she passed Theac herding two small children. A strong wind had kicked up, flipping back her cloak so the driving rain got underneath, soaking through her coat and shirt.

The next two houses in her street were empty, and by the time she got to the fourth house, the water was rising above her ankles. She glanced down towards the river—it was flowing freely over the banks, the entire road along the bank now under water. It was beginning to collect debris and send it flooding down the streets too, bits of wood, plants, other rubbish. Rain continued to fall and the waterfall roared. Dread clutched at her chest.

This was going to get much worse before it got better.

She waded through murky water in the next house, helping a

mother and two children out and up to the bridge. The mother was sick, racking coughs shuddering her too-thin frame. Talyn didn't like leaving her to make the trek to Town Hall unaided but something told her there would be others in worse condition and she wanted to preserve Tiercelin's strength for them.

In the distance was Halun, his bulk wading easily through the water, a shivering man in his arms. He'd found a makeshift raft from somewhere and was dragging it behind him with a piece of thick rope. Two young women sat on it, soaked and pale, faces tight with fear.

Corrin shepherded a group of beggar children out of a ramshackle building close to the riverbank. More residents were making their own way out as it became obvious the water level was going to keep rising and they saw the Wolves escorting people to higher ground.

"Could we use boats?" Talyn asked Halun when they came together, liking his raft idea.

"I thought of that, Captain, but most of the fishing vessels moored nearby have either been washed away or are too large to use in these narrow streets. And looking for others could take a lot of time."

The water had soaked through Talyn's boots and added weight to her legs as she waded back through to the final houses in her street. Many of them were derelict and hadn't been lived in for months. She waded from door to door, calling out for anyone who remained. They were all empty.

"This one's done," she shouted to Halun as she waded back out to the main road.

He nodded, voice lifting over the waterfall and rain. "Then we've cleared all the streets leading off this main river road. We can start moving further back."

Theac came sloshing over before she could go anywhere. "Look."

She and Halun both glanced up at the bridge where Theac was pointing. People were streaming onto it now, all coming from farther back in the quarter. Parents carried or led children, older folk supported each other, while others moved under their own steam. All were soaked and shivering, most of them too-thin and not properly clothed, but they were alive.

"Someone's warning the rest of the slums." Halun's voice rang with relief.

"That's Zamaril's work." She couldn't help her smile. "Come on, let's make sure nobody gets left behind."

SHE RESCUED two small children before the water rose to her waist. Shivering wracked her soaked body—despite the physical exercise, the wind was growing cold, and so was the water she was wading through.

When next she saw Tiercelin, he was struggling. He'd continued to fly those who couldn't walk unaided to Town Hall, and she wondered at the strength it must take to battle the strong winds while carrying the weight of another human. His grit bolstered her, and she waded determinedly further back into the Poor Quarter.

Several steps later, she was almost knocked off her feet as a wave of water washed right up to her hips. She gasped at the coldness of it, then gritted her teeth and pushed open the door of the next house.

This one was empty too, though she wasted precious time slogging through waist-deep water to check every room. A heavy object—a wheel torn from a cart, it looked like—hit her in the legs as another wave of floodwater washed through the front door when she attempted to leave, knocking her off her feet.

She went down, water rushing over her head, choking as muddy water ran down her throat. It took a few seconds to get her feet back under her and then lift her head clear. The water steadily continued to rise, and her teeth were beginning to chatter.

Talyn checked the final house on the street and found it empty, before struggling back up to higher ground, where Tiercelin stood at the bridge, trembling. His arms were wrapped tightly around himself, hair slicked to his skull, great grey wings bedraggled.

"It's rising too fast," he said. "I don't think you're going to have time to check them all."

Talyn glanced with dread down at the cold, dark water that inched higher with every second that passed. What terror must anyone still left in the quarter be feeling? Movement caught her eye—Corrin staggering up, one arm wrapped around an elderly man hobbling along gamely beside him.

The stream of people from further inside the quarter had slowed significantly, but two men were dragging a small boat down from the bridge and onto the water. Once they were onboard, they began rowing towards a series of buildings Talyn and her Wolves hadn't gotten to yet.

"Shadowhawk's people," Zamaril said at her side, having arrived without her noticing. "They'll deal with the southwestern area. We just have to focus on this part."

"I'm going to have to start swimming," she said, pulling off her heavy cloak and unlacing her boots. The tunic went too, until she was clad only in her wet shirt and breeches. "Damn, it's getting cold!"

"We've been colder before." Sari's voice offered cheerfully, before disappearing as quickly as she had come. They had. Even now, it was more the change from such thick heat that made her feel cold. Compared to winter in the Twin Thrones, it was still warm.

"I'm not sure that's a good idea," Tiercelin said worriedly. "What about the debris? The current looks like it's only getting stronger."

"It's not over yet," she said. "There could be more people trapped down there."

"The captain's right," Corrin added. "Living in the Poor Quarter doesn't make them worth less than anybody else. We can't save everyone, but we should go on as long as we can."

Zamaril simply began yanking off his boots.

Tiercelin nodded. "You get them out of those houses, and I'll get those that can't walk to safety. Deal?"

The three of them smiled at the winged man. "Deal."

Tiercelin stepped forward to take the man Corrin was leading, and then lifted into the air without another word. Corrin saw Talyn had stripped and began doing the same. He didn't miss Talyn's concerned look.

"Don't worry. I spent my boyhood free diving in the bay with my da for fish. I'm a strong swimmer." His confident smile was at odds with his soaked, shivering frame, but it lessened her concern nonetheless.

Together they waded back into the water. As soon as it reached her chest, Talyn began to swim. It was easier to manoeuvre this way, and faster too, though she was forced to expend extra energy on avoiding the various debris being carried along by the floodwater.

She swam towards the houses most in danger, diving under the water to get through the door then surfacing inside the house. There was a man in this one, but he was already dead, floating amidst a tin cooking pan and a wooden basket. His skin was blue. Talyn's heart clenched in despair, but she had no choice but to leave the body there and keep looking.

She ran into Theac a few moments later. He had stripped and was swimming also, clearly looking for her. They tread water in the middle of the street. She hoped she didn't look as blue with cold as he did.

"I've just been up on the clear ground," he shouted. "It's going to get too dangerous down here soon. Once the bank bursts completely, the river will turn into rapids, and that's going to make this flooded area a whirlpool of dangerous currents, especially if the wind doesn't die down."

She nodded. "We'll keep going as long as we can."

"Captain." His hand reached out to grab her wrist. "We are responsible for the safety of our wing."

His words checked her like a slap to the face. She wasn't a Callanan warrior, responsible only to her partner anymore. She couldn't use the lives of her wing as recklessly as she might use her own. Guilt hammered at her, along with a surge of fear of making another mistake.

"You make the call when to pull them out," she said, meeting his eyes. "I'll trust the decision to you."

"Aye, Captain." He let her go, and they parted ways.

Talyn swam into another house. Her teeth had stopped chattering, which probably wasn't a good sign, and her limbs were becoming sluggish. One look at her hands showed blue, wrinkled skin. Gritting her teeth, she forced the lethargy away.

Then she saw the small boy. He was struggling, trying to keep his head above water, but beginning to tire. Talyn surfaced beside him, and her heart clenched at the look of utter relief on his face. She took a strong hold around his waist.

"Can you hold your breath while we swim under the door? It won't be long."

He nodded, eyes fixed on her face. She smiled reassuringly at him and kicked down, taking him with her. She swam as quickly as she could out the door, then surfaced on the other side. The boy started breathing again immediately, though his teeth chattered with cold.

Back where Tiercelin was waiting, the water was now up to his knees. He took the boy securely in his arms and smiled in reassurance. The boy smiled tiredly and snuggled into his chest.

"Wait until I return before you go back in, Captain." Tiercelin gripped her shoulder, forcing her to meet his eyes. He was haggard, his face pale and wet, his eyes showing dark shadows. His arms and shoulders trembled with the strain of carrying so many people. "You're too cold. Stay out a few minutes and warm yourself up or you'll be no good to anyone."

He was right, reluctant as she was to admit it. She busied herself rubbing arms and legs vigorously, restoring warmth as much as was possible in the wind and rain. Halun appeared, sloshing out of the water. He carried a woman in his arms, and a girl hung off his back with her arms locked around his neck. Clinging to the waist of his pants was a skinny youth. Theac, Zamaril and Corrin were behind him, leading or carrying another three people each.

"We've got them all," Theac said wearily. "This lot are the remaining inhabitants. They'd all gone to shelter together at some place they thought would be safe."

"The Shadowhawk's people are out too. It's getting too dangerous even for the boat," Zamaril added. "I think we've covered as much as we can. We just have to hope those living on the eastern side of the quarter have stayed on high ground."

He stood with his head hanging, shoulders sagging forward. Theac and Corrin were hunched over their knees from pure exhaustion. Talyn felt like doing the same. Halun stood tall, a tower of strength.

"Take a breather," she said. "We'll escort them up to Town Hall together when Tiercelin gets back."

It wasn't long before Tiercelin appeared in the sky, battered about by the wind as he fought to fly a steady course. This time when he landed, he was out of breath, his entire body trembling.

"This is it," she told him. "Why don't you take a break from flying and walk back with us?"

"Sounds... good." He gasped, waving a hand when she gave him a concerned look. "Just... catching my breath."

They had no sooner begun walking over the bridge when a man came running towards them from the direction of the city, eyes wide with what looked like panic. He was middle-aged, too thin as with many of the folk she'd seen tonight, his brown hair plastered to his skull.

"My babies," he cried. "Have you got my babies?"

They were all momentarily frozen by the man's approach, minds sluggish from cold and exhaustion. All except Halun. The big man stepped forward and laid a hand on his arm.

"What's wrong, sir?"

"My babies." He was distraught. "I left them... I was working in the city tonight... I left them here at home. Did you find them? Where are they?"

"How old are your children? Tell me what they look like," Halun commanded gently.

He scrubbed at his face, struggling to focus. "Twins, ten years old. They both have blonde hair, curly, too long, it always needs cutting..." He took a shuddering breath, as if realising he was rambling. "Their names are Miekl and Lana. Please tell me you found them?"

Talyn shot a questioning glance at the Wolves—she didn't recognise those descriptions. They shook their heads too. "They must still be down there," she said quietly to Theac.

Her second nodded and turned back to the man. "Which house do you live in? We'll go and get your children for you."

"That one." He pointed to one of the houses, only four blocks back from the river. The water was almost up to the roof. Talyn cursed inwardly—how had they missed it?

"I'll get them," she said quickly, sharing a look with Theac. It was too dangerous to allow anyone else to attempt. "The rest of you head to Town Hall."

"It's too dangerous," Theac said flatly. "I'll go."

"Theac, I'm Callanan. I know you don't understand what that means, but trust me, I've been trained for situations like this. I'm ordering you to leave. I'll see you up at Town Hall."

"Captain!" Corrin raised his voice to capture her attention. "There isn't enough time. Look at the waterfall."

The cascading water was now at least triple its usual volume. On the western bank of the Rush, the river had risen over halfway up the levee. There was no more eastern bank—the river had turned into a churning beast, full of debris and powerful currents. It flowed down into the Poor Quarter, seething around buildings and streets alike.

"Go!" she shouted. "That's an order."

She didn't stay to argue further, wading back into the water and diving under before coming up and swimming strongly towards the house the man had pointed out. A distant roaring sound came to her ears—the rapids were getting worse.

She dug deep, increasing her speed. The water lapped at the roof of the house. She took a deep breath and dived down, seeking the doorway with her hands. Eventually she found it and swam through. Her breath burned in her chest, and spots danced before her eyes. She kicked upwards, desperately seeking air. Finally, her head broke through, mere inches from the ceiling. She looked around, seeing nothing in the living room.

Another few gulps of air and she was diving again, heading for where she hoped the children's bedroom would be. She swam for what seemed like forever in the black water, eventually surfacing in another room at the back of the house.

There were two dark shapes in the corner. Shouting the children's names, she swam towards them. A small cry answered her back. She came up beside them, relief flooding her.

"Are you all right?"

"We were waiting for Pa to come and get us." The twins chattered over each other in their fear and exhaustion. "So we were floating, like he taught us at the beach."

"I'm going to get you out of here." She summoned a reassuring smile for them. "I want each of you to grab my shirt, and don't let go."

The walls shuddered, and fear spiked in Talyn. She managed to get the children out the front door, and then looked wildly around. The flooding waters had turned into a raging torrent. There was no way she was going to get herself and two small children back to high ground before it hit.

One of the houses nearby was larger than the rest, its roof still above the water line. She made sure the twins were still holding on tight, then towed them towards the roof.

"Can you climb up there?" she asked, trying to keep the urgency from her face and voice so as not to panic them. Her teeth chattered loudly and her limbs were growing numb. They nodded, afraid despite her forced confidence. Lana went first, her feet digging into Talyn's shoulders as she climbed up and onto the roof. Miekl followed after. The twins huddled at the edge, arms wrapped tightly around each other.

"Climb right up to the highest point," Talyn shouted as the onrush of rapids screamed towards them. "As high as you can. Hurry!"

It hit Talyn before she could climb onto the roof too. The force of the rushing water slammed into her body, tearing her away from the house. She struggled, then cried out in pain as her knee slammed into something hard and unyielding.

Water was everywhere, over her head and rushing into her mouth and nose. She choked, spitting out muddy water, and tried to float, but the water was too rough. The fierce current held her in its grip, and she wasn't strong enough to swim out of it. Again, the water covered her head, and she had to exert all her strength to struggle back to the surface.

Her reserves of strength were almost gone. She'd fought hard against the currents for what seemed like hours now, and the cold had sapped the energy from her muscles. Her head began to sink again, and she didn't have the will to rise. Her arms struggled weakly for a few moments, but then she began to sink, water running into her nose and mouth. Blackness appeared at the edge of her vision.

Realisation finally hit that she might die here. Without thinking she opened her mouth to shout Sari's name, instinct telling her that her partner would be nearby, already coming to help. Instead water rushed into her lungs.

Because Sari was gone, dead because of Talyn. Because she'd been overconfident. The knowledge was crushing and for a moment she stopped fighting entirely, the absence of her partner a deep, gnawing grief, a hole in her chest that would never heal.

Her eyes slid closed.

CHAPTER 31

Strong arms wrapped about Talyn's waist, and she was hauled bodily towards the surface. Her head broke into clear air, and she gasped for breath, the arms still locked bruisingly tight around her. The water in her lungs stifled her breathing and she convulsed, gagging.

Focused on the burning in her lungs, the choking need for air, she barely noticed as she was towed through the water. Her rescuer struggled against the strong current, but he or she was fresher than Talyn, and managed to drag them both out of the water's grip and up onto higher ground.

The arms loosened from her waist, and she slumped into the mud, spitting and retching river water until her lungs were clear.

Her entire body trembled—she'd been inches from death.

Once she'd emptied her lungs and stomach of muddy river water and could breathe again, she dragged herself to her hands and knees, then forced herself to her feet, wanting to know who'd plucked her from the river. A man stood nearby, as soaked and covered in mud as she was, watching her carefully. His face was hidden by a dripping black mask. The usual cloak hung, soaked through, around his tall form. How had he swum in that?

LISA CASSIDY

"Didn't realise you had a death wish, Captain Dynan."

Shocked, she backed up a step, the effort launching another coughing fit. "*Shadowhawk?* What are you doing here?"

Instead of responding, he looked her over. "Are you all right?"

"I'm fine, thanks to you." She paused, then a sudden, urgent thought occurred to her. "What about the children? Were they swept away too? Are they all right?"

He nodded, raising a hand to forestall her flood of desperate questions. "I got them clear before you, though it meant you almost died before I could get back to you. They're safe, just over there."

She glanced at where he pointed; the twins sat with their arms wrapped around each other, looking scared and cold but very much alive. Her shoulders sagged with relief.

Another few deep breaths and she had the strength to lift her head and study him for a minute. Despite being as dishevelled as she was, he was breathing easily. "I... you saved my life."

"I did." He nodded. "Are you all right? No crippling injuries?"

"No." She visually checked herself over. "I'm fine. What are you doing out here?"

"Well, you *were* the one who sent Zamaril to rouse my network to help clear people out of the slums." He flashed a smile. "Thanks for that, by the way. But I'm here the same as you, Captain, to help where possible."

"You saved their lives as well as mine." She gestured to the twins. "Thank you."

"All in a day's work." More glibness. "Now, there are fishermen stuck out at sea who were returning with the day's catch when this wild weather started up, so if you can walk, I'm going to leave you to get the children to safety and try and round up some more of my network to go and help them."

She hesitated. She should be doing more, asking him questions, but she was still exhausted and shaken, and the children were in danger of getting ill if they stayed out in the wet and cold too much longer. So instead she just nodded. "I'll make sure they're okay."

"Goodbye, Captain Dynan." He paused as he turned away, glancing back. "And thank you for your help tonight. You and your Wolves saved many lives that I could not."

He strode off before Talyn could say another word.

TALYN LIMPED THROUGH DOCK CITY, a twin clinging to each hand. She avoided Wharf Street in the hopes Patrolmen would be busy sandbagging and not wanting to interrupt them. Since the Wolves had left Corrin's home hours earlier, someone had been out lighting covered lamps along the main thoroughfares of the Market Quarter. Not that she could see anyone. Rain drove across the empty streets, pattering incessantly on the cobblestones.

Her knee was swollen and aching and her body wouldn't stop trembling. After what felt like an interminable period of trudging through the sleeting rain, the twins helpfully calling out directions, the hall came into sight.

The road curved upwards to where a large brick structure stood on a section of high ground close to the base of the wall. Lamps lit up the area surrounding it, and she trudged towards it gratefully.

A wall of warm air and the hum of conversation greeted her as she walked through the open door. People filled the large space inside, most sitting huddled in small groups, many wrapped in thick blankets. Fires had been lit at both ends of the hall, casting a rosy glow over the interior. Talyn shivered, eyes closing momentarily as warm air brushed over her skin.

The twins' father had been hovering anxiously near the entrance. At the sight of them, he let out a cry and opened his arms. The twins let go of Talyn's hands to bury themselves in their father's embrace.

Tiercelin appeared in front of her, wings rustling in agitation, relief evident on his features. "Thank goodness you're okay. You took so long... we were afraid... well, we—"

"Captain!" Corrin's shout of greeting almost drowned out Tiercelin's words, given even more effect because he was usually such a quietly spoken youth. Theac strode at his side, Halun not far behind. She was surprised by how relieved they seemed at her appearance.

"How's the sandbagging going?" she asked.

"You can worry about that when you get warm." Tiercelin waved at a nearby man and muttered a few words. In a few moments he was back, carrying a thick blanket. "Here, get this wrapped around you."

"What about the—"

"Warm first," Tiercelin said firmly. "The Shadowhawk has organised some of his network to help here. They've arranged dry clothes and blankets for the survivors and are getting started on hot soup and drinks."

She took the blanket Tiercelin was insistently proffering. "The Shadowhawk?"

Corrin smirked. "The City Patrol are too busy sandbagging Wharf Street or looking after their own homes to notice."

"Okay then, we need to—"

"I sent Tye to go up and check in with the Falcon. Figured the lad was the least likely to offend anyone up there," Theac said. "The Falcon assured him that Prince Cuinn is safe—he's posted some Falcons to keep an eye on him until the weather calms down."

Her mouth opened. Closed. "You did?"

He nodded briskly. "Prince Cuinn is still our responsibility, Captain, and it's my job to take care of things when you're not available."

Talyn swallowed, reaching out to grip his shoulder in silent gratitude. She'd almost died earlier, and now she was suddenly, truly, wonderfully glad she hadn't. That realisation rocked her, made her grip tighter than she'd intended, but he didn't seem to notice. "Thanks, Theac."

TALYN FOUND a quiet room and quickly changed out of her dripping clothes into some dry ones Corrin found for her. When she was done, she felt a little better, but her knee throbbed painfully. She limped out of the room, surveying the scene before her.

Halun was lugging huge piles of chopped wood in to keep the fires going. Theac was deep in conversation with Andres Tye and another man she thought must be the Wall Quarter patrol commander. Zamaril had appeared—carrying mugs of steaming drink to those who didn't have any yet.

And most surprising of all, Tiercelin moved between those laid out on pallets, attending to injuries without hesitating over the fact it was humans he was helping. A flush of pleasure warmed her body. Her Wolves were good men. She was proud of them.

She looked around for Corrin, and spotted him approaching her, carrying a steaming cup. "Here, drink some of this."

She cupped both hands around its blissful warmth and took a long swallow of the deliciously sweet kahvi. Its warmth spread through her, and the blanket and dry clothes helped, so that she felt she might finally get warm again.

"Shall I get you another one, Captain?" Corrin offered once she'd drained the cup.

"No, leave it for everyone else here. That's plenty for me."

"Captain?" Tiercelin approached them, concern still written in his face as he studied her. "I noticed you limping before, did you hurt yourself?"

"I got swept away by the rapids. My knee smashed into something."

"Sit down here, Captain." He motioned her to a crate, and she did as he bade, glad to rest her aching legs. Once she was settled, he pointed to her left pants leg. "Do you mind?"

"Go ahead."

Tiercelin knelt gracefully before her, wings resting loosely on the floor to either side of him, and with deft fingers rolled her pants up above her knee. It was swollen and purple, the bruising livid. His hands were cool as he gently palpated the injured area. "You've strained some ligaments, but I don't think you've done any permanent damage. I'll give it a treatment now, but you'll probably need a couple more before it will be fully healed."

His hands moved gently around her injury, eyes sliding closed in concentration. Talyn began to relax as warmth spread through her knee and the sharp ache began fading. She let her head loll back to rest on the wall behind her, eyes on Tiercelin as he worked.

Suddenly his head flew back, eyes wide with shock, and he made a cutting motion with his hands, physically shifting away from her. She was so languid it took a moment for her to realise what was happening. By then Theac had already barked, "What is it, Tiercelin?

"Captain, your magic..." His voice trailed off, something like shock and horror and wonder all mixed together filling his voice.

"What magic?" She blinked at him.

"You're..." He frowned. "There's a wound in your magic—a wide, gaping wound that festers."

"What are you talking about, lad?" Theac demanded.

Ignoring him, Tiercelin turned pleading grey eyes to her. "What happened to you?"

"I don't know what you mean," she said, genuinely puzzled.

"You must," he insisted. "My healing magic... it uses my body's energy to help heal your physical wounds. But *your* magic is torn open just like a physical wound, like a ragged gash deep inside. It's not healing. Captain, I've never seen anything like it."

Her gaze caught on his, not knowing how to respond to his obvious distress. "I don't know, Tiercelin. My Callanan magic allows me to create a shield of light like you've seen, that's all. It's not winged folk magic."

Tiercelin looked up and around, seeming to notice that the other Wolves were staring at him in concern. He turned back to her and whatever it was he'd been thinking or feeling faded away. He cleared his throat and shifted closer to her. "I'm sorry, Captain, maybe I'm wrong. I'll keep working on your knee if that's okay?"

"Please, do," she encouraged him. Whatever he'd been doing had felt wonderful.

Tiercelin's face was a mask of concentration as he worked on her knee. She wasn't exactly sure what he was doing—his hands performed quick movements around her knee without actually touching it.

"It's aural healing."

Talyn looked up as Theac spoke, lifting an eyebrow in query.

"It's part of winged folk magic. Some of them have the ability to heal by working on the aura of a person. It's far more efficient and powerful than normal healing practices. Tiercelin is very talented." There was no dislike or even the usual hint of contempt in Theac's voice as he spoke of the winged Wolf, just a surprisingly genuine respect.

Even so, Tiercelin flashed him a mildly irritated look. "There's actually a lot more to it than that. But yes, Captain, those are the basics."

Tiercelin finished a few moments later. He made a cutting motion with his hands, then stood, his wings flaring for balance. The swelling around her knee had lessened substantially and the pain had dulled to a faint throb. Even the bruising didn't look as severe. She flexed it gingerly—no pain, just stiffness.

"That's amazing." She smiled in wonder. "Tiercelin, you're a marvel!"

Halun appeared before he could respond, a frown on his face that drew the pattern of his slave tattoo tight over his cheekbones. Andres Tye was at his side. He gave Talyn a smile of welcome despite the grim note to his voice when he spoke. "The Patrolmen and the townsfolk have managed to block up Wharf Street and Parlour Road, but the levees flooded just a short while ago, and now the flood is threatening via another route."

"Sailor Road?" Corrin asked.

Tye nodded. "But we don't have enough to hold it. The men sand-bagging in the other two locations are only barely keeping the waters back. The rest of the Patrol is still up at the citadel. We can't spare any of them to go to Sailor Road."

Talyn stood, expecting her knee to hurt, but it didn't. "We'll go. Five of us is better than nothing. Hopefully the rains will stop soon and cut us a break."

"There are *six* of us, and you aren't going anywhere on that knee," Tiercelin said, suddenly assertive.

She shook her head. "You need to stay here to look after the sick and injured. My knee will be fine, it doesn't hurt anymore."

"No." He shook his head stubbornly. "I'm one of the Wolves. That's what you keep telling us, right? That we're a wing?"

Talyn hesitated, the same warmth from earlier filling her chest at Tiercelin's declaration. A lump appeared in her throat, and she had to clear it before speaking. "Yes, that's right."

"Then I'm coming with you. Give me a few minutes and I'll find something to strap your knee with."

Tiercelin hurried off, not noticing the stares of the other four Wolves on his back. None of them said a word, but something indefinable had shifted. Theac cleared his throat, turning back to Talyn. "These people are wet and exhausted, and some of them ill or injured. Who's going to hand out blankets and hot food and drink if we go?"

"I think I can manage to run things here," Tye interjected with a smile. "And let's have some faith in the city folk to help out their own."

"He's right," Talyn said, shooting Andres a grateful look. "It's warm and dry in here, that's the main thing. They're all going to be in a lot more trouble if Sailor Road floods."

Halun reappeared. He was carrying Talyn's Callanan cloak and boots. "We carried these back with us when you went after the children. I've managed to mostly dry your cloak. You'll probably need it."

"Thanks," she said gratefully, replacing her blanket with the cloak. She felt better as soon as its weight settled around her shoulders.

Tiercelin arrived soon after, efficiently strapping Talyn's knee with some odd sort of stretchy material she'd never seen before. He caught at her arm as she went to follow the others, his voice dropping to an undertone only she could hear.

"I can't fix that deeper wound, Captain. That will take time and skill that I don't have—but I know you were lying back there. From what I saw... I honestly don't know how you function day to day with a spirit wound like that."

Spirit wound.

Sari.

She'd been a fool not to realise what he was talking about. The knowledge swept through her like a tide and she had to fight not to rock back on her feet. Unable to speak, she simply gave Tiercelin a nod and hurried after the others out the door.

THE RAIN WAS FALLING AS STRONGLY AS ever. It beat at her the moment she stepped out, and she glanced longingly back at the warm interior of Town Hall. Then they turned a corner, and all was darkness.

"How are we going to get sandbags down to Sailor Road quickly enough to be effective?" she asked Theac.

"We're not in the Poor Quarter anymore, Captain," he said, a note of bitterness to his voice. "When the sandbag storehouses were set up, the planners put them close to the danger points in the Market, Dock and Wall Quarters. Sailor Road is the main link between the west bank of the Rush—where a lot of the smaller fishing boats dock—to the residential area of the Dock Quarter. There's a storehouse right where we're going."

Not long after, they rounded a corner to see the water lapping up a wide road sloping downwards towards the western bank of the river. The warehouse stood at the top of the street. Theac's quick shove showed the doors were locked.

Talyn glanced at the rising water level, then at Halun. "Can you break them down?"

The big man cracked his knuckles and nodded. He walked to the doors and leaned against them, pushing all his considerable strength into busting through. The wood bent inwards but didn't open. Halun strained harder, and Theac joined him, but it wouldn't budge. After a moment they stepped back.

"It must be barred on the inside," Theac said. "Solid steel, I'd say."

"You're serious?" She stared at him. Six thrices! The insanity of it killed her.

Zamaril swore, gave the doors a good kick. It didn't help.

"I don't fancy standing in the rain and staring at the door while the water laps at my ankles," Tiercelin said. "And here I was just beginning to think humans might be as smart and capable as us winged folk."

331

"Zamaril can do it," Corrin said suddenly. He had been standing a little apart from them, gazing up at the windows.

Zamaril spun, the surprise on his face turning into a secretive little smile. Corrin matched the smile with a grin. "You're telling me the best thief in Dock City can't climb up there, break in through a window, and unbar the doors from the inside?"

"Those windows will be locked," Theac said.

Zamaril and Corrin both turned to give him a scornful glance, but it was Zamaril who spoke. "I've gotten through a hundred windows a lot more secure than that."

"How will you get up there?" Talyn asked, genuine concern in her voice. She'd seen Zamaril's agility firsthand, but the rain was still pouring down and visibility was limited at best in the dark.

He studied the wall with a practiced eye. "If Halun can give me a leg up to that drain, I can shimmy up to reach the lowest window. Once I'm there, it will be easy."

Without a word, Halun stepped forward and lifted Zamaril bodily onto his shoulders before moving to stand beneath the drainpipe. The thief gripped it firmly and scrambled upwards until he was just below the lowest window. Air gusted past Talyn's head as Tiercelin leapt into the air to hover beneath Zamaril.

The thief twisted around to stare at him. Tiercelin gave him a little nod, then spread his arms—as if to say *I got you if you fall.*

Zamaril gave a tiny nod in return, then focused his attention on the window, which he had open in seconds. Talyn and the others stood huddled outside, hunched in their cloaks, trying not to shiver. It took the thief several minutes, but he finally managed to unbar the doors from the inside. He emerged covered in dust and coughing, shooting them an indignant look as they pushed past him to get inside out of the rain.

When Talyn took a deep breath, she also started coughing. The sandbags had evidently been in the warehouse for years and there was dust everywhere. There were plenty of them, however, stacked from floor to ceiling. She glanced back outside. "Does anybody have any sandbagging experience?"

"We'll need to line them up between two solid points, so the water can't flow around," Theac said. "I'd suggest between the wall of this building, and that house across the street. They both have solid brick walls."

Without a word, Halun hefted two bags and turned to head back outside.

Then stopped dead.

Three men stood at the warehouse entrance, framed in the backdrop of darkness and sheeting rain, making it hard to see them properly.

"Six people isn't enough to sandbag this road as fast as it needs to be to keep ahead of the rising floodwater." The Shadowhawk's voice rang out. "Want some help?"

Halun turned back to Talyn, one eyebrow raised. She gave him a little nod. The big man tossed his two sandbags to the Shadowhawk. He caught them and headed back out into the rain without a word. The two men with him moved inside, heading to grab their own bags. She recognised one of them—he made kahvi at one of the cafes in Dock City. Corrin had taken her there once.

Petro? Or something like that.

He gave her a little nod of acknowledgement as he passed her. She shook off her curiosity and went to get some sandbags.

They had a flood to stop.

THE NINE of them worked in a line, each stacking sandbags in their own section to make a wall across the road. Talyn worked at the end of the line, a wall on her right and Halun on her left—the former dock worker knew how to stack and could carry about six bags each trip, so his section of the wall rose far more rapidly than the rest of them.

They were already exhausted from their rescue efforts earlier in the evening, so now they set a slow but steady pace. Too tired to talk or sing, the Wolves and the Shadowhawk's people nonetheless worked in silent accord.

It wasn't long before Talyn's back and shoulders were aching, and her knee began hurting again. Her section of the wall grew waist high, and the flood water lapped about half way up. They were just managing to keep ahead of the flow. Halun noted her renewed limp and began dumping half his load next to her each time he came back from the warehouse.

"You shouldn't be walking on that knee, Captain," he said with a rare smile. "I can carry enough for both of us."

The night passed into the early hour before dawn, and still they worked. It became a sheer effort of will to keep mechanically stacking the bags that Halun dropped beside her. They just barely kept ahead of the flooding waters.

Then, as blue light started filtering across the sky, the rain stopped.

One moment it was pouring down on them, and then there was nothing. The wind died almost as quickly, so that a sudden silence descended on the road. Talyn kept sandbagging for a few moments before she realised, then Halun touched her shoulder. She looked up groggily. The flood waters were lapping near the top of their wall, but they'd stopped rising.

The Shadowhawk straightened too, lifting his gaze to the sky before it returned to land on hers. "I think that's our cue. It's been a pleasure, Wolves."

He was gone without another word, the two men of his network following suit. All three separated at the top of the street, going in different directions. Talyn straightened, swearing as her back and shoulders cracked painfully. Zamaril let out an almighty groan and collapsed against the wall, rubbing his shoulders.

"Is it really over?" Corrin whispered, his voice dry. He swayed on trembling legs, dark hair plastered to his forehead, eyes hollow from exhaustion.

Theac gave his soaked-through cloak a dark look. "I think I'm about to start sprouting moss."

For some reason, they all found his comment hilarious. Tiercelin started it, laughing out loud at the words. Corrin joined in next, shaking so much with laughter that he had to sit down. Soon they were all sitting there on the wet cobblestones, sagging in exhaustion against the wall of sandbags, laughing themselves silly.

"I need some sleep," Theac said eventually, when the laughter stopped. "And some kahvi."

"And some dry clothes." Zamaril smirked.

Theac snorted and allowed his head to thump back against the sandbags.

Talyn dragged herself to her feet. "As much as I like the idea of sitting out here in the wet and cold, I like the idea of a hot fire better. Our work here is done."

Zamaril groaned loudly as he rose to his feet. "How far is it back to Town Hall?"

THE HALL WAS JUST as they left it; warm and dry. Exhausted as they were, they consciously quickened their pace when it came into sight around the corner. Talyn stopped dead just inside the doorway.

All the children were sitting together wrapped in blankets in a semi-circle around a small group of musicians at the top of the hall. They sat on stools. A couple were playing fiddles, one a small guitar. Another sang softly. The sick and injured had pulled their pallets closer so that they could listen, and they lay there watching with sleepy eyes.

The healthy adults were tending the wounded and passing around steaming mugs of kahvi and hot soup. They tapped their feet to the music as they walked around, singing along to parts they knew.

Talyn wondered at it. At how music was like breathing to Mithranans—and it wasn't just a winged folk thing, despite how some of them had magic in their voices.

Andres came straight over, calling out to a few of the helpers to bring some food for them. "You made it."

"Just." Talyn smiled. "Thank you for handling things here."

He waved a hand. "I had the easy job. Your wing saved a lot of homes and lives last night, Captain."

As the Wolves were gratefully accepting mugs of hot soup, starving after the long night, the Patrolmen who had been sandbagging Wharf Street and Parlour Road began trickling in. Despite their extreme weariness they stood together in groups around one of the fires in the hall, sipping soup and chatting quietly.

"All I want to do is fall into my bed and sleep for a month." Corrin yawned. "But there's absolutely no way I could manage to walk up the wall."

Talyn was summoning the strength to inform them that yes, they were going to have to make the walk back up the wall when she was forestalled by a deep voice behind them.

"If I may?" She spun to find a huge bear of a man, complete with a neatly trimmed but bushy beard and a receding hairline. The amiability of his expression belied his intimidating appearance.

"Mayor Doran." Theac straightened. Something in how quickly he'd responded told Talyn he liked and respected this man.

"Theac." The mayor nodded, then offered his hand to Talyn. "Captain, it's a pleasure to finally meet you. I'm the mayor of this fine town. I can't thank you enough for the help you and your Wolves provided last night." His lips twitched as he spoke, as if in some private amusement. "Justus Doran."

"Talyn Dynan." She shook his hand, hers almost entirely swallowed by his firm grip. "And we just pitched in where we could. It was a bad night weather-wise."

"To be frank, you all look exhausted. My wife and I are going to be here most of the day helping to sort things out, find shelter for those who have lost homes and so on. I'd be pleased to offer you my home to go and clean up and get some rest. Theac knows where it is."

"We couldn't possibly, sir." Theac looked horrified at the thought.

"On the contrary, it's the least we can do," Doran said gently. "There are guest rooms on the second floor, you're welcome to all of them. And feel free to make use of our bathing rooms and the well-stocked larder. I suspect once you've cleaned up and rested, you'll be looking for something to eat."

"Thank you, sir," she agreed with alacrity, delighted that she wouldn't have to walk all the way back to her bed in the citadel. "That sounds wonderful."

The mayor's house was a block away from Town Hall, a brick home rising three stories high. One of the mayor's servants, warned of their arrival, let them in and showed them the way to the second floor. The remnants of adrenalin faded as they trudged up the stairs and separated into individual rooms.

Talyn chose a room in the corner of the house, looking out on the street below and the sparkling ocean beyond. The view occupied her for only a few seconds, however. The large, double bed looked far more enticing. She dropped her cloak in the middle of the floor, tugged off her boots, and crawled under the blankets.

She was asleep before her head hit the pillow.

CHAPTER 32

*T*alyn awoke late in the morning, pleasantly warm and sleepy. After a few moments of dozing, she stretched out languidly, pleased that her knee was only slightly sore. She threw the covers off and loped to the window. Her back and shoulders had stiffened during her sleep, and she stretched out, trying to work out the soreness. Then she caught a whiff of herself and grimaced. Her muddy clothes smelled *bad*.

Exploring the room, she found a door leading into a bathing area. It was tiled in pure white, and a small bathtub sat under the window. A fluffy white robe hung on the back of the door. Not wanting to bother the servants to bring hot water for the tub, she stripped off her muddy clothes and washed with the large jug of cold water by the sink.

This was the first instance she'd seen of wealth in Dock City. The mayor's home was large, but for guest rooms to have their own individual bathing rooms… that spoke of money. It made her wonder what the source of the mayor's wealth was. He'd seemed a lovely man, but first impressions weren't always correct, and she couldn't help but think of comments Theac and Tye and others had made, how some city officials took bribes from the winged folk.

Once done, flesh chilled, she leaned over the bath and poured the remnants of the jug through her hair, rinsing it as best she could. Then, mostly clean, she shrugged on one of the thick white robes and brushed the knots out of her hair, then left it out to dry before venturing out of her room to see if anybody else was up and about. The floor was silent and empty. She padded down the hall, the carpet soft on her bare feet.

At the top of the stairs, a delicious smell accosted her, wafting up from below. Her stomach rumbled, reminding her that she was starving. She followed the smell to the bottom of the stairs, through a comfortable living area, and into the kitchen.

Halun stood by a cooking fire, deftly scrambling eggs in a pan. Theac was beside him, heating water for tea and monitoring several slices of bread grilling near the eggs.

"Morning," Talyn greeted them, taking in a deep breath of the delicious smell.

"It's actually almost afternoon," Theac grumbled, but it was good-natured. "We were about to come and wake you for breakfast. It's almost done."

"Are there any other supplies around?"

Halun nodded and pointed silently to the larder. She smiled at him and went to investigate. Halun's reluctance to speak had become a natural part of the wing, something she—and she guessed the others too—found a comfort. It was nice to not always be chattering. Not that she hadn't noticed Halun spoke more often as time passed. But only when it was just them. He remained mostly mute when they were around others.

She raided the larder for a small pile of ingredients, then lugged them back into the kitchen and dumped them next to the cook fire beside Halun's. The kitchen was so big that she had plenty of room to work, throwing together her ingredients and stirring thoroughly.

"Where did you two learn to cook anyway?" she asked as they worked.

Theac gave her a sour look. "I'm making toast, Captain."

A trill of laughter inside her head. *"I don't remember a time you made toast without burning it to a crisp."*

"Yes, all right," she said good-naturedly. "Even so. I've been told I am incapable of successfully toasting bread."

"My mother taught me to cook."

As always, Talyn was a little taken aback by the cultured smoothness of the big man's voice, and in this case, even more surprised. She hadn't expected him to answer. She and Theac carefully remained silent and casual as he continued.

"I had three sisters and four brothers, and Mama was a slave too, so she had to try and make the food rations she received enough for all of us until we were old enough to start working too. Then we could earn our own rations." Halun kept turning the eggs. "Eggs were her favourite. Mine too."

Talyn thought she might snap the handle off her pan, the fury that swept through her was so powerful. Yet anger wasn't going to help Halun. From Theac's suddenly stiffened shoulders, she suspected he was feeling the same way. She cleared her throat. "Did your mother make them with oil or butter? I always preferred oil."

A little smile flickered over the big man's face. "Me too, Captain. But she loved butter."

"Butter is so much better."

"Shush, you."

A moment of comfortable silence fell, but then the tell-tale rustle of feathers sounded at the doorway.

"Pancakes!" Tiercelin's voice rang out a moment later, gleeful with delight.

She glanced at him. Had she finally found a food both winged folk and humans ate? "Would you mind flipping these while I make more mixture so there's enough for everyone?"

He came to stand beside her, flicking wet hair out of his eyes. She glared at him when she was showered with water droplets, but he only grinned back at her and began to rather clumsily flip pancakes. She swallowed a smile. It was unlikely Tiercelin had ever had to cook in his life.

Corrin and Zamaril appeared soon after. They took in the scene in the kitchen and went to investigate the larder for themselves. When they re-appeared with their own supplies, Halun looked at his eggs and sighed thoughtfully. They were cooked, so he shovelled them into a tray and kept them warm over the embers of his fire. Then he went back into the larder to get more eggs.

None of them made snarky or otherwise negative comments about the well-stocked nature of the mayor's larder, though she kept anticipating Zamaril or Theac to come out with something at any second.

So they liked the mayor despite his wealth. Interesting.

A half-turn later, they all sat down to a meal of Halun's eggs— some with butter, some with oil—Theac's toast and tea, Talyn's pancakes, Corrin's cold ham cuts and Zamaril's fried mushrooms and tomatoes.

The Wolves ate, chatted and laughed, all picking on each other's food, especially Theac's overly sweet tea. Halun consumed about three times more than the rest of them, then sat back in his chair with a satisfied sigh.

For her part, Talyn sat mostly silent amongst it all, muscles aching pleasantly with weariness, food warm in her belly, and for a moment, not weighed down with grief.

Eventually, Theac pushed away his empty plate with a regretful sigh. "We should get going if we're going to fit our afternoon training in. We've already missed the morning session. I want to make sure we get that *sabai* sideways shuffle perfected before the game."

"Right." Corrin nodded, picking up his own plate and Halun's and heading to the sink. Chairs creaked as Tiercelin and Halun rose to help him clear up. "The game is the day after tomorrow."

Talyn eyed them suspiciously. Where was this sudden enthusiasm for training coming from? "No training today. We need rest after last night, or we'll never make it through a game."

Theac cleared his throat. "Mayor Doran sent a message while you were sleeping. He says he and his wife will be busy at Town Hall until late, so we're welcome to rest here for the afternoon."

All gazes swung to Talyn. She certainly didn't feel up to the wall walk yet and was happy to accomplish that after some more rest. "Then it's sorted. We'll rest this afternoon and head back up this evening."

SHE WAS DELIGHTED to find a library in the house and spent the early part of the afternoon curled up in the living room reading. Outside the sky was a cloudless blue, as if the heavy rainclouds of the day and night before had never been. The humidity had returned with a vengeance too.

"Just a preview of what's to come," Theac said when she expressed surprise. "Although the amount of rain we got yesterday and last night will be spread out over a week or more once the monsoon season arrives properly."

One of the mayor's servants had washed all their clothes, and after hanging out in the hot and humid morning sun, they had already dried.

Andres Tye stopped by mid-afternoon to let them know that the floods were quickly receding now the rain had stopped, and the rest of the City Patrol had been released from the citadel.

"Not that many of mine are pleased about being told to help mop and sweep with the clean-up. Lucky Captain Finnus is home with the gout once again and left me in charge," he said cheerfully. "Speaking of which, I'd best get back to the Market Quarter and make sure they're not slacking off."

"Has Captain Doljen set his men to helping too?" Theac asked. "The Dock Quarter was probably the worst hit outside the Poor Quarter."

Tye shook his head. "Some of his off-duty men are helping out, but that's all."

"He's a good lad," Theac said as they watched Tye leave from the front porch.

Talyn flashed him a smile before going back inside. "I'm not surprised. It was you that trained him."

. . .

HALUN JOINED her in the lounge, nose deep in a book entitled *Farming in Arid Conditions*. Theac, Corrin and Zamaril sat a little further away, playing what sounded like a complicated and contentious game of cards. She had no idea what Tiercelin was doing.

Later in the afternoon, she decided to go out for some fresh air. She took her cleaned and dried clothes upstairs to change before making her way to the back door, which led out to a beautiful garden. High brick walls enclosed the space, she assumed to keep intruders out.

She strolled through the garden slowly, letting the warm air and scent of flowers clear her mind, and turned her thoughts to the alleya game.

Considering the superior strength, speed and mobility of the winged folk, Talyn's strategy centred on stamina and agility. If the Wolves could outrun and outlast the winged folk, and if they could use Callanan fighting *sabai* to match some of their opponents' natural grace and magical ability, they might have a chance of putting up a good fight.

And if *she* played, well... the Shadowhawk had been right. She suspected there were few Falcons that could take her on in single combat and come out the winner. But she was still in two minds about how much she should involve herself, having taken both Theac and the Shadowhawk's warnings to heart.

A rustling caught her attention, drawing her out of her musings. She looked up, catching a flash of movement high on the wall through the trees. Before her mind could put together what was happening, the twanging of a bow cut the thick air.

Her breath lodged in her throat, muscles turning rigid with panic.

And then something slammed into her shoulder.

She stumbled backwards, swearing aloud as hot pain flared down her right side. Panic warred with the need to respond inside her. It scrambled her thoughts as she glanced frantically around, trying to work out where the attack was coming from. A figure disappeared over the wall, human, face covered by a black mask and form hidden by a dark cloak.

She staggered, faint with shock and sudden pain.

What...?

An arrow protruded from her right shoulder. Bright red blood—her blood—was already flowing through the hole in her shirt.

The sight of it—of blood seeping and a fletched arrow embedded in flesh—brought memory crashing mercilessly down around her.

Sari. Lying prone on the rocky ground. Arms askew and face turned to the side, the odd cloudiness in her brown eyes already telling Talyn what had happened even before she could scream, could run un-heeding of danger across the clearing to slide to her knees beside her partner.

Two arrows slamming into the ground at her feet before the other Callanan with them could rush in to take out the archer.

Fumbling, crying, unable to breathe properly, desperately checking for a pulse. But the arrow had gone through Sari's heart and she'd been dead in that instant. No time for a final goodbye. No time for anything. Just gone.

She'd been alive, laughing, fighting with as much exuberance as Talyn. And then she was gone.

No. A scream lodged in her throat, a panicked, aching gasp replacing it. Talyn sank to her knees, the fingers of her uninjured arm clutching at the grass, seeking a way to hold on, to keep a grip, to stop herself drowning in the grief of that day. The pain was insistent, but it barely registered. In her mind, she was back in that warm summer's afternoon, trying to understand the fact that her partner, her best friend, the most important person in her world was gone.

They had tried dragging Talyn away, to a more secure location, but she wouldn't leave. Two Callanan had to carry them both. She'd barely noticed.

Chest heaving with broken sobs, tears streamed down her face. She swayed on her knees, fell forward to the ground, gasping for air, fingers curling uselessly in the grass. Pain stabbed bright and hot through her.

From where she'd fallen she could see the hazy outline of the back of the house through tears and shock. Zamaril was coming out the back door, a questioning look on his face as if he were looking for her. His eyes widened in horror as he caught sight of her. "What happened?"

She could only close her eyes, bite her lip against the agonising pain in her shoulder and the even more agonising grief of memory. Her vision blurred, blood loss making her dizzy.

"TIERCELIN!" Zamaril shouted the healer's name at the top of his lungs, running to Talyn's side. "What can I do?" He looked helplessly at the blood pooling on the ground under her shoulder.

A wave of dizziness passed over her and she shook her head. She heard him distantly as he swore repeatedly under his breath.

"TIERCELIN!" he screamed again.

Everyone inside had heard his first panicked shout, and all four Wolves appeared as he yelled the second time. They ran through the back door and slid to a halt at the sight of Talyn bleeding on the grass.

"Shit." Theac was the first to recover from stunned shock— reacting as quickly as *she* should have when she'd first heard the intruder. He grabbed Tiercelin's arm and dragged him over to her. Tiercelin snapped out of his shock at Theac's rough touch, dropping to his knees and focussing his brown eyes on her shoulder, one hand hovering just above it.

"Will she be all right?" Corrin asked in a shaky voice. He and Halun were crouching nearby, wearing identical panicked expressions. Talyn's vision worsened, their voices turning distant.

"She's going into shock," Tiercelin's voice sounded faintly.

"Is that bad?" Zamaril demanded.

"I need to stop the bleeding," Tiercelin said quickly. "Then we'll worry about the arrow. Halun, I need her inside and on a flat surface."

A moment later Talyn was gently turned then lifted off the ground, so softly it was like she weighed nothing to the big man. Even that small movement sent agony spearing through her, and she cried out.

"Corrin, Zamaril, go and heat some water and get me clean towels and a sharp knife," Tiercelin snapped, in control now.

"I'll go after the bastard." Theac growled low in his throat. "Captain, did you see where he went?"

345

Theac's words dimly penetrated her fog, but not strongly enough for her to properly process them or understand. Something inside her fought for clarity, knew she shouldn't be numb like this, but it failed.

Halun carried her to the long table by the fireplace in the lounge area. He laid her down and tenderly tucked her hair behind her ears, his eyes and touch communicating his worry for her in a way that words never could.

While Corrin and Zamaril gathered what Tiercelin needed, the winged man worked on stopping the blood flow. His hands moved over her shoulder at a frantic pace. Corrin and Zamaril re-entered the room with loud steps and panicked questions.

"Should we go and fetch a healer?" Corrin asked worriedly, hovering over Talyn.

"I can go." Zamaril volunteered immediately.

"The only person better than myself to work on Talyn is another of the winged healers. I know of none who will come here to treat a human," Tiercelin said tersely.

"The Falcon could make one of them come," Zamaril argued.

"There's no time. This wound needs treating now," Tiercelin snapped, but then his confidence seem to fade. "I don't know... the wound in her magic is worse somehow. I don't know if I can..."

His face swam above her, pale despite his brown skin, and something about the worry and panic on his beautiful winged folk features reached her. She fought for the strength to reach out to him. "Tiercelin?"

"Yes, Captain?" He bent closer to hear her.

"Trust... you."

He huffed out a hopeless breath, but when she wouldn't release his gaze, he gave a nod and straightened. "Zamaril, I'm it. I can take care of this. You with me?"

"We both are." There was no hesitation in Zamaril's voice as he looked at Corrin, then nodded at Tiercelin.

"Good. The bleeding has stopped for the moment. I'm going to cut the arrow out and stitch the wound. I'll also need to investigate whether any ligaments have been damaged." He gave them a look.

"The bleeding will increase the moment I start cutting—one of you needs to keep pressure on the wound site to slow it down."

"That's going to hurt," Talyn protested in a whisper.

"Here, I found this in the cupboard." Zamaril held up a bottle of spirits. He poured a cup and gave it to Talyn. She gulped it down, trying not to choke, and the fiery liquid warmed her insides. "I can staunch the blood flow—just tell me what to do."

"Have you cleaned the knife?" Tiercelin looked at Corrin.

Corrin nodded. "It's my sharpest. I rubbed it in alcohol. You won't even feel it, Captain, you know how sharp my knives are."

Talyn silently blessed the young Wolf. The sharper the knife, the easier it would cut, the less it would hurt.

"I'm going to need you to hold her down, Halun. Zamaril, stand right there please and use that towel to staunch the bleeding—it's going to hurt but you'll need to apply pressure, as hard as you can." Tiercelin's brisk confidence was calming everyone down. Talyn's eyes drifted closed. She was in good hands. "Corrin, raid the cupboards for any sort of healing herbs, or medicine. See if one of the servants knows where they're kept. Also, I'll need strong twine and a needle to stitch this up once I'm done."

Halun leaned forward and gripped her forearms firmly, giving no leeway for Talyn to move. When the knife cut into her skin, she roared in pain. Halun didn't let up and Tiercelin kept going, working quickly and efficiently to cut the arrow out. Zamaril pressed a towel hard into the areas Tiercelin wasn't working, and she wasn't sure which hurt more.

Talyn cursed him endlessly as agony tore through her. It was unbearable, and just when she thought she couldn't take any more, Tiercelin lifted the knife and pulled gently on the arrow. There was a chilling sucking sound, and then it was out.

She sagged into the table, covered in sweat and exhausted. The memories continued to swirl around her, the scent of sweat and blood and fear drawing them like a lure.

"Did you get what I asked?" Tiercelin asked Corrin.

"I got the twine and needle, and I found some herbal paste in the larder. It was prepared by your healers—the name Greencrest is on the jar. Is that okay?"

"Perfect. She's one of my teachers and she specialises in healing herbs."

Tiercelin smeared plenty of the sweet-smelling paste into the open wound, then set about stitching it up. The entire process hurt like blazes. Talyn lay there gritting her teeth and gripping Halun's hand for support.

Eventually it was over, and the agony slowly faded to a dull throb in her shoulder.

Tiercelin directed the others to clean up the mess, then began using his magic on her shoulder. His face was a mask of concentration as his hands worked above the newly stitched wound. Gradually the pain eased and Talyn's rigid muscles slowly relaxed.

When Tiercelin stopped, he was pale and exhausted, bracing himself on his arms as he leaned over her, sweat-slicked and breathing hard. Part of her realised what he'd just done for her, what he'd given, and she swallowed, managing a whispered, "Thank you."

"You're welcome." He smiled. "Now rest. You'll be fine, I promise."

"My arm?"

"You'll regain full mobility, but only if you keep it immobilized while it heals." He frowned. "You won't be able to play in two days."

The front door slammed open and Theac stomped in. He looked livid, directing a fierce glare at Tiercelin. "Is the captain okay?"

Tiercelin straightened to look at him. "I think so, yes."

"Did you find who did this?" Zamaril demanded.

"No. I followed witness sightings across the town and back and ended up nowhere," he said angrily. "Dammit!"

"That's all right," Halun said calmly. "You can't do more than your best."

"Did you find any traces of the attacker at all?" Tiercelin asked.

Theac explained his search in more detail while Tiercelin wrapped Talyn's arm and shoulder in bandages and then fashioned a sling to keep it still. After that Halun carried her over to the couch and Corrin disappeared into the kitchen. He came back with a mug of steaming tea.

"Drink this. It should help with the pain." He smiled shyly. "It's what my father always used to make for me when I hurt myself."

Talyn drank slowly, her head drooping back against the cushion. She felt terrible. The flashbacks left her emotionally wrung out while Tiercelin's work left her physically exhausted and in lingering pain. The conversation raged around her as the Wolves sat in chairs surrounding the couch.

"One witness said they saw a man running from the back wall wearing a mask like the Shadowhawk was wearing last night," Theac said.

Zamaril snorted. "That's right. He saves her, and lots of other people, then comes to try and kill her today. I don't think so. It's more likely one of Prince Azrilan's Falcons. They don't want the captain in the game tomorrow because she could outplay any of them. Notice it's only a disabling wound, not aimed to kill."

She stirred, dizziness making her thoughts foggy. Zamaril had already guessed how much of a difference she might make? It was hard to find the motivation to follow that thought and she didn't try.

"We don't know that for certain. Whoever it was might be a bad shot; an inch down and they'd have hit her heart," Tiercelin said.

"It's not the Shadowhawk," Corrin said, certainty filling his voice. "The arrow that shot her wasn't his. There's no lightning mark on it."

A brief silence fell.

She shivered, trying to hide her hissing breath. Again she saw the flash of Sari lying there, arrow through her heart, as if she were right back there in that clearing. A tear slid down her cheek and she had to close her eyes for a moment.

Either they didn't notice, or they pretended not to. After a moment Halun kept talking.

"I'll put the word around on the docks." There was an edge of menace to the big man's soft voice she hadn't heard before. "If anyone knows anything, I'll get it out of them."

"What about the game?" Corrin said. "Clearly she won't be able to play."

"We'll play," Theac said. "We've got enough players."

"I think we should call the game off," Talyn said weakly. "Without me, all five of you will have to play the full game. You're exhausted after last night. I appreciate your sudden willingness to play, but I don't want any of you to get hurt."

"You trained us better than that, Captain, and you know it. We'll play," Corrin said.

"It's not brave unless you're scared and you do it anyway," Zamaril said determinedly. "Right?"

She bit her lip, fighting back more tears, and then the exhaustion and pain won, sucking her down into deep blackness.

CHAPTER 33

*H*e dragged himself home at dawn. Once the initial crisis was over and it was clear the floods weren't going to rise any higher, it had been time for him to disappear. It wouldn't be long before the Patrolmen started paying closer attention to who exactly was helping out.

Besides, he was utterly exhausted and there really wasn't much more he could do. For now, at least. With so many businesses damaged or destroyed, basic supplies would become even more sparse, and it was doubtful the winged folk would do much to alleviate that.

There would be more work for the Shadowhawk in the weeks and months ahead.

For now he put that out of his mind, managing only to strip off his mask and soaked clothing and stuff them somewhere well-hidden before dropping onto his bed and falling instantly asleep.

He awoke several hours later, muscles stiff and sore, but inwardly chafing until he could get free again later in the day. The moment he was, he went out wandering through the streets of Dock City, keen to check on the aftereffects of the flood and see whether any further help was needed.

The residents seemed to be responding well. A lot were out in the warm afternoon, working busily on fixing damage to their homes and businesses. Water slicked the cobblestones in the main streets and turned the narrower ones into sludgy bogs. The combination of that, rotting produce, and the heat of the afternoon contributed to an especially delightful smell in parts of the Market Quarter.

His steps slowed as he came to the Poor Quarter, pausing halfway over the bridge. The raging waters had settled, despite the water level still being much higher than usual. And gazing east—large areas of western and central Poor Quarter was still under water. Far to the east though, where the homes flowed into the beginning of the forested headland, he could just make out tents on any spare bit of flat land and multiple small boats moving around to collect belongings or materials to construct shelters from.

Some enterprising few were moving back into the drier areas to claim something of their homes back, or loot them, but Town Hall would be sheltering many people for some time until the waters receded completely. He hoped that happened before the monsoon season arrived properly.

Turning back around the way he'd come, he quickened his stride. It was about the time of day the izerdia workers returned but tonight Shale Street was empty—the barred entrance to the tunnel was unguarded. Presumably the tunnel had partially flooded too.

Eventually he arrived at the inn he'd been aiming for the whole time. In the Wall Quarter, but close to the border of the Dock Quarter, it had avoided significant damage in the floods, and already a handful of its patrons had returned.

He stepped around the waiter sweeping water out of the entranceway and walked straight to the end of the bar. Without making it obvious, he leaned back slightly on his stool, glancing at the underside of the damp bar top.

A second chalk mark had appeared next to the one he'd made two nights earlier. Surreptitiously he wiped both marks off, then waved the barman over to order a drink. Young and clearly bored, the man lingered to chat once he'd brought the Shadowhawk's drink over.

"Big night," he remarked. "Did your home survive?"

The Shadowhawk nodded, took a sip, tried not to spit it back out. The ale tasted more like cat's piss than anything resembling drinkable alcohol. "A bit damp but I've still got a roof and walls."

He nodded equably. "Same. Worked out lucky the missus picked a home on higher ground in the Dock Quarter. Less lucky her sisters didn't. Looks like they'll be staying with us a while."

The Shadowhawk made a sympathetic face, but said nothing, wanting to be left alone. The barman didn't get the message and continued chatting.

"Those poor bastards in the slums are lucky the foreigner lady brought her men down to help. Have to admit I thought it a bit of a joke when I heard they'd been drafted into the WingGuard, but they went over and above last night."

The Shadowhawk shrugged, keeping his face disinterested and gaze on the ale before him. Taking a breath, he summoned the courage for another sip. Even worse the second time. He struggled to swallow it without betraying how disgusted he was.

"You heard what happened this afternoon, though? Someone wasn't happy about the foreigner helping out."

"What happened?" His voice snapped out before he could stop it, his gaze shooting up to the barman.

"Someone shot her with an arrow." The barman grinned at finally catching his customer's full attention. "She and her men were staying at the mayor's place. I heard she was taking a walk in the garden when it happened."

He should be relieved. She was a threat to him and his work and if someone had decided to take care of her, that was a good thing. But he wasn't relieved. After last night he was incandescently furious. Countless lives had been saved because of the actions she'd taken. It took a moment before he could speak without a snarl ripping out of him. "Who?" he ground out.

Something of what he felt must still be in his voice because the barman took an unconscious step back. "Not a clue." Another customer walked in and the barman's attention wavered. He went to go and serve the new arrival but the Shadowhawk reached over the bar, grabbing the man's arm.

"Is she dead?"

"Alive and breathing from all accounts," he said, flicking an uneasy glance between the Shadowhawk and his arm. "Arrow took her in the shoulder most say. Janie next door says she heard the captain nearly lost her arm. Rogo down the street reckons the arrow was poisoned but the winged healer in the wing saved her life."

"Thanks," he muttered, letting the man's arm go.

Before he'd reached his new customer the Shadowhawk was gone.

THE SHADOWHAWK PUSHED through the door of the abandoned house they usually met in, but instead of banging back against the wall it stopped halfway, water sloshing. He glanced over his shoulder at the alley behind him. There weren't many roaming about the Poor Quarter tonight and those that were out were more likely than not to be dangerous.

He almost wished one of them had come at him though, given him an excuse to let loose some of the anger that was raging inside him. On his way, he'd left urgent messages in three different spots for Zamaril.

He'd saved her life and then someone else had tried to take it away. He wanted to tear them apart, whoever had done it. They'd saved so many lives last night. Talyn Dynan and her Wolves deserved honour, not a cowardly attack.

"Ten points for a discreet entry." Saniya's voice drawled. "What the hell do you think you're doing?"

"Where were you last night?" he snarled, shoving the door closed against the tide of ankle-deep water. She sat on the room's only chair, booted feet up on the room's only table, clear of the water. An unsheathed knife rested in her lap.

"Making sure my people were safe and riding out the storm." She didn't move, voice blunt but calm in the face of his anger. "What's gotten into you?"

"Your people? Don't you mean *our* people? I didn't see any sign of you last night while I was out trying to save people from their flooding homes."

She didn't reply for a moment, instead slowly swinging her legs to the floor and standing up. "I was doing what I had to. As were you. Now, you wanted to meet. What is it?"

He took a breath, trying to keep his voice even. "I've been warned the WingGuard are looking to set a trap on a shipment of flour arriving soon. But that's not so important now. After the floods, supplies are going to be in even shorter supply than usual."

"The queen isn't a complete fool. She'll make sure extra is sold to the merchants in Dock City. The last thing the Falcons need is hungry citizens rioting."

"And we both know sufficient supplies for everyone to eat, and sufficient supplies for the wealthier citizens—and those in the Falcon's pocket—are two different things."

She nodded acknowledgement of that. "We'll leave the shipment of flour alone."

"Just like that?"

"You can do as you like, but my priority is survival, Shadowhawk. Let the WingGuard waste their resources setting a useless trap for us. We'll be ready for the next one."

She was right. It was the smart move. But he hated it all the same.

She smiled at the look on his face. "I have no idea what's eating at you, but it's going to get you killed if you don't get control of it. And if you become a liability to me, our working relationship is over."

He snorted. "You need me."

"I don't *need* anyone." She paused at the doorway. "I'll make sure my people free up some of the usual storage locations. We'll be ready if and when more 'supplies' need liberating."

"They will," he said firmly.

"Then I'll see you soon, Shadowhawk."

For the briefest of moments, he toyed with following her. He was fairly confident he could do it without getting caught—night had fallen outside, and darkness was his friend, his shield.

But no, he didn't have the patience for it tonight. His emotions were flaring too hotly to manage the razor-sharp focus he'd need to successfully shadow someone like Saniya.

So he turned and left, strides quick and angry despite knowing he should keep them calm and unbothered.

DESPITE THE LONG walk from his meeting place with Saniya, he was still fuming as he entered the apartment. The fury burned through him—the thought of her hurt, almost killed, after he'd saved her life the previous night. He paced the room, fists clenched.

Who had dared attack a WingGuard captain? It wouldn't have been a human, he couldn't see any possible motive for one of them to attack her. Unless one had been contracted to do it. There were those, mostly from the Poor Quarter, who sold themselves as killers for hire.

But who amongst the winged folk would pay a human to do it?

He forcibly stopped his pacing and took a deep, steadying breath. Saniya had been right, he needed to let it go. It wasn't his concern. Talyn Dynan was able to look after herself, and her Wolves had been beyond impressive the previous night. Without them many more lives would have been lost.

He needed to start planning his activities over the coming weeks. Once monsoon season arrived it would be harder for him to move about discreetly, and logistically harder to steal and store things.

He'd sent a message to his Dock Quarter contacts—find out what shipments were coming and when. Maybe Navis could tip him off to the Falcons' plans, whether they intended holding back anything that was coming in.

Speaking of... familiar footsteps coming up the stairs had him crossing the room to yank the door open and haul Navis bodily inside. As soon as the door closed behind him, he demanded, "Who went after Captain Dynan?"

"I don't know. Or care." Grey eyes met his, unafraid and slightly irritated. "And hello to you too."

"If this was you…" the Shadowhawk warned.

"You have absolutely no reason to think that, so I'd appreciate it if you'd stop your angry posturing. I merely came here in anticipation of my services being required after the flood." Navis straightened his cloak. "Not that I understand why you're so upset. She's a big problem for you—it would have made things easier if the assassin had succeeded in killing her."

He shook his head. "If she was a problem for me, it would have manifested itself by now. She'll only come for me if I threaten her charge, and I don't give a flea's shit about the prince of song."

"Perhaps. From what I've heard, the descriptions of her attacker sounded interestingly like you." Navis paused. "Have you stopped to consider that you're being set up?"

That stopped him cold. "Set up by who? For what purpose?"

"After the floods, she's become quite popular. Someone trying to turn public opinion against you might think framing you for attacking her a smart way to go." Navis raised a hand as the Shadowhawk opened his mouth to speak. "Or perhaps someone might be looking to set her against you."

The Shadowhawk shook his head in frustration. "She knows it wasn't me."

"Does she?" A single arched eyebrow.

"It doesn't matter. None of this has anything to do with me. There could have been many other reasons someone went after the captain," he said. "And you were right to come. After the floods, I suspect there will be more shortages than usual this coming winter. Can you get me information on what the royal family might be trying to hold back? Any secret shipments the dock masters won't know about?"

Navis silently held out a hand.

Mouth tightening, the Shadowhawk walked over and opened the drawer in the room's table. He opened the bag of coins sitting there, then dropped two gold coins into Navis's open hand. "I'll double that if you bring me something I can use." He paused. "And add another gold piece if you bring me information about who went after Captain Dynan."

Navis's hand closed over the coin and it disappeared too quickly into his cloak for him to mark where. The Shadowhawk made a mental note to hide the bag of coins somewhere else in the room as soon as Navis was gone. "I'll do my best."

Once the information broker had gone, the Shadowhawk dropped into a chair, rubbing a tired hand over his face. He had to go back; sleep would be impossible now, and anyway, if he didn't return to his routine somebody would eventually notice.

He didn't even consider stopping.

CHAPTER 34

Talyn managed sleep in her room that night, thanks to Tiercelin's ability to relieve the pain in her shoulder, and despite her frustration at having to miss the alleya match. The panic attack she'd suffered on being shot had left her wrung out and her eyes slid closed the minute her head touched the pillow.

She awoke early in the morning when her shoulder started to ache, her other muscles registering their complaints too from the sandbagging and swimming. That wasn't unfamiliar though. She'd awoken stiff and sore—and injured—plenty of times in the past.

This time, it only served as a stark reminder that she wouldn't be limping downstairs to the mess to be teased by her partner and friends, to endure the good natured ribbing about getting too old to be a Callanan, or how she'd only gotten hurt because she'd been too slow.

She wouldn't be dishing out the same kind of teasing. No, all that was gone.

It was difficult to dress with her arm wrapped in a sling, and by the time she'd dragged her shirt and breeches and boots on, her shoulder throbbed with a fierce ache she did her best to ignore.

She limped over to her little kitchen. Her knee was also aching, so she made herself a cup of tea and added some pain herbs Tiercelin had given her. She'd just taken the first sip when a sharp rap sounded at her door.

Ravinire stood there, eyes going straight to her sling. "Talon Parksin informed me of what happened yesterday. Are you all right, Captain?"

"I'll be fine. Tiercelin did a good job," she assured him.

"I have written a formal missive to your king and First Shield Ceannar, apologising for what happened and assuring them of your full recovery." Ravinire seemed uneasy, as if he worried that she—or her uncle—was going to blame him for what had happened. "I hope you can accept my apologies too, Captain. I assure you it won't happen again. I will assign some Falcons to—"

"I appreciate that, sir, but I don't need Falcon protection," she cut him off politely. Her uncle would be concerned to hear that she'd been hurt, but she doubted it would affect diplomatic relations, as Ravinire seemed to fear. "Do you have any information on who was behind the attack?"

"No." His fidgeting increased. Perhaps more than worry over how the Twin Thrones might respond was unsettling him. This was the second event to happen in the space of months his Falcons had no explanation for. "However I have ordered the City Patrol to prioritise identifying the perpetrator."

She speared him with a look. "The Wolves thought perhaps somebody wanted to prevent me playing in today's game."

Ravinire's expression tightened. "I disagree. Your wing isn't going to win today, with or without you. There's no need to hire someone to attack you. I can only assume it must have been a mistake of some sort."

That stung, but she kept her face bland. "It was full daylight when it happened, sir. Not easy to mistake me for someone else."

"Even so. It wouldn't have happened if you and your wing hadn't stayed down in the city to help with the floods. Not to mention one of them could have been hurt ahead of the game. At the very least they must still be exhausted."

"I'm sure they are," she said equably. "But they, and I, judged lives and homes more important than an exhibition game they've been set up to lose anyway."

"I've already warned you to be careful, Captain Dynan." He stepped away, wings spreading wide. "Don't make me do it again. I'll see you this afternoon."

SEEKING out a distraction from her soreness and lingering emptiness of spirit, she made her slow way down into Dock City. As usual it was a beautiful, sunny morning. The birds were singing again, and the sun held the promise of uncomfortable warmth later in the day.

The streets were as busy with people as they always were, though today many of them were working to clear up flood damage. From snatches of conversation she caught as she walked by, the main topic of discussion seemed to be the festival the following day. Some of them recognised Talyn and gave her a wave and a greeting. She smiled back, the simple human interaction breathing some life back into her.

The city had pulled through. Some lives had been lost, many more homes, but it could have been much worse. And Talyn had been part of the reason for that—her and her Wolves. She repeated that to herself like a mantra as she walked.

It took her some time, but she found the café Corrin had taken her to before. Inside she asked for a mug of kahvi and a sweet pastry. While waiting for the kahvi to be made, a familiar young man appeared from out the back, stilling at the sight of her. "Captain."

"I never did catch your name?" She lifted an eyebrow.

"It's Petro. I own this place." He moved out from behind the serving counter, offering a faint smile. "Best kahvi in Dock City."

"Is that so?" She smiled, then lowered her voice. "I just came to say thank you."

Surprised flashed over his face, then the small smile stretched to a full one. "You're the one that deserves the thanks, Captain Dynan. How's that shoulder?"

"Sore, but it will get better."

The woman behind the counter passed over a steaming cup along with the pastry, but when Talyn went to pay, Petro refused to take it.

"A kahvi and pastry is the least we can do in thanks."

"Are you sure?" She was a little taken aback. What she and the Wolves had done the previous night was what any warrior would have done back home.

He nodded eagerly. "Come back sometime, Captain. Those pastries are even better when we manage to get a supply of apples to make them with."

She ate and drank as she strolled towards the wall. The pastry was delicious, buttery and hot and seasoned with cinnamon. The kahvi gave her a fresh jolt of warm energy, and Talyn made a note to go back. Petro hadn't been unfairly bragging about the quality of his kahvi.

She reached the wall path and made her way up slowly, taking care not to exert her knee. The sun was already warm enough that she'd worked up a sweat by the time she reached the top. Far below, Feather Bay was a glittering spectacle, as if the day and night of floods had never been.

Negotiating the citadel was difficult now her muscles were tiring. She had to climb ladders one-handed and cross their swaying bridges without both arms to balance with. Eventually she came to the small bridge that led across to Prince Cuinn's tower.

Her shoulder was throbbing again, and her knee hadn't liked the ladders much. She limped across the bridge and knocked on the door.

A moment later it was yanked open from the inside, and Cuinn appeared in the doorway.

"What happened to you?" he asked, amusement dancing in his emerald eyes as he looked her up and down, absolutely no trace of concern in his face or voice.

"I fell down the stairs," she said dryly. "Can I come in?"

He stepped back and gestured her inside. The amusement on his face as she walked past made her grind her teeth in irritation.

"You're annoyed with me again," he said. "What have I done now?"

Talyn cursed his ability to read emotions for the thousandth time and reined in her irritation. "I'm not annoyed with you."

There was movement at the top of the spiral stairs leading up to Cuinn's bedroom level, and a beautiful winged woman appeared, wrapped only in a sheet. She smiled politely at Talyn and directed a fully-fledged grin down at the prince.

"Good Morning, Zanna." Allure oozed from his voice. "Do you mind leaving us for a minute? I need to speak to my captain."

"Don't be long," she said seductively, returning to the bedroom and closing the door.

"I'm sorry, did I interrupt something important?" Talyn fought to keep sarcasm from her tone.

Cuinn waved his hand dismissively. "Her? No, not at all. How can I help you? You might start with explaining how you got those injuries. I can be somewhat dim-witted, I'll admit that, but I'm not quite stupid enough to believe you fell down some stairs."

"I was shot by an arrow."

He grinned, as if he thought she were making a joke. "Seriously?"

"It was yesterday afternoon, while I was walking in the garden of Mayor Doran's home. Tiercelin got the arrow out and stitched me up, but I can't use my arm at all, so I can't play today."

He managed an expression of mild concern. She figured she should be grateful for that. But it was quickly gone, replaced by puzzlement. "Are you sure? Why would anyone shoot you?"

"Yes, I'm quite certain I was shot by an arrow." She kept her voice calm with an effort. "It's possible that somebody doesn't want me playing in the game today. Maybe someone thinks the Wolves can't win without me?"

He snorted, dropping onto his sofa and stretching his long legs out before him. "That somebody figured right."

"Not if you play."

"What?" Incredulity sent his voice a full pitch higher than normal.

"You've boasted to me on numerous occasions how often you play alleya and how good you are. We could use another winged man on the team, especially one with your skill and experience. The Wolves are *your* wing, after all."

"Never going to happen," he said flatly.

"Why not?"

"A prince playing a game of alleya with humans against a team of winged folk? You realise Azrilan himself won't be playing?" He laughed. "Imagine how stupid I'd look. I don't even have warrior magic, Captain."

"Do you *want* to be humiliated in front of your brothers, when Prince Azrilan's team destroys yours? Isn't that Prince Mithanis' goal? Make you an even less likely candidate for the throne."

"It would be far more humiliating to actually be playing *with* the losing team, Captain," he said languidly. "At least this way I can distance myself from the whole ridiculous affair."

With an effort, she reined in her temper. But her control faded as quickly as it had come. "You don't deserve them, *Prince*."

He lifted an eyebrow, utterly unbothered by her tone. "Is there anything else you wanted, *Captain?*"

"No," she snapped, striding to the door and firmly ignoring the pain from her knee. "I wouldn't want you to have to put yourself to any sort of effort. I'll see you at the game."

Her ire quickly faded as she limped away from Cuinn's tower. She would never dream of speaking to a charge that way back in the Twin Thrones, and not because she would be whipped for it, but because duty and respect would hold her tongue. She was ashamed of herself. She was still so raw, and her once masterful control seemed to fade entirely around Cuinn.

"*He doesn't deserve anyone's respect,*" Sari muttered.

"*That doesn't matter, Sari. I'm Kingshield. I should let his behaviour wash over me—my only job is to protect him.*"

"*I know.*"

Talyn had asked Tiercelin to show her the alleya stadium weeks earlier.

As with most things made by the winged folk, it was an absolute marvel of architecture. The grassy, rectangular field where the game was played was situated on a level section of the forest floor far below the citadel.

Tiered seating cascaded down, enclosing the field completely from the forest outside. The stadium was built from the same creamy marble that the great wall was made from.

He'd pointed out where the royal family would sit in a viewing balcony close to the field, and other spots where noble families owned balconies. The one he'd rather sheepishly pointed out as his family's was closer to the Acondors' box than any other he pointed out.

"And you winged folk let the humans in here to sully all this magnificence with their presence," she'd noted dryly.

"Only once a year." He'd smirked. "And the seating is sharply demarcated. Humans on the western side, winged folk on the east."

She tried to imagine what that empty stadium must look like today as she headed inside at a lower level. The Wolves had been assigned a room in the western section of the stadium to wait for their appearance. The room formed part of what seemed to be a rabbit warren of corridors and rooms built in underneath the seating.

There were no windows, but the sound of thumping feet penetrated the roof above them from people moving to their seats. Occasionally the sound of cheering and clapping drifted down the hall outside.

As soon as she appeared, Tiercelin came over to inspect her shoulder. "How are you feeling?"

"My shoulder and knee are both a little sore," she admitted.

"I can fix that for you," he offered.

"No, you need to save your energy for the game. I'll be fine." Injuries like these were part of the life of a warrior. She'd gotten through them before and would do so again.

He tossed her a packet of herbs. "At least make yourself some tea with those later. It will help."

"I went down to talk to some old Patrol contacts this morning,"

Theac said. "They have nothing on who attacked you yesterday. Whoever the masked, cloaked man was, he disappeared good."

"And I'm sure the Patrolmen are trying extra hard to find him," Zamaril muttered.

She doubted they would ever find the man. The attack had been high risk—dressed so distinctly, in a wealthier area of Dock City and in full daylight... yet the opportunity to catch him had been right away. By now that cloak and mask was gone, and unless anyone had actually seen him disappear, they weren't catching him.

"Doesn't matter," Corrin said cheerfully. "We have another plan to deal with whoever it was."

"What's that?" she asked suspiciously.

"You'll see." He turned his attention to lacing up his boots.

"Please don't forget that you're protective guards, not Patrolmen," she addressed the room. "Your focus should be on the protection of Prince Cuinn, nothing else."

"Which it will be, if he ever lets us near him," Theac assured her.

He was far too cheerful. They all were. None of them looked depressed or apathetic as they changed into their Wolf uniforms, grey on white. Halun wore his sleeveless vest with breeches and boots. Theac wore the whole uniform, as did Tiercelin. Zamaril and Corrin wore their shirts with the sleeves rolled up.

Once they were ready, Talyn led them through extensive stretching exercises. Considering that they had no spare players, they could ill afford to get injured.

By the time a Falcon came in to get them, her stomach was a tight ball of anxiety. Already on edge from the emotional fallout of the flashbacks caused by her injury, she had little ability left to manage the anxiousness she felt on behalf of the Wolves.

Before being led out, they lined up in front of her in a neat row.

"I know you believe that the WingGuard intend to do their best to humiliate you all out there today," she said. "But I want you to hold your heads high, no matter what." She hesitated. "What we did together the other night, what *you* all did, that was real. Today is a game of sport, and no matter what importance the winged folk attach to it, I know, and you know, and *every* human out there knows your worth." She cleared her throat. "You might lose today, but it won't matter. Because you'll know already that you're better than they are. Better men, and better warriors."

There was a silence as the Wolves stared at their shoes, clearly embarrassed by her heartfelt speech. Then Theac spoke. "We'll do our best for you, Captain."

"Wish us luck." Corrin smiled.

Halun gave her the crispest salute she'd ever seen as he passed her. Zamaril's expression was unreadable.

"Don't worry, Captain," Tiercelin tossed confidently over his shoulder. "We'll do you proud."

CHAPTER 35

*T*alyn found her way to the viewing balcony on the eastern side of the stadium where Ravinire and several of his other captains were gathered. The Falcon stood apart from them, talking quietly with the overall commander of the protective flight—Flight Leader Iceflight. Talyn had only spoken to the flight leader once, but they saw each other every week at Ravinire's captains' meetings. She'd taken one look at the lack of feeling in those grey eyes and the supercilious smile on his face when he'd greeted her and decided she didn't like him any more than he apparently liked her.

He hadn't deigned to speak to her since that first introduction. She'd returned the favour.

The viewing balcony jutted out slightly over the field but was well behind the game's boundary lines, the grass a good ten foot drop below. It gleamed a deep emerald in the afternoon sun.

She glanced around, mouth falling open.

Thousands of people were filling the stands. Both winged folk and human—the skies above were a riot of colour as those winged folk not seated hovered in the afternoon thermals. Their conversation filled the air with noise. It was like nothing she'd ever seen before.

Before she could properly take it all in, Ravinire came over, thankfully leaving Iceflight behind. "Your men are ready?"

She nodded.

"I hope I don't need to remind you—"

Before he could finish, his words were drowned out by a roar from the crowd. On the tails of the roar came a series of trumpet blasts. Eight Falcons appeared in the air above, spiralling down onto the field. The eastern half of the stadium greeted them with a massive cheer.

Azrilan's team, wearing the teal and scarlet of the WingGuard.

The Wolves walked out onto the field next, backs straight, heads up. The humans leapt to their feet, roaring at the top of their lungs, even louder than the winged folk. The Wolves looked up, startled at the acclamation. The western stadium vibrated with the force of the crowd's fervour.

The winged folk came to their feet in competition, musical voices lifted in song and cheers, and the sound sent the blood racing through Talyn's veins. She wished desperately that she was playing.

The cacophony of screams, cheers, whistles, singing and stamping feet came to a reluctant end as Ravinire lifted into the air and raised a hand for silence. The two teams gathered in the centre of the field while he formally went over the rules of the game. They listened carefully, then moved apart.

Halun and Tiercelin moved towards the southern goal, where Azrilan's team would be trying to score, and Corrin and Zamaril moved towards the northern goal. Three of Azrilan's team flew over to the side of the field—lining up just under the viewing balcony where Talyn stood—to await substitution into the game, and the other five moved into their positions.

A rustling murmur ran through those on the balcony with Talyn. Princes Azrilan and Mithanis were arriving in the viewing balcony immediately adjacent. Several Falcons, their protective guard, stood arrayed behind them. Neither looked at Talyn as they sat beside their mother.

Prince Cuinn already sat on the other side of the balcony, apart from his family. He sprawled in a wide chair, wings resting on either side of him. As Talyn watched, he looked up and shared a laugh with one of his female companions. She wasn't sure he'd even noticed the Wolves walking out.

The ball was brought out and placed in the centre of the field. The cheering started again, slow rhythmic chants. Some spectators had brought along white and grey banners with the stylized image of a wolf etched in blue. They unfurled in the afternoon breeze, white, grey and sapphire flickering all along the western stand directly across from her.

Talyn barely heard the whistle. If she thought the crowd had been loud before, it was nothing compared with the absolute riot of noise that was inspired by the start of the game. Both Theac and his opponent leapt forward, but the Falcon was winged and younger. He reached the ball first, picking it up and swooping into the air.

Tiercelin lunged for him, but in a practiced move, the Falcon passed it to his companion, who moved around the Wolf, shouldering him hard as he did. Tiercelin half fell-half flew back to the ground. In another second Azrilan's team had scored, bringing a roar from the eastern stand.

The Wolves seemed to take this quick score without concern. They nodded at each other and moved back to the centre point. It was now Theac's ball. Ravinire blew his whistle to begin.

The Falcons almost scored again after the very first display of winged folk warrior magic Talyn had seen in Mithranar. A winged man dived at Theac, but he twisted away at the last second, kicking the ball down to Zamaril. The thief caught it deftly and kicked it on to Corrin. His aim was slightly off, and Corrin had to run for it.

Before he got there, a swooping Falcon made two sharp throwing gestures with his right arm. Bright balls of scarlet light, each the size of an apple, flew from his hand and slammed into the grass between Corrin and the ball. Two loud cracks reverberated through the afternoon air at the impact. Corrin reared back, throwing one hand up to shield his eyes from the brightness before sliding to a halt.

The Falcon took advantage of his distraction to scoop the ball up and launch back into the air. Corrin reacted quickly. He threw one of his knives, deliberately blunted and edged with wax for the game. It caught his opponent in a glancing blow on the wrist. Cursing in pain, the Falcon dropped the ball.

Corrin picked it up and looked for Zamaril. The thief, however, had been attacked by one of their other opponents and had to use his sword—the steel of the blade also blunted—to defend himself.

Corrin turned and tried to run but didn't get anywhere near the goal before two Falcons dived on him. He crashed to the ground, giving up the ball. It was swiftly relayed back to the other end. This time, Tiercelin didn't fly quickly enough to intercept. It looked as if his shoulder was paining him.

Halun was there, though. He stood directly in the flight path of the Falcon swooping in towards the goal. The winged man managed to dodge Halun in time, but it was awkward, and the ball flew out of his hands and out of bounds. The umpire whistled, and the ball was returned to the centre.

As the first half progressed, the Falcons scored another two goals and were prevented from scoring more by a series of lucky circumstances more than the skill of their opponents. The Wolves didn't even look close to scoring.

They tried to implement some of the moves Talyn had been teaching them, but the Falcons were too quick, not giving the Wolves any time to think about the best way to proceed, and using their warrior magic to distract the Wolves and keep them from maintaining concentration. Their magic was a critical and unrelenting advantage, particularly since *sabai* hadn't become instinctive to the Wolves yet.

Worse, the Falcons never gave them an opportunity for a one-on-one fight, and the Wolves weren't quick enough to force them into it. Any time the ball got down the northern end, the Wolves didn't have time to do anything before they were swamped by Falcon defenders.

The mid-game break couldn't come soon enough.

Azrilan grew cockier as the game wore on, his laughter and taunts floating piecemeal to her between the loudest cheering. Even

Mithanis was smiling, clearly enjoying the display. Talyn had to grit her teeth to stop herself from losing her temper and doing something ill-advised. Only decades of mastering her cool self-control prevented it.

And Cuinn. One of the winged women had moved onto his lap, and Talyn counted at least four glasses of sweet wine downed so far. At this rate he'd be passed out drunk by the end of the game. Disgust curled through her at the behaviour of all three princes.

But the human spectators hadn't given up. They chanted constantly, giving a lusty cheer every time a Wolf touched the ball, and booing loudly every time a Falcon scored.

Finally, Ravinire whistled for the mid-game break—they would play for two half-turns.

The Wolves waved up at Talyn and the crowd as they filed back into their break room for water and a quick rest. Despite her heart sinking on their behalf, they seemed in good enough spirits. Azrilan's Falcons drifted by directly under her into their room. They didn't look up once.

Part of her was glad the rules prevented her and Azrilan from talking to their teams during the break—she wasn't sure she could face her Wolves and their despair knowing they were about to lose badly. The cowardice shamed her.

When they came back out a quarter-turn later, Tiercelin had his bow and blunted, cloth-tipped arrows strapped over his back, but otherwise they hadn't changed anything. Talyn studied them carefully. They didn't look tired, only sweaty from the hot sun. All of them held their heads high. She'd been certain the score would demoralise them, but that didn't seem to be the case. They moved towards the centre of the field and lined up in front of Theac.

There was a sudden break in the chanting from the opposing crowds. Into the brief silence a group of spectators in the western stand howled in concert.

A wolf's howl.

Another took it up. Soon the entire western half of the stadium was breaking out in howls.

The Wolves glanced at each other. She frowned, struck. They were focused, determined, seemingly unbothered by either the score or the raucous crowd. Then her gaze moved to the princes opposite her, and she froze.

The easy smile Mithanis had been wearing all afternoon was gone. Now his dark eyes were quietly contemplative as the howls echoed around him. The queen looked outright furious. A smile toyed at the edges of Azrilan's mouth while Cuinn nuzzled the neck of the woman on his lap.

A contempt-filled term used to denigrate the human population of Mithranar was being turned into a cry of strength.

And the queen and prince of night didn't like it.

A shiver went down her back. Maybe it wasn't such a bad thing that the Wolves were about to lose. Ravinire whistled and the players moved back into their positions, Theac and his opponent three paces back from the ball. The score stood at three-nil.

The Falcon whistled the start of the half.

The howls reached a crescendo.

The same thing happened as at the beginning of the game. Theac's opponent was quicker, getting to the ball first. He spread his wings and leapt into the air.

Then, suddenly, the winged man faltered mid-leap. Her eyes swung to Theac—he'd pulled a rope from around his waist and lassoed his opponent's ankle as he flew upwards. Talyn's second yanked fiercely on the rope and the Falcon cried out in pain, wings fluttering as he dropped back to the ground.

Theac snatched the ball and ran. He had a few seconds before the rest of the Falcons—already high in the air—realised what had happened and flew after him. Two dived at him, and in the second before he was tackled to the ground, he kicked the ball down to Zamaril, timing the move perfectly.

The thief caught the ball and sprinted for the goal. The two Falcons who'd dived on Theac wasted precious seconds untangling themselves from him and each other and getting back to their feet.

At the northern end of the field, Azrilan's two defenders swooped towards Zamaril, one of them lifting an arm in preparation to send his crackling warrior magic at the thief.

Corrin, nearby and unseen, hurled his knives in quick succession, his hands a blur of movement. The first hit the Falcon about to use magic cleanly on the wrist, sending his arm askew and the orange energy burst flying harmlessly off course. The second smacked into the first defender's ribs mid-dive, forcing him to double over, half-winded. Two more hit the other defender in the exact same place. The hits knocked the Falcon just inches off course—Zamaril dodged violently to one side and sprinted through.

Seconds later he scored the Wolves' first goal.

The humans leapt to their feet, screaming their joy. Talyn simply stared—stunned.

Zamaril performed an elaborate bow, and the human crowd began chanting his name. Corrin collected his knives and the ball returned to the centre. The Falcons started with the ball following the Wolves' score. Theac's opponent threw it straight up in the air to a Falcon who was too high for Theac to lasso.

The Falcon winged swiftly towards the goals. Tiercelin dropped out of the sky, angling towards him. Another moved to fly up and intercept Tiercelin, but Halun grabbed him, wrestling him off his feet and dropping him to the ground where his wings were pinned beneath him and he couldn't get away.

Tiercelin intercepted the Falcon with the ball. They spiralled towards the ground. At the last moment, the Wolf pulled out of the dive in an exquisite display of timing. The other Falcon crashed heavily to the ground, dropping the ball.

Azrilan leapt to his feet, signalling for a time out. Ravinire caught the gesture and whistled. The prince shouted commands, and the two injured Falcons limped off, to be replaced with the substitutes.

Talyn barely noticed, instead staring open-mouthed at the Wolves. She couldn't quite understand what was happening—after weeks of endless apathy and fear of humiliation, they were fighting back.

It was Wolves' ball. Tiercelin started with it down near Azrilan's goal. Three Falcons came at him at once, but Halun planted himself in front of them. One slammed right into him and fell like a stone. The other two dodged around, but by then, Tiercelin had leapt into the air and was moving upfield with the ball.

The Falcon centre rose in front of him, sword drawn. Tiercelin stopped, shrugged, then pulled his own sword. The man moved forward to engage, and the moment he did, Tiercelin tapped the ball down to Corrin, who had snuck up behind. Now engaged with Tiercelin, the Falcon couldn't follow Corrin, who darted up the field.

Tiercelin pushed his opponent back with a series of quick strikes, giving himself enough time to dart to the side and slam a shoulder into one of the two Falcons who'd dodged Halun and were now going after Corrin. The Falcon spiralled to the ground, where Theac was ready to pounce, axe swinging. The second got around Tiercelin, who was then left to defend himself from his original opponent.

But that left only one Falcon chasing Corrin and one standing between him and the goal.

Zamaril was waiting closer to the goal, and he and Corrin ran at the final defender together, kicking the ball between them so the Falcon wouldn't know which of them would make the ultimate shot on goal, and sprinting fast enough their pursuer couldn't quite catch up.

In vain, the Falcon trying to catch them sent bursts of scarlet energy slamming into the ground around their feet and the ball. The violent crackling of energy snapped through the cheering and the roars, but neither Corrin or Zamaril let it distract them, focusing entirely on each other and the ball.

The Falcon defender ahead of them was concentrating so fiercely, arms lifted in preparation to use his own magic, that he didn't see Tiercelin raise his bow and nock an arrow. It flew between the two Wolves and hit the Falcon right at the base of his sternum. The cloth-tipped arrow didn't penetrate skin, but it hit hard and the Falcon reeled back, gasping as air whooshed from his lungs.

This time it was Corrin who shot the ball neatly through the goal.

The score was now three-two, with still a quarter-turn to go in the half. The two crowds competed wildly against each other to be the loudest and most effusive. The stadium reverberated with stamping feet and chanting.

Talyn could barely hear herself think.

Azrilan was on his feet. A frown creased his handsome features as he spoke emphatically with one of the Falcons below the viewing deck. Mithanis's face was dark as a thundercloud, he and his mother murmuring to each other. Cuinn appeared oblivious to it all. He was still sprawled in his chair, leaning across to speak to the woman beside him while the one on his lap nuzzled at his neck.

The Falcons pulled together after Azrilan's quick instructions were relayed. They swapped another injured man for a fresh one, but even so the ones left on the field looked to be tiring fast—sweat poured off them and their wings hung limply at their sides. If Talyn's experience with her energy shield was anything to go by, their use of magic had likely drained them, not to mention the effort they expended in flight.

Both teams spoke together in separate huddles for a few moments before Ravinire called them back to the centre.

As the game progressed, the Falcons pushed the Wolves hard, making them run and work for everything. The Wolves did the same. The two teams strained together for a while, nobody scoring. The Falcons' use of magic faded and then stopped entirely. Sweat slicked the skin of all players as the sun beat down over the field.

Theac was slashed in the leg with a not-so-blunt knife, then Halun was knocked in the head with a sword hilt. A tense few moments passed while Ravinire called a brief timeout and Tiercelin kneeled beside the big man. The crowd roared when Halun clambered back to his feet.

The Falcons almost scored just after that. Their attacker's throw missed the goal by less than an inch. Then it was the Wolves' ball from the boundary line. Tiercelin picked it up and kicked straight out. Theac caught the ball at the same time a Falcon swooped down on him.

Talyn's chest clenched, but then Theac did the unthinkable. He stepped to the side, body spinning gracefully in a classic *sabai* move, avoiding the dive and keeping the ball. The Falcon landed and leaped for him, but not before Theac smoothly kicked it down to Corrin.

The youngest Wolf made it to mid-field before being accosted by two Falcons. Zamaril was there, though. He came running up from behind, launched himself into the air, flipped in front of Corrin, then landed lightly on his feet and drew his sword. The cocky grin that followed the move was the icing on the cake.

What the...?

Talyn stared in astonishment. She'd yet to see any of them successfully execute a flip in training, let alone one as smooth and flawless as what Zamaril had just done. All of a sudden the thief was brimming with confidence.

One of the Falcons lunged at him with his sword. Zamaril ducked under it the way Talyn had taught him and came up underneath, smacking the flat of his blade against his opponent's chest. Simultaneously he lashed out with a kick to the man's knee, dropping him hard.

Corrin took advantage of the distraction. He picked up the ball and in two strides launched into another *sabai* move, flipping over the whole group and landing on the other side, coming up running. Zamaril engaged the second Falcon to stop him following, but the Falcon with the damaged knee leapt into the air.

"CORRIN!" Zamaril yelled in warning, fending off a series of quick attacks with astonishing ease. Talyn was agape. The Wolves were moving like a seamless fighting unit. When had that happened amongst the groaning and reluctance of the past weeks?

The young man kept going, increasing his speed until he was sprinting all out down the field.

"Corrin!"

Talyn hadn't even noticed Halun run up the field, but somehow his shout was audible over the crowd. Corrin passed the ball just as the injured Falcon dived on him, then dropped to the ground, rolling away before he could be tackled. Halun took the ball, tucked his head in, and charged for the end of the field. A final defender landed on his back, beating at his head and shoulders.

Halun merely tucked his head in and kept charging forward until the ball was in the goal. When he looked up his mouth and nose were bloodied, but he was otherwise fine.

"YEAH!" Talyn screamed, jumping up and down on the spot, heedless of the surly Falcon captains around her. Iceflight had his arms crossed, jaw locked, the chill in his bearing a perfect match to his name.

The human spectators were delirious with excitement. There was every chance now that the Wolves could win. All they had to do was score another goal in the final minutes of the game.

The Wolves knew it too. They gathered in the centre of the field as the ball was brought back up. Mithanis raged at Azrilan's team, shoving his brother aside to do so, livid with anger. The Falcons returned to their positions with renewed determination in their eyes.

The ball was with the Falcons. Their best attacker stood with it in the middle of the field until Ravinire blew the whistle. Before the sound had died, he rocketed straight into the air, Theac's lasso just barely missing his ankle.

Once they were up in the air, the five players of Azrilan's team joined together, forming a flying V shape with the ball holder protected in the middle.

Talyn's heart sank. They were in an unbreakable formation. All they needed to do was to fly straight for the goals like that. Halun couldn't touch them, and the four players surrounding the ball holder could easily deal with Tiercelin.

It was a sound strategy—if the Falcons scored now, there would be no time for the Wolves to score before the end of the game.

Whoever scored now would win.

The human crowd booed at this unfair tactic, but Azrilan was back in his seat, wings relaxed, that little smile playing at the corners of his mouth again. Mithanis prowled at the railing. Their mother's overt anger had faded to a cool watchfulness.

Halun ran over to Tiercelin, taking the winged man's arm and murmuring something in his ear. Tiercelin glanced between Halun and the oncoming Falcons and gave him a little nod. Corrin's hands dropped to his knives, but they were too far away for him to do anything—he was at the other end of the ground. Still, he and Zamaril moved forward, closer to the centre, just in case.

Talyn's gaze went back to her single winged Wolf. Tiercelin's face was set, hair damp with sweat, bow and arrows hanging loosely down his back. As the Falcon formation approached, he spread his massive grey wings and leapt into the air.

Hope flickered in her. She knew what he was going to try and do.

Tiercelin climbed quickly to their height, then hung in the afternoon sunlight, facing the Falcons down as they flew inexorably towards him. Her fists clenched of their own accord, her heart racing. "Come on, Tiercelin," she whispered. "You can do it."

Time seemed to slow to a crawl. Then, Tiercelin held out his arm, palm outwards. As if holding their breath, the whole stadium fell suddenly silent, so quiet you could hear a pin drop. Talyn didn't even notice.

Then, with a snap-hiss that was heard across the stands, Tiercelin summoned his first Callanan energy shield. It was a great living shield of silvery grey light, shot through with sparks. He held it there, face twisted with the effort.

The Falcons were almost too late to avoid it. They veered away, tangling with each other, dropping to the ground. Halun, Corrin, and Theac converged on the group, throwing themselves at the Falcons so they couldn't leap back into the air.

In a grasping, physical, brutal tangle they fought it out, each trying to get the ball. Tiercelin hung in the air, panting, clearly too exhausted to do anything more.

It was hard to see who had the ball in the scrimmage that followed. One of the Falcons had hurt himself in the fall and was out of action. The others fought bitterly with Theac, Halun and Corrin. Talyn suddenly realised Zamaril wasn't there, and looked for him.

"Clever," she whispered.

The thief had used his brain. Instead of getting involved in the brawl that the other Wolves were able to handle, he hung back, out of the way. Sensing his presence in the way only a tightly melded team could, Halun, Theac and Corrin worked at getting the ball out to him.

The stadium remained utterly silent, both east and west holding their breath in an absolute paroxysm of anticipation. Then, Corrin managed to roll his slim body out of the pack, the ball in his hands. Without hesitation, he threw the ball to Zamaril.

The thief took the catch cleanly, but wavered a moment, his confidence deserting rapidly.

Talyn hung over the balcony and screamed. "GO ZAMARIL!!!! I KNOW YOU CAN!! *GO!*"

Somehow he heard her. He turned on his heel and ran for his life, ball tucked securely in his arms.

Now the Wolves' superior conditioning began to show. Both teams had been fighting for an hour, but whereas the Falcons were exhausted, the Wolves had more to give. Zamaril sprinted down the field at his top speed, determination etched across his face.

The Falcons disentangled themselves from the pack, desperately looking to try and chase Zamaril down.

Theac and Halun eschewed weapons and flung themselves on two of the Falcons, using their superior strength and skill to wrestle them to the ground, keeping them pinned there.

Corrin fought the third, going at him with a sword so quickly the Falcon was forced into a flurry of counters. Their swords flashed, and Corrin kept up the furious pace, using sabai, using everything Talyn had told him, not giving the Falcon a moment to gather himself and leap into flight.

Tiercelin dropped out of the air, using his falling momentum to slam into one of the two Falcons that managed to lift off. The two crashed hard into the ground, then lay there, gasping. Neither looked to have the strength to fight anymore.

Just one Falcon defender left.

The western crowd had started roaring the minute Zamaril had moved. The thief poured his heart into the run. Talyn was screaming, yelling his name, urging him on. The Falcon swooped through the air after him. Talyn's breath caught—he was going so fast, he would catch Zamaril before he reached the goal.

The winged spectators were on their feet now too, roaring in unison with the humans, urging Azrilan's Falcon on. Zamaril heard the crowd's warning and glanced up and back. The Falcon was taking no chances. He lifted his arm, made a throwing motion. Talyn held her breath.

A bright blue light flashed, faded, winked out of existence.

The Falcon's magic was too drained. Making a frustrated gesture, he drew his sword instead and dove hard and fast at the thief.

Zamaril dodged at the last minute, rolling along the ground. The sword flashed, slamming into the ground where Zamaril's head had just been. The thief rolled lithely to his feet and the two opponents faced each other warily. The Falcon was armed, and Zamaril had his hands full with the ball.

The Falcon went at Zamaril with a series of quick, stinging attacks. Zamaril stepped out of range of each one, though the last managed to scrape along his cheek, and bright red blood dripped down his face. Talyn snarled—those weapons were supposed to be completely blunted. She'd personally made sure the Wolves' weapons were.

The winged man struck again. This time Zamaril moved aside only an inch. He dropped the ball and stepped inside his opponent's guard. Before the Falcon knew what was happening, Zamaril had gripped the hilt of his sword and twisted it out of his hand in a classic *sabai* move. In the next second, Zamaril drove his elbow into the man's sternum. The Falcon dropped, hunched over, gasping, hand pressed to his chest.

Zamaril picked up the ball and ran for the goal.

The humans screamed like nothing Talyn had ever heard before. She found herself screaming with them as the ball sailed through the goals, kicked neatly from Zamaril's foot. The crowd lost their minds in a cacophony of singing, stamping and clapping.

Zamaril looked as if he couldn't believe his eyes. She stared as it slowly sunk in that they'd won the game. A wide grin spread across his face, and he set off at a run back down the field, face alight with excitement.

An icy trickle whispered down the back of her neck, tearing her momentarily from stunned joy.

She glanced to her right. Mithanis's dark eyes were on her, something unsettling in the quality of his stare. Like he was assessing her and didn't quite like what he found.

Whatever it was, she didn't like it. She met that stare without hesitation, a little smile of triumph spreading over her face. He'd tried to embarrass and humiliate them and he'd failed. Miserably.

She held his gaze for a moment longer, then dismissed it. As her attention moved away, it fell on Cuinn—surprisingly, he'd been watching the interaction between her and Mithanis, and a little smile of amusement curled at his mouth. He shifted, and it almost looked like he was about to give her a nod, but thought better of it and turned away, dismissing her from his attention.

Then the roaring of the crowd broke through the bubble of silence that had settled around her and the princes, and the smile on her face widened into a grin. She swung off the balcony onto the grass below, ignoring how the jolt thudded painfully through her shoulder.

The Wolves were gathering in the centre of the field, yelling and backslapping and grinning like madmen.

Halun saw her first. His face split into an enormous grin. Then she'd reached them, and Corrin was chattering excitedly while hopping from foot to foot, and Tiercelin was looking right at her, pride flashing in his grey eyes.

"I did it," he said excitedly. "Did you see my shield? I did it!"

"It was one of the best shields I've ever seen," she told him. "I'm so proud of you. I'm so proud of you all."

"We actually won!" Zamaril looked as if he still couldn't believe it.

"You did well, lad," Theac said gruffly. "You all did. I've never been as proud of any unit I've ever led."

She didn't say it aloud, but she couldn't say with any certainty she'd ever felt this scorching pride for any comrades she'd fought with before.

"You did it, Tal. Look at them. They're on their way to being an elite Kingshield protection unit." Sari's voice rang with excitement and pride. Pride for her.

It took everything she had not to start bawling like a baby right where she stood.

CHAPTER 36

*W*ith the ebullient cheers of the crowd echoing in their ears, the Wolves headed off the grass and back to their room. Talyn followed, smiling at their excited chattering.

"Did you see the look on those Falcons' faces when we won?" Zamaril crowed.

"This will show them," Corrin said, his face flushed with excitement. "We aren't so inferior after all."

Talyn opened her mouth, wanting to warn them. The winged folk weren't going to take this well. But the looks on their faces stopped her. They looked so proud and excited, she couldn't ruin that. There would be enough time for warnings later. Instead, she asked, "Something changed in the second half. You started playing better, well enough to win. What was it?"

"I thought an accomplished warrior like yourself would have recognised our strategy, Captain," Tiercelin drawled.

"I—"

"Remember how we mentioned an alternative plan to deal with your attacker?" Corrin interrupted.

"Yes." She frowned, not sure what that had to do with the game.

"Since the aim of shooting you was most likely to prevent you taking part in the game to ensure we'd lose," Zamaril said, "we decided the best way to get revenge was to win the game."

"So we sat down and worked out a strategy to win," Theac said gruffly.

"We played terribly in the first half on purpose," Halun said. "For two reasons—to gauge the skill of Prince Azrilan's team, and to give them false confidence."

"Then in the second half we came out fighting," Tiercelin said. "And gave them a big shock in doing so. The momentum carried us through the first two goals, which was the plan."

"We had to fight for the last two goals," Corrin said. "But this time we didn't hold back, using everything you taught us."

"Our thief here has a mind for this sort of thing. Most of the strategy was his, and Theac helped polish it." Halun gave both men a firm nod.

"I see." She nodded, trying to give herself time to come up with an appropriate response. If she hadn't been utterly floored before, now she was downright shocked. Now that they'd explained it to her, she could see exactly how the game had flowed to a perfect plan—all those little things in the first half she'd put down to chance, it had been the Wolves, cleverly baiting the Falcons into thinking they were useless, while not allowing them to score too highly that they couldn't come back. If she was honest, she hadn't seen this in them.

"Maybe not, but your instincts were spot on."

Before she could say anything, Corrin spoke up. "Captain, you told me once that you look out for those under your command. It runs both ways, you said. We're a team, we look after each other, and that means we've got your back too. Always."

"You're our captain," Tiercelin added, scowling in a perfect imitation of Theac. "Nobody touches you without consequences. There was no way that we were going to lose today."

"I…" She trailed off, then took a deep breath. "Thank you."

An awkward silence descended, none of them comfortable with the sudden level of sentiment hanging in the air between them.

It was Zamaril who broke it, clearing his throat loudly. "I don't know about the rest of you, but I think that win requires celebration. I know this great little place in the Dock Quarter where the ale is cheap and delicious. Anyone care to join me?"

"You don't mind if I come?" Tiercelin said hesitantly, his wings ruffling.

"Should anyone speak against it, I'll introduce their heads to a steel pole," Halun spoke, the smoothness of his cultured accent at odds with the blunt words.

Corrin nodded in violent agreement and Zamaril jerked a thumb in the big man's direction. "What he said. Come on, let's go."

They crowded for the door, excitement still spilling out of them in waves, then turned to look at Talyn expectantly when she didn't immediately follow.

She opened her mouth. It was on the tip of her tongue to say yes, to follow them out the door. But then it hit her. She *wanted* to. She wanted the high spirits and camaraderie of a night out drinking after winning a particularly difficult battle. And she wanted to do it with her Wolves.

She'd started to care about them.

Panic closed over her chest so tightly she almost gasped. "I..." She cleared her throat, swallowed. "You should all go. I need to stay."

Their faces fell, and the sight of it ripped at her. But she couldn't do this again—she had to keep her distance.

"Have fun," she managed, doing her best not to let them see how broken she was. "And no drill in the morning. You've all earned a day off. I'll see you in two days."

Corrin opened his mouth, clearly intending to protest, but Halun grabbed him firmly by the shoulder and shoved him at the door. Tiercelin's laughter trickled out as the youth almost went headfirst into the door and Theac barked an admonition. Zamaril gave her a small nod and followed them all out.

The door swung shut behind them and she took a deep, steadying breath.

It was better this way. Safer.

CHAPTER 37

*H*e sat in his seat at the stadium for a long time after the game was over. Others were doing the same. Many were families. Husbands and wives and children excitedly recapping what they'd just seen and not wanting to leave and let the magic die yet.

It had been a late afternoon game and night was falling quickly—the sky black and full of stars above.

They'd won. And it had fundamentally changed his world.

Somehow, some way, the Wolves had beaten Prince Azrilan's Falcons and for the first time ever had won a victory for the human folk. He'd been unable to believe his eyes when he'd seen the way the Wolves fought back in the second half.

They hadn't been weaker, or less skilled, or in any way inferior to their winged opponents. The Wolves had met the Falcons head to head and defeated them on equal terms. Fierce hope had bubbled up in him as he watched them fight with the heart of true warriors.

And all because of Captain Dynan.

Any lingering doubts he had about her intentions in Mithranar had faded. She had turned a rabble of human criminals into warriors and—albeit unintentionally—used them to prove the worth of humans to a winged population that stubbornly refused to see it.

She might refuse to admit it. Might deny it even to herself. But she was just like him.

He wasn't alone.

It was heady; the fragile hope that maybe there was someone he could trust, that maybe for the first time in his achingly lonely life there might be someone else who wanted the same things he did. He crushed that hope before it could take root; it would hurt beyond measure if he was wrong.

Still, he needed to talk to her.

Soon.

CHAPTER 38

*T*alyn had barely finishing bathing—made slower and more difficult with her bandaged shoulder—when a firm knock came at her door. Night had fallen, her room lit only by a handful of lamps. Outside the Mithranan evening was warm and heady with the scent of flowers.

She opened the door to find Theac there, a large flagon in one hand and small sack in the other. Her eyebrows lifted in surprise.

"Apple juice," he said before she could say anything. "Mind if I come in for a moment?"

She sighed. "Theac, you should be out celebrating with the Wolves. You deserve it."

"Yeah, well, me being around so much ale probably isn't the best idea." He shrugged. "Apple juice is safer. It's also a lot more expensive, so best let me in so it don't go to waste, Captain."

She wanted to tell him no. To retreat back into her room and be alone with her painful memories and despairing thoughts. Instead she found herself letting him in and waving him over to the sofa by the unlit fire. Her lounge windows were open, letting in the warm air and light from the torches lit in the walkway outside.

"Not much privacy up here in the citadel is there?" he grumbled. "Windows and open-aired spaces everywhere."

"Plus, flying people who can drop in on you any time." She smiled wryly, dropping onto the couch.

Theac said nothing for a moment, busying himself emptying the sack and pouring them both a glass of juice. Along with two small cups and plates, the sack held half of a pie of some kind and two sweet-smelling pastries.

"The pie is Errana's." He barely fought a smile. "She thought Corrin might be hungry after the game. The pastries are cherry—my favourite—I get them at a small bakery in the Market Quarter whenever they can get their hands on the fruit. I've been going there since I was a boy."

It wasn't until she began eating that she realised how hungry she was—she hadn't eaten since a small breakfast. They ploughed through the food in a strangely comfortable silence. Once finished, Theac leaned forward to re-fill both glasses before settling himself back on the couch.

"So, who did you lose?" he asked gruffly.

"Theac, I—"

"I've seen it before, of course. Happened to me once or twice," he said. He was looking at his cup instead of her, giving her space.

"I don't want to talk about this." Despite his effort at gentleness, her body had turned rigid, and she stared straight ahead, not wanting him to see what was on her face.

He was silent for a long moment, then, "Did you ever wonder about the blue we chose for the symbol of the wolf on our uniforms? The colour of our captain's eyes. You said it was tradition in your Kingshield, and we wanted to honour that."

"Theac, I can't—" She was mortified when her eyes flooded with tears. Had they really done that for her? She didn't deserve that kind of loyalty.

"You said we're a team, and we help each other out. Now, I understand you might not want the lads to know your personal business, but I'm your second. More, I've been a Patrolman many more years than you've been a warrior." He paused. "I'll leave now, if you want me to, nothing further to be said. Or I can stay a bit. And you can tell me who you lost."

"My partner." The words were barely audible. She wasn't sure she'd ever said them aloud, not since Sari's death. He said nothing, giving her space to tell as much or as little as she liked, and once she'd gotten those first two words out, she found the rest spilling out of her. "Callanan partners are close. We train together, fight together, *think* together. It's like having an extension of your own body. Losing her was..." She shook her head. There were no words for it.

"And you blame yourself."

Her head whipped towards him, and his mouth creased in a bitter smile. "I'm all too familiar with that look of guilt and self-hatred, Captain."

"It *was* my fault. Sari and I... we were good. They called us the best, and it was true. There wasn't a mission we couldn't complete, a battle we couldn't win. It made us cocky. It made *me* cocky. One day I made a decision, went against protocol because I thought we could handle it, and she died." Misery choked her last few words.

"Maybe that's true and maybe it's not. Either way, it's now something you have to live with every day." He cleared his throat. "But it *is* okay to live, Captain."

She said nothing. The words were kind, but even now she couldn't find it in herself to accept them.

"I've been thinking on this a bit," he started again. "How Tiercelin reacted when he tried to heal your knee the other night... what he said. Now, these Callanan of yours obviously have some kind of winged folk magic." A wry look crossed his face. "I imagine Tiercelin has filled your ears with his thoughts on that?"

She huffed out a laugh. "He has."

"It set me to wondering." He cleared his throat. "You're grieving, Captain, and rightfully so... but what you just described about how Callanan partnerships work... could it be that your magic also connects in some way? It would explain why Tiercelin sensed such a wound in yours, and why your partner's death has hit you so hard."

"Maybe." She wrapped her arms around herself, shivering as the conversation headed back into too painful territory. "What does it matter?"

"I imagine if I'm right, the lad might be able to help heal your magical wound. It might make coping with your grief easier."

She shook her head. "That feels too much like letting go. I can't let go of her, Theac."

He cleared his throat, hesitated, then said gruffly, "You *need* to let go of the guilt, Captain."

She said nothing, staring ahead into the unlit fireplace.

"The first time I lost a lad after an order I'd given—he was barely twenty and I'd only been a watch officer for a few weeks—it took me months before I could go out on Patrol again," he said. "They almost kicked me out then. Would have, if I hadn't been fortunate enough to have a sympathetic patrol captain."

"Why?" She managed the single word.

"The idea of giving another order, of going out again, it filled me with panic," her second said simply. "I was terrified of making another mistake."

Her eyes filled with tears. She swallowed. "What did you do?"

This time it took Theac a moment to reply. When she summoned enough courage to look at him, he was looking at her with an expression full of regret. "I started drinking. Not too much at first, just enough to take the edge off. But as the years passed and the mistakes and losses piled up... it just got worse. Two years ago, my brother died falling out of a tree while on an izerdia work crew. I went completely off the rails after that, was kicked out of the patrol within three months. Soaked in my grief and guilt until the day you walked into the pardonable cells." He cleared his throat. "You're stronger than I was, Captain."

"That's kind of you to say." She didn't tell him she'd actively sabotaged her Kingshield posting, that she might freeze at a critical moment if Cuinn were ever attacked in her presence, that the sound of an arrow firing sent her into a panic. "I'm sorry about your brother."

"And I'm sorry about your partner, Captain." After a moment he rose, clearing up the plates and cups. "I'll make sure the lads are aware that not going out with them tonight wasn't anything to do with them. And I'll help you keep your distance, if that's what you need."

"Thank you," she said gratefully.

He nodded. "I'm your second. So, I'll see you the day after tomorrow for drill then?"

"You will."

"Night, Captain." And he was gone, shutting the door quietly behind him.

"You've got a second, Tal."

She did. He was a grizzled, bad-tempered, too-old, stubborn alcoholic, but he was *hers*. And she wouldn't have it any different for the world. That knowledge was terrifying and exhilarating all at the same time. Maybe, just maybe, she *was* starting to live again.

She grabbed hold of that flicker of hope and sat curled on the couch, sipping Theac's apple juice and willing that hope into life.

CHAPTER 39

When Talyn walked into the barracks' common room two mornings later, she found Theac sitting at the central table with a pile of parchment stacked in front of him. He was glowering, as per usual, but the sight made her smile. "What are those?"

He looked up. "Enquiries about enlisting with the Wolves."

"You're kidding?" Talyn walked over and dropped beside him. The pile was inches thick. Theac handed her a bunch and she flicked through. "There are winged folk names in here." She frowned. "Are you sure these aren't some sort of prank?"

"I wish," he said sourly. "The Falcon delivered them this morning— you just missed him. Apparently he started getting enquiries the day after the floods. He was just writing their names down initially, then when more and more came in, he started making them fill out proper applications."

"Before we won the game?" Her eyebrows shot upwards.

A smile briefly lightened his dour expression. "I couldn't tell whether he was more surprised at Dock City humans wanting to join the WingGuard, or their audacity in traipsing up to his precious citadel and approaching his Falcons in the first place."

"I can't imagine they got a warm reception," she said dryly.

"I suppose we're going to be able to train up a full wing. Sixty guards plus talons," Theac said, slight disbelief in his voice.

"It looks like it." She scarcely believed it either. After all the time and work she'd put in since arriving in Mithranar, could things finally be turning around? That flicker of hope burned momentarily stronger.

"There are over fifty names here," Theac muttered.

Shit. That sobered her quickly. She'd gone from reckless Callanan warrior to Kingshield guard to now suddenly responsible for building a full wing of warriors. Sari would have laughed if she'd seen her now.

"Kahvi, Captain?" Tiercelin ducked his head in from the kitchen doorway.

"Please." She didn't look up from the parchment in her hand. "And bring the others, we need to have a meeting."

"What, no run this morning?" Zamaril strolled in, stopping and whistling when he saw the pile of parchment. "Have we run out of kindling for the fire or something?"

"They're applications for enlistment."

"Oh." He paused. "Why do we have them? Shouldn't they be on the Falcon's desk?"

"They're applications to enlist with the Wolves."

"Oh," he said again, then started, eyes widening. "With us? Seriously?"

"Did I just hear right?" Corrin appeared with Tiercelin and Halun behind him. "People suddenly want to enlist?"

"They do." Talyn thanked Tiercelin as he handed her a mug of kahvi, then motioned for them all to sit on the chairs around the table. "And we're going to look at the applications together."

Beside her, Theac coughed. She turned to him, dropping her voice. "They've earned the right to be involved in this decision."

"Yes, of course." He nodded, amusement flashing over his face.

She gave him a look, then turned back to the others. "We'll do interviews with all of the applicants we consider. I don't care about previous experience, or what they do for a living. If they've got what it takes to be a Wolf, we'll accept them. That's how you all got here, and that's how it will stay. It's what makes you different from the Falcons, and in my opinion, it's what makes you better. An applicant must have the full agreement of all six of us before we take them. Agreed?"

A series of nods. Everyone but Tiercelin still looked rather floored.

"We are also going to ignore the WingGuard's ridiculous rule that women can't become warriors. If they've got what it takes, we'll have them, male or female."

Nods around the room.

"We're also going to accept winged folk, if they want to join and we think they're a good fit," Talyn said carefully.

"If they're half as decent as Tiercelin, I'm all for that, Captain," Zamaril said quietly.

Everyone stared at him, and Tiercelin looked unaccountably touched. His arrogant tone vanished momentarily as he spoke. "Thanks, Zamaril. And for what it's worth, the Falcon offered me my pick of Falcon wings last night. I chose to stay with the Wolves."

"Good lad." Theac gave him an approving look.

Talyn wondered when the last time that had happened in Mithranar, a human giving a winged man an approving look. Or a winged man smiling back with genuine affection. The hope wriggled inside her again.

"Life isn't going to be any easier. I'm going to demand the same high standards from you and the new recruits, and eventually you'll have guard duties added to your training." She spoke over the lump in her throat. "If any of you have decided that this life isn't for you, you've earned your discharge along with a pardon." She hadn't gotten Ravinire's permission for that yet, but if any of them wanted it, she would do whatever it took to *make* him agree. She no longer wanted Wolves that had no choice but to be where they were.

"I'm staying," Corrin said fervently, words tripping over themselves, he spoke so quickly.

"Me too." Halun crossed his arms over his chest.

Tiercelin's wings rustled. "I already told you I'm staying."

"Same here, Captain," Theac muttered.

Unable to help herself, her gaze went to Zamaril. Her most reluctant and cynical Wolf. He'd hated being caged by the wing. If he wanted to be free, she wanted nothing more than to make that happen for him.

He was watching her, pale blue eyes for once stripped of derision. She sensed him wrestling with himself, making a choice between trust and a new life, or going back to the life he'd always known.

The other Wolves said nothing, letting him come to his decision. A smile threatened to break free when she noticed them all unconsciously leaning towards him. Even Theac's hand had curled into the fabric of his breeches where it rested on his knee.

"I'd like to stay, Captain," he said so softly she barely heard the words. Almost instantly the room relaxed. Tiercelin leaned over to punch him in the shoulder. Theac gave him an approving nod. Corrin beamed from ear to ear.

"Well chosen, Zamaril," Halun spoke with his usual quiet dignity.

She was struck by the strength of the bond that had developed between them—she hadn't realised how strong it had grown. Sadness licked at her. Such a bond was a wonderful thing, but it could hurt too.

"All right then." She made her voice brisk and began dividing up the parchment into six piles. "Let's start reviewing these. The ones you like, put them in a pile on the left, the ones you don't, a pile on the right. We'll interview everyone in the left pile."

There was a brief silence, then, "I can't read."

It was Zamaril who had spoken, and it wasn't the words that surprised her, but the lack of self-contempt or challenge in them.

"I can't read either," Corrin admitted. "I've started learning from my sisters when I visit, but I can only recognise basic words."

"In that case, how about we work in pairs?" Tiercelin suggested. "I'll work with you, Zamaril, and I'll read each application aloud. Halun can work with Corrin."

"Could you..." Zamaril hesitated. "Maybe you could teach me as you go?"

"You promise not to start spitting and snarling at me, and I'd be happy to."

"As long as you don't get all superior, I'll be patient." Zamaril scowled.

Talyn glanced at Theac. "That sounds like a plan. And from now on Theac and I will be down in the mess a half-turn after dinner each night if either of you wants extra reading lessons."

"Actually, Captain." Halun spoke quietly. "I've some teaching experience. I'd be pleased to run lessons of an evening. Writing too. For the new recruits as well."

"Thank you, Halun." Talyn smiled at him. "Let's get down to it."

The sound of shuffling papers filled the room as the Wolves settled back into their chairs, brows furrowed in concentration, Halun and Tiercelin's voices sounding as they read their applications.

Talyn took a moment to smile at their focused concentration, then turned to her own pile.

BY THE FOLLOWING MORNING, they had a shortlist for interviews. Many were poorer humans from Dock City, some seeing a way out of their difficult lives, others wanting to repay what the Wolves had done during the flood. But there were also wealthier humans amongst the applications, and a handful of winged folk.

A week later, she and her Wolves had spoken to all of them and chosen who they wanted to take on.

Ravinire frowned at her when she handed him the list of twenty names. "A full wing has six details of ten warriors, plus a talon for each detail, Captain."

"Yes, sir. However, given we have limited resources to undertake training, I thought it better we start with a smaller number—two full details of ten guards. Once they're up to speed—I'd say six weeks for basic training—we'll accept another intake of twenty, assuming you continue to get more applications." She paused. "And then a third intake once the second has completed training. With that timing,

Prince Cuinn will have a fully manned wing by the time my posting has finished in Twelvemonth."

"Train two full details at a time." He considered that for a moment, then his face cleared in surprise. "You want to keep Theac as your second and promote each of the existing Wolves to talon."

"Eventually, yes. I think you'd be surprised with how well suited they are for it, sir."

He nodded. "Very well, Captain. I'll send out the enlistment notices today and ensure the barracks are properly equipped for the new recruits, including uniforms and weapons. They'll be ordered to report in two weeks, if that suits you?"

She considered that for a moment. Two weeks meant they'd finish basic training by early Ninemonth. "Yes, sir. Thank you."

He gave her a long, measuring look. "I will admit to being thoroughly surprised, Captain. The way your Wolves played, the skill they showed... well, to be blunt, I would have called it impossible. You're everything that was advertised."

So she'd passed his test. She was surprised how little that mattered anymore. "I'm not anything if you can't get Prince Cuinn to let us guard him, sir. Without that, the Wolves are a well-trained protection wing with no purpose."

"Understood." He hesitated, jaw working. "And while I respect what you've managed to do with your wing, you need to be careful, Captain. You've been here long enough to understand why, I hope?"

"I do." It was her turn to hesitate. "What will the consequences be, for our win?"

"I hope there will be none." Ravinire was grim, suggesting he didn't believe his own words. "As much as it rankles you, Prince Cuinn's utter disinterest where the Wolves are concerned will help. Still, there are a lot of unhappy winged folk. I recommend you all keep your heads down."

"Thank you, sir. I understand."

CHAPTER 40

*T*wo days after her conversation with Ravinire, Talyn was summoned to attend the queen. A young Falcon came swirling down towards Talyn as she and the Wolves finished up drills for the afternoon.

She gave him a nod of acknowledgement when he landed beside her. His wings were an entrancing violet in colour, and he held himself with the same casual arrogance that Tiercelin did, indicating he was nobility too. "Can I help you?"

"The queen would like to see you right away, Captain," he said formally.

Talyn frowned. "What for?"

"I don't know. The order came via the Falcon."

Talyn sighed and waved Theac over, stepping away so she could speak to him privately. "The queen has summoned me and apparently it can't wait."

Concern flashed in Theac's dark eyes. "Be careful, Captain."

Talyn dropped her voice. Gone were the days when she discounted what her cynical second had to say. "You think I should be worried?"

"The royal family is a pit of vipers, Captain, and the queen rules them," Theac murmured. "And we just showed up her WingGuard in an alleya game."

Then there had been her conversation with Ravinire. He'd warned of consequences too. Dread swirled in her, but she tried her best to ignore it and clapped Theac on the shoulder. "I'll be fine."

The Falcon straightened as she crossed back to him. "You'll take me to her?"

"Yes, Captain." He hesitated. "Can I ask... well, that is... you taught Lord Stormflight how to do that shield?"

"I did."

He frowned. "But how is it that a human could teach one of us how to use our magic?"

"I think you'll find that humans aren't quite as hapless as you winged folk seem to think." She kept her voice light. "Are you interested in learning... I'm sorry, I don't know your name?"

"Ronisin Nightdrift." He gave a smooth bow. "But I couldn't possibly... I mean, I was just curious."

"Well, you're welcome to come and join us anytime, Ronisin." She gave him a smile. "I suppose we'd best not keep the queen waiting any longer."

He flushed. "Of course. If you'll follow me, Captain."

RONISIN DIDN'T SPEAK another word as he led her through the palace, though she frequently caught him glancing sideways at her. His arrogance hadn't bothered her overly much—she considered it progress that he'd even expressed interest in what she'd taught Tiercelin to do. She wondered if he'd take her up on her offer, or whether it had been smart of her to make it. She hadn't forgotten Tiercelin's warning from months earlier about not displaying her magical ability in Mithranar. It might be best if Ronisin's winged folk pride held him back. The last thing she wanted to do was create more waves before leaving.

When they reached the area of the palace Talyn recognised as the queen's, Ronisin left her with another graceful bow at the open doorway to a sitting room before winging away. Talyn stepped inside, training and experience leading her to scan her surroundings as she did each time she entered an unfamiliar space.

The queen was arranged comfortably on a sofa, lilac wings hanging loosely over the back, an untouched plate of fruit and pastries laid on the small table beside her. Ravinire stood behind and to her right, back straight and face expressionless as always. An unfamiliar winged woman sat to the queen's left, and the two were talking softly.

Talyn stood just inside the entrance, stance loose, hands behind her back, and waited. The queen didn't even look her way. Ravinire stared at the wall beside her head.

"Is she trying to be rude, or just making the point that she is queen and you are very much her inferior?"

Talyn stifled a smile. *"I doubt that much thought has gone into it."*

Sari's laughter tinkled. *"If only she knew you were one of the Dumnorix."*

"I suspect now isn't the time to reveal that information. It might be misconstrued."

"Yes." A disappointed sigh. *"Your uncle won't be pleased if you create a diplomatic incident. Although given he signed off on sending you here, I'm not sure you could be blamed."*

"Stop trying to cause trouble." Talyn squashed her partner's voice, ignoring the indignant squeak that followed.

Several more minutes passed before the queen deigned to look up and acknowledge her presence. "Captain Dynan," she said, a polite smile gracing her beautiful face. "Thank you for coming."

Mindful of Theac's warning—and Prince Cuinn's passing references to threats of whipping—Talyn kept her expression bland and voice polite. "You summoned me, Your Grace?"

Piercing blue eyes watched her for a long moment, and Talyn endured the scrutiny stoically. Training to be a protective guard had its benefits—fidgeting was frowned upon and quickly beaten out of any recruit. "Yes. It occurred to me that I had yet to officially meet the woman in charge of my youngest son's safety," she said eventually.

"Or she finally noticed you were here after your Wolves trounced her WingGuard at alleya in front of the whole population," Sari muttered.

Talyn stifled a smile, managed a smooth bow. "I am sure you are very busy, Your Grace."

"Tiercelin Stormflight's parents came to see me recently. They were very upset." That blue gaze was unrelenting.

Although Talyn couldn't detect a question in there anywhere, the queen was looking at her expectantly. She cleared her throat, trying to come up with something polite but not inane. "I'm sorry to hear that. Can I ask what upset them?"

"Since he distinguished himself so well in the alleya game, he has had offers from the captains of several accomplished Falcon wings to join them," she said. "It seems that he's turned them all down to remain with your Wolves."

"I'm sorry, Your Grace, I don't think I understand your concern." Talyn couldn't help the edge in her tone, and winced internally, fighting to keep her expression deferential. "The Wolves *are* a part of the WingGuard."

"It's a problem because my subjects—my *friends*—do not wish to have their son brought down amongst a group of humans. It does not reflect well on them."

The whip of anger that swept through her at those words was as surprising as it was strong. Talyn hesitated a moment, trying to choose her words carefully. "Your Grace, I didn't force Tiercelin to remain with my wing. It was his free choice to make."

The queen's gaze narrowed. "Be very careful where you tread, Captain Dynan. I acceded to Ravinire's request to bring you here because Cuinn is my son and of course I wish him to be safe. However, he is the youngest, and as such, least important son where my throne is concerned."

A lie. Talyn's gaze flicked to Ravinire. As usual his face was impassive. He hadn't requested her. But of course they weren't the only ones in the room—the queen's friend was listening intently while she daintily ate a pastry and pretended not to be, and several Falcons were just outside the door.

"*Figure it out later. The queen is staring at you!*" Sari hissed.

Swallowing, she returned her attention to the queen. Aware she was on shaky ground, she attempted to be honest and diplomatic at the same time. "Your Grace, I would like you to understand that because Prince Cuinn is my charge, he is my priority."

Something unreadable flickered in the queen's eyes. "Be that as it may. Tiercelin Stormflight will return to the WingGuard."

Talyn frowned. "Your Grace, his choice is to remain with the—"

"His choice has nothing to do with it." The queen's mouth thinned. "And neither does yours. Tiercelin goes back to the WingGuard. Am I clear, Captain Dynan?"

Her fists curled at her side, but she forced them to unclench and used every bit of control she possessed to keep her face calm. "The Falcon assigned me to the protection of Prince Cuinn. I am trained for this, Your Grace, and I assume that is why my presence was requested in Mithranar. However, I can't protect your son properly if I'm held back from doing my job. Tiercelin is an integral part of—"

"No winged man is integral to any wing of humans." The queen cut her off, voice cold and cutting. "You think you've proven something by winning a game of alleya? In a real fight your humans wouldn't have stood a chance against my Falcons."

Anger burned through Talyn so strongly she went rigid with it. For the very first time in her life, her Dumnorix blood surged. She wanted to claim it, right here and now, tell them who she was and demand Tiercelin's return.

Ravinire's wings flared, ever so slightly, but just enough to draw her peripheral vision to him—to the warning written in his face.

"You would have single-handedly destroyed those insipid winged excuses for warriors in a real fight," Sari spat.

Fuelled by her partner's rage along with her own, Talyn ignored Ravinire and held the queen's gaze, wrestling with the anger that wanted to break out. Her fury must be unmistakable, no doubt her Dumnorix eyes blazing with it.

And then the blood drained from the queen's face, eyes widening in shock and something like fear. It shook Talyn, broke the hold her anger had over her. Some clarity returned.

"Your Grace?" Ravinire asked in concern. "Are you all right?"

The horror vanished from the queen's face as quickly as it had come, and the coolly arrogant mask returned. Talyn wrestled a grip on her anger and forced it down deep. Her Dumnorix name wasn't going to change anything for Tiercelin, and it might anger them enough to send her home.

"I'm fine," she snapped. "Captain Dynan, I hope I have made myself clear."

"The decision is yours, Your Grace." Talyn inclined her head.

Her mouth thinned. Talyn hadn't managed to entirely hide the edge to her voice. "I understand you are in the process of enlisting new recruits for your wing. Any winged person who applies will require the permission of their family," she said. "I hope I've made myself clear, Captain."

"Yes, Your Grace."

"Good. You're dismissed."

She turned and left before the words had even finished coming out of the queen's mouth.

SHE COULDN'T hear anything above the angry thud of her boots on the marble and the noise in her head—a furious scream that had had no outlet back in the audience chamber.

"Captain!" Ravinire had to shout as he flew up behind her.

"What?" she snarled, spinning on him, still seething.

"The two winged names on your list—Liadin Skywing and Lyra Songdrift. I've already spoken with their families on your behalf. They've been given permission to enlist with the Wolves."

She huffed a furious breath. "So you knew this was coming? You said *nothing* when we spoke the other day."

"That's my prerogative." His voice warned her she was stepping close to the line.

She stiffened. "Excuse me, sir. I have to go and deliver the news to Tiercelin."

"He already knows."

"What?"

"His parents sent the order while you were in with the queen. He'll be gone by the time you get back to the barracks."

She gritted her teeth, a wave of sorrow sweeping over her at the thought of anyone but her delivering that news to Tiercelin. "Where will you put him?"

"He'll stay in the protection flight and go into the wing assigned to Queencouncil members for now, though he'll struggle to be accepted amongst the other Falcons after being a Wolf. Once a spot opens up in one of the elder princes' wings, his family name will ensure he gets transferred in there."

Talyn speared Ravinire with a look, saying flatly, "What a waste. But you agree with what she's done, don't you?"

"I do as my queen commands. That's my job. I think you're forgetting that's also your job while you're here."

"Oh, I'm under no illusions about whose *command* I'm under." She hadn't forgotten the way the prince of night had looked at her immediately following the Wolves' victory, and anger made her reckless. "Are they really the queen's commands, or Prince Mithanis's we're all following?"

His eyes flashed. "You go too far, Captain."

She shrugged. "I don't care."

"You should, unless you want to see the rest of your wing disbanded and sent back to the cells."

That checked her like nothing else could. She was responsible for others now, not just to herself. She took a deep, shuddering breath. "You don't actually agree with her, do you? That in a real fight those Falcons would have beaten my Wolves."

Ravinire's face hardened, but he looked away from her. "I am glad, Captain Dynan, that our two kingdoms are allies. I would not like to face you in war."

"You could make them better. Your Falcons."

He gave her a bitter smile. "Not if I wanted to keep the winged folk happy. Now please, Captain, that's enough for one day. Leave before you make things worse."

. . .

SOME OF THE life was gone from the barracks when Talyn stepped into the common room a short time later. Theac stood by the fire, glowering, while Corrin, Zamaril and Halun sat morosely in chairs.

Theac's eyes went straight to her. "There's nothing you can do?"

She swallowed. She'd never felt more powerless or helpless in her life. "No. I tried, but... no."

"This is because we won." There was no life in Zamaril's voice.

"Yes," she said honestly.

"What about Liadin and Lyra?" Corrin asked.

"They've been given permission by their families to join us."

Theac barked out a bitter laugh. "Because they're both younger children of winged families with no ties to the nobility."

Halun heaved his bulk out of the chair. "This isn't right," he said, then stalked from the room.

Zamaril followed without a word.

Talyn looked helplessly at Theac, but there was no reassurance there. His glower deepened and he left too.

"It's not your fault," Corrin offered.

She shook her head. "Then why do I feel like it is?"

CHAPTER 41

*T*he Shadowhawk's right boot sank into a puddle and he cursed at the soft splash it made. It was an uncharacteristic error. The darkness was his shield, where he felt safe, where he could move without a whisper when he focused properly. Tonight though, he was tired, close to the end of his strength, which was dangerous in and of itself.

His quarry caught the sound and glanced back, copper mask flashing. After weeks of waiting and searching—running himself ragged in the process—he'd almost caught a killer in the act. Not in time to save the victim, whose blood spilled hot into the mud of the alley, but while the culprit still lingered, ensuring his victim was dead.

The shadowy figure had run the instant the Shadowhawk appeared, fleeing into the night. He pursued without hesitation.

Now the killer led him deeper and deeper into the rabbit warren of alleys in the Poor Quarter. The night was warm, thick, and sweat slicked his skin. The scent of refuse and sewerage filled his senses, lingered in his sweat and on his tongue. It was a smell he'd never grown accustomed to, one that threatened to turn his stomach unless he focused utterly on the darkness.

Ideally, his quarry would lead him to whoever was behind the killings, or at least where they were based. But he doubted they would be that foolish. The best he could hope for was to catch this one and demand some information. His mind shied away from what that might involve—he doubted it would come easily.

On and on they ran, the Shadowhawk slowly closing the distance, his long strides and familiarity with the dark making it impossible for his quarry to elude him. He wasn't sure where they were now, the houses and ramshackle buildings looming on either side, the river far behind them.

The more they ran, the clearer it was that the killer wasn't leading him anywhere. He was simply trying to get away.

It was time to end this.

The Shadowhawk sped up, closing the distance in a single bound and crashing into the killer from behind. They hit the ground, his quarry moving as they fell, throwing an elbow which hit the Shadowhawk clean in the jaw. He swore, reeling back as pain flared through his face. The man almost squirmed free but the Shadowhawk wrestled himself back on top, trying to pin him to the mud with his weight.

A knife flashed. Grunting, the Shadowhawk knocked it aside, lunging to his right to do so. The weapon clattered away but he was off balance, and the killer brought his knee up into the Shadowhawk's ribs. The breath whooshed out of him and he fell back, pain spearing through his chest.

The killer was on his feet in an instant. The Shadowhawk lunged for his leg, locked a hand around his ankle and yanked. The man stumbled, falling again. He leaped at him, forcing him back down, struggling, underneath him. For a moment the Shadowhawk had his quarry pinned with the weight of his knees and left arm, his right hand free to reach for the knife at his back and use it to properly quell the man.

Instead he hesitated.

The man under him sensed the hesitation and renewed his struggles with more vigour. They wrestled in the mud for a few more moments but eventually the killer slammed his head back into the Shadowhawk's jaw, sending stars flashing through his vision.

Then he shoved the Shadowhawk off him and ran.

Wheezing, the Shadowhawk sat up, biting his lip at the pain throbbing through his jaw and ribs.

"Not much of a fighter, are you?"

He pushed himself to his feet, incredulity filling his voice. "Saniya? What are you doing here?"

"I was out and about, got curious at the sight of you running past. Who was that guy?"

"He killed someone," he gasped, took a moment to steady his legs under him. Damn, his chest was on fire. It hurt even to breathe. "And that's a bullshit answer. You didn't just *happen* to see me."

It was hard to tell in the dark, but he thought amusement flashed over her face. "You hunt down murderers now?"

He said nothing, just stood there catching his breath. He had to focus. Focus. If he slipped, even for the briefest...

"Well, my curiosity is officially at an end. See you around, Shadowhawk."

"What were you doing here?" His voice lashed out, sharp enough to have her turning back. Something in her expression made him ask, "Do you know who these guys are?"

"What guys?"

She sounded genuine. He didn't believe it. "You know what I'm talking about. Your crew... don't try and tell me your leader isn't aware of a new group operating in Dock City."

"And if we did?" she challenged.

"They're killing humans. Murdering them."

"And I'm supposed to care about that?" She lifted an eyebrow. "I don't know why you're bothering. Humans die all the time in the Poor Quarter."

"I'm trying to make Dock City better for those who live here. If some new gang has their sights set on killing people for fun, then I'd like to stop them."

"And what makes you think they're doing it for fun?" Her eyebrow lifted. "You know who the victims are, don't you?"

He stilled. "Who?"

Her bitter laugh echoed in the dimness. "I figured you would have worked it out by now. You *have* noticed none of the victims are poor, right?"

"Right."

"Then let me ask you a question." She stepped a little closer. "Where do you think these well-off victims have gotten their wealth from?"

His mouth tightened. "You're telling me they all took bribes from the Falcons?" Suspicion flared at the little shrug she gave. "You know who these killers are, don't you?"

"My people know enough to know we don't need to worry about them bothering us, and that's all we need to know. You should consider doing the same."

It was a fair point. He should be focussing on his usual work, especially after the floods, but something about this new group made him highly uneasy. "Tell me, Saniya, were you out following *me* tonight, or the killer?"

A short, considering silence. "I was asked to keep an eye out. Make sure they wouldn't be a problem for us, like I said. And my report will reflect my belief that they won't be as long as we leave them alone."

He pinched the bridge of his nose to try and alleviate the headache forming there. The cautious hope he'd felt after the alleya game was already fading. Talyn Dynan wasn't down here in the streets with him. Saniya and his network were. Despite his suspicions about Saniya's motivation, her people cared about nothing beyond avoiding the Patrol and getting their cut. And he refused to risk his network members—normal people with regular lives—in anything that could hurt them. "Will you tell me if you learn anything more about them?" he tried anyway.

"You know better than to ask me that." She flashed him a grin that held no warmth, then backed away into the shadows, calling back a short, "See you soon."

He waited until he could no longer hear her footsteps before sinking to his knees and running his gaze over the ground. It didn't take him long to spot the knife lying in the dirt a short distance off. Bending, he picked it up, angling the metal so it caught the faint moonlight from above.

It was a finely worked blade. Expensive. And distinctive too. There were many smiths throughout Dock City—one of them would recognise the work.

The Shadowhawk straightened and tucked the knife into his tunic. Now he had somewhere to start.

CHAPTER 42

*T*iercelin's absence from the wing was a physical and emotional ache for all of them. Talyn's fury over the queen's arbitrary and unjust ruling seethed through her, refusing to fade even a few days later. After a gloomy practice, where the remaining Wolves had put in a full effort but without any cheer whatsoever, she returned to her room to find a courier had been and left a letter propped against her door.

It was sealed with the black seal of the Kingshield and written on fine parchment. Curious, she tore it open, kicking the door shut with her foot as she walked into her room and started reading.

Guard Dynan,

Commander Ravinire has informed me that you were injured in the course of your duties. I hope you are recovering well, and that the Falcon was honest in his account of the fullness of your recovery. Should that not be the case, the king has made it clear that you are to exercise your discretion and return home at once.

This missive serves as notice of a reduction in your posting length, as per Kingshield policy on injuries sustained while on active duty. Ship passage has been booked for your return home

AT THE END OF EIGHTMONTH, RATHER THAN TWELVEMONTH. I HAVE
ALSO WRITTEN TO THE FALCON TO ADVISE HIM OF THE CHANGE.
  I LOOK FORWARD TO SEEING YOU ON YOUR RETURN TO RYATHL.
  REGARDS,
  FIRST SHIELD LARK CEANNAR

Talyn stared at the letter in astonishment. She sensed her uncle's involvement amongst Ceannar's carefully worded letter. There was no such Kingshield policy she'd ever heard of. The king was upset she had been hurt and so Ceannar had fabricated an injury policy to bring her home while saving face for everyone.

The old Talyn would have rankled at this interference into her affairs by an overly concerned Dumnorix relative, but now she wasn't sure what she felt.

She was going home early.

"*Good news, or bad?*" Sari enquired.

"I've absolutely no idea," she muttered, then her anger swept back in. "Good news. I can get out of this stupid, arrogant, feathered world sooner than expected."

And return to FireFlare, to Leviana and Cynia and Tarcos. To the cooler climes of Ryathl and not being sneered at on a daily basis by every winged person she dealt with.

"*But that also means leaving the Wolves.*"

The Wolves.

The end of Eightmonth was less than two months away. The new recruits would only have just finished training. Theac would have to take on the next two lots himself.

"*He'll be fine, you know.*"

"*I know. But they've just lost Tiercelin. And now I'm going to walk out on them too.*" Her heart clenched at the thought. She tried to tell herself that they already knew she wasn't in Mithranar permanently, but somehow that didn't make her feel any better.

Behind her, someone cleared their throat loudly. She spun, right hand dropping to her sai.

Prince Cuinn leaned casually against her bedroom archway, an amused grin spreading over his face. Today he wore a violet silk vest

—were those buttons made from pure silver?—and fitted ivory pants that fell to his calves. No shoes. Silver-blonde hair carefully styled to enhance his natural beauty. "Not here to kill you, I promise," he drawled.

"I'm sorry, I didn't hear you knock," she said pointedly. Her momentary surprise turned to anger in a blink. This winged man annoyed her more than most people she'd ever met. He regularly tested her otherwise masterful self-control, which only irritated her even further.

He shrugged. "I didn't."

"Well." She folded Ceannar's missive. "Where I come from, that constitutes bad manners."

The amused smile widened. "Don't take your bad mood out on me just because you're angry at yourself for not hearing me come in."

Her mouth tightened. But her control reasserted itself and she said nothing, merely staring at him with a cool gaze.

He sighed dramatically and moved backwards into the living room. "Is there ever a time when you're *not* angry at me, Captain Dynan?"

She bit down an angry retort. "Did you want something, Your Highness, or were you just dropping by for a visit?"

"As genuinely entertaining as needling you is, I did have a reason for coming here." Cuinn shrugged. "But you've diverted me, Captain, and I'm now far more intrigued by what's in that letter you're clutching. Good news?"

"Yes. I'll be leaving sooner than expected." There was no reason not to tell him. After all, he was her charge. "At the end of Eightmonth."

"You have a lover back home." He loped over to one of the front windows, staring out, his back to her. "You miss him."

Where had that come from? She hadn't even been thinking about Tarcos. In fact, her attention had been on his wings—despite spending so much time amongst winged folk at the citadel, it seemed rude to stare, and they were unwelcoming enough as it was. Cuinn's caught the light, a myriad of shades of silver and white. She might even call them beautiful if he weren't such an unlikable person. "Who

I may or may not take to my bed is none of your concern, Your Highness."

"There's more," he murmured, voice turning distant. "Part of you doesn't want to go home. Underneath, so much..." He stopped abruptly, eyes flashing open. For a moment she saw true annoyance in his face, the first real emotion she'd seen from him. "Why don't you answer any of my questions?"

"Because I don't *have* to answer any of your questions." She forced calm on herself, putting a wall around her emotions so he couldn't read them. "My only responsibility is to keep you alive. Even when your mother takes away my wing members."

"So nauseatingly honourable." He frowned, ignoring her pointed comment about Tiercelin. "Why would anyone sign up for something like that? Potentially sacrificing yourself for a person you might not like or respect."

"You wouldn't understand," she said coolly.

She swore he flinched, even though it vanished in a heartbeat, replaced by a roll of the eyes and bored huff. "I've been informed that by early Ninemonth you'll—well, Parksin now, I suppose—have two full guard details in rotation. They may attend me overnight, but I'll not be bothered with them during the day, and they will remain outside the tower."

"Overnight, *and* at formal events and any occasion you leave the citadel," she said firmly.

"I believe that's the current arrangement."

"Good," she said. "They'll be ready."

He made a face as he walked to the door, waving a dismissive hand. "Don't rush on my account."

"Are you really sure he's a Dumnorix?"

Talyn huffed out a breath, part laugh, part sigh. "I suppose he has to be."

SHE TOLD the Wolves first thing the next morning, knowing if she didn't do it immediately, she'd probably never get around to it. Their faces when she lined the five of them up before her indicated they already knew the news she had wasn't good.

"I'll be leaving sooner than expected," she said, passing Theac the letter. "At the end of Eightmonth. Orders from home. I don't have a choice."

Theac glowered down at the parchment in his hand. Zamaril scratched his head. Corrin stared at his shoes. Their mood plummeted even further, if that was possible. Hers followed suit. After everything she'd done to build them up, she hated that circumstance was trying to tear them back down. She hated even more that it was partially her fault.

"We always understood you didn't belong to us," Halun said with quiet dignity. "But you will be missed, Captain Dynan."

Corrin lifted his head, looking at the big man, then her. "And we're happy for you. That you get to go home."

"The lads are right," Theac said gruffly. "Now we'd best get back to practice."

She nodded, searching for but failing to find anything more to say. Zamaril was the last to peel away, but he caught her gaze and gave her a little wink.

She swallowed. She was going to miss them too.

CHAPTER 43

he monsoon settled in, a constant pattern of short downpours followed by light showers and quick snatches of dry. The new recruits started—eighteen humans and two winged folk—and joined daily training with the Wolves. Several weeks passed as they settled into their new world without Tiercelin, and Seven-month turned into Eightmonth.

The ex-Wolf remained scarce. Talyn went looking for him one day, wanting to see how he was, but she'd been turned away by his new wing captain—a terse individual who'd told her she had no business in his barracks. She hadn't tried again after that, not wanting to make trouble for him.

One rainy afternoon, Talyn headed into Dock City once training was over for the day. A recent ship arrival had carried letters from Leviana and Tarcos and her plan was to go to Petro's cafe and read them while enjoying a mug of kahvi.

Set on higher ground near the border of the Market and Wealthy Quarters, Petro's little establishment not only had the best kahvi, but its tables sat along a narrow terrace that looked out over the docks and Feather Bay.

There were many lovely cafes in the citadel too, some with breathtaking views, but the last thing she wanted was to spend more time amongst the winged folk. She continued to rage about Tiercelin being taken from her wing, though she knew some of that anger was covering the guilt she felt over it, *and* over her sooner than expected departure. She had to keep telling herself she wasn't abandoning them, even though that was exactly how it felt.

Theac, the Shadowhawk, Ravinire, they'd all warned her what would happen if the Wolves won the alleya game. Yet she'd trained them to win anyway. And the consequence had been losing Tiercelin.

Petro welcomed her with a smile as she walked through the door, cloak dripping all over his floor. "After the usual, Captain?"

"Yes, please. I'll be out on the terrace."

She chose a table in the corner that had a nice view without being crowded in by other patrons and remained dry under the terrace overhang. The waters of Feather Bay were grey, reflecting the drizzly afternoon. The flags of the docked ships hung limp.

She chatted a few moments with Petro when he brought out her kahvi, then opened Leviana's letter. Her mouth quirked in a smile at her friend's cheerful, witty description of events since she'd last written. She was particularly excited about the birth of her new baby brother. According to Leviana, Darkon Seinn was the most gorgeous baby ever born in the Twin Thrones.

Talyn's smile turned to a frown when the tone of the letter changed towards the end.

I don't really want to tell you this, because I know you'll worry, but if I don't tell you, you'll be angry with me. With a healthy baby boy delivered, my parents have cast me off completely, Tal. They've told me not to return to the family home and taken my inheritance. Just like that, I don't have a penny to my name aside from my Callanan wages.

Oh, well, it's all for the best I suppose. I never wanted to be their heir, anyway, and I wouldn't give Darkon back for anything. I miss you Tal, and Cynia and I can't wait until you come home again.

All my love,

LEVIANA.

Talyn sat back, leaving the letter lying on the table. There was no doubt Leviana had kept her letter deliberately light, despite how awful she must feel. To be completely thrown aside by your parents would be heartbreaking.

Sighing, Talyn leaned forward and opened Tarcos's letter. His was much lighter. He wrote mainly of his experiences with Ariar in the mountains, and it was clear he was enjoying every moment of his time there. She was glad for him—Tarcos took everything seriously, too seriously, she'd often thought. It was time he lived his life, rather than spending every moment considering his every word and activity and how it might reflect on his family.

Sighing, she rubbed at her eyes, shaking off some of the glumness that was creeping over her at reading Tarcos' account of life fighting the brigands.

Going to Ryathl after Sari's death hadn't helped in the way she'd hoped it would, despite the presence of Dumnorix relatives easing the edge of her distress. Leaving to go so far away—facing the difficulties she had in Mithranar, they'd helped her distance herself from what had happened.

Yet only a handful of weeks remained until the end of Eightmonth. And maybe that was a good thing. She would be able to see Leviana, be there for her friend properly. She would reunite with FireFlare, with long gallops through the forest and plains around Ryathl. And she missed her family. Not only her parents but her Dumnorix relatives too. The Wolves would be fine. Theac was a solid commander and she'd left them with enough foundation to build a strong detail— and depending whether the Callanan remained interested in the Shadowhawk, the First Shield might even send a replacement for her.

But going home meant going back to her old world again too. And while part of Talyn still wanted that, a greater part of her couldn't imagine ever doing it without Sari.

She was so busy with her tangle of emotion, she didn't notice the man sitting down at the table beside hers, his chair facing out over the view. When he cleared his throat, she looked up, startled.

"It's me, Savin," he spoke quietly.

A quick look confirmed it was indeed the man who'd snuck into her bedroom claiming to be a spy for the crown. His hair was covered by a cap, and he wore glasses with thick rims. She waited silently while his eyes roamed casually over the bay. "I thought it was time to check in with you."

"You heard that I was attacked?" she asked.

A little nod.

"Do you think the same perpetrator was behind the break in at the palace?" She asked the question not because she necessarily thought there was a connection, but to test him. What he was willing to tell her. How good his sources were.

"Unlikely." He spoke the word decidedly, clearly confident in his answer. "One was an attack directed at you, likely aimed to prevent you from playing in the alleya game. The other was an attempted break in—nobody was attacked or hurt."

"And you've nothing further on who was behind the break in?" She allowed impatience to fill her voice. "It happened six months ago, Savin. I thought you were supposed to be a spy."

There was a stilted silence, then, "My inability to learn anything more about the break in is… troubling."

She leaped on that. "So it was a professional move by skilled perpetrators staged to look otherwise. Either that or you're just not very good at what you do."

"The first," he ground out.

She still thought the break in had all the signs of being a recon-naissance, a way to test the defences of the citadel. That fit nicely with professionals being behind it. "Find out who in Mithranar has that skillset and match that with who would have motivation for breaking into the citadel."

Irritation coloured his tone. "I do know how to do my job, Captain."

"Then do it." She paused, hiding her puzzlement about why he'd come to see her. As with their first encounter, she got the distinct sense more was going on than he'd admitted. It had been two months since the alleya game and the attack on her. Why come talk to her about it now? She sighed, dismissing her concerns—it was a puzzle she was unlikely to be able to solve given her imminent departure. "I'll be leaving soon. If you were telling any part of the truth when you said your job was to protect the royal family, then you'll report any information you learn regarding Prince Cuinn to Theac Parksin."

Silence met her words, and after another moment went by without a response, she turned around.

Savin was gone.

She wondered if he'd already known she was leaving.

With a sigh, she rose to her feet. Her kahvi was finished and a breeze had whipped up, sending the rain into her face. She waved a farewell to Petro and pulled her cloak over her head as she stepped out into the street.

"Captain!"

Talyn spun, recognising Tiercelin's voice instantly and stunned to see him waiting for her on the opposite side of the street. He wore plain clothing and stood under a roof out of the rain.

She crossed straight over to him. "How are you? Is everything all right?"

"I'm all right." He gave a little shrug. "I'm sorry I haven't been around."

"It's all right. I'm so sorry for what happened." The words came out in a rush. "I know it was my fault, and if I—"

He touched her arm, stopping her apologies. "I wouldn't take back our win for anything in the world, Captain, so please don't apologise."

"Are you sure?" She searched his grey eyes.

A small but genuine smile curled at his mouth. "Certain. And once my new wing mates get a bit more used to me, I'll be back around visiting, don't you worry. I did hear that you're leaving soon?"

She nodded. "In a couple of weeks. Is that why you came down here? I hope you don't think I wouldn't have come to say goodbye."

"No, actually." His face turned serious, voice dropping. "I overheard a few of my new wing mates talking the other day in the mess. What they were saying... I thought you might be interested to know."

"What was it?"

"Remember the break in? How the Falcon told us that those who broke in tried to access an old storage room in the barracks?" Tiercelin shifted closer. "Captain, I think that particular room had been used to store izerdia."

Her eyes shot to his. "They were after izerdia," she breathed. "That would make so much more sense."

"That's what I thought too," Tiercelin agreed. "You said you thought they were professionals. If that's the case, then they were most likely looking to sell for a profit."

"Then it probably has nothing to do with Prince Cuinn or his safety, but it's useful nonetheless." She smiled at him. "Thanks for letting me know."

Another smile flashed over his handsome face. "Any time, Captain. And make sure you do come and say goodbye before you leave."

"I will," she promised.

"*Odd, Talyn. A professional group of thieves—which by the way, Zamaril claims doesn't exist—break in to the citadel to steal izerdia, only it's been moved before they get there.*" Sari spoke as Tiercelin lifted into the sky with a wave, scepticism filling her voice. "*So they're professional enough to get in, but not to know the izerdia's been moved?*"

"*And why send someone to Cuinn's tower in the middle of the break in attempt?*" Instinct continued to nudge at her. Izerdia may have been a goal, but she didn't think it was the primary one.

"*Exactly. They learned that despite the WingGuard's lax security, they still couldn't get deep into the palace without being spotted.*"

"*Which might explain why they haven't tried again, even though they didn't get the izerdia.*"

It probably didn't matter. She was leaving soon, and anyway, the Wolves' job wasn't to police Mithranar's izerdia supplies. Still, she made a mental note to mention it to Theac.

"*You know what I want to know?*"

"*Hmm?*"

"*If Savin's as good a spy as he claims, and he truly does work for the royal family, then why didn't he tell you about that storage room being used for izerdia?"*

Excellent question.

CHAPTER 44

Once done eating dinner in the mess with her Wolves—a much busier affair now they had twenty new recruits—Talyn headed for the Falcon barracks on the opposite side of the palace. Ravinire had ensured they had a full supply of training swords and similar weapons, but like with Tiercelin, Talyn wanted her two new winged Wolves to be trained with a longbow.

So, request form filled out and clutched in her hand, she moved quickly through the various walkways. Her shoulder wound had fully healed by now thanks to Tiercelin, and it was a relief to be able to swing herself up ladders and balance on swaying bridges without one arm strapped to her chest.

The Falcon barracks was actually a series of smaller buildings inter-twined together and sprawling down the slope adjacent to the royal quarters. Tonight, Talyn took a longer route, walking up from the lower levels. She wanted to avoid passing throngs of Falcons who were off duty, not sure her recent temper could handle the dark looks and muttering that inevitably broke out at her presence.

She was halfway along an open-aired walkway that would bring her to a wide set of steps leading up to the central area of the barracks

—only a short walk from Ravinire's office—when the sound of a scuffle caught her attention.

She slowed. The sound had been soft, and she wasn't entirely sure she had... no, there it was again.

The night of the break in came flooding to her mind, and she quickly folded up her request form and tucked it into her belt before reaching back to slide her right hand around the hilt of a sai. Then she stood, listening, until the sound came again. This time she caught a soft cry.

The distinct undertone of fear in that cry pushed Talyn into movement. The sounds were coming from a narrow walkway that branched off just ahead of where she stood. Quick, long, strides brought her to the corner and she stepped into the walkway entry, poised for whatever might be there.

The light beyond was much dimmer, the walls on either side so close together they cut off the moonlight coming from above, so it took her a moment for her eyes to adjust and realise what was going on.

A winged man had a woman pushed against the wall. She was struggling, but not hard enough to cause him any problems as he held her there with his body weight and superior strength. Her blouse was torn, exposing her breasts. The man's hand was on one of them, the other on his breeches as he fumbled to undo them.

Fear leaked from every movement and sound the woman was making, leaving Talyn in no doubt that what was happening wasn't consensual. So far neither had noticed Talyn's appearance.

And the woman was human.

"Cut his balls off, Talyn."

"Oh, I intend to."

"Am I interrupting something?" She kept her voice crisp as she walked into the alley, keeping one hand on the sai.

The woman froze at her appearance, but the winged man turned towards her with a snarl of anger.

Then it was Talyn's turn to freeze.

Shit.

The man was Idrian Iceflight, flight leader of Ravinire's protection wing. She hadn't been able to see his face from so far away, only the colour of his wings.

"This is none of your business, foreigner," he said coldly. "Leave. Now."

"I'll leave when you let her go." Technically a superior officer or not, Talyn wasn't going anywhere.

"This is personal business." He repeated, voice turning even colder. "Go before I decide you're refusing to obey orders."

"You're not my superior officer. The Falcon is." She took a step closer. "And I don't know what your idea of consent is here in Mithranar, but that woman is not giving it. Let her go."

He shoved the woman hard into the wall then turned to take a step towards Talyn. Fury turned his shoulders and face rigid, and Talyn drew her sai. Iceflight looked ready to attack her. She glanced at the woman, trying to urge her to run while she had the chance. Instead she huddled against the wall, drawing her dress up to cover her chest.

"You attack me and you're a dead woman," he said softly.

"I'm not going to attack you," Talyn said evenly. "But if I'm forced to defend myself, you're not going to end up the winner. Leave now, and all that happens is that I report this to the Falcon."

He frowned in momentary confusion, then an incredulous laugh huffed out of him. "You think the Falcon is going to care about this?"

"What's going on here?"

Both Talyn and Iceflight snapped their attention to the winged man walking towards them from the opposite end of the walkway. Talyn's grip on her sai turned white-knuckled as she recognised the prince of night.

"This is going from bad to worse."

"Stay calm. Play the situation as it develops," Sari advised quietly.

"Your Highness!" Iceflight gave a snappy salute, a note of subservience entering his tone. "I'm just dealing with a disciplinary matter. Captain Dynan was refusing my order to leave."

Mithanis's dark gaze turned to her, contemplative. "Is that so?"

"I came upon Flight-Leader Iceflight attempting to rape this woman," Talyn said calmly. "I refused to leave until he let her go."

The prince of night looked at the woman still huddled against the wall, utterly frozen with terror now that he'd appeared, then down at the hand holding her sai. "You drew a weapon on my flight leader?"

The danger in that softly uttered question was distinct and almost had Talyn drawing her second sai. A cold smile settled over Iceflight's face.

"Your Highness, as I said, the flight leader was—"

"It's none of your business what the flight leader is doing in his spare time. You are a foreigner and a guest here and he outranks you in every way imaginable." Mithanis moved towards her, swift as a striking snake. He lifted a hand, and her eyes were drawn to the black energy crackling around it. Winged folk warrior magic. He opened his palm, bringing it close enough to her cheek that the energy snapped against her skin, making her uncomfortably aware of what it would do to her if it touched her.

"He'll kill you, Talyn. Don't push." Sari leapt to life in her head.

Talyn's glaze flicked to the woman.

"Don't even think about it," Mithanis murmured. "I am a prince of Mithranar, and you don't dare lay a hand on me. Now, sheathe that weapon and walk away."

He shifted even closer, using the magic in his voice and wreathing his hand to dominate and quell. It worked. She'd never faced song magic before, not used like this, where he could find the emotions he wanted in her, the fear and vulnerability and instinct to run, and bring them out, exaggerate them.

She found herself sliding her sai back into its sheath and stepping away. Unbidden, her gaze went to the woman.

There was nothing she could do. She couldn't gainsay both Iceflight and Mithanis. She couldn't stop them, either.

She hated this goddamn country.

"Go," Mithanis said, a smile curling at his mouth as he realised he'd won the battle of wills. "And I recommend against mentioning this incident to anyone. Including the Falcon. You don't want your precious wing sent back to City Patrol jail, do you?"

She turned on her heel and strode away, hands curling and uncurling at her sides, the impotent rage so strong she almost had to scream to let it out.

Just over a week until she was to go home.

It couldn't come soon enough.

CHAPTER 45

*H*e debated with himself over and over. Almost turned back three times on his way there. And when he arrived, he hesitated again, telling himself he was just making sure nobody was around. But the walkway outside the guest wing was utterly empty and had been for some time.

Snarling at his own indecision, he reached up to check his mask was firmly in place, then headed down the walkway, blowing out lamps as he went. It wouldn't do for one of the winged folk out enjoying the night's thermals to glide past and see him approaching her quarters.

He rapped a single, sharp knock, then shifted to sink into the shadows by the door. When Talyn opened it, it took her several moments to spot him. Her gaze instantly flashed from him to the dark lamps and she stiffened.

"Not here to kill you," he murmured. "But if you could let me in before someone sees me, that would be safer for both of us."

She hesitated, then stepped back from the doorway, closing the door behind him as soon as he was inside. He studied her for a moment, frowning. She was different from the last time he'd seen her face to face. Before the alleya game.

She held herself stiffly, banked fury in her eyes, as if she was holding back from screaming… or attacking something. The emotion hit him like a slap in the face, almost sending him staggering back a step.

"Did something happen?" he asked before he could stop himself. And then he realised. Of course—the removal of Tiercelin from the wing. He'd heard about it, but even though he'd seen firsthand how she cared about her wing, the level of fury he saw in her now seemed odd given how much time had passed.

Her mouth thinned. She was clearly in no mood for pleasantries. "If anyone learns you were here, I'll be arrested, if not worse. So whatever it is, spit it out, Shadowhawk, and then leave."

He couldn't help himself. "Which begs the question, why *did* you let me in?"

"I'm not in the mood for games," she warned, voice low and deadly.

He faltered. "What happened?"

There was a beat of silence. She took in a deep, steadying breath, then shook her head. "Nothing you would care about."

"Fine." He stiffened at her dismissive tone. "I've come across some information and I thought you should know it too."

Her gaze snapped to his. "Is it about Prince Cuinn?"

"No."

She relaxed. "Then what is it?"

"There have been a series of murders over the past several months." He told her what he knew, how he'd chased one of them down and taken the man's knife. "It's taken me weeks, but I found the smith who made it. He said that the customer who purchased it wasn't a regular and hasn't been back since. But here's the thing—the customer came in with another man. This other man recently put in a large order for weapons. Knives, swords and arrows."

She frowned. "For what purpose?"

"He didn't know. Or he was too scared to say. I'm not sure."

"When was this?" Her voice was crisp, the questions quick and incisive.

"A month ago."

431

She turned away, thinking. "What do you think it's all about?"

"I have no idea. That's why I've come to you."

She huffed out a breath. "I'm not part of your crusade. I'm only here to—"

"Protect Prince Cuinn, I get it." He stepped closer. "But something about this feels off, doesn't it? Such a large weapons order—thirty of everything, he said. For what purpose?"

"I agree. It doesn't sound good. But it's not my problem." She shrugged.

He stiffened. He hadn't expected this. "So you won't help me?"

For a long moment she wavered, glancing briefly over her right shoulder. Then she straightened, as if she'd come to an internal decision. "I don't know what it is you expect me to do."

"Something more than tell me it's not your problem," he said flatly.

"Well, it's not. And I'm done with trying to meddle in the insane society you have here in Mithranar." The anger was back, and strongly enough that she turned away to pace across the room.

Bitter disappointment filled him. Why had he thought this would go any differently? He was a fool. "Fine." He nodded and headed for the door, hauling it open. "Thanks for nothing, Captain Dynan."

BACK DOWN IN the city he strode through the tangle of the Poor Quarter, trying not to let his black mood take over. He'd sent another request for a meeting with Zamaril—his seventh in a row with no response—and approached their meeting site with little hope the thief would be there.

Instead he was astonished to find the man waiting for him on the doorstep of an inn that had closed down a month earlier. When he saw the Shadowhawk approaching, he pushed open the broken door and stepped inside.

The Shadowhawk glanced around, making sure there weren't any watching eyes to see him go in, then followed the thief. A faint patch of moonlight shining through a broken window filled the middle of the open space but otherwise it was all in darkness.

"You finally deigned to respond to my messages."

"I only came to tell you to stop sending them," Zamaril snapped. "I'm not spying for you anymore."

He let a beat of silence pass. "May I ask why?"

"I'm a Wolf now. My loyalty is to my captain." He gritted the words out, as if he couldn't believe he was saying them any more than the Shadowhawk could.

"You're serious? Zamaril Lightfinger, Dock City's best thief, renowned for working alone."

"Things change," the man said softly. "Stop sending me messages. Besides, she's no threat to you."

"Oh, confident of that, are you?" The words snapped out, full of his irritation.

"Not entirely." Zamaril shrugged, stepping closer. "But she's my captain. I'm hers to command, not yours, Shadowhawk."

"She's leaving though, isn't she?" he spoke in a cutting tone, still angry over her rejection of him earlier. "What good's your loyalty then?"

"I'm a Wolf now." The words were spoken with quiet dignity. "And that's that."

A long breath escaped him. Understanding. He nodded at Zamaril. "She's lucky to have you."

The thief barked a laugh. "It's the other way around, actually. Good luck to you, Shadowhawk."

The thief was gone before he could say another word, using the shadows almost as well as he did.

He stood there alone in the abandoned inn, head hanging down. For a moment he was utterly lost. He didn't know what to do next, how to fix the problems that needed fixing. He was one man, and one man wasn't enough—that was becoming increasingly clear. And one day, well, he couldn't hide forever.

They'd find him eventually.

But not yet. He forced himself to straighten, lifting his head. Someone was out there with weapons for thirty fighters. Perhaps a new gang, perhaps something more nefarious. He had enough contacts in the Poor Quarter that he'd be able to confirm quickly enough if it was a new gang.

And if it wasn't... well, perhaps he'd leave it for the WingGuard to deal with. Winter was coming soon and more people would struggle this year after the destruction the floods had caused.

He'd make sure it was easier for some of them, at least.

That was something.

CHAPTER 46

$\mathcal{T}$alyn looked up with a sigh of irritation at the loud knocking on her door. It was early evening—she'd just bathed and was relaxing with a book after the day's training. It was one she'd brought from home, an instructional book on advanced fighting techniques with a sai.

Reluctantly, she rose to open the door. If this was the Shadowhawk again... surely, she'd given him the message clearly enough the other night? She wasn't going to risk further consequences for her wing by having anything to do with the Shadowhawk. If the Callanan wanted more information, they certainly hadn't asked her for it.

"Theac!" she said, surprised to find her second at the door instead. "What is it?"

"I was hoping not to find you here," he said tersely.

She lifted her eyebrows. "Where exactly *did* you hope to find me?"

"With Prince Cuinn."

"Okay." Talyn was puzzled. "What's going on?"

"He left the citadel with a party of friends earlier today. He's gone to the Acondor family retreat on Sparrow Island."

"He..." She frowned. "Sparrow Island?"

"It's a few hours sail off the east coast—most of the island is home to several hundred human Mithranans, but it also houses a private retreat belonging to the royal family." Theac was wearing his usual scowl, but Talyn sensed a note of something different in his voice. He was worried.

"Did he take any Falcons with him?" she asked.

"No."

"Does Ravinire know?"

"I've no idea, Captain. I only just heard." Theac hesitated. "Tiercelin sent a message to let me know."

"Right. Well, there's no need to be concerned." She said the words for both their benefits. "There's no threat to Prince Cuinn that we're aware of, and he's been unguarded most of the time I've been here."

"Right." He nodded.

Why hadn't Ravinire told her? Why hadn't Cuinn? They supposedly had a deal—he took a guard whenever he left the citadel. Annoyance flickered, and she was tempted to tell Theac to go back to bed and leave the prince to his amusements.

But then she remembered the Shadowhawk's visit. Weapons for thirty warriors. Warriors linked to a series of murders in Dock City. A month ago.

"Plenty of time to put together an assassination plan."

She shook her head. It was a crazy thought. *"Yes, but he said it was humans who were murdered. And one at a time. That's a very different operating behaviour."*

"But Theac's here for a reason. And your instincts are screaming at you."

"And a group of professionals tried to steal izerdia from the citadel," Talyn said.

"You wouldn't need so many weapons if you had izerdia and knew how to turn it into an explosive. But if you'd failed to steal some izerdia..."

"And the break in... what if they learned they couldn't get into the palace so they're trying the island instead?" Talyn shook her head. She was being overly paranoid.

Even so. Sari was right. Her instincts were telling her something was off.

She fought down the instinctive tide of panic with reason. She knew how to do this. "We'll take the Wolves and go." She made the decision, nodding at Theac. "What's the quickest way for us to get to Sparrow Island?"

"By boat." He hesitated, clearly reading the disquiet in her face. "What is it, Captain?"

"A few days ago I was told that someone recently made a large weapons purchase in the Poor Quarter—enough for thirty warriors."

Theac's eyes widened. "Where is this information from?"

"Someone I can't afford to ignore," Talyn said.

He nodded. "That's good enough for me."

"Go and gather the Wolves—not the new recruits—arm up and meet me at the top of the wall walk. Quickly, now!"

He left without a word. Talyn ran back inside her room, dropping the robe she wore and snatching a clean uniform from a drawer, dragging on her boots. She strapped and holstered her weapons as she ran full pelt for the top of the wall walk, almost barrelling into a number of people in her headlong flight.

She beat the Wolves there, and promptly began pacing, unable to keep still, failing to ignore her unease. There was no need for this. Cuinn was just taking a trip, as usual not informing his guard. There was absolutely no reason to think any danger beckoned.

"Except the idea of thirty armed warriors out there."

"Cuinn is the last member of the royal family any assassination team would go after." She tried to reassure herself.

"Captain!"

She spun, shoulders relaxing slightly at the sight of her Wolves, then stiffening again when she spotted Tiercelin with them. His longbow and quiver hung down his back between his wings.

"He's one of us." Zamaril spoke before she could get a word out. "And if there's danger out there tonight... well, we're a team, Captain. Let him come."

If she hadn't been so taken aback by Zamaril's heated plea on Tiercelin's behalf, she might have refused quickly and firmly. Instead she shifted her gaze to the winged man. He regarded her steadily. "I'll do whatever you order, Captain."

She hesitated. "Are you on duty at the moment?"

"Not until tomorrow afternoon."

"Fine. You're in." She turned. "Halun, we're going to need a boat. A fast one."

"I know just the one," he said, life animating him at her approval of Tiercelin. "Don't worry, Captain, I'll get us there as soon as is humanly possible."

"What about the Falcons?" Theac asked.

She hesitated. "I don't have any evidence that something is wrong, and if there is, I don't want to waste time trying to convince Ravinire. Besides..." After the incident with Mithanis and Iceflight it had become blindingly clear how little influence or capability Ravinire had.

Theac's voice dropped. "You don't trust him."

"I don't trust anyone other than us." She stepped back and raised her voice. "Come on, let's get moving. Halun, you lead the way."

Corrin hesitated. "We've never fought before, Captain."

"And you likely won't have to tonight. But you said you wanted to stick around and be a Wolf." She kept her voice brisk. "This is what it means. Now hurry!"

HALUN LED them at a swift jog out to the Dock Quarter, taking them to where the smaller, private boats were moored. Eventually he stopped outside the door of a narrow house—one of a cluster along a sandy street.

"The man inside runs a business trading supplies up the east coast. He's not always legal with what he carries, but he's the best sailor I know, and he's got a fast, reliable boat," Halun explained, one eyebrow raised in question.

"Fine." Talyn nodded.

He thumped loudly on the door. A few moments later, it swung open to reveal a short man with a slight paunch and thinning brown hair.

"We need you to take us on a run, Lifer," Halun said. "Right now."

"I just came back in a couple of hours ago. I'm not going back out for another two days." He shrugged. "I can take you then, if you like, but it will cost you."

Halun nodded amiably, as if accepting what the sailor was telling him. Then, with a move as fast as lightning, he reached out and grabbed the man by his shirt collar, hauling him bodily out of the door. There was a tearing sound as the cloth ripped.

"You're going on another run, tonight, and you're taking us with you. No charge. Orders direct from Prince Cuinn." He showed teeth. "Agreed?"

He tightened his hold on the man's clothes until he squeaked an agreement. At that, Halun let go. Lifer promptly dropped to the ground, then scrambled to his feet with an ingratiating smile. "Chatty tonight aren't we, Halun? Where are you going?"

"Sparrow Island," Theac barked. "As fast as you can get us there."

Lifer nodded. "It'll take a couple of hours, depending on the wind. I also need to worry about rocks once it gets dark."

Theac said, "Just get us there fast."

Talyn moved in front of her second before his bad temper provoked Lifer into refusing to help. "I know it's late and cold, but trust me when I say we wouldn't be doing this if it wasn't of the utmost importance. We really need your help."

He stared at her for a moment, jaw clenched. "I owe you all one anyway, from the night of the floods. I'm tired is all, haven't slept in a couple of days."

"Then you should lay off on the illegal leather trading, my friend." Zamaril grinned, clapping him on the back, restoring the light mood.

"What, and go straight like you lot?" Lifer snorted.

"It has its benefits." Zamaril winked at Halun, who smiled.

The boat was small, but sleek and well kept. The Wolves piled into the back while Lifer put up the sail and undid the mooring rope.

Luck was with them. The wind blew steadily from the south, pushing the little boat along at a good speed. Lifer guided the boat out of the bay and then up along the eastern coastline, his eyes constantly roving the water for rocks.

Talyn ran her eyes over the Wolves—they looked calm enough, though Zamaril's fists were clenched and Corrin was staring at his boots.

Her own fear stirred, raising the spectre of doubt. Nearly two years now since she'd fought in a real battle—the break in at the citadel didn't count. She didn't have the battle sharpness she'd once had, and Sari's death had ruined all her supreme confidence in one blinding moment.

What if she froze again?

Theac's gaze shifted to hers, eyebrow raised, and she looked away.

A QUARTER-TURN INTO THE JOURNEY, just as Lifer began tacking away from the coast and out into the ocean, it started to rain. At first it was a light drizzle, then became slowly heavier, turning into a steady downpour. Lifer rigged up a tarpaulin over the back of the boat to keep them dry, then rummaged in a locker for his wet weather gear.

Theac relayed Talyn's information to the Wolves in quick, blunt terms. All eyes flickered to her one by one.

Tiercelin shifted. "Captain, you don't think the izerdia...?"

"It's a leap," she said. "But there's a possibility—if an attack of some sort is being planned—that the same people were looking to get their hands on izerdia."

"And work out how easy it would be to get into the palace," Zamaril added. "You think an assassination team is going after Prince Cuinn, don't you?"

"I think it's one of many possibilities of what those weapons might be for, and not the likeliest one," she said. "But we're his protective guard, so we don't take chances."

The Wolves sat in silence.

Talyn wavered between confidence that she was worrying over nothing—that she was being overcautious in heading out to this island in the middle of the night—and fear that her instincts weren't wrong, that something was going to happen and that Cuinn was facing danger without her there. Ultimately, no matter what else had happened in Mithranar, no matter her Callanan mission or training the Wolves, her one and only job as a Kingshield guard was to keep a member of the Dumnorix family safe.

When terror of failing in that mission threatened to become over-whelming, she switched to worrying about the Wolves instead. If the worst happened, they'd never faced a real fight before. Would they stand firm and fight as they'd been trained, or would they panic and forget everything under the pressure of having their lives in danger? It could go either way.

An alleya game was one thing. Having someone come at you with a sharp blade intent on killing you? The smell of blood and screams of pain? That was something else entirely.

"We're not far now," Lifer shouted, jolting her from her thoughts. "It's just around this headland. I don't usually go anywhere near it because of the Falcon patrols, but the family has a small dock for their private boats. I'll take you in and drop you off."

"Don't wait around," Theac told him. "Drop us off and get out of here."

His eyes flickered nervously between them. "Is there something going on?"

"Probably not." Theac glanced at Talyn. His gruff confidence reas-sured her. "But it's best to be safe."

She looked ahead through the curtain of falling rain. "We'll be fine."

CHAPTER 47

*D*espite the rain and the worsening seas, Lifer delivered them safely to the small jetty which jutted out from a sheer cliff face. Squinting, Talyn could just make out a narrow gap in the cliff at the end of the jetty, and what looked like a path heading to a steep stairwell clinging to the side of the cliff face.

Perched high above on a rocky outcropping was a house shrouded in darkness and rain. As far as she could tell, the rest of the clifftop was covered in trees.

The retreat was isolated.

Perfect territory for an assassination attempt by a skilled and well-prepared squad, especially once they realised it would be too difficult to try and sneak into the palace without being seen. It would only be a matter of patience and waiting until their target came out here.

The Wolves clambered out onto the rain-soaked wood behind Talyn. Lifer stayed in his boat, eyes tracking them as they ran along the jetty. She'd forgotten about him by the time they reached the wet sand at the base of the cliff and started straight up the stairs.

The rock was uneven and slippery from the rain, the darkness making it hard to see the way properly. Tiercelin leapt into the air without being asked, hovering close in case one of them slipped and fell. At the top, they were greeted with a narrow, paved path leading in the direction of the house, though the structure wasn't visible through thick trees.

Tiercelin landed, wings furling at his sides, and began walking along the path, but Talyn stopped him, motioning for the Wolves to gather around her. "We need to scout the area before we go charging in blind. Follow me and try not to make any noise."

They nodded without hesitation. She tried not to fear for them—if there was indeed an assassination team here, one of them could get hurt. Ruthlessly, she shoved that fear away, along with the fear that she might not be up to this anymore.

Whether or not she was, she was doing it anyway. Some core part of her simply wouldn't let her do otherwise.

She stepped off the path and began moving through the dripping forest, heading in the general direction of the house she'd spotted at the top of the cliff. Slowly the trees thinned, and the house came into sight, a dim outline against the night sky. Three stories high and surrounded on three sides by a wide veranda.

An area the size of an alleya field had been cleared around the house—perfectly manicured lawn lit by the watery light of a moon mostly obscured by clouds.

Shit.

"You won't be sneaking up on that house," Sari offered helpfully.

Talyn knelt behind the tree line and the Wolves followed suit without a word. For a long time, they watched the house, rain pattering around them. Some of the tight anxiety in her stomach loosened when nothing moved. There were a handful of lights on inside, but the house was mostly dark. It was well after midnight, and likely everybody was abed. There were no unusual sounds above the rain.

Then, Tiercelin stiffened. Talyn's heart thudded when he pointed to a shadowy figure that appeared from around the left side of the house, swung up onto the veranda roof and crouched there, as if waiting. Tiercelin's winged folk vision had been first to catch it.

"Shit," Zamaril cursed in a whisper. "Do you think they're already inside?"

"Could it be one of the guests?" Corrin said.

"Climbing onto the roof?" Zamaril hissed back.

"Prince Cuinn would have only winged folk with him," Theac said quietly. "They wouldn't need to be climbing onto the roof. And any human servants in there wouldn't be either."

"Theac's right." She was reassured by his quick analysis. Theac knew what he was doing, and she had to allow herself to rely on that. "The better question is where did he or she come from? We've been here a half-turn and nobody has come past."

"They must have climbed the cliffs to the south." Halun's voice rumbled.

"Then they were out there on a boat too." Corrin's voice was full of dread. "We're lucky we didn't run right into them."

Thirty warriors. A cold chill shivered through her. Thirty assassins and she had herself and five Wolves. All she could hope was that the Shadowhawk's information had nothing to do with what was happening. That this was something else.

"Can you make out where the others are, Tiercelin?" Talyn asked, shaking her head as Zamaril went to open his mouth. "The person on the roof is a lookout, watching for anyone approaching the front of the house. You don't have a lookout unless there's more than one of you."

"I can't see anything else," Tiercelin responded a moment later.

"They might still be climbing the cliffs," Theac said in an undertone.

"They're setting themselves up. It's what I would do if I were planning an attack here." Talyn's eyes never stopped, constantly roving the area before them. "I'm going to go in first and take out their observer. We go in quiet through the front, delay how long it takes them to learn we're here."

"We're possibly facing superior numbers, so we pick them off one by one if we can." Zamaril nodded.

She glanced at him. "Exactly. Tiercelin, do you know where Prince Cuinn's bedroom will be?"

A firm nod from the winged man. "Third floor, eastern side, corner suite. I've been here before."

"Good. Once the observer is dead, Tiercelin, I want you in the air covering the others as they cross the open ground to the front door. You see anything move on them and you shoot to kill, understand?"

Her met her gaze steadily. "I will."

Anxiety tore at her—they could already be in the house, already making for Cuinn's room—but if she made a mistake here and rushed in, they'd all die along with Cuinn.

She took a breath. "Once we're in, Theac, you and Zamaril go straight for Prince Cuinn—don't stop for anything. Extinguish any lamps in his room and keep him still and quiet. Corrin and Halun, stay together but spread through the ground floor of the house and take out anybody you come across that has a weapon. I'll do the same with the second floor. From there we move up to the third, clear it on our way to the prince's room."

"And me?" Tiercelin asked.

"You stay up high in the air—shoot anyone armed who comes running out here, or follows us in. I'm assuming Cuinn has friends staying with him. If any of you come across them, or any servants still awake, tell them to stay in their rooms and barricade the door. Any questions?"

They shook their heads one by one.

Talyn sensed their nervousness, but also their determination. "If you get caught and you need help, remember the whistle I taught you. Don't hesitate to use it." She paused, talking to herself as much as them. "Things will get chaotic and scary in there, and when that happens, just go with your training and your instincts. Take a deep breath, relax as best you can, and all those endless hours of training will take over."

"We'll be all right, Captain." Theac nodded. "Now go."

Talyn rose to her feet and rounded the house, not leaving the trees until she was directly east of the veranda. Then she dashed out, running low and keeping to the shadows. Nothing moved on the roof.

One light step up onto the veranda and she paused, utterly still, making sure there wasn't anyone else around. Nothing moved. As she'd suspected, the man on the roof was the front sentry—meaning the others were probably coming up the cliffs and in through the back. Once confident she was alone, her eyes turned to the section of the roof where the lookout was crouched.

Her right hand reached for her sai. She pulled it silently from the sheath, balanced it in her hand, then moved into a light run, her feet touching the wooden veranda floor without sound.

Judging her move with instinct born of years of training, she launched herself upwards, right arm extended. The sai she gripped in her right hand slid through the thatched veranda roof—deadly sharp —and into the chest of the man who crouched above.

He didn't make a sound as he died.

And it had been as easy as breathing.

Talyn landed lightly, sheathing her bloody sai and making a sharp gesture to the Wolves watching from the trees. Tiercelin was a blur of movement as he launched himself into the night sky.

The others emerged from the trees at a run, but Talyn didn't wait before going to the door and pushing it slowly open. Her eyes scanned the interior. A lounge area, lit by a dying fire.

The slight click from the shadows on the other side of the room was all the warning she got. Talyn launched into a run, at the same instant summoning her bright sapphire energy shield. The energy drain was immediate, slowing her steps a fraction. Two crossbow bolts zoomed towards her and sizzled harmlessly into the shield.

Before he could reload, she was across the room and moving into the darkness beyond where the crossbowman crouched, bow aimed at the front door. Along with the copper mask covering his face down to his mouth, he wore all black.

Another lookout. Whoever they were, they were most definitely professionals. An interesting detail to think on later.

Right now she was more interested in removing the threat they posed to her charge. As the shooter hastily tried to reload, she stepped in and drove the point of her sai into his throat.

A clean, silent kill.

Withdrawing the sai, she straightened, a distant part of her thoroughly relieved the man had been firing a crossbow, not bow and arrow. There'd been no tell-tale hiss to send her spiralling into a panic.

A sound behind her had her spinning, sai raised, but it was just the Wolves coming through the front entrance. Zamaril and Theac headed straight up the staircase to the left of the door, weapons drawn but moving as quietly as she'd taught them.

She stepped back into the light, then gestured sharply to Halun and Corrin. The young man's eyes widened at the sight of the dead man at her feet.

"Another lookout," she murmured. "He was here to kill anyone coming through that front door. There are likely to be more, so move quietly and check every room before you enter it."

"We will." Corrin was pale, mouth in a tight line. "Go, Captain. They might already be upstairs."

She nodded and left them, running back through the lit room, and taking the stairs that Zamaril and Theac had disappeared up. If the assassins were coming through the back of the house, then there must be a second staircase—the lookout position at the front stairs likely there to stop anyone surprising the attack team from the front.

On the second floor landing she paused, allowing her eyes to adjust to the dimness. A long corridor stretched ahead and to her left, both dark, both holding a series of closed doors. She took the one straight ahead.

She tensed as she approached the end of the hall where it intersected with another that ran the length of the back of the house. She was five steps from reaching it when two masked figures appeared from the right, padding on silent feet, swords held ready.

They saw her quickly, catching her movement in their peripheral vision.

She didn't stop her forward movement, lifting her right sai to catch the swinging blade of the closest swordsman. A practised twist of her wrist yanked the sword from his hand and left his torso momentarily open. In a breath she'd stepped into him and buried her second sai in his heart.

As he dropped, she stepped away from the other man's lunge, sheathed her remaining sai and ducked down to sweep up the fallen sword in one movement. Her attacker followed, pressing her further back down the hallway with a series of controlled slashes.

She parried each of them, then shoved his blade to the side before swinging back and slicing the tip of her sword through his neck. His hands rose to his ruined throat as he fell. Blood sprayed in a wide arc. Warm droplets of it spattered over her face and hands.

It was over in seconds. She was breathing hard, muscles trembling —the burst of adrenalin keeping her on her feet.

She kept the sword, yanked her other sai from the dead man's chest, and went to the end of the corridor—several paces to her right was the landing for the second stairwell. Two more swordsmen were coming up at a run, clearly alerted by the sound of fighting. At a shout from below, they veered sharply to each side of the staircase.

Another crossbow twanged and several bolts came flying up the stairwell at her, directly between the two swordsmen.

Swearing, Talyn summoned her shield, slamming it into place. Both swordsmen hesitated, shock flaring in their eyes at the sight of her shield. Then the sound of fighting from below—the thump of a knife hitting flesh, Halun's low growl.

"We've got the shooter, Captain!" Corrin called up, voice admirably steady. "You're clear."

She dropped the shield, heart thudding at the effort it had taken, before turning her focus to the first assassin to reach the top of the stairs. She lashed out with a booted foot, sending him tumbling back down the way he'd come.

"Incoming!" she shouted, even as she ducked under the second man's swing and ran her sword through his chest.

A loud echoing whistle sounded—Zamaril from somewhere above.

Leaving the sword impaled in the dead body, she spun and took the stairs up to the third floor at a sprint. The whistle came again as she reached the landing—from one of the rooms at the end of the corridor. The eastern suite, like Tiercelin had said.

Talyn ran, sprinting down the corridor at top speed, then shouldered her way through the double doors of the room at the end. A sai in each hand, she surveyed the scene, looking for her charge.

Cuinn was in the corner of the room to her right, chest bare, golden hair in disarray. A winged woman crouched naked behind him, wrapped in the bed sheet. All three arched windows were open, shutters swinging out in the breeze.

Theac and Zamaril stood between Cuinn and three masked attackers. Two bodies already lay bleeding on the floor. Theac's axe and Zamaril's sword were dripping blood, and both men were breathing hard.

"They came through the windows," Theac shouted unnecessarily.

Three masked heads shifted her way, then glanced at each other. One moved on her. She killed him before he could take a step with a throw of her sai. Zamaril's blade flicked as the thief took advantage of his opponent's distraction, disarming the man and opening up his throat. The third hesitated, then moved on Cuinn. Talyn's second sai took him in the back.

"Are you all right?" Talyn snapped at Cuinn as she moved quickly to retrieve her sais.

He nodded. "Zamaril and Theac arrived just as they burst through the windows."

"Unlocked, were they?" she snapped, then dismissed him before he could respond and looked at Theac and Zamaril. "You two okay?"

"A few cuts, nothing serious," Zamaril said, then looked at the dead bodies, his skin pale and spattered with drying blood. "Killing's a rather messy business, isn't it?"

Theac gripped his arm. "You don't ever get used to killing, and that's the way it should be."

"Is the prince okay?" Corrin appeared in the doorway, panting. His hands were splattered with blood and gore, but a determined light shone fiercely in his green eyes. Halun was behind him, axe slick with blood and brain matter. He, too, was a grisly sight. They'd killed more than just the crossbowman below. Pride flared briefly in her chest—her Wolves hadn't folded, they'd fought.

"For now." She nodded briskly. "Is the ground floor clear?"

"We took out the shooter and the man you kicked downstairs, plus another two creeping in through the kitchen. But then we came as soon as we heard the distress signal, so we didn't get a chance to clear the whole ground floor." Corrin spoke quickly, words falling over each other.

She did a quick count in her head. "That's what, ten dead? I'm betting there's a second wave out there somewhere, if not already in the house. *Sari?*" It didn't matter that her partner wasn't physically present, not now when her charge's life was in the balance.

"A good possibility. Plan for it." A second's thought. *"They know where Cuinn is, so first thing to do is get away from there."*

She nodded, faced the Wolves. "First we get the prince out of this house—if there are more, they'll be coming straight at this room." She was bitterly regretting not telling Ravinire where they were going as she glanced around, eyes falling on the open windows. "We'll go out the windows, make straight for the cover of the forest. Once clear we'll plan where next. Halun, you first. Go!"

The big man didn't protest, making straight for the windows.

"What about my friends staying here?" Cuinn demanded suddenly. "We're just going to abandon them?"

She gave him a flat look, motioning for Zamaril to follow Halun out. "Yes. Your life is our priority and we can't save everyone. Besides, the assassins are after you, not your friends. Hopefully they'll be left alone."

"Hopefully? That's not good enough." He was upset. She found it both annoying and surprising—when had he ever displayed a shred of caring about anyone else?

"Too bad," she said, ice-cold. "Maybe if you'd let us bring a full guard here, we could protect more people. Now out the window. Stick close to the wall and don't leave Halun's side until we're all down."

His mouth thinned, but he did as she asked, wings rustling as he leapt after the other two. Theac went next, then Corrin, Talyn shooting anxious glances at the doorway, expecting more assassins to burst through at any moment.

But none came, and then she was out, shimmying down the drainpipe to land in the damp soil. It was dark in the shadows by the house, and she relaxed a little. Hopefully they were staying ahead of the game, doing what their adversary wouldn't expect.

"Now what?" Cuinn asked, irritation colouring his voice. He kept glancing up at the house, whether to see if they were being followed, or out of concern for his friends, she couldn't tell.

"Halun leads, you directly behind. We stick to the shadows, over to the servants' quarters there." She pointed. "Then stick close to the shadows by the building, and a short dash into the forest by the cliffs. You don't stop for anything. Am I clear?"

"Crystal, Captain."

"Go!"

She scanned the skies for Tiercelin as they ran, but the sky was cloudy, and the rain didn't help visibility. Ignoring worry, she kept pace behind the others as they scrambled for the servant's quarters, then inched along the southern wall before sprinting over to the trees.

She didn't take a proper breath until they were inside the dripping forest without any shouts of alarm coming from behind them.

"Theac, thoughts?" she snapped.

He looked up. "We could go for the cliff path and head out on one of the family's private boats. Your Highness, you know where they're stored?"

"I do." Cuinn nodded. Strangely enough, the prince didn't look afraid, just shocked by the attack. "There's a path down the southern cliff face, not far from here actually. It leads to a private beach and the boathouse."

"I—" Talyn opened her mouth to agree, but a faint screeching cry caught her attention. It sounded familiar, something she'd heard before. But where… Sari answered before she could recall.

Tal, that was a niever.

"What?" In her shock, she spoke the words aloud. "That's impossible. What would a niever be doing here?"

"Captain?" None of them had noticed her muttered words. Their gazes were fixed on the southern horizon, just out beyond the cliffs.

Where a small cluster of dark flying shapes was heading straight for the house.

"Niever-flyers," she breathed. Another screech sounded, closer this time, another quickly following on its tail. The cries held an edge of anticipation, of hunger, and she'd heard it before from nievers flying into battle.

"What in the sodding flea-bitten shits is a niever-flyer?" Theac barked, losing a hint of composure for the first time.

She ignored him, her eyes instantly going to the skies over the house, heart pounding in growing terror. The skies where Tiercelin was, where she'd told him to stay.

Nievers would tear a winged man to shreds in seconds.

Theac reached out and bodily hauled her back as she went to run back out into the open. "What are you doing?"

The sharp movement jolted some clarity back. If she ran out into the open, she'd be flagging Cuinn's location for anyone present. The same if she shouted for Tiercelin.

"They're flying creatures, a bit like bats, but much bigger," she said, failing to hide the dread in her voice. "Firthlanders ride them in battle —archers. Like our SkyRiders, only ours are eagles. But I don't understand why they'd be here."

"Doesn't matter," Zamaril snapped. "Tiercelin's up there."

"No he's not." A musical voice sounded behind them. "He saw you all creeping out of the house and followed."

As one they spun to watch Tiercelin step out of the trees behind them. The utter relief that filled the space was palpable enough Talyn thought it might be possible to cut it with a knife.

He gave them an odd look, but then waved a hand. "Anyway, no time for chat. I've been scouting the area. There are more of them waiting down by the boatshed—I almost missed them in the dark. They're hiding, waiting to ambush you, I'd say."

"Then we'll—"

"Nope there's more. Another twenty at least. They're on horseback and combing the forest from the north. It won't be long before they stumble across us."

"Plus those things." Corrin pointed a hand at the niever-flyers, now rapidly approaching the house.

Talyn took a breath. All their potential escape routes had been cut off. And if anyone tried to fly... well, those niever-flyers weren't out here in the rain for no reason.

They were trapped.

CHAPTER 48

"*Tal, this is no simple assassination attempt. This is a full assault, and one that has planned for every contingency.*"

She ignored Sari's voice—that would be something to contemplate later, if they managed to survive this.

Theac was the first to regain control, his experience and level-headedness coming through. "Captain, you'll have to take Prince Cuinn and run—veer around the riders in the forest. We'll stay here and draw them to us, delay them as long as we can while you and the prince run north for Harbridge. It's the largest town on the island and has its own City Patrol contingent."

Another deep breath. Theac was right. Even if she could manage twenty assassins with the Wolves' help, the jetty option was too risky —a dangerous cliff path in the dark and one that would make them completely exposed to the niever-flyers overhead.

Overland was better, a wider space to deal with and the potential of losing their adversaries in the trees. And in the trees and dark they would be able to hide from nievers searching above.

But what he was suggesting…

"No." She shook her head firmly. "You'll all be killed. You can't hold off such a large number and survive."

"Doesn't matter," he said stubbornly. "What matters is that the prince survives. You know our duty, Captain."

She shook her head. "You all take Prince Cuinn, and I'll stay here to hold them off."

"Not even you can hold them off as long as five of us can, Captain." Tiercelin joined in the argument. "And the prince's safety is paramount. That's what *you* taught us. We don't have time to stand here arguing."

"Go," Corrin urged. "While you still can."

"You..." She faltered. They were right, but she couldn't. It was like all the air had been sucked from her lungs. She couldn't leave them to die... not the five men who she'd turned into loyal comrades and warriors. After everything they'd been through, this couldn't be the end of them.

But they were right.

"Sari, I can't."

"I don't know what to tell you." Sari hesitated. *"I can't think of another way."*

Cuinn had stayed aloof from the argument, but then he seemed to notice the sickening acceptance in her eyes. "Hold on, this is insane. There has to be another way."

"There isn't," Talyn said flatly. "We're sworn to protect you, no matter whether you like it or not."

"You're not listening to me," he said, and his voice trembled with some emotion she couldn't name. It wasn't fear, though. "I will not allow any of you to die for me tonight."

"You don't control our actions, Your Highness," Theac reminded him respectfully. "We are your WingGuard protection detail. This is what we trained for. This is our job."

"You are humans," he whispered. "And you're willing to do this for *me?*"

"No," Zamaril spoke. "Not for you. For us. Because this is who we choose to be."

"Wait!" Talyn's head snapped up. She'd been desperately trying to come up with another way, another option, and Tiercelin's words had finally filtered through. "Tiercelin, did you say they were on horseback?"

He nodded, hopping from foot to foot, wings rustling. "Captain, they'll be on us any moment. We don't have time to—"

"Are they separately combing the forest, or are they riding in a pack?"

"They're scattered around, like a net, waiting for us to run into them. They could stumble over us any minute." Panic edged his words, though he was visibly fighting it. Halun reached out and laid a hand on the winged man's arm. Almost instantly his wings relaxed.

There was a sickening lurch in her chest; despite their fear, they were not hesitating to offer their lives.

She wasn't going to let them.

"Tiercelin, take Corrin and find one riding alone. Corrin, take him out with one of your throwing knives—it needs to be a clean hit, mind, so he doesn't sound the alarm. Bring his horse here. Bring his clothes too. Can you do that?"

Corrin nodded, swallowing. "What if they find you before we can get back?"

"If you're quick enough, they won't. Tiercelin, you stay on the ground, am I clear?"

"Very." Furling his wings in tight behind him, he set off at a run, Corrin falling into step behind him.

Once they disappeared from sight, Talyn looked up at the trees around her. "Everyone climb a tree, but don't go too high. Stay still and quiet. If any of them ride through, they hopefully won't look up."

She waited until the others were already climbing before following Cuinn up into the tree he'd chosen. He sat hunched over, enfolded in his wings, staring out over the ground, face taut with misery. In moments they were settled in position, surrounded by rain and darkness.

Her heart leapt into her throat when a series of loud, challenging screeches came from the skies—it sounded like the nievers were directly overhead. The leaves above them rustled, but the dark shapes in the sky flew on without stopping.

"I've heard of your SkyRiders," Cuinn muttered. "But those things are like nothing I imagined."

"Shush!" she quieted him.

Moments later she froze when hoofbeats thudded and a horse appeared below, but this one was rider-less, and being led by Corrin. She dropped from the tree and landed in front of him, snatching the dead man's clothes he carried and dragging them on over her own. The others came down too.

"What are you going to do?" Tiercelin asked.

"I know a little something about horses. I'm going to draw them all away from you while you take Prince Cuinn and run straight for Harbridge." She turned to the prince. "Where will you be heading?"

"On a straight line north, veering a little to the west. That's the most direct route to Harbridge."

"Then I'll lead them northeast."

"On a horse?" Zamaril asked doubtfully.

She flashed a grin. Insanely, she meant it. "Damn right, on a horse."

"Captain?" Tiercelin's voice was tight. "You know we need help. Even if we make it to Harbridge, we can't be certain they won't keep coming and the City Patrol aren't skilled fighters. We need the Falcon and more WingGuard."

"Tiercelin—"

"I can fly back to the citadel and have Falcons here by the time the others get Prince Cuinn to Harbridge."

"You don't understand," she snapped. "Nievers have talons as long as your arm and their riders are excellent shots."

"I'll run to the clifftop and drop down to fly just above sea level—they won't see me against the dark ocean," he said steadily. "You know I'm right. We need help. I need *you* to trust that I can do this, Captain."

"I..." She faltered.

"Trust in what you built. If you don't trust him, trust yourself, now, or you'll never be able to."

She nodded sharply. "Be careful. You die, and I'll never speak to you again."

A grin flashed over his beautiful features. "Right back at you, Captain."

He was gone before any of them could protest further, sprinting into the night, making a beeline for the eastern cliff edge. The rest of the Wolves tracked him too, the same worry on their faces as she felt deep in her chest.

She pushed aside her fear for him before it could incapacitate her, and gripped the horse's saddle before leaping up into it—it was like coming home. All at once her confidence returned.

She pulled the soaked woollen hood up over her face, inhaling the bitter scent of its previous owner. In the dark and rain, they should mistake her for one of them. "Move as fast and quietly as you can. Remember what I taught you and keep safe."

"Captain. I…" Halun's face worked. He clearly wanted to say something but couldn't get the words out.

"I'll be fine, I promise. Now go!"

"Captain?" Cuinn's voice stopped her. His green Dumnorix eyes—just like starlight— luminous even in the dark.

"What?" she snapped.

"It's not your job to die for me, not tonight. I forbid it."

She almost laughed, but he was so serious, scowling at her through the rain. "It *is* my job, Prince Cuinn, you just don't seem to realise that."

His scowl deepened. "I have the power to take away your free will, Captain Dynan, and unless you promise me that you are not riding off to certain death right now, I will use every inch of that power to stop you."

"No, you won't." Talyn stared back at him, pitting her will against him for the first time ever. "Because I am Kingshield—and you will never take my duty from me, no matter how powerful you are."

Corrin stepped in front of the prince, beseeching her. "Please, Captain. There are twenty of them out there, maybe more. You can't…"

"This is the life you chose, Corrin. That goes for all of you." She looked at each of them in turn, even Zamaril, who didn't shy away from her gaze. "Now go, and do *your* duty."

"Captain's right," Theac barked. "Let's go. Halun you take the lead, Corrin and Zamaril each side of the prince. I'll bring up the rear. Hurry now!"

Cuinn didn't even look at her as they all turned and ran into the darkness.

THE TREES WERE dark and silent. She sat in the saddle with her eyes closed, using every sense she possessed to try and judge the location of the riders out in the forest. They were near, but not near enough to spot her. And she had to draw them to her before her Wolves ran into them.

Taking a deep breath, she raised her hand and erected her bright sapphire energy shield. It lit up the night, showing her location for miles around.

Hoofbeats sounded as horses closed in on her from left and right almost instantly.

"I saw them!" she screamed. "They're going this way. Follow me."

A distant niever shrieked.

Letting loose with the characteristic ebullient whoop of the Aimsir on muster, Talyn dropped her shield and kicked the horse into a gallop.

Driving rain blinded her vision as her mount careened along in a north-westerly direction, slipping frequently on the muddy and uneven ground underfoot. She held her seat easily enough, but the horse under her was no Aimsir, and the other riders kept up easily, thinking she was leading them to their quarry.

Exactly what she wanted.

It didn't take them long to figure out she wasn't one of them. A shout came from behind her as she led them deeper into tangled forest, away from both the house and the route towards the populated areas of the island. But by then they were fully engaged in the chase.

Less welcome were the nievers sweeping in low over the treetops, drawn by the growing group of riders racing through the forest. The first arrow flew well clear of her, slamming into a tree trunk moments before she raced past it. Her stomach clenched, but she kept riding, forcing aside the panic.

Her charge's life depended on her and she refused to fail.

More arrows sailed through the night, one close enough she heard the hiss as it passed within inches of her left ear. Her hands curled so hard around the reins the leather cut into her skin and it took everything she had to keep focused, not to flinch, not to hesitate.

Eventually the frequency of the arrows coming at her faded—the riders pursuing her were contending with the dark, the obstructing trees, and not wanting to hit their comrades. Besides, she knew from Callanan training that nievers couldn't hover... their riders had only single, brief opportunities to shoot as they flew past or over a target.

So she used the terrain to her advantage. She managed to keep *just* ahead of her pursuers as they followed, and she led them on a merry ride through the rain.

One rider on a better horse pursued her doggedly, closing the gap slowly but steadily. She slowed her horse a little to allow him to get close. Then, judging her moment exactly, she dropped the reins and leaped upwards out of the saddle. Rough wood scraped over her palms as she gripped an overhanging branch for a few seconds, then dropped to land in the saddle behind her pursuer. She slammed the hilt of her sai into his temple and shoved him off the horse.

As she regained her seat, an incline appeared ahead, steep and made dangerous, the rain turning the ground into little more than muddy sludge. She didn't baulk from it. Her horse slid half way down, falling heavily on his side. She rolled with the movement, continuing all the way to the bottom where she landed on her feet and turned to face the first attacker riding her down.

Time slowed.

Her breath came fast, her grip on her sais sure, stance loose and ready.

An enemy rider bearing down on her.

And in that moment, in the deep of pre-dawn and the rain and dark, Talyn came back to herself.

The adrenalin of battle thrummed through her veins, hot and powerful. It was like Sari was back at her side again and they were facing down a brigand assault together. She even caught a snatch of her partner's wild laughter in her ears—the sound she always made when the odds were against them but she knew they'd come out victorious anyway.

Then time snapped back into focus.

She stepped aside at the last moment, gripping the stirrup as the first rider galloped past and hauling herself up behind him. He shoved his elbow back into her chest, but she twisted aside before thrusting her sai deep in between his ribs. He coughed blood, sliding out of the saddle and hitting the ground with a crash.

Talyn wrenched the horse around, spraying mud everywhere. More riders converged on her from every direction. She rode like an Aimsir, using her sais to kill two riders before finding a fallen sword in the mud and sliding half out of the saddle to scoop it up.

At first she fought as if Sari was still at her side, protecting her back as always, each instinctively knowing where the other was. She lost the horse that way, lamed by an attacker's blade from the side. A deep slash down her right bicep caught her unawares when she rolled clear of the falling mount.

Her body moved at its utmost limit of agility, dancing through the mud. She felt every pull of muscle, each rasp of breath in her lungs, the slickness of rain on her face and the cold grip of the sword in her hands.

And she began to adjust. To fight like she had no partner. To turn that little bit faster to protect her back, to hold back rather than overextend and leave her side vulnerable.

Every step part of a dance. Parry, slash, drop, weave. Lose the blade, gain another with a quick *sabai* move. Bring her shield to life. Drop it again. Breathe in. Breath out. Feel the damp air rush over sweat-soaked skin. Teeth bared in a silent snarl the whole time.

She had no idea how much time had passed before she killed a man and stood, chest heaving, staring around her. Rain continued to fall, tapping on the leaves in the sudden silence.

No more pursuers loomed out of the dark. The nievers were gone.

She was alone in the forest, bodies strewn unmoving around her. Her breath steamed in the cold air. Blood, gore and mud covered her from head to toe.

The adrenalin began to fade, leaving her with the exhausted satisfaction she'd always felt after a fight. She knew her eyes would be glowing.

She'd missed this. She'd missed this more than breathing. This was who she was.

A snatch of Sari's laughter sounded again, and she clung to it. *"You got this, partner."*

Maybe she did.

And the tears began streaming down her face.

CHAPTER 49

*J*alyn headed steadily north through the forest as quickly as she could, figuring from Theac's description of the island she'd hit a town or the ocean eventually.

She needed to get to Cuinn.

The niever-flyers had disappeared somewhere during the fight. She assumed they'd realised that she wasn't their target and had gone after Cuinn. Hopefully her Wolves had kept hidden and silent underneath the canopy.

Hopefully, Tiercelin had made it clear away before one of the bat creatures had seen him.

Water dripped down through the leaves. The downpour of earlier was slowly easing to a faint drizzle. Her knee throbbed with every step, and blood seeped through the makeshift bandage she'd wrapped around her right bicep and another cut over her left ribs. Her body complained at each movement—what had once been easy was now pushing her limits. Exhaustion and soreness leached strength from her bones and muscles.

She'd felt like this before. But where before there had once been Sari and other Callanan, healers and ale and the bright warmth of satisfaction, now it was just her and the dripping forest and the uncomfortably humid air of Mithranar.

But maybe that was okay. It wasn't what she'd had. It wasn't what she chose or what she wanted more than her next breath.

But it also might be the first step towards the new beginning she needed.

Dawn was turning into full morning as she finally emerged from the forest into a cleared patch of high ground. A pink glow bathed the northern coastline laid out at her feet.

And just to the east, less than a full-turn's walk away, was a large town, settled along the turquoise beach. In the faint distance in both directions were more villages, but this one was clearly the largest.

If that wasn't enough to convince her she'd found Harbridge, the cluster of bright wings circling the sky above the town did. She counted at least a full flight of Falcons.

Relief almost crumpled her where she stood.

Tiercelin had gotten word to Ravinire. He was okay. And if the Falcons were hovering above Harbridge, then Cuinn was most likely safe in the town.

Her sore knee had turned her gait into a heavy limp by the time she made it across open fields to what appeared to be a main road into the town. She was confused by how empty the road was—it was early, and she assumed it would be busy with those travelling to and from the town.

The reason for the empty road was clear as the road approached the first outbuildings of Harbridge. It wasn't walled, but three Falcons stood on the road just outside the entrance, barring anyone coming or going.

Their eyes widened in unison at her bloodied, mud-covered state.

"I'm Captain Dynan," she told them, figuring she was close to unrecognisable in her current state. "Is the Falcon here?"

One of them nodded reluctantly. "He's with Prince Cuinn at the *Leaky Boat*. Centre of town, you can't miss it."

She nodded. "Why the lockdown?"

"Prince Cuinn was attacked last night." He gave her a look, as if it was the stupidest question he'd ever heard. "By humans. They must have come from Harbridge. The town is locked down until we find the perpetrators."

Talyn huffed a laugh, waving a hand in the direction she'd come. "The perpetrators are all back there. Dead."

He lifted a single eyebrow. "All of them?"

"Yes." She doubted the niever-flyers were coming back. Not in full daylight. And she certainly wasn't giving either of these men that information anyway. "There's no need to shut down the town."

"They would have had supporters here. They need to be flushed out."

"You don't know that." Even as she said the words, part of her acknowledged they might be right. The Falcons' rudeness was irritating, but an operation like they'd faced down last night must have had help, and she doubted it had come from the winged folk.

"We have our orders, Captain."

Without a word, she pushed past them and limped her way into town.

THE LEAKY BOAT was easy enough to find thanks to the sight of a haggard-looking Corrin standing guard on the front door. A breath of relief escaped her. Despite his obvious exhaustion, he looked whole and unharmed.

She'd almost reached him before he recognised her limping up the road, then his mouth opened, his eyes widening with surprise. A moment later, his shoulders slumped in relief. "You made it! We thought there was no way you could..."

When he trailed off, she flashed him a weary smile. "None of you have seen a Callanan in action before."

He didn't respond, instead striding for the door, pushing it open, and shouting for Theac. The Wolf appeared an instant later—as if he'd been waiting. He stared for a moment, the same astonishment and relief flashing over his face. Then he recovered, snapping, "Inside, now."

Talyn found herself hustled to a chair by the fire, Theac speaking the whole time. "Zamaril and Halun are watching out back," he assured her. "Liadin and Lyra are up in the sky keeping an eye on the approaches to town."

"I think the full flight of WingGuard should do the trick," she said dryly. "Let them rest, Theac."

"I don't trust anyone but us."

She gave him a look but didn't dispute his words. "The prince?" In the warmth and comfort of the chair, the last of her adrenalin was ebbing away, replaced by exhaustion and pain from each of the myriad cuts and bruises she'd sustained in the fight.

Theac's glower returned. "In the private room out back. His friends followed him here... he's entertaining."

Corrin appeared then, passing a small healing kit to Theac. "I got this from one of the Falcons."

Talyn sank back in the chair as her second cleaned and dressed her cuts, including the deeper ones to her ribs and arm that needed stitches. He was much rougher than Tiercelin but seemed to know what he was doing. Corrin hovered, directing ferocious glares at any loitering Falcons who dared even look their way. The inn otherwise had no customers that she could see.

"They're making people stay in their homes too?" She winced as Theac started on her arm.

"Nobody is allowed out on the streets until the Falcons are satisfied the threat is contained," he grunted.

"I think they're over-reacting." She swore as he jabbed the needle a little too hard. "The human assassins are all dead, and those niever-flyers are long gone."

Corrin shuddered. "Those things are nasty. They almost found us a couple times last night."

She looked to Theac. "Did you mention them to Ravinire?"

He shook his head. "I thought that best left to you."

Just as he was finishing up, the inn door slammed open and

Ravinire appeared, his gaze searching the room until it landed on her. Talyn swore under her breath, wincing as she forced herself to her feet.

He did not look happy.

"You're hurt," he said curtly, wings rustling in agitation as he strode over. Corrin and Theac melted away into the background, leaving her alone to face the Falcon.

"Nothing serious, sir." She hesitated. "Can I ask for a status update?"

His mouth thinned. "The island is secure. Nobody is getting on or off without being thoroughly searched and interviewed by my Falcons."

"Sir, I—"

"Don't think for a second I'm not furious at your conduct, Captain," he snapped. "You took Tiercelin from his post and came here with four humans to face an assassination attempt without warning me first."

"I wasn't the one who ditched his guard to travel to an isolated house on a god-damned island," she said, barely holding her temper. "We followed as soon as we learned Prince Cuinn had left and arrived in time to forestall an assassination attempt. Tiercelin—"

"Has already been given his orders. He remained at the citadel and will be suspended from duty."

"Sir, if I may?" Theac was suddenly at her shoulder, tone polite and deferential, speaking just as she was about to completely lose her temper. "We had no information to suggest the prince was in danger last night, no evidence to bring to you. Captain Dynan's conduct was exemplary—I don't think you understand the circumstances. She left us to draw away a twenty-strong team of adversaries so that we could bring Prince Cuinn here safely. She risked her life for the prince's, sir."

Theac's intervention had given her time to get her temper under control, and she spoke before Ravinire could negate what he'd said. "Sir, Theac is right, but it wasn't just me. Tiercelin helped save the prince's life last night too. If you want to keep Prince Cuinn safe, then I suggest you stop taking away my best warriors."

467

"Prince Cuinn wasn't the target," Ravinire bellowed. His voice was loud enough to carry through the entire room. It was the first time she'd ever seen his iron control break, and it took the wind out of her remaining anger.

"What?"

"The queen was supposed to be here last night, not Prince Cuinn. She changed her mind yesterday afternoon, and the youngest prince decided to travel instead on a whim." The words were tight, angry. "An assassination like what your wing described takes weeks of planning. They were after my queen, Captain."

"Either way, we foiled the attempt," she said quietly.

"You got lucky," he said. "Now, I want you all back at the citadel. There's a boat out there ready to take you. You're off duty until I say so. My Falcons will watch the prince until then."

She understood how he was feeling, understood well enough that his anger no longer bothered her. His queen had been under threat. She'd be raging too. "Sir, there's more you should know. There were a handful of niever-flyers out there last night."

"The Firthlander flyers?" He frowned.

She nodded. "Like you said sir, the attack was well planned. If the Falcons had been here with the queen, the nievers would have torn them apart. The danger Tiercelin risked flying to the citadel to warn you..."

She let the words trail off, satisfied by Ravinire's flinch. His shoulders sagged momentarily. "I don't understand. Why would Firthland attack our queen?"

"They wouldn't," she said firmly. The last thing they needed was an international incident because Mithranar thought the Firthlander warlord had attacked them. "But there should be questions asked, nonetheless." In fact, she'd write to Tarcos the moment she was back at the palace. But she couldn't exactly let on to Ravinire that she was on personal terms with the likely heir to the Firthlander throne. "There are also twenty or so dead bodies out in the forest just north of the house. You might want to search them, see if there's any evidence of who they are or where they're from."

He regarded her for a moment. "They're all dead?"

"Yes, sir. And roughly ten more bodies in the house."

"Thank you, Captain." There was something odd in his voice, but she couldn't recognise it. "I'll take that under advisement."

"Yes, sir." She saluted and went to find her Wolves.

LEAVING Theac to collect Corrin and find where their boat was, she went to get Zamaril and Halun. To do that, she had to pass through the back room. It was full of winged folk drinking and laughing.

Cuinn sat in the centre, sprawled in a chair and with the young woman from the night before on his lap. The prince noticed the instant she walked into the room, and he sat up in a single move, almost sending the girl tumbling from his lap. But instead of concern, all she got was a curious, "Captain, you got away?"

"What are you doing?" She tried to contain her temper. "It's early morning."

"It's never too late to party, Captain, especially when you've had a brush with death."

She stared at him. "That's seriously all you have to say to me? To your Wolves? They were prepared to die for you last night."

"Well, as you've pointed out to me on a number of occasions, Captain, that is their job." He dismissed her with a wave of his hand and turned his attention back to the girl on his lap.

Her dislike of the prince hardening into something more like hatred, Talyn turned on her heel and went out the back where Zamaril and Halun were managing alertness despite their obvious exhaustion. Both brightened at the sight of her.

"Good to see you, Captain," Halun's smooth voice welcomed her. "Are you all right?"

"I'm a little banged up, but Theac's butchered me up nicely. Come on, we've all been dismissed by Ravinire. Back to the citadel for us."

Zamaril gave her an arch look, gaze lingering on her bandaged arm. "The Falcon's displeased, I take it? Even though we saved his precious prince last night."

Halun crossed his arms over his chest, nodding at the thief's words.

"He is, but I don't think his anger is entirely about us." She explained what he'd told her about the queen being the target.

Surprise and understanding rippled over Halun's face, but Zamaril wasn't appeased. "No matter who the target, we saved their damned prince."

"And you should be proud of yourselves. *I'm* proud of you. But we don't do this for validation," she said pointedly. "And I don't know about you, but I'll happily take the excuse for some time to rest and get some sleep."

THEAC CAME to sit beside her as one of the town's fishing boats drifted away from the dock, beginning the trip back to the citadel. His glower was firmly in place. "Last night was like no assassination attempt I've ever seen."

She raised an eyebrow. "And you've seen many, have you?"

His expression settled into a scowl, and he made no reply.

Talyn sighed. "They had multiple teams, planned for the eventuality of us getting out of the house and somehow managed to acquire some niever-flyers. They wore masks and dressed uniformly in black. And I'm betting Ravinire finds nothing identifying on any of the bodies." She paused, looked at him. "I've been part of operations like that as a Callanan."

"That's true." He frowned. "But Captain, they weren't highly skilled warriors. Competent, yes, but you handled them easily, and they weren't too much for us, either."

She smiled at him, giving him a nudge with her elbow. "Nice observation. The Wolves are going to be fine once I'm gone, Theac."

He scowled. "I'm nothing special, Captain."

"You're more wrong than you could know," she said softly.

And I'm going to leave them. The thought summoned a wash of guilt, but if she'd learned anything in the past day and night, it was that she'd trained the Wolves well. Cuinn would not be without capable protection when she left.

If Ravinire let them do their jobs.

Yawning widely, Talyn huddled into the blanket that Corrin had found for her and allowed the rocking of the boat to send her into a light doze.

NIGHT WAS FALLING by the time they tied up at the sprawling docks outside Dock City and trudged their way up to the citadel. Talyn dismissed the Wolves to their barracks to rest, then headed for her quarters, desperate for sleep herself. She'd been awake for almost two days.

Her neck prickled as she stepped into her dark bedroom, but Savin appeared out of the shadows before her hands reached her weapons.

"That's quite a skill you have there," she noted.

He didn't seem to be in the mood for small talk. "I heard what happened. You saved the prince's life."

She nodded. "Just barely, but he's fine. Ravinire tells me it was the queen who was supposed to have been there last night."

"I am... yes, that's true." He paused.

Silence fell. She was exhausted and in no mood for playing games with Savin, so she waited for him to say what he'd come to say and leave, so she could sleep.

Eventually he spoke again. "You did a good job. Your wing has done impressively well, considering." The words sounded awkward, but genuinely meant.

"Why are you here, Savin?"

"For the obvious. I wanted to hear directly from you what happened out there." He paused. "I am ashamed to admit I had no idea such an attack was brewing."

The Shadowhawk knew. It was on the tip of her tongue to say it aloud, but caution stopped her. If he hadn't come to her with that information... she may never have gone out to Sparrow Island. She'd been annoyed enough with Cuinn to leave him out there alone.

And for that alone she owed the Shadowhawk a large debt.

"There were at least thirty men involved in the attempt, Savin, all with weapons and some mounted on decent horses," Talyn said instead. "Whoever was behind it wasn't messing around. They wanted the queen dead. If it wasn't for a bit of luck, Prince Cuinn *would* be dead."

A long, weighted, silence, then, "That many. How did you come out alive?"

"We fought our way out," she said tersely, then, "Will you report to Theac once I'm gone, like I asked?"

"I can do that," he said quietly. "As long as he remains the only one that knows about me."

"Fine," she said. "Now I'm exhausted and would like some sleep."

His silent departure was her only response.

"Again, he told you nothing, Talyn. He was only here to find out what you knew."

"I know. But I'm too tired to worry about it now. I'll make sure I warn Theac before I leave."

TALYN WAS SUMMONED to Ravinire's office the next morning. Expecting a sharp dressing down not unlike the one she'd already received, she straightened her uniform and squared her shoulders before presenting herself at his office.

"Tell me what happened," he demanded without preamble, waving her to a seat in front of his desk. "Theac gave me a good account yesterday, but now I want your detailed report."

Talyn sat and ran through everything, in simple, concise terms.

Once she was done, Ravinire's face betrayed no reaction to her account. "You knew something might be wrong. If not, you would never have approached the house in the way you described. You went in there expecting a fight. Why?"

Talyn shifted in her seat. Admitting to having contact with the Shadowhawk would have worse consequences than a sharp dressing down, so she told him a half-truth. "What Theac told you yesterday was true, I didn't know anything, not for certain. But a few days earlier an informant told me one of the smiths in the Poor Quarter had received a large order for weapons. It didn't seem relevant to Prince Cuinn's protection at the time, but when I heard he'd gone off alone to an isolated location... it just didn't feel right, sir. I decided to take the Wolves just to make sure everything was okay."

His face tightened. "You're running informants without my knowledge?"

"Yes, sir." She shifted, brazening out his anger. Her emotional breakthrough in the fight, while doing nothing to remove the heaviness of grief still resting at her core, had begun to dull the edges of her self-doubt. And with that, some of her old confidence was returning. It would likely never come back in full, but that was okay too. "My responsibility is Prince Cuinn's protection. Informants are by their nature secretive. You gave me no orders against running sources."

"All true, Captain, but you should have kept me apprised of the fact you were running a source. I didn't need to know their identity."

"Yes, sir."

He sighed when she gave him nothing further. "Captain Dynan, you've removed any doubts I may have had when you arrived about the calibre and skill of the Twin Thrones Kingshield. However, I find myself almost relieved that you're leaving soon. I remain deeply uncertain of the benefit of having you here. The aim certainly wasn't to cause political problems for the queen."

"I'm sorry sir, I don't understand." Talyn frowned. "What problems have I caused Her Majesty?"

"The Wolves are a wing dedicated to the protection of Prince Cuinn. They are not meant to be used as an emblem of pride for the human community of Mithranar, or as a tool to show up the Wing-Guard. You've used them to do both of these things."

"That was not my intention, sir, and you know it," Talyn said hotly. "It is not my fault that the winged folk treat the humans in Mithranar as if they are worth less than the dirt on their shoes, and it is not my fault that the Falcons are so poorly trained that they can be beaten at a game of alleya by humans with only basic Callanan training."

"Captain!" Ravinire rose from his chair, voice rising to a shout. His wings unfurled behind him with a whoosh, an intimidating sight.

"No!" She shot up too. The old Talyn rose within her, the one that had been cocky and direct and afraid of nothing. "I came here to do a job, and I've done it to the best of my ability. If you hadn't noticed, you still have a third prince because of me and the men *I* trained. Maybe if you tried treating the human folk like equal citizens, they would have seen the alleya game as a fun afternoon of sport instead of a chance to prove that they aren't as worthless as you winged folk seem to think."

"You take an indignant tone with me, but we both know you're too smart not to understand what winning that game meant." His words were cold, cutting. "What it will mean when it spreads through Dock City that a human wing took down an assault force and saved a winged prince's life in doing so."

Her mouth curled. "I'm sorry sir. Next time I'll let him die. Wouldn't want to show up your WingGuard."

"That's enough!" Ravinire furiously shut down her tirade, one clenched fist slamming on his desk.

"Yes, it is," she said, equally coolly. She'd gone well over the line with a superior officer, but part of her didn't care. She should care. She was Callanan no longer.

"Tiercelin has returned to his WingGuard unit with a mark on his record. You try anything like you did with him the other night again, and I'll toss you out of Mithranar the very next day, no matter what your king thinks of it. Am I clear, Captain Dynan?"

She stiffened. The threat was moot, she had only days left anyway. And she was increasingly glad of that fact. "Perfectly. Is that all, sir?"

"It is."

Talyn rose and went to the door, pausing before leaving. "I had hoped you called me here today to discuss arrangements for Prince Cuinn's guard rotation. Even though the attempt seems to have been intended for the queen, it might be wise to ensure that he has a round the clock guard from now on. Obviously, I was wrong, and you've clearly got that situation under control."

"The WingGuard aren't as useless as you might think, Captain."

"I hope not, for Prince Cuinn's sake." Talyn hesitated. She was worked up enough that she was tempted to bring up the incident with Iceflight, just to see what Ravinire's reaction would be, but she hadn't forgotten Mithanis's threat to the Wolves and in the end that stayed her tongue. She went to leave, but Ravinire's voice stopped her. "Sir?"

"The Wolves have been very well trained, that is inarguable. I am assuming that you will leave Theac Parksin in command when you leave?"

"That would be my recommendation, yes."

"You might want to have a word with him about his role, and what will and will not be condoned. Are we clear, Captain?"

"Yes, sir."

It took all of Talyn's self-control not to slam the door on the way out.

CHAPTER 50

*A*fter some searching, Talyn eventually found Cuinn alone by the royal pool. As usual, it was a beautiful sunset, and the water glowed in an ethereal blue light. The prince stood by the railing, gazing into the distance. Talyn was struck suddenly by a powerful sense of loneliness. He glanced over and saw her a moment later, and instantly the emotion vanished.

It took her aback. She'd never seen that in him before.

"I take it from the glum faces I've been seeing all week that it's finally sinking in with the Wolves that you're leaving?" He raised a golden eyebrow.

"You noticed. I'm shocked." She leaned against the rail, watching in awe the breathtaking beauty of the burnished sunset. "Theac will captain the Wolves now. They respect him, and he is a solid commander."

"But not as good as you." Cuinn smiled with amusement, cocking his head. "I will have to learn to shield better, at least until their misery dies down a little. I think you are breaking their hearts, Captain."

"My time here was only ever going to be temporary," she said uncomfortably.

"And you're too smart to imagine that you can just walk away without consequences after everything you put into building that wing," he said, slight rebuke in his tone. "You won them to you, heart and soul."

"You're one to talk!" Her temper flared, ignited by her guilt and his words. "We're nothing more than an amusement for you."

"Which I've made perfectly clear to them, and to you," he pointed out.

"Even now?" she asked softly. "After they stood there that night and offered their lives for yours?"

"Oh, Captain." He chuckled, regarding her as if she were being particularly obtuse. "They weren't offering their lives for me. They were sacrificing themselves for you... they wanted to give enough time for *you* to get away, and they knew the only way to get you to do it was send me with you."

"I—"

He raised a hand, cutting her off. "I could feel every beat of their emotions that night, and I have no reason to lie to you. Did you truly imagine those humans would sacrifice themselves for *me*? A winged man they despise?"

She swallowed. No, they wouldn't. Not Zamaril, not Halun. Tiercelin maybe, even Corrin, because she asked it of him, but not the others. Hot tears flared at the back of her eyes and she took a long moment to wrestle her emotions under control. Cuinn watched her the whole time, no doubt reading everything she was trying to hide.

"Good luck, Prince Cuinn," she said eventually, keeping her voice brisk. "If you let them, the Wolves *can* keep you safe."

"And you, Captain Dynan." He gave her a little nod, a smile curling at his mouth. "I hope you find what you've been looking for ever since you came here."

Before she could think about saying any more, his silver wings spread wide and he leaped into the sky, warm Mithranan air gusting over her as he did.

Talyn watched him go. This was likely the last time she'd ever see him. She still wasn't entirely certain Ceannar was right that he was a

Dumnorix. Eight months, and she still hadn't felt that instinctive kinship, not even in the dark and the rain when all their lives had been in danger.

She wondered what would become of him.

She'd only been back in her rooms a few moments, had only just opened her duffel to begin packing it, when Willir appeared at her front door. He had a note for her, flashing a cheerful smile as he passed it over.

"Who's it from?" she asked.

His smile faded a little. "I'm not to say, Captain."

She stiffened. "And what's in it, then?"

"I don't know. I was to ensure only that you read the note, then tell you to burn it once you had."

It contained a few neatly written lines on a single scrap of parchment. A request to meet, a location, and a rather imploring request to tell nobody of the note or the meeting.

She didn't recognise the handwriting.

Immediately she considered telling Theac. It was tempting. She trusted nobody else in Mithranar like she'd come to trust her second. But she was leaving, and reluctant to drag him into something that could get him in trouble once she was gone.

Then there was the potential that it was a trap. Perhaps she'd survived eight months in Mithranar only to be killed the night before she departed.

Smiling to herself, Talyn crumpled the note and tossed it into the fireplace. They'd better bring more than twenty warriors if they truly wished her dead this time.

She almost got lost trying to find the meeting location. She'd memorised the instructions before destroying the note, but the route led her through areas of the citadel she wasn't familiar with.

Eventually she found herself deep into the western half of the hill city, stepping out off one of the spanning walkways and onto the surface of a hillside. Her leg muscles burned as she hiked up a barely visible path that curved around the side of the hill until the citadel faded from view.

Her surroundings appeared deserted, nothing but the call of the night birds and the gentle swish of the breeze through the trees. Until she stepped into a clearing where two figures waited for her.

Both winged.

One cloaked and hooded. The other dressed in plain civilian clothing but otherwise instantly recognisable.

"Commander Ravinire," she said dryly, hiding her surprise. This whole time she'd been expecting Savin. "This is an odd place to meet."

He didn't reply. Instead the other figure stepped forward, pulling back the hood of her cloak. Talyn sucked in a breath, eyes flashing to Ravinire before settling back on the queen of Mithranar. "Your Grace."

"Thank you for coming, Captain. I understand how odd my note must have appeared."

"*Your* note?" Talyn glanced around the deserted hillside. "Why are we meeting like this?"

"I wanted to make a personal appeal to you, Captain. To stay here in Mithranar. Continue leading my son's guard."

"*Well that's unexpected.*"

Talyn stared at her. "You want to make an appeal? In the middle of the night on an isolated hillside where nobody can see us. Forgive me, Your Majesty, but this feels much more like an ambush."

"I've been told you're not a fool, so I'll be plain." She stepped forward, one sharp gesture sending Ravinire moving several paces away, out of earshot. Even so, the queen's voice lowered. "I know what the Kingshield is. I know they only protect the Dumnorix. It's why I requested they send one of you here. Why I had Ravinire assign you to create a wing for Cuinn despite his protests that he could protect my son with his own Falcons."

"*She knows!*"

"*Quit the commentary. I need to concentrate.*"

479

"I'll be quiet like a mouse," Sari's voice promised. *"And eavesdrop."*

"Why?" Talyn asked flatly. "Why now and not before, if you've truly known all this time who your son is?"

"Because I'm getting older. And that means the day I have to name my heir is growing ever closer."

Talyn glanced between the queen and Ravinire, several things becoming clear. Despite the break in at the citadel, dangerous floods and an attack from a numerous and well-organised assassination squad, there had only been one single occasion during her time in Mithranar that Talyn had felt truly afraid, felt her life genuinely in danger.

Those moments in the narrow walkway when Mithanis had confronted her.

The queen had requested a Kingshield, worked to give Cuinn a guard that was free of the ties and influence of the Mithanis-controlled WingGuard. Because the true threat to Cuinn was his eldest brother. And she and Ravinire were the only ones in Mithranar who either saw that or cared to do anything about it. It also told her where Ravinire's loyalties lay—with his queen. Clearly the only one she trusted to be out here tonight. Yet even then, she hadn't trusted him with the knowledge of her son's father.

"Will you stay, Captain?" the queen asked when Talyn said nothing.

"No." There was no point prevaricating. She stepped back, raising her voice so that Ravinire could hear. "The both of you have done nothing but stymie my efforts and hold back information since I arrived. You took Tiercelin from me and you treat me and my wing with contempt."

"Eight months and you still have no understanding of how things work here," the queen hissed. "I've done what I could for you within the narrow limits I have. I have a country to rule, Captain, and for that I need the support of my most powerful nobles. Tiercelin's family demanded my action, and so I took it. I allowed you to have other winged folk in your wing where I could."

For the briefest of moments she wavered. Her Wolves had been willing to sacrifice themselves for her, and she wasn't going to deny that she'd truly loved working with them, building them, developing the trust and rapport they had.

"Let me ask you something," she said, gaze shifting between them. "Two weeks ago I came across Flight-Leader Iceflight attempting to rape a human woman near the Falcon barracks. I tried to stop him, and Mithanis appeared, warning me off. He threatened to send the Wolves back to the cells if I reported the incident to you, sir." She paused, looking straight at Ravinire. "Is that what would have happened?"

The shared glance between Ravinire and the queen was all the answer she needed. "I could deal with the daily contempt and scorn that my Wolves and I face—it doesn't really matter what Falcons think of us, after all. But that woman was hurt and victimised because she was human, and you both think it's okay that Mithanis has the power to allow that to keep happening. Worse, you can't or won't do anything to stop it. I'm not staying in a place like that."

"Your moral high ground is offensive, Captain, and irrelevant to the matter at hand," the queen said coolly. "People do what they need to do to survive, and don't try and tell me you don't know that already. You are a Kingshield, and you and I both understand what that means in terms of your responsibilities. I'm asking you to stay here and live up to them."

"If you request it, another Kingshield guard might be sent to replace me." Talyn was unmoved by her words. "If my king agrees, I will ensure they are fully briefed on the situation before they arrive."

"That's not good enough. I want you, Captain."

"Why?"

The queen met her gaze for a long moment. "I have my reasons. Please, Captain, I truly want you to stay. Protect my son."

But she couldn't. It was time to go home. She'd found the first steps of a new life here in Mithranar, and now she had to go home to claim that new life. She wanted that so much. To stop living in despair and fear. To have only the grief to carry around.

"I'm sorry, Your Grace, but my posting is over and I'm going home." She softened her words. "It's where I belong. I'm happy to take your formal request for a replacement with me."

The queen nodded, glancing over at Ravinire before returning her gaze to Talyn. "Fine. Good night, Captain."

Ravinire gave her a long, searching look but turned to follow his queen without a word.

"GOOD LUCK AND KEEP SAFE," Talyn told her gathered Wolves with a smile.

Halun crossed the distance between them in two strides and lifted her into a bone-crushing hug. She yelped with surprise, then threw her arms around him. When he let her go, his jaw was clenched. "If there's anything you ever need," he said gruffly. "You know where to find me."

"Me too," Corrin said earnestly. "I'll never forget what you did for my mam and my sisters."

"Good luck with your next assignment, lass," Theac growled. "Hope your next lot aren't as troublesome as we were."

"Well at least my next lot won't complain about having a female captain," she teased him. "And they won't be thieves and dock brawlers. *And* they won't whinge about a tiny little run up a wall."

Zamaril had stayed quiet until now, but at this he stepped forward. "I'm not a thief anymore," he said quietly, uncharacteristically serious. "I'm a Wolf, and that's because of you. Thank you, Captain."

"It's been a genuine pleasure to work with you all, and I couldn't be prouder of what you've accomplished." She met each of their gazes in turn. "Remember what you've learnt, and you'll do well."

"Would you write us, Captain?" Theac asked, clearing his throat.

"Plan on lots of letters," she promised. "Because I want to hear every detail about how the new recruits are going."

"Make sure your replacement knows *sabai*," Zamaril said. "It gives us an advantage we need, and we're barely beyond the basics."

Talyn winced internally. She wasn't sure the Callanan would be entirely approving of their unarmed combat method being taught in another country, but maybe there was some way she could wrangle another Kingshield who also had a Callanan background. "I'll do my best."

A heavy silence fell then. Neither party wanted to be the first to go.

She straightened her shoulders, hefted her bag, pasted a cheerful smile on her face. "I'll see you again one day. Promise."

"If we don't see you first." Corrin beamed.

It was harder than Talyn had thought it would be, walking out through that gate and leaving them behind.

But she did it. Time to go home.

She stood at the prow of the ship as it left Mithranar, the ocean beyond the headlands beckoning. She was steadier now, some of her self-doubt gone. She'd proven something to herself here, that she could still be a warrior, could still come through when it mattered.

"Captain!"

She spun as the musical voice sounded behind her, eyes widening in surprise to see Tiercelin standing there. "I know I said I would say goodbye." The apologetic words came out in a rush before he could say anything. "But I worried it might make things more difficult for you. Ravinire was so furious and your captain hates me and..."

Her words hung there for a moment. Tiercelin came closer then stopped. He was frowning, and his great grey wings hung limply from his back. He seemed to be looking for words to say. In the end, he simply lifted his head and looked at her.

"Before you came, I was lost. I was consumed by fear of disappointing my parents, and my own lack of confidence and purpose. You gave me pride in myself and my abilities. You made me see that I am important. You showed me what comradeship can be like, and how it warms your life." Tiercelin's face worked as he stepped a little closer. "You stripped me of my arrogance and my ignorance, and you gave me a life. That is no small thing, Captain. Never forget it."

"Even though they took you away from us?" she whispered.

"Even then," he said steadily. "Because I won't change back to who I was. And I can take everything you taught me wherever I go."

"I'm glad," she said, fighting to keep tears from her eyes.

"You will always be welcome here, if ever you wish to return." He smiled now, cheekiness returning. "And if you ever want to learn more about your winged folk magic, you know where to find me."

"Tiercelin, I don't have…" She stopped. "I'll see you. Good luck."

He nodded, lifting a hand in farewell before spreading those great grey wings and leaping into the sky.

She turned back to the prow, staring out over the blue ocean, eyes already seeing the plains of Ryathl in her mind's eye.

"We're going home."

Sari's cheer brushed like a warm breeze through her mind.

CHAPTER 51

𝒯he Shadowhawk stood before the mirror in his bathing
room. It was night, and the only light came from the lamps
lit in the bedroom just beyond the open door. His face stared back
at him.

Her ship had left that afternoon, and he'd stood on the wall and
watched it sail out of the bay. A peculiar mix of despair and longing
ate at him. The Kingshield guard from Calumnia had changed things
so fundamentally in her short time in Mithranar—she had done more
in eight months than he had in years.

She'd represented the hope that maybe he wasn't the only one
trying to make things better, that maybe others thought and felt the
same way. But now she was gone.

The idea crushed him, as if the air had been sucked from his lungs.
He would miss her, would miss what she did for the humans and
winged folk. But if a foreign warrior could help so much in such a
short space of time, then surely he could do even more. He needed to
fight past his crippling fear, the people of Mithranar deserved better.

His people deserved better.

Taking a deep breath and rolling his shoulders to loosen them, he
dug in his pocket for a piece of chalk. He'd go down into Dock City

later tonight and leave the mark to set up a meeting with Saniya. Her people clearly had resources—maybe there was more he could do to utilize those resources.

He'd just tugged the chalk loose when a knock came at his door. Sighing, he pushed it back down deep in his pocket.

"Cuinn? Come on, you're late for the alleya game. Irial sent me to get you."

He stared in the mirror, the human features of the Shadowhawk dissolving from his face as he let go of his magic. His wings flashed into sight at his back, no longer concealed. Another deep breath, then a close look to make sure there wasn't any residue of his glamour.

Glamour. The magic no winged person had been born with for generations. Until him.

The knock came again, harder this time. Prince Cuinn Acondor settled a lazy smile on his face, then turned around and walked out to greet his friend.

It was time to play some alleya.

To be continued...

A Tale of Stars and Shadow is continued in *A Prince of Song and Shade*.

* * *

* * *

Sign up for Lisa's newsletter to keep up to date with the details on her upcoming books, special content for her followers, and invites to her events (as well as her advance reader team). You also get some great free stuff when you sign up, including:

- A free ebook with a collection of short stories from *The Mage Chronicles* Universe;
- A free download of maps from the world of *A Tale of Stars and Shadow*
- A free download of *We Fly As One* - a song written and recorded for *A Tale of Stars and Shadow* by Peny Bohan

Sign up at Lisa's website
tatehousebooks.com/bonus-content

ALSO BY LISA CASSIDY

The Mage Chronicles

DarkSkull Hall

Taliath

Darkmage

Heartfire

A Tale of Stars and Shadow

A Tale of Stars and Shadow

A Prince of Song and Shade

A King of Masks and Magic

A Duet of Sword and Song

* * *

Consider a review?

'Your words are as important to an author as an author's words are to you'

If you enjoyed *A Tale of Stars and Shadow,* or any of Lisa's other books, she would be humbled if you would consider taking the time to leave an honest review on GoodReads and Amazon (it doesn't have to be long - a few words is all).

Reviews are the lifeblood of any book, and more reviews help make sure Lisa can keep writing books!

ABOUT THE AUTHOR

Lisa is a self-published fantasy author by day and book nerd in every other spare moment she has. She's a self-confessed coffee snob (don't try coming near her with any of that instant coffee rubbish) but is willing to accept all other hot drink aficionados, even tea drinkers.

She lives in Australia's capital city, Canberra, and like all Australians, is pretty much in constant danger from highly poisonous spiders, crocodiles, sharks, and drop bears, to name a few. As you can see, she is also pro-Oxford comma.

A 2019 SPFBO finalist, and finalist for the 2020 ACT Writers Fiction award, Lisa is the author of the young adult fantasy series *The Mage Chronicles* and epic fantasy series *A Tale of Stars and Shadow*. She has also partnered up with One Girl, an Australian charity working to build a world where all girls have access to quality education. A world where all girls — no matter where they are born or how much money they have — enjoy the same rights and opportunities as boys. A percentage of all Lisa's royalties go to One Girl.

You can follow Lisa on Instagram and Facebook, where she loves to interact with her fans!

Also make sure you head to her website, where you can sign up for her mailing list and get spoilers, bonus content and advance info on all her new books!

tatehousebooks.com/Lisa-Cassidy